To Paul
_my ????_

Perfidia

By

Dodie Hamilton

With Love

Dodie H
_xx_

Dedication:
For good friends Pat 'Zebedee' Jay, for Lone wolf, the US Navy Seal, and for Brian the Lion Harris.

Acknowledgments:
For Julie Dexter, who is always there for me, for John and
Josie Lewin, founders of Spirit Knights Paranormal
Investigation, and for the author, Simon Richard
Woodward – the magic behind the word.

Book One

It Wasn't Meant to Be Like This

Prologue

Sophie tied up her hair, scraping it way off her face and into a high ponytail. Didn't want it flapping in her eyes. When you're going on a date there's nothing more annoying than your hair flapping in your eyes.

Okay that's done now for the lips. She hunted through the make-up box searching for the lipstick. Not just any lipstick! No soggy pinks or maudlin mauves. The reddest, shiniest, brassiest, Woolworth's Counter *rouge a lèvres* she could find, the one she borrowed from Lola, the exotic dancer at the New Revue, the one she keeps for such an occasion, the run around the Great Park.

Three times applied and blotted her mouth is now seriously red. Not a Coco the Clown mouth! No, luscious and inviting, the way she likes it when dancing, or rather, the way *he* liked it. Several coats of jet black mascara, her lashes are curled, combed, and swept and flutter like bat's wings.

A last slick of gloss possibly?

'Easy with that,' drawled a voice from the adjoining dressing room. 'You'll be passin' the wild cat enclosure. We got the new Bengal tigers today. It's a good six hours before feedin' time. Needless to say they're pretty upset. I don't want them seein' juicy red meat and leapin' the wires, at least not until I've tripled your life insurance.'

'Funny,' said Sophie and continued glossing.

This touch of the theatrical, this nightly ritual, must be carried out in a manner befitting a ritual, with gravity and care, because for God's sake, it is grave situation! No one, not even the man standing through there can ever know exactly how grave.

She's dressed. Grey cotton vest and leggings, Nike running shoes, a loose sweater tied about her waist in case it rains, and it usually does this time of night, it's hardly most glamorous outfit. Sophie doesn't care. It's practical, an essential stage of the ritual and has been so twelve years.

'You ready to go?' the voice calls, casual and yet as ever so very concerned.

'Yes I'm ready.'

'Then I guess you'd better go.'

Sophie pushed opened the doors and stood for a moment on the veranda overlooking the Italian Gardens. It was a beautiful night, the stars silver filigree and the moon a great copper disc hanging low on the horizon.

A great wail of sadness, silent yet audible to all, passed over her heart. Why, she thought, must it be like this? Why like so many pieces of jigsaw am I spread over and about the world? Why remind myself of yesterday?

Silence, there was no reply from the house, only the clink of cufflinks in a box and the rustle of a linen shirt being dropped into the laundry basket.

Come on, Sophie, she urged. Get on with it. There'll be no rest in this house until you're back here again.

Down stairs she ran, along the corridor, and out through the Great Hall, down the passage, through the brick pantry and out a side door and under the loggia.

Pausing she listened, so quiet, no one stirring, not a dog barking or a mouse squeaking.

The dew heavy on the grass, her shoes kicking up water, she ran out onto the Mound. Twice she'll run round the Park. If he's there waiting they'll meet. If he's forgotten, or moved on, or if it truly is as she was told, that he is no more than a dream in her head, a memory, then she'll return. She'll shower and sleep. The sun will rise and another day, and another life, will begin.

Chapter One
The Problem

'So, let me get this straight!'

He pushed back the chair and the interview was over. With the exception of Sophie's mother, no one, not even Madame de Valois of the Royal Ballet, remains seated when General Alexander Stonewall Hunter is on his feet.

Eyes of flint, he faced them down. 'A short time ago you considered my daughter an exceptional dancer. "Gifted, articulate, and with original flair, we may be looking at a new Fonteyn," *this* was your latest appraisal. Now at the point of graduation you say she has no future in the ballet?'

The administrator was abashed. 'I am sorry about the letter but not sorry for considering Sophie a world class ballerina. My regret is that such hopes were ever set down on paper. Considering the times we've been disappointed by spurts of adolescent growth we should have known better.'

The co-director nodded. 'Indeed, the Czechoslovakian girl last season is a case in point, so much promise and all to nothing.'

The Director nodded. 'And the girl from Tokyo.'

'Excuse me!' Alex Hunter cut through the chat. 'I'm not interested in your regrets. It is my daughter's disappointment that concerns me, namely, why after so much time and effort she's not to be given her heart's desire.'

'It is as we said, Sophie has a height problem.'

'No, madam! My daughter does not have a problem with height, you do!'

'Yes, it is our problem. Regrettably, in terms of ballet it is also hers. She is a beautiful young woman, elegant and graceful.' Heads nod in agreement. 'In the world of fashion her height can only add to her charms but in our world…forgive the 'our', it's the only word that fits…the mandatory ceiling for the ladies corps-de-ballet is five-eight. Sophie at last measuring was five-ten.'

'Two inches?'

'Two inches.'

'And that is the problem?'

'Believe me, we would have it otherwise. It's not our wish to part with gifted dancers, the Company's time and effort being equally precious. Sophie graduates with honours. We will offer her a place yet, conscious of her dedication to the art, felt it only right to acquaint you both with the facts.'

'And what are the facts?'

'Sophie's talent will suffer if she stays. We couldn't use her corps de ballet, the line would be spoiled, neither would she be considered for senior roles. The painful truth is that unless there's a sudden influx of male dancers with a corresponding rise in height and less vanity, I doubt there's a soloist willing to be her partner.'

'Because the mighty two inches will overtop him?'

'Yes.'

'You have gotta be kidding!'

'No, General, I wish I was. Balance, technique, and muscular stress, there are many reasons why a female *coryphée* needs to be shorter than the male. I'm afraid the system is not yet bold enough, or brave enough, to choose a-right.'

It was then Sophie whimpered. Such a sad sound it brought her mother to her side. 'Darling, don't give up! It's not decided yet, is it, Madame?'

The room was silent.

'Is it decided?' Alex Hunter looked to the Director. 'Has the hard work and dedication of a girl's life been for nothing?'

Madame de Valois pursed her lips. 'Your daughter's future is still very much in her hands. It's my hope she'll direct her talent elsewhere.'

'You mean to another company?'

'Height restrictions in all reputable companies remain the same, however, the world of dance has many paths and as my colleague pointed out Sophie is a beautiful young woman. I doubt she'll let this hurdle stand in her way.'

'A colossal hurdle, wouldn't you say, Madame, the loss of a life-long dream?'

'Yes, but one that must be gotten over!'

'You said you'd offer her a place.'

'That has been suggested.'

'But not by you.'

'I have spoken with your daughter. She knows my thoughts on the matter.'

'And what are your thoughts?'

'Perhaps you should ask Sophie?'

As one they turned. Heart sick, unable to answer, she shook her head.

'Then,' said Madame de Valois, 'I'll tell you what I told her. Ours is an elite world. If she accepts a post within the Company her career is on hold. She is a wonderful dancer and as such would for a time be regarded as a show piece but with none of the major roles open to her. Time and again passed over for a dancer of less talent, her life would consist of touring the suburbs or back row corps-de-ballet when the ranks are reduced.'

'Your words are harsh.'

'Yes but true.' Ninette de Valois took Sophie's hand. 'Do you recall what I said to you? I asked if you could live in so constrained a world. Could you thrive on the meagre crumbs shed from a particularly barren table?'

Alex Hunter turned, loving blue eyes gazing into tearful blue. 'And could you, Sweet Pea?' he said, already knowing the answer. 'Could you live like that?'

'No, Daddy.' A tear slipped down her cheek. 'It would kill me.'

~

She emptied her locker. 'Don't cry, Soph,' Becky Ryland hissed. 'The Mice are gathering and you don't want them to see you.' Beyond crying, Sophie dropped several pairs of *pointe* shoes into the bin. Patched and mended, yet lovely maintained, her dreams were like these shoes. Now they're nothing.

It was always the ballet. Bobby Rourke, her stepfather, said she was born to dance. What would he think if he were here today? He'd probably say, 'don't worry. There'll be another company willing to take you.' But as an Ace pilot during the war, one-of-the-few, he would know this is the Royal Ballet and that having tried for the highest mountain a lesser pinnacle wouldn't do.

'Oh, do get a move on!' Becky breathes down her neck. 'Your parents will be wondering where we are.'

'I'm done.' Sophie slammed the locker door. 'I've got everything I need from here. There are just a few bits to collect from the Abbey.'

Becky narrowed her eyes. 'Why there? It's London and the ballet you're leaving not the Beauforts.'

The Abbey at Midwinter Down has for the last few years been a bolt-hole during weekends and short vacs. Becky loves it there. A tricky childhood, coming to England opened a whole new world to her, a world she wants to hold onto, and who can blame her. A beautiful seventeenth-century manor house in the heart of England where one is cosseted by Lord Beaufort and his wife, Lady Joanne, two of the kindest people in the world – no one wants to give up on that, especially Becky, who, mad for their son, dreams of bridal gowns and coronets and doesn't want Sophie rocking the boat!

'You don't need to move your stuff anywhere.'

'I don't see how I can keep it there with everything changed.'

'The Abbey hasn't changed,' said Becky. 'Uncle Charles hasn't changed. He and Lady Jo are always glad to see us.'

Sophie would sooner not visit but Joshua, her brother, is there. They go to collect him to bring him home. Also, there will be questions and sympathy, and awfully nice people trying to be kind and Sophie's not sure she can bear it- not that any of this matters with Becky determined to stake her claim.

'I know you're feeling bad, Sophie. It's rotten getting chucked like that. If it was me I'd be tearing my hair. Chucked or not I can't let you get between me and the Beauforts. You know I'm always scratching about for cash. The Abbey is the one place I can go without worrying how I'm going to manage. And it's not just cash-flow! I need to be among people who care whether I live or die.'

'Your mother cares whether you live or die.'

'Yes, when she's around, but when is she ever! I need the Abbey. I need my attic suite and cosy truckle bed. I need Nanny Foster's cocoa, and Lady Jo's hugs and Uncle Charles's enthusiasm. I need his name! I love the way it makes people sit up and beg! I know he's not my uncle – Becky Ryland niece of an English Lord, don't be absurd! I know he's on loan and that I got him through your ma's connections. But I still need him to be a little bit mine.'

'Heaven's sake, Becky, don't make a drama of it. My leaving England won't affect your chances with Johnny.'

'Johnny?' Becky snapped her jaw. 'What's he got to do with it?'

'Everything I'd say.'

'This isn't about Jay Beaufort. He's a fantastic guy and I do like him but that's as far as it goes. It's the Abbey I like, and I don't know how you can say your leaving doesn't affect me. You're my buddy. We do everything together.

Can't you at least visit the Abbey? You can't stay away from England forever.'

'No, and I don't intend to.'

Sophie was a toddler when she went to America, she and Mother left England on the promise of a new life. They found lies and shadowy corners in a broken down Mill-House in Fredericksburg, Virginia. In '48 her real father became known, and from then, torn between love of her step-father and fear for Mother, she never felt safe. Bobby Rourke died in '48. Then followed the Korean War and Dad a POW. In '53 they moved to Vermont, and there, at a private school attached to Bennington, she passed the Royal Ballet audition.

Ten years they boarded here, two skinny kids sharing the same dorm and same hopes, the first five years were at White Lodge among cold sheets and stiff British accents, the rest at Baron's Court where Sophie happily embraced her roots, as English now as strawberries and cream. Nothing challenges Becky's Virginian drawl. She hangs on to her heritage and with it her hopes of Johnny Jay Beaufort. 'So what will you do, Soph, when you're Stateside?'

'I haven't a clue.'

'You're on vacation first, aren't you?'

'Yes, Switzerland, hopefully then my parents will stop worrying about me.'

'That ain't gonna happen. They love you and are always going to worry. Say, did your pa lose his temper back there?' Becky snickered. 'I wish I'd seen their faces when he marched in. I bet he had 'em all peeing their pants.'

Sophie turned away. Who cares what they felt? She's sick of the whole damn business! Ten years she's studied here! Ten years gazing into multiple mirrors at multiple Sophies, and all too gawky, too shy, and now too tall.

It is six months to the day since she saw 'the problem', namely, a frill of curls jutting above everyone else. Ten minutes later she saw the problem echoed in the ballet-mistress's eyes, saw her pause, stare, and walk out of the room returning with Madame. 'Miss Sophie Hunter!' was the call: 'A moment of your time in matron's room, if you please!'

Sophie didn't want to believe it, neither did Mother. 'It'll be okay. Your father is a giant but I'm only five-seven.' Nanny Foster at the Abbey offered similar advice. 'They've got it wrong, dearie. You've done all your growing.'

How she'd longed for it to be true, every day praying, 'Lord, let me not grow anymore.' The Lord wasn't listening – ten years, two inches, and it's all over.

~

Word has spread, students – the 'Mice', as Becky calls them – are whispering in the corridor. Sophie now one less rival to worry about, the Mice have a particular look in their eyes; sympathy shot through with glee.

Down in the quadrangle an army staff car waits with pennants flying, her parents as always in their private world. A surge of love and frustration rose up in Sophie; all that nonsense in the office, everyone kow-towing, she might have been invisible.

Daddy has a long reach. His sons revere him, Tim at the Academy and Joshua not far behind, Sophie would die for him but wishes him a little less mighty.

A heroic, if somewhat shadowy figure, on his rare visits to London he arrives in a staff car whisking Sophie and friends for tea at the Ritz. Then he's gone in a khaki-clad cloud. As for Mother, if Royal Ballet Admin is in awe of the General then the whole of Upper School is dazzled by the onetime GI bride who left everything she knew and crossing an ocean inherited a nightmare.

The nightmare is over yet, it left a purpling bruise that if not visible to the eye is felt by the heart. Mother is not well. It's partly why they visit England, an appointment with a Harley Street specialist.

A breeze blew up, Daddy tucking Mummy's collar close about her neck.

Becky spoke from behind. 'You are lucky, Sophie.'

'Lucky?'

'Yeah, lucky! You have folks that love you.'

Yes, in that she is lucky. She knows where she stands in her father's love. She is his little girl, his Sweet Pea. Brother, Tim, and younger brother, Joshua, are his best boys. But Mother is his reason for living. No one can rival her in his affection. She is the light-of-his-life! And should that light diminish – should her cough become more ragged and loss of weight pronounced – then his light will diminish accordingly.

~

Alex Hunter clenched his jaw. 'That Madame gives me the pip!'

'She is rather a cool sort of person,' said Adelia. 'But she does try to tell the truth and you can't ask more than that.'

'I suppose! But did you see our little girl's face? She's flattened, all squashed down and no place to go.'

'I know. It's awful.'

'I blame myself.' Agitated, he pushed his hands through his hair. 'Tall is in the family. Dad had it and father before him. Tag's got it, and I guess looking on the other side of the fence Josh will have it too. Hunter men have always been lofty. I assumed you being a cuddly babe Sophie would be okay.'

'She is okay. She's a daughter to be proud of.'

'Sure, but that's all you. It's nothing to do with me.'

'It's everything to do with you. You are a wonderful man, high, wide, and handsome. I'm proud of every blessed inch and wouldn't want you less, and the Royal Ballet, and Madame de Valois included, can go to blazes.'

'Hey!' He laid his hand against her lips, fingers shortened stumps, souvenirs of a Korean inquisitor. 'Don't get worked up. You know what the doctor said.'

'Oh pooh! I get a little breathless, that's all. If I can't get worked up about my own daughter when her dreams are in tatters then I don't know what.'

Alex frowned. 'I should've got more worked up. Two inches for Chrissakes! No one ever died because of two inches. Cockamamie British red tape!'

'Excuse me, General Hunter, don't forget I am British.'

'You're not British. You're international. Okay, you were born here but that's all. Ain't no stiff English broom stuck up my wife's backside.'

'I'm glad to hear it.'

'But you gotta admit what we witnessed back there was bullshit of the first order. They make petty rules and then they're stuck with 'em. It comes of centuries of living in rundown castles and wearing moth-eaten ermine.'

'I didn't know you were such an Anglophobe.'

'I love England. It gave me you. I'm saying the Royal Ballet is hog tied by its own red tape, and if that's not enough we're off to Suffolk exchanging one arcane institution for another. Impoverished gentry, I can do without them!'

'Hardly impoverished. They have Van Dykes on the walls.'

'Uh-huh, and rusty water in the bath.'

'We Brits are not consumed by creature comforts. We are more circumspect.'

'That old pile is circumspect. Do you recall the last time we were there, a pipe burst and water came through the ceiling and dripped on the beds?'

Adelia laughed. 'Yes and there were mice in the tapestries.'

'I like hot water in my pipes and Johns that flush. Much like London Bridge, Lord Beaufort and his manor house are one stone away from falling down.'

'Darling, why say that? You like Charles, you know you do. He's a good man, exceptionally kind to Sophie and Becky. Look at the help he's been? The times they've stayed during weekends and long vacs? We couldn't have asked for a safer environment, a real home-away-from-home.'

'Your home, honey, not mine. Sure, he's a good guy, but I've had enough of globe-trotting. I need to be back on my own territory, to feel the ground under my feet. Have my girls where I can keep my eye on them.'

Adelia sighed. 'First there's Switzerland. Still, perhaps when we're rested the two inches won't seem so baleful and you'll be able to plan ahead.'

'Yes, if you're able to plan ahead with me.'

'I shall be.'

'Promise?'

'Promise.'

'And you'll try to get well?'

'I shall do my best.'

Eternally anxious these days, Alex shuffled his feet. 'I don't know about Switzerland and all that snow. Maybe we should go to some place hot, a couple of months in California. Get heat into your bones. You're always so chilly.'

'I am English, dear heart. I was born chilly.'

'You were born beautiful. I love you.'

'Love you too.'

'Come rain or shine?'

'Come rain or shine, but hush now, darling, they're coming. Becky's rather done up, but then, bless her, she has her eye on the moth-eaten ermine.'

'You don't say? I thought Johnny had his eye on Sophie.'

'He does but is currently drawn to Becky.'

'And why not. She's a great looking girl.'

'She takes after her mother.'

'Talking of her mother is Sue still rolling around in Brazil?'

'Sue is recouping her losses.'

'Affirmative, recouping with a monthly cheque from my wife's allowance.'

'How did you know about that?'

'I know everything. I am the eyes and ears of the world.'

Adelia's mouth turned down. 'Now where have I heard that before?'

'Hush, baby. You don't want to be thinking of him, not after all these years.'

'Time has nothing to do with it. Where Bobby is concerned there will always be regret.'

'And it's those regrets that are doing you no good!' He curled his fist. 'Six foot deep and still hurting you, I swear to God he'll bury us both.'

'Never mind that!' She took his hand. 'Did you know Sue's last millionaire turned out to be a dud?'

'She should've stuck with the funeral parlour and Frank.'

'Frank is fine. He's married to Beth and with girls of his own.'

'Sure, but Sue was his first love and you don't get over that.'

'No, and thank God we don't. The girls are coming! Now remember, darling, let Sophie do the talking. No pumping and probing.'

~

The car turned into the approach, the Abbey appearing through the avenue of leafy trees as a rose-tinted jewel box. A decade of exploring its many secrets and yet Sophie still finds mystery under that pink tiled roof. Virginia creeper invading diamond studded windows and dusty bricks, it was begun in 1589 and added on throughout the centuries it is a maze of twisting staircases and narrow spaces, and of hidden priest holes and dark cellars, of warmth and sudden cold places where aristocratic faces gaze down from every wall.

Alex Hunter grinned. 'This is some place then, Sophie.'

'Yes.'

'You and Becky come here a lot.'

'Whenever we can. We love it.'

'I admit it is kinda cute.'

'Cute?' Adelia grimaced.

'It is cute, honey, like a picture in a kiddie's story book.'

'I can think of better words.'

'Like enchanting,' said Becky.

'And magical,' said Sophie.

'And noble.'

'And peaceful, with nothing and no one around for miles.'

'Hey!' Alex took Sophie's hand. 'You're twenty and gorgeous. Why would you want to be peaceful? You and Becky should be out shaking your bones in a jazz cellar with a couple of lads, never mind peaceful.'

'Ash!' Adelia Hunter tutted. 'What a thing to say.'

'What's wrong with it?'

'Nothing if you believe it.'

'And you don't?'

'Not a word and neither does your daughter. It's contrary to everything a father wants for his daughter.'

'My girl won't do anything crazy. She has her head screwed on.'

Sophie gazed out the window. The last time they drove down the Avenue conversation was all about ballet. Now, unable to pursue that topic, her parents try making her feel less of an outsider. What they don't know, and what she'll never tell, is that in company of the General and his wife everyone is an outsider. Together they create a bubble that no one can penetrate, no obvious word or gesture of affection yet all the while conveying adoration. Sophie is used to it but today she feels truly on the outside.

The car swung through the archway into the courtyard.

The family were on the steps, their faces wreathed in smiles. John Beaufort, heir to the Estate, more observer than participant, stood to one side.

Ten years and Sophie doesn't know the Abbey – fifty years and she'll not know that man. He doesn't want to be known. Born late to his parents, and adored by Clare and Julia, his sisters, he stands aloof, staring down his patrician nose, probably viewing Sophie and family as more of the nuisance fee-paying public who are to trample the grounds and worry the animals in the Park.

Becky's mad for him. He's all she talks about, how witty and intelligent. Sophie wouldn't know. Hear no evil, see and speak none, he doesn't seem to notice her, animals and sexy blondes his preoccupation.

Drawling voice forever clipping consonants, he's known for 'huntin', shootin', and fishin'' but with a camera rather than a rod and gun. Tall, fresh faced, with brown hair and hazel eyes he is good-looking, of that he is sure, and *noblesse oblige*, strolls the grounds blessing every blade of grass beneath his booted feet. Gossip talks of a dark side, the Hon John directing traffic. Society columnists love him, though never quite as scandalous as the Profumo affair, yet hot and spicy, his name linked with single and married women alike.

Last summer there was the fete in the Park. Sophie wandered into the orchid house. There he was, jeans unzipped and a certain politician's wife with her hands down his pants. Since then she'd often catch him staring, a challenging look in his eyes. Becky can have him. She's welcome to him!

'At last, you're all here!' Charles Beaufort smiles, the warmth of his welcome carrying them en masse into the Great Hall. 'We thought you'd never come.'

Becky bounded up the steps laying claim to Lady Joanne.

Afraid to find sympathy in their eyes Sophie was slow to follow.

Warm lips touched her cheek. 'Hello, dear girl,' Charles Beaufort took her hand. 'It's so good to see you.'

Rooted to the spot Sophie couldn't move. It's here among a familiar smell of ancient walls, dry rot, and potpourri. She must leave this and go back to a life and country she no longer knows. The loss was suddenly unbearable.

A hand grasped her elbow. 'Come!'

John Beaufort took her hand and ran. They raced across the Great Hall, up a flight of steps and along a corridor into the Long Gallery, on and on, images flickering by, scandalized ancestors frowning down from dusty portraits, blue and gold lions *regardent* pawing the air and flag-draped Beaufort battle-honours, the weight of centuries woven into walls.

Caught between laugh and sob she ran, she'd no choice, on through bedroom after bedroom, musty canopies hanging from rickety four-posters, until a downward flight of steps and the sudden sunshine of the loggia.

'Okay then, Goody Two-Shoes!' Hands about her waist he lifted her onto the wall. 'Sit awhile and rest. You've had a busy day.'

Head down, she sat trying to get her breath back. A tobacco tin from his pocket, he leaned against the wall rolling a cigarette. 'I got a new cat yesterday bedded down on drips,' he said. 'I got the local vet to take a look.'

'What did he find?' said Sophie finally managing to speak.

'Chronic kidney disease.' He shrugged. 'I'm not surprised. Cooped up in a cage all this time and fed potato chips by moronic tourists is enough to kill anythin'.'

'People think they are helping.'

'They're not! They're makin' a bad situation worse.'

'They don't know that.'

'Well, they should! See a wild cat in a cage and the gen pub can't resist stuffing toffees through the bars. I complained to the authorities but don't expect anythin'. Call that place a Zoo? It's more a fuckin' abattoir.'

'Don't swear.'

'Oh did I swear? Sorry about that. I got carried away for a minute thinkin' I was talkin' to a human bein' not a Goody Two-Shoes.'

'Why do you call me that when you know I hate it as I hate foul-mouthed swearing? It reminds me of the past.'

'Maybe that's why I do it, to shake you up. Can't have you red-eyed and mopin'.' He blew smoke into the air. 'If not Goody what should I call you?'

'Sophie like everyone else!'

'But you're not like everyone else.'

'What am I like?'

'What are you?' Ponytail of hair swiping his collar, he leaned back. 'A few sticky expressions spring to mind, mummy's little darling and daddy's Sweet Pea.'

'You really do think I'm a spoiled brat.'

'Maybe not a brat but certainly spoilt.'

'Thanks very much.'

'I'm only tellin' it as it is. Honest John, they call me.'

'That's not what I've heard.'

'And what have you heard?'

'Probably best I don't say. I must go in.' Sophie pushed off the wall. 'Dad will want to avoid traffic and I need to collect things from my room.'

'What things?' he said echoing Becky. 'Tacky toe shoes and gnarly knickers?'

'Yes, if you like.'

'Take what you need but leave the best behind. Keep a lid on this, Sophie. Too tall my arse! Seems to me the Royal Ballet is talkin' through theirs.'

'That's what Dad thinks.'

'Your dad is right. Forget 'em! Their loss is another company's gain.'

'Unfortunately, it doesn't work like that.'

'Whatever, do not leave here thinkin' not to come back, though I've probably fucked up the conjugate, Latin never my subject, *quia domus mea, domus tua*. My house is your house. Leave your best hopes here. I'll guard them with my life, a notice on the door "property of Goody Two Shoes'', no admittance.'

Sophie stared. 'Why are you being so kind?'

'I'm always kind. I can't help it if you don't see it. Remember, chucked out of the ballet doesn't mean chucked out of here, my word as an Englishman.'

'Oh don't!' She put her hands over her eyes. 'Don't be kind to me, Johnny, or I'll fall apart. Stay who you are for heaven's sake.'

'And who am I?'

'Honourable John, Lion tamer and all round smart ass.'

'Christ!' He seemed startled. 'Is that how you see me? I had hoped for another view. Still if being a smart arse keeps you at the Abbey I'll stay smart.'

~

On the plane ride home Sophie tied her hair back, twisting the heavy curls up on her head. Then she resumed a letter to Ethan. Every night she adds to it, nothing heavy, a bit of this and that, something he might enjoy. Usually the pen flows. Tonight there's little joy to convey.

Letters from Sophie have been passing back and forth across the world since she was a child. It started with Dad posted missing in Korea. She wrote to him via US army post, her letters shared among the troops. Most replies were scribbled signatures on the back. One contributor remained constant even after the war – Ethan Winter, son of Jane Winter, Boston, Massachusetts.

It was Major Jane Winter, a US Navy nursing sister in a MASH unit, in '51 who started the communication, gentle *billet doux* reaching back into the heart of a child. Autumn '58 the notes ceased. Ethan took over, a couple of lines straight to the point. '*Hi, Sophie Hunter. Mom got sick and died last month. I'll drop a line now and then if you like. Stay safe, Ethan Winter the Third.*'

Years on and still they swap a letter a week. His start '*hi, Sophie…*' and ends '*…stay safe, Ethan Winter, the Third.*' She's no idea what he looks like, though his letters, brief and to the point, offer an image of a compact human-being with pointed head and stubby legs. He has one photograph of her as a cygnet in Swan Lake, taken on the day she was accepted into the Royal Ballet.

Pen-friends are comforting but distant. Tonight with the moon shining through the plane windows, Joshua snoring, and Mum with her head on Dad's shoulder, Sophie could've used a hug.

Ethan is very bright. Post graduate in physics currently cramming in Russian and Cantonese, his ambition is to be an astronaut. While puzzled as to what use Russian or Cantonese might be to Men from Mars Sophie's life pales in comparison. Her news is always of the ballet, and as any balletomane will tell you, news anywhere at the moment is Rudolph Nureyev.

Last January outside the Opera House Sophie bumped into the man. Snow falling, she'd stopped to lace up her boots. Waving hands and manic eyebrows, he cannoned into her. The morning of February 21st found an envelope in her pigeon-hole, an apology for rudeness and two tickets for *Giselle*.

Tickets for Nureyev and Fonteyn were gold dust, thus followed a frantic search for an evening frock, Becky's RADA friends coming to the rescue with a key to the RSC wardrobe – Becky a modern day Cleopatra in gold wrappings, and Sophie as Titania, paste sapphires in her hair and aquamarine wings.

Such magic being of the past she must find something else to do. Johnny Beaufort had a suggestion. He cornered her in the Library.

'My word as an English man was clearly not enough to keep you?'

'I beg your pardon?'

'You emptied your suite.'

'I left a couple of bits.'

'Yes, but not your heart.' With that he'd turned away. 'If you can't find a job back home you could always work here as Junior Lion-tamer. Leather thigh-boots and a nasty looking whip, you'd be a sensation.'

Weary, Sophie yawned. Dawn is breaking. Sunlight gilding the Eastern horizon it looks like it'll be a nice day. Time to finish the letter.

'Well, it's happened, Ethan Winter the Third. My pretty little world, as you are wont to call it collapsed. Thanks to two inches I am unemployed and so if you're not too busy with Russian and physics, and the other things you do, please keep your eyes open for

*a suitable vacancy. Mail-person or tea-girl I am available because
I don't see myself as taming anything yet, lion or man.*

*Sophie Hunter, ex-pupil of the Royal Ballet and failed
ballerina.'*

Chapter Two
Memories

Back with Granma Ellen and the boys, Sophie couldn't help thinking she should count her blessings; nine-year-old Joshua sprouting in every direction and Tag coming up thirteen and polishing the lintel with his crew-cut, she should be glad 'the problem' was only a matter of inches as opposed to feet!

Tag, Timothy Alexander William George, grinned. 'Hi Sis, how's it hanging?'

'How's it hanging?'

Voice ripping through five octaves he laughed. 'I meant, how are you?'

'Then please say so instead of sounding like one of those moronic BSA chaps on a Venturing rally.'

'For your information I *am* one of those BSA chaps who happens to be on his way toward Eagle Scout and so less of the moron.'

The brief spit-spat was conducted in the age-old younger brother, older sister fashion, plenty insults plus plenty reassuring grins. Sophie played her role; that she is miserable, doesn't mean Tag has to be. Besides, beneath the freckled exterior hides a sensitive male. Then there's Josh shooting out and up in the Hunter way yet with mother's heavy gold hair and his own heavenly eyes. Joshua Robert Hunter! So beautiful people stop to look and animals come to be petted. He spends a goodly part of his life in England where, when not being spoiled at the Abbey in Oxford, he's with Uncle Gabriel and Julia.

Johnny Beaufort and Josh are inseparable. See them in the Great Park together, the man with the mane of curly hair and the golden-haired lad, and you see Androcles and the Lion, their ambition to free every captive creature in Creation. A former champion of the cause, forever trying to raise funds for animal welfare, Lord Beaufort acknowledges their commitment with a sigh. 'It's a battle they can't hope to win. It'll break their hearts as it broke mine.'

Charles Beaufort is quick to detect a broken heart. The last day in England Sophie spent time with Nanny in the South Wing and then walked via the Cloisters to the Orchid Room, one of her most favourite places.

Charles Beaufort will never walk in on Johnny and his paramours - he warns of approach scraping his shoes outside the door. That evening, having announced his presence, he spoke with Sophie. 'I've been trying to mend that,' he said of a broken pot, 'but it doesn't want to stick. It's a rare piece, been in the family generations but will have to go. Some things are not meant to mend.'

Sophie must have muttered something because he continued. 'You and Rebecca have brought a deal of happiness to the Abbey. Youth and beauty bring life to a house. We had it when our girls were young. Now we have it with you. Lady Joanne loves to see you as do I. You have a home here.'

If she came close to breaking down it was then, Johnny stopped her, an earlier whispered aside: 'No crying over spilt milk, Goody. Get your virginal arse out into the working world and earn your own bowl of cream.'

The belt-and-braces chat is his forte. It is in the rare moments of kindness he's most dangerous, luring you into a trap only to slap you down. Money and how to get it is his constant worry. You need cash to save endangered wildlife and ready cash the Estate does not have. Treasure and trash in every corner, the Abbey is a Dolly Mixture house. Woolworths or Faberge, you never know what you're looking at. Once, Sophie took a toffee from a dish on the table by the Wedgwood Sitting Room fireplace returning the wrapper to the dish.

Johnny threw the wrapper on the fire, his drawling tones echoing round the room. 'Qing Dynasty, that dish can buy and sell the village. It's one thing to carry M&S coffee-creams, quite another to be stuffed with wrappings.'

Sophie wanted to crawl through a crack in the floor, her humiliation made complete when George Allen, the major domo, took up arms against Johnny.

George is butler to Lord Beaufort, he and his wife Betty with the family for years. That day hearing the remark he slammed a heavy tea-tray on the same table. Up went the dish, toffees scattering. George caught it and set it back. 'How's zat, sir!' Charles Beaufort was heard to murmur.

Johnny was studying to be a Vet then as well as busy at the Abbey. Becky took his part. 'He didn't mean it. He's fed up of going to his pa for cash.'

Sophie didn't care. 'He should get a job.'

'He has a job. He's a Viscount.'

'That's not a job. That is a matter of birth and this is not the twelfth century! If he needs money he should earn it.'

It seems Johnny was outside that day and heard every word. She is sorry about that but he is too bossy by half. It comes of being pandered to by older sisters Clare and Julia. Clare is married to the Reverend Thomas Glossop who is currently spreading the word in China, and Lady Julia to Gabriel Templar, the guardian angel who for so many years stood between Mother and danger.

Blond and handsome, Gabriel has his own miniature angelic likenesses in twin sons, Charles Junior and Michael. Dad says we should always be honest, especially with ourselves. Sophie remembers the violence of early years in Virginia. She remembers electricity zapping from Gabriel to Mother and back again. If she were being honest she might wonder why equally blond and angelic Joshua spends so much time in England, and why her parents allow it, and why Dad is never at ease when the name Templar is mentioned.

'*Things happen in wartime. People get thrown together. Some never come apart.*' Nanny Foster said that one night. She was watching Gabriel when she said it who in turn was watching Mother. Lord Beaufort suggests certain objects are not meant to mend. Nanny says they are unable to break, differing points of view of the same mystery.

~

If Sophie thought her brothers grown then Aunt Sarah's sons were a shock. 'Hi, Sophie,' a handsome string-bean with red hair grinned, David, the younger brother studying medicine at University College.

'Hello, Peter.'

'Ah come on, Sophie!' he said. 'It can't be that long since we met.'

'I'm only teasing. I knew it was you. I couldn't miss. You have the intern look, pale and sadly loitering.'

'Yeah, pale from lack of sunlight but not from loitering. I've just completed a 90 hour rotation. Not once set my ass on a chair.' He grinned again, 'though you being a refined young lady I should omit the word ass.'

'You should.'

'How are things then, coz? You're looking well.'

'Thanks, I am well, and thanks again for *not* asking how I'm hanging.'

David laughed. 'That'll be Tag. I saw him the other day. That boy has been badly bitten by the military bug. He tried signing me up for the Medical Corps. So how's the ballet? Gotten any major roles lately and if not why not. You're beautiful, Sophie. I'd pay to see you breathe never mind dance.'

A compliment from Davy!? There must've been a role reversal. It was always Petey studying girl-catching lines. David was into Outer Space. 'You sure you're David Parker? The David I remember wouldn't have trotted out that line.'

'That's no line. You are beautiful in a cool British way. I'm half in love with you already. Speaking of love…(he did the twitch of the head thing inherited from his father, Maurice Parker, the neurosurgeon) How's Becky?'

This is the real Davy. Nuts over Becky, he'd follow her around like a puppy.

'She's fine. I had a call from her this morning. She's been accepted into the Company.'

'I guess that means she'll stay in London.'

Conversation fell flat, Davy disappointed his dream-girl was still out of reach and Sophie because talking about the ballet brought back the hurt.

~

With news of President Kennedy's assassination, Dad is called away but phoned to say he'd be back in time for the trip to Switzerland.

The nation's grief hasn't stopped Granma Ellen fussing. Mother is having some sort of crisis and returned from lunch with Uncle Maurice saying she is flying to Virginia tomorrow. 'I'm taking the eight am hop.'

'Why would you want to go back there?' said Granma. 'Wouldn't you be better waiting until after Switzerland or at least until Alex is home.'

'I'm not bothering Alex and neither will you, Ellen.'

'But you're ill and ought not to travel alone,' Granma persisted. 'I would come with you but can't at such short notice.'

'I'm not asking,' said Mother, a backed-against-the-wall look in her eyes.

'I'll come with you,' said Sophie.

~

They arrived in Fredericksburg just after nine and took a taxi.

'Where to, ma'am?' said the driver.

'Perhaps you might take us on a mini tour?'

They drove along Main Street; memories opening up as pages of a colouring book. 1946 Sophie travelled this route, a toy monkey in her arms and sleepy-dust in her eyes. Uncle Gabriel collected them from New York Harbour. It should've been Bobby, but afraid to show his face, he sent the handyman. Some handyman! Gabriel was a Marine in those days, strikingly handsome in uniform yet scorned by many as an illiterate bum. Adelia Challoner, dazzling beauty in second-hand clothes, came to America on the promise of love. Love was waiting at the Harbour and, though now married to another, continues to love. It is as Nanny Foster said: some things can't be pulled apart.

They passed the store where Becky's mother used to work - Sue's gorgeous face and momentous cleavage mesmerising every red-blooded male in town. It's where Mother bought fabric for curtains and endless tins of 'Spring Blush' emulsion. Sophie remembers the smell of paint, the buzz of a sewing machine, and relentless criticism from Bobby's mother.

Mother was always busy, if not sewing drapes then digging potatoes. Keeping busy was her sanity: Bobby and the Mill proving all kinds of disappointment.

The cab turned left. The Mission Hall where the annual ballet recital was held is a supermarket now. The Hall is gone but memories of a night in '48 remain in Sophie's heart under the heading of '***The Night I learned the Identity of my Real Father.***' It is all so long ago yet, when hearing the opening bars of Mendelssohn's Midsummer Night's Dream, her skin prickles. She feels the swish of a tutu. Then a little girl runs onto the stage and poised in the spotlight the opening words are on her tongue: '*How now, Spirit, whither wander you?*'

At that point the memory usually collapses supplanted by another - Captain Robert Rourke DFC lurching down the centre aisle, a stick in his hand and murder in his heart. That's the trouble with eidetic memory; you must take it all, the good, the bad, and the sickening.

Mother is ahead of Sophie. 'Darling, do you remember that night?'

'Yes.'

'Everyone squashed in those hideous infant chairs?'

'Yes, everyone but Gramps. He demanded a proper chair.'

'So he did! I'd forgotten that. Oh dear Bill, how I miss him!'

'Me too.'

'That night you stood in for Puck and never hesitated. You knew every step and every line. That's your daddy coming out in you, photographic memory. Do you remember how you felt when you ran on the stage?'

'Yes, scared and excited at the same time.'

Eyes dark and heavy, Mother turned. 'Would you do it again? Would you go through it all if you knew what was to come?'

Her question isn't about a child's ballet recital. It is about a decision made years ago, a choice of life or death, whether to stay in England or come to America. Mother is asking herself if it had been worth it.

~

There have been changes since they were in Virginia, busy highways where there once were open fields. The Eyrie, what they could see of it from the road, appears to be the same beautiful black-and-white Tudor style house made more beautiful by Dad's love for Mother.

The cab turned the corner.

'Oh!' Mother gasped. 'They've cut down the wisteria!'

'Oh no!' It was true. The mass of pendulous blossom that once a year gave life to the South Wall had been stripped away. 'How could they do it? It was wonderful. It filled the bedroom with scent.'

'…and crept under the tiles and was a general nuisance. It used to drive your father crazy always having to get ladders out.'

'He would never chop it down.'

'No, he wouldn't.'

They stayed and they stared. Moved by the look in Mother's eyes the cabby had long since cut the meter. 'Let's just call it a job lot, shall we, ma'am.'

The cabbie got out for a cigarette. Sophie couldn't sit in the cab, not with Mother taking mental snap-shots of the house and surroundings. She hated what it implied, the gathering of memories before saying goodbye.

Uncle Maurice Parker is a professor at Johns Hopkins hospital. After Dad he's mother's closest friend and has been since he and Aunt Sarah spilt in '54. They lunch together, talk on the phone, giggle and tell one another dirty jokes.

Giggling is not what went on yesterday. She saw Maurice to talk of her health.

Sophie got back inside the cab. 'We should go.'

'I'd like to see the Mill.'

'Oh must we?'

'You don't have to. You can be dropped in town. But I must.'

Mother must have phoned ahead because when the cab pulled into the drive they were met by a house agent. A key changed hands. The next Sophie knew the cab and the agent are out the gate with a promise to return in an hour.

The silence after the cars left was intense, the air heavy with yesterday. Slowly sound crept back, a blackbird in the Cypress and the familiar creak of sails. They might have been back in '46 and Sophie a three year old. The only thing missing is a squeaky pushchair - Oh, and a black Russian sable!

That coat! The times she's slept under it, perfume clinging to the pelts! It wasn't the first. There were two sables both with the name Adelia Rourke embroidered in the lining. The first accompanied them to America wrapped in brown paper, a Custom's officer goggling: '*Some coat you got, lady. What's it doing in a paper bag?*'

'Shall we go in?'

They approached the door. Mother was trembling, tremors passing down into Sophie's hand. The key turned, the door swung open, and the past rolled out like a dusty red carpet. 'Oh! Oh!' Mother started back. 'I can't do it.'

'You don't have to.'

'But I should! I owe it to him. I owe to the house! One last look!'

'No,' Sophie shook her head. 'You don't have to do anything. It's all been said and done a long time ago.'

'It's not so long ago, not in the scheme of things.'

'Come.' Sophie led her away, suddenly incredibly frail. It was strange and rather terrifying. Adelia Hunter nee Challoner was always so strong.

'It's all wrong, Sophie,' she said. 'I should at least say goodbye.'

'Look! There's a summer house over there. It wasn't here when we were and so doesn't have history. You can sit and rest without worrying.'

'I bought these.' Mother drew out a posy of rosebuds from her bag. 'He liked roses. These are only just born. I thought the house might like them.'

'And so it will.' Gently, Sophie wrested the posy away. 'It's okay. I'm not afraid of the house. Bobby wouldn't hurt me then. He won't hurt me now.'

~

The door closed behind Sophie and it's not the polished parquet circa '63 she sees, it is broken black and white tiles of 1946 and Mother's voice echoing down the years. '*We'll wait. I'm sure Daddy won't be long.*'

In '46 it was warm in the hall and musty-smelling, soupy light filtering through heavy green blinds. A mirror is on the facing wall. Birds pass back and forth outside, their shadowy shapes reflected in the glass.

A clock chimes. A dark shape blurs the light.

Someone, something, crouches on the stairs!

Toddler Sophie slides off her mother's lap and runs to the gate.

'That you, Daddy?'

'Come away!' says Mother. 'It's dangerous.'

'But I want my daddy...my daddy...my daddy!'

Sophie opened her eyes and it is parquet again and a metal hall stand with umbrellas and a table bearing a blue vase of dried Delphinium.

That's how it went throughout the brief tour of the Mill - the embroidery of yesterday draped over today. Open a door and a shadowy figure would pulse into view. It might be the storybook wicked witch and failed grandmother, Ruby Iolanthe, who hated the English usurpers and would snap at the hand that fed her, and who wore hideous hats and stank of liquorice toffees she wouldn't share, then it might be Mother up a step-ladder, a hammer in her hand and drawing pins in her mouth, and Gabriel - dear Uncle Gabriel - in the window seat mending a fishing-fly and humming under his breath.

Gabriel hums a melody and the walls hum with him, they breathe with him, wistful, suspiring. People talk of love, their voices raised in anger or in muted adoration. A dog barks, Biffer, sad little dog with sad ending. Music plays, a record on a wind-up gramophone, *'ain't misbehaving, saving my love for you..!'* And ever and always in a thousand permutations there is the man himself, Bobby Rourke, Battle of Britain Hero doing a soft-shoe-shuffle, back bent and a cigarillo drooping from his lips. *'Hiya, Sophie!'* She can hear him now. *'How's my beautiful princess? Man, have you grown! You're a perfect tintype of your mother. How's your father, the General, the miserable son-of-a-bitch?'*

What is it she sees? Is it eidetic memory or more the living ghosts of the past? Half in and half out has been this way all of Sophie's life. Inherited from her parents, she sees it a gift and not a curse. She's not afraid of empty houses, and this is empty, the new people, whoever they are, have no lasting presence. Their stuff is here, cups in the dresser, and towels in the cupboard, but not them. Former tenants of the Old Mill have a tale to tell so blisteringly hot they suck the place dry, and when they left took the heart of the Mill with them.

It took a while to decide where to put the roses. They should be left in the tower where Bobby spent so much time, auditioning, he would say, for the *Hunchback of Notre Dame*. Sophie found a better place, the greenhouse - Bobby's favourite hidey-hole where he was most at peace.

Straight way she saw him perched on an upturned bucket in a ratty cardigan he always wore. Swigging from a bottle of beer, Biffer curled up at his feet, he was talking to the plants, telling them of his buddy, Alexander Hunter, the best friend any man ever had, and how he, Bobby - sick bastard - betrayed him.

She let herself out and locked the door. One-by-one images of yesterday faded. Sunlight remained, and starlight, and dusty answers.

Bobby is buried under the blue Spruce, the grave marked by the statue of an eagle in flight, Gabriel Templar's work, a peace-offering to a troubled soul.

Mother was tidying the grass. 'He got it wrong, you know,' she said.

'Sorry?'

'Gabriel and the poem.' She stroked the eagle's wing. 'See what it says? '*Age shall not wither them. At the going down of the sun and in the morning we shall remember them.*''

'I see it.'

'It's wrong. The quote should read "*age shall not weary them.*" Gabriel got it mixed up. He said he was thinking of me when he did it, a quotation about Cleopatra. "*Age cannot wither her not custom stale her infinite variety.*" When the Press pointed it out he was upset. I told him not to worry.'

Mother turned her cheek wet with tears. 'I said Bobby wouldn't mind. In fact he'd prefer it. It made him a winner again.'

Chapter Three
Star-Pattern

After that trip it seemed Mother was taking mental pictures. You could almost hear the audible click of a shutter as her eyes settled on an image. She might be looking at Tag in his new scout uniform or maybe Josh plunking on the piano. Then again it might be Sophie she aimed to capture, most of the time it was at Dad she stared and he, conscious of her gaze, would look up.

It was contagious. On the plane to Switzerland Sophie began to do the same, to gather memories. By the end of the holiday, on the last day, she was wishing she could stop. Praying she could stop!

Mental photography kept her from brooding. Since being back home no one has mentioned the 'problem', not even Aunt Sarah, Dad's sister, the classiest, and most inquisitive, lady in Georgetown. Usually she and Granma are quick to bring family worries out into the open. They're probably thinking Sophie will talk when she's ready. She's never going to be ready. The ballet was her life. Can one change horses midstream without losing one's balance?

On the subject of change, a moment ago a strange thing happened. Tag and Josh ride up front in the cockpit with the pilot. A window seat to herself, Sophie grew used to seeing her face reflected in the glass.

Davy Parker said she is beautiful in a British way. She didn't feel beautiful. She felt awkward. And what is British beauty? Sophie rather hopes it means someone like the fashion model, Jean Shrimpton. They share the same high cheekbones, the wide eyes and plentiful hair.

As befits a ballerina Sophie wears her hair parted in the middle and scraped into a bun. Waking from a nap a moment ago she glanced at the window and there she is big eyes and sorrowful mouth. Then it happened – the glass shimmered, and instead of the classic ballerina profile there was a stranger.

More Las Vegas than Sadlers Wells, this Sophie had the same blue eyes yet now heavily made up with long, sweeping lashes. There was the same mouth yet with seriously red lips. As for her hair, it tumbled in curls about her shoulders and was crowned by a headdress of feathers.

'What?'

One-one thousand, two-one thousand, three-one thousand, the image lasted five counts, the eyes in the glass widening in shock and the arched eyebrows lifting. Then it was gone.

Once upon a time she would have run to Mother and told her of this Other Sophie but not now. Though not confirmed, per se, it is understood Mother is very sick – it's what the mental snapshots are about, she is harvesting time.

Dad does it all the while, the Camera, his army codename.

Sophie doesn't know what her father does. No one knows. When not on active service he spends time in the study, headphones on, blinds pulled, and Mother steering everyone away.

Sophie asked once what he was doing. 'I'm looking at things,' he'd said clicking off the Dictaphone.

'What kind of things?'

'Things people and countries and governments may not want me to see.'

In that moment he'd stopped being her father and became a stranger. Sophie never asked again.

'*Dearest Dad!*' She always knew when he was going into danger. She'd wake to find him in the doorway, his mouth soft and his eyes full of love.

'Going away, Daddy?' she would whisper.

He would nod. 'Take care of Mommy while I'm away will you, Sweet-Pea?'

He'd pause, lashes flickering click, click. Then he was gone.

Sophie doesn't do the eyelash thing. Her inner camera works a different way. Exactly how different she once told General Jentzen, Daddy's boss.

Hard to describe but let's say she works from a given point out. Suppose she wanted to remember the posy of rosebuds in the greenhouse? She'd focus on one rose and one petal, and then another petal, and another, adding more until she not only had the posy she had the greenhouse *and* the Mill.

The General was impressed. 'It sounds like a lengthy process.'

'It isn't. It takes longer to describe than do.'

'You are one chip of a military block, Miss Sophie, a mini Box-Brownie. I shall keep my eye on you. You'd be useful in my line of work. Tell you what,' he'd offered a card, 'if you ever run out of things to do call me on this line.'

The General was at the house the other day enquiring after Mother. He saw Sophie and smiled. 'How's my mini Box-Brownie?' When he was leaving he said. 'There's a camera on the market called an Instamatic. One click and you got it. Keep polishing your particular lens and one day we will have a chat.'

~

The holiday progressed and Sophie began to feel better. The hotel was comfortable and the food delicious. The slopes were clean and there was a cute instructor who seemed to think she was cute. Out on the slopes, the swish of the skis and air rushing by and nothing but blue skies above is like flying.

A thought came into her head, Bobby's voice. 'Say, Princess, if you're looking for somethin' to do why not fly a plane? That Beagle Pup is still on the airfield.'

Flying was his life. He lived to fly and died flying. 'Come on,' he'd scoot her into the passenger seat, Biffer squashed in behind. 'Let's go shoot the breeze over Chesapeake Bay.'

Up they'd go, the airfield and houses below like green and grey lozenges. More often than not he'd been drinking, the cockpit sodden with the smell of beer. There would be trouble when they landed, Mother white-faced and furious.

'If you take her up in that condition again we're on the next bus out of here.' He'd laugh, 'what's a matter with you? You know the kid's safe with me. Drunk or sober I'm a better pilot than any flier in this 'burg.'

Beer left him soft and sentimental. Whisky made him crazy. He died trying to save Biffer and in his Will left Sophie one hundred thousand dollars, a love of flying and animals, and a detestation of booze.

Becky goes drinking with her RADA Shakespeare buddies. They rehearse in the theatre and then order wine at the Russian Bar in Floral Street. Sophie used to go with them, but Miss Goody-Two-Shoes, as Johnny Beaufort would no doubt say, would settle for a Cola.

'I don't know what you see in booze,' she'd say. 'It tastes like vinegar.'

Becky would bat her eyelashes as the waiter heaped extra cabbage on her plate. 'It is vinegar but it helps goo to go down and the stodge to clear out.'

Cabbage and more cabbage! High on gas and low on satisfaction, they were always on some kind of diet. It drove Mother crazy. 'What are you two eating? There's nothing of you.' Dad didn't care what they ate but wasn't keen on them sharing an apartment in London. 'It's a big city and you're little girls.'

Mother worried about gaunt faces until she saw them dance. Then she understood. 'You have to do this,' she said. 'You're wonderful both of you, so alive and with such purpose.'

Across the aisle Mother sits with eyes closed and fingers entwined with Dad's. Perhaps I'll change my mind about doing a solo spot at the RBS Gala, thought Sophie. I'll take back the Saint Saens Swan. Mother loves that piece. It would make her happy.

~

They should be going home today but have got an extra day's holiday. The plane scheduled to fly them home has engine trouble, and Robert Whitney, a friend of Dad's staying at the same hotel, offered a ride back in his jet. 'So what do we do?' said Dad. 'We got an extra day, let's use it well.'

There was much talk across the board, Tag has made a friend of Bob's son, Karl Whitney, and is for the Upper Slopes again. Sophie prefers not to ski. Josh wants to visit an Observatory top of one of the mountains. Dad wants Mother to rest and so Josh won the day.

'We gotta go! A guy I was talking to said they've got a 1.93 telescope and a high resolution spectrograph and that on the right day you got a terrific view of a wide star-pattern.'

'Gosh! A wide-star pattern?' Mother smiled. 'We can't afford to miss that.'

'Top of a mountain?' Dad was still thinking on Mother. 'How do we get there? We don't want anything strenuous.'

Eyes sparkling, Mother laughed. 'Sweetheart, I'm fine.' And she did look well. 'Honestly I am. I've felt never better.'

'There's no climb, Dad,' said Josh. 'It's cable car all the way. You get a lift up to the point and then take a car the rest of the way.'

Dad nodded. 'That's not so bad. You reckon you can manage that, honey?'

'Try holding me back.'

It was decided; Tag to go with the Whitneys, the rest to the observatory.

~

They were three hours at the Observatory gazing out into endless sky. Josh was in his element. Mad to understand exploding stars and quasars, and how men can travel in Space, in terms of career it looks like a toss-up between becoming a lion-tamer or astrophysicist.

Talking of astrophysics, Sophie's had a letter from Ethan Winter; he talks of a career change, and is not happy about it. She'll write him a nice, long chatty on the plane home tomorrow to dry his tears. In fact, now she has so much time on her hands she may even suggest a meeting.

Oh, if only she'd known what was to come, that it would be Sophie needing to dry her tears!

They were on their way back down when it happened. Looking back the signs were all there, the warning signals. It's just that nobody picked up on them.

It started with Josh suddenly feeling unwell.

'What's the matter?' Mother asked him.

'I feel kinda spooked.'

'Spooked?' Dad asked. 'What do you mean spooked?'

'I don't know. I just want to get out of here.'

'I thought you wanted to be here?'

'I did – I do – but now I want to get out.'

'Then we'll go,' said Mother. 'You do look rather pale.'

Poor Josh! He'll never forget the day nor forgive himself. 'I should've spotted it,' he was to say later. 'I should've known Gabriel was trying to warn me. I could hear him shouting inside my head but couldn't make sense of it.'

Sophie tries telling him it's not his fault – no one could've known what was to happen. 'Someone did know,' Joshua will insist. 'Gabriel knew.'

The cable car came out of the mist like an overweight dragonfly, people pushing and shoving to get on. The car lurched away from the platform and was practically down and engaged with the lower landing stage when Josh started to yell. 'Get off!' He shouted. 'Mom! Dad! Sophie! Get off!'

So traumatised is he by the memory, he doesn't realise that but for him everyone would have died. So loud were his screams – so insistent – people at the front of the car panicked, and were leaping the gate and clawing their way to the other side even as a loose piece of machinery came crashing down.

A loose piece of machinery! That was the cause, so Sophie was to learn at the inquest, cables intertwined and the oncoming machinery severing another.

People pushing and screaming, it was mayhem. Then Sophie felt hands about her waist and heard her father yell. 'You there, catch my daughter!'

Then she's flying through the air and is caught against a stranger's chest.

Someone screamed. It may have been Sophie, she's not sure.

She recalls struggling in the stranger's arms, fighting to look back.

Everything seemed to slow down then, tick-tock, second by second.

'Daddy! Mummy!'

They died in slow motion.

'Oh God!'

The scene is imprinted on her brain. The car begins to tip. Dad is trying to keep his balance. He has Joshua in his arms, and is lifting him by the waist and scruff of the neck. He's leaning back, whoosh, Josh is flying through the air. A man catches him, Sophie doesn't know who, only that her brother is safe.

The car is tipping, sliding back down the mountain.

Sophie saw it happen, saw the moment her mother chose to let go.

'No Mummy!' she whispered, 'please don't do it!'

It was too late.

Adelia knew they couldn't both get out. There wasn't enough time therefore there wasn't a choice. It was here, clear in her husband's beloved eyes. And so when his hands went about her waist – hands she'd known and loved these twenty years – hands she couldn't live without, the choice was easy.

'Oh no, darling, I don't think so.'

'Honey, please! I can lift you! I can save you. You know I can!'

'I know you can but I don't want to be saved, not without you.'

'But baby! It's only a matter of inches!'

'Just hold me.'

His arms went about her. She looked back once at the children, saw their beloved faces and knew they were safe. Smiling, she turned away breathing in his familiar smell – warmth, love, honour, safety and endurance.

It is enough.

Chapter Four
For Mother

Sophie's waiting to go on stage. All the noise and bustle you'd think she'd be nervous but she's calm as to be invisible. A year has come and gone since she quit school. Worrying about how tall she is and whether she dare nibble a sausage is yesterday's problem. Traditionally she's not entitled to share a stage at this year's Gala, yet beneath the starched tutu of the Royal Ballet there beats a tender heart, consequently she's here warming and stretching her muscles ready to fulfil a promise made to a pair of coffins.

Copper caskets strapped in the belly of a military plane, and so cold to the touch, her spirit shrank away. Copper caskets and military bands? Mother would've hated it but Granma, so utterly defeated by the death of her son no one had the heart to deny her. 'Wounded in one war! Three years of another in a POW camp. He comes home, has a couple of years with his family and is killed on vacation? Don't talk to me of God. There's no justice in this world.'

The journey home from Switzerland was managed smoothly, General Jentzen pulling rank. Sophie elected to accompany her parents. Joshua and Tag left for the States, carried back to Vermont in the loving care of the Whitney family.

'Sophie is staying a good idea?' asked Diana Whitney. 'It'll be days before things are sorted. Would you like me to stay with you?'

Sophie declined the offer. She couldn't have engaged in conversation, and she wasn't alone – Daddy Bobby was with her.

At first he was a voice in her head. 'Hi, Princess,' he'd said that first terrible night in the hotel bedroom. 'It's me, your old pal Bobby.'

She heard him but couldn't see him – her eyes sore from watching the cable car tumble afraid she might see her parents tumble with it.

'Nah,' he'd said. 'That wasn't going to happen. Your pa would have held on so tight to your ma nothing would've torn them apart.' He was right. They were found with their arms about one another. 'Never seen anything like it,' a rescuer was heard to say, 'her head on his chest like they were sleeping.'

A man from the US consulate arrived. Questions were asked and forms filled in. Sophie moved about the hotel in a daze. For once she has no true memory of that time, only of sitting at the window watching birds peck at a nut-feeder.

That's when Bobby appeared, soft drawl whispering, *'I'll keep you company.'*

It's alright. She's not crazy. She understands her imagination is working overtime. It's not new, from a child she's seen things that weren't there and heard words that were never spoken. Born into another family she might've worried but who can worry when, given time to listen, Dad can – could – converse in any language. Then there's

Mother who, after an air-raid in '42, suffered recurring amnesia which left her chatting with shadows on the wall. The boys have their own bugaboo, Joshua with an 'early-warning system', and Tim (who from a lad's point of view could not be more normal) can often find lost items simply by thinking of them.

Throughout the plane journey home Bobby was a misty figure in the opposite seat, still the step-father she knew, a bottle of beer in one hand and cigar in the other — not at all reformed – heaven made so little difference that when a stewardess suggested a pick-me-up he offered the thought: '*Yeah, a Tequila Slammer with a cherry on top!*'

At the airport she was met by Uncle Gabriel, a statue of grief honed by his own hand. At that, Bobby had faded away. '*You'll be okay now*,' he'd said. '*Gabe will get you through the next couple of days.*'

From then on time moved in drags and spurts. It might've been better if she could cry. Gabriel on the other hand never stopped crying. Not a single tear fell on his cheek yet his body quaked in sorrow. Later she heard that in the moment of Mother's death he laid back his head and howled.

The caskets were rolled into separate cars, army pennants flying. Sophie and Gabriel followed in a car driven by Franklin Bates. Frank used to live with the Hunters in Fredericksburg, Dad's closest friend they served together throughout many campaigns. 'You okay, Miss Sophie?'

'Thank you.'

'If you ever need me I am here. The Guvnor would want it.'

'Thank you.'

Yes and no, please and thank-you were the only words available. Tim and Joshua were equally closed off – though on the issue of blame Tim is voluble.

'I don't wanna talk. I just wanna kick the shit out of the guy responsible. A thing like that, support cable breaking, it shouldn't happen. And the automatic safety system off! If it takes all my life I'll get to the bottom of it.'

Joshua had questions. 'Could Mom have made it out of the cable-car? I mean, could she? I wouldn't like to think she chose to leave us.'

Dad always said, if you have to lie make it a good one; Sophie lied and lied good. 'The car was at tipping point. They were way off-balance. And whatever she did, Joshua, she did for love.'

'Such a fool.' Joshua struggles with guilt. 'The voice in my head wasn't saying get out of the Observatory. It was saying stay out of the cable car. I misread it.'

'Rubbish!' said Sophie. 'You misread nothing.'

He'd smiled then. 'You sound like Mom.'

That comment was to be repeated during the funeral. 'My dear, how like your mother you are. You have your father's hair and eyes but it's your mother's elegance and complete beauty of soul I see. We shall miss her.'

Sophie misses her. With Mother gone a curtain has fallen – darkening every room, and no matter what anyone says or does the darkness won't lift. The only way to survive is to run and run hard. Back home she runs in the morning and the evening. One night an unseen visitor joined her. Not Bobby – a Genie in the Lamp, he vanishes the moment her sneakers appear.

Now when she runs Sophie hears the slap of shoes alongside, sometimes it's sneakers, other times boots pound the pavement and a military cadence rings in her head like the one Dad used to sing when he and the boys went running.

The first time she heard the ghostly chant in back of her mind she was terrified. It is one thing for imagination to provide a phantom long-distance runner quite another to hear the phantom sing.

'Your baby was lonely, as lonely as can be,
Then Jody provided her with company,
Ain't it great to have a pal who
works so hard to keep up morale.
Sound off, 1- 2, Sound off, 3- 4,
Sound off, 1 -2- 3- 4, 1-2 ---3-4!'

It got so she heard the cadence every time she ran and so for a time didn't. Then, contrariwise, she missed the exercise, *and* the chanting, and started up again. Faded t-shirt, hair tied back and sweat dripping, she chases the blues away. For a time they stay away but sooner or later return. This ballet solo is an offering to her parents and to the magical Pool of Lethe in the hope that memories of the tragedy will sink never to rise again.

A skin tight-lace bodice overlaid by white silk, and a skirt six layers of the stiffest tulle, Sophie stretched the classic requirement as far as she dared, and in a Last Woman Standing mood, she also enhanced the make-up, gold and tawny bronze shadow on her eyelids and ditching the usual pale lipstick for a vivid slash of scarlet.

If she's going to be seen let's be seen. It's likely she'll never dance again.

Miss Gabriella hurries forward. 'Do you think you're able to manage? You've only to say if you don't feel up to it. The Saint Saens is a demanding piece and we wouldn't want to overtax you.'

'I'm fine, thank you.'

'Okay then. We'll leave you to it.'

People were taking their seats. They chat and cough and rattle programmes. Behind the curtain, graduates are warming up for their *Bluebird pas de deux*

The lights go down. The orchestra plays the opening chords of *Dance of the Cygnets;* Becky and her three partners link arms, and offering a smooth Shiva-like profile of tulle and swansdown, enter stage right.

They say tragedy enhances strengths and exposes weaknesses. It exposed a weakness in the Hunter/ Ryland friendship. Sophie must accept her share of blame. She knew it was failing but lost in grief did nothing. Distance, no place in the Company, suddenly they seemed to have nothing in common.

Becky's mother Sue arrived in Vermont the day before the funeral. Stunning in a black pant suit and wide-brimmed hat, she alighted an ancient Packard with hot-house lilies in one hand and a cosmetic purse in the other.

'I loved your mother,' she'd said in that liquid treacle voice. 'She was a friend to me when most folks turned their back. I'm here to take care of her.'

'Take care of her?' Granma Ellen was appalled.

'Yes, ma'am, no discussion and no argument! Adelia Challoner was born beautiful. I'm here to make sure she goes out the same way she came in.'

Aunt Sarah accompanied Sue to the funeral parlour. 'Not that Sue needed do anything,' she said. 'Adelia looked as she always looked – the face of an angel.'

Sue left Vermont on a cloud of Dior perfume. Becky stayed in England. It is a long way to come but no condolence card or phone-call? Can that be right?

'It ain't her fault,' said Sue. 'Her pa shot hisself and took a long time dying. She was with me when we found him. She ain't got over it so go easy on her.'

A porcelain doll fragile as tensile steel, Becky is coming off-stage. She offered a smooth cheek to kiss. 'I hear you're taking flying lessons.'

'A few, nothing too serious.'

'Does that mean you'll be able to nab across the Atlantic when you fancy, because if you do, me and Jay will find that real handy.'

'I thought Johnny flew his own plane.'

'He does but can't afford to do it too often. Mind you, if this TV thing comes off he'll have more cash than he can handle.'

'TV thing?'

Becky set a finger to her lips. 'A wildlife programme in the offing. They fly him to Kenya, film him in action, and run it as a weekly programme. It'll go down a bomb. He's a great looking guy. Women will go crazy for him. Say, I like your hair long like that. It's geometric cuts here in the West End. I'd have mine bobbed but have a part in *Much Ado* with the RSC so I need it long.'

Ah yes, the Royal Shakespeare Company. Becky is proving a disappointment to Madame. She is out all night and late for practice, and quote, 'doesn't show the commitment needed to maintain a position with the Company.'

Becky doesn't care – as always her commitment is to the Abbey and as Granma says, 'hooking His Lordship Junior.'

Johnny Beaufort is out front. Since the funeral Sophie thinks kindly of him. That day they were waiting for the car when Frank poked his head round the door. 'A guy outside needs a ride. He looks like a hobo but sounds like a Toff.' Long hair, boots and spurs, it was Johnny. All through the funeral he stood at her side, hand under her elbow and handsome face sombre. Then he left. 'Don't forget,' he said. 'The word of an Englishman, my house is your house.'

Granma was not amused. 'If that's British aristocracy then all I can say is hoorah for Founding Fathers.' Sue Ryland, on the other hand, shared her daughter's hopes. 'Nothing a little Virginian magic won't tame.'

'So?' Becky is staring at Sophie. 'Are you visiting the Abbey while you're here or flying straight back? The Beauforts are awful busy. The Horticultural Society is running a competition in the Under-spire: who grows the best orchids. Needless to say Uncle Charles is in with a shout.'

'Are you suggesting I'd be in the way?'

'Of course not! Just pointing it out.'

So here it is, a fifteen-year-friendship exposed to the footlights.

'Josh and Tim okay?' said Becky, examining her nails.

'Tim's in college. Joshua's here in England. I see Johnny in the audience.'

'Jay out front?' Becky peered through the curtains. 'So he is and in the Royal Box sitting with Nureyev.' She laughed. 'That's typical of him, must have the best seat. I wonder why he didn't say he was coming.'

'Perhaps he wanted to surprise you.'

Becky and Johnny are pictured together in Society columns, shots of them at the races or *Annabelle's Night Club*, Becky smiling into the camera while snuggling into Johnny's shoulder; '*The Beaufort heir with gorgeous partner, Miss Rebecca Ryland, rising star at Sadler's Wells.*'

Becky was still at the spy-hole. 'He's with that TV guy. They must be filming here. That'll be why he's wearing a penguin suit. Have you anyone out front?'

'No.'

'Not even one of the Parker boys, Petey, for instance?'

'Peter's engaged.'

'No! Is Little Peter Parker engaged?'

'If he's anything like David I doubt he's little.'

Sophie peeped through the spy hole. There was a large party in the Royal Box. One of the men drew her gaze. 'Who's the chap in the corner?'

Becky looked. 'Why, are you interested? If you are I can find out.'

'It's okay. I just wondered. He seems familiar.'

Becky laughed. 'I can't believe Jay's here. He hates ballet, says he'd sooner eat shit than watch pansies in tights.' She stepped back. 'I'm not sure about ballet. They've got me doing R&J running from one scuzzy town to the next.'

'It's all experience.'

'And one I can do without! Anyway, as I said I've been offered a play.'

Sophie was shocked. 'You're not thinking of giving up!'

'I'm not thinking of giving up anything.' Eyes like glossy blueberries against the white cygnet make-up, Becky spread her arms. 'I want the ballet and the theatre. I want life with a capital L. I want furs, diamonds, and pearls. I want love and adventure. I want to travel the world. And…!' she paused.

Sophie filled in the gap. 'And you want Johnny Beaufort.'

'Yes, I do and I don't care who knows it,' said Becky, her face suddenly stern. 'I want him so bad I'll run over anybody who gets in the way.'

The remark hung quivering in the air. Then she laughed. 'Look out, here comes Gabriella. Good luck then. I'm off to get ready for the party.'

'Is there a party?'

'Yeah, here at the Garden…a private party. Don't say anything but Rudolph Nureyev is rumoured to be dropping by.' Becky darted away. 'Lighten up, Sophie. You can't cry forever. I learned that when my pa blew his brains out. Eat, drink, and take whatever's coming.'

'You ready, Sophie?' The stage manager looked at her. She nodded.

There are moments in life when hidden energy comes to the fore. People do extraordinary things – a mother drags a car from an injured child, a man dives into a river to rescue a dog – miraculous moments when the soul is released.

Sophie had her moment that evening.

'And house-lights down, 10, 9, 8…'

The stage manager counted the lights down

The harp began to stroke the first tentative chords. Then the cellos came in. The stage was in darkness, a single spotlight following Sophie onto the stage.

There is much said about this piece. Non-ballet people associate the solo with *Swan Lake*. It's not from that work. It is a piece devised by Mikhail Fokine using music from Saint Saens' *Carnival of the Animals*. A swan is dying. The ballerina is required to convey the struggle of death. Sophie spent hours researching the work and as far as she is concerned there has only ever been one Swan, and that the Russian Prima Ballerina Assoluta, Anna Pavlova.

The film she watched was old yet the beauty of the dancer shone through. When Sophie stepped on the stage she knew she could never hope to emulate such skill and yet, she could show the audience what the piece meant to her.

It isn't about dying, or even the struggle to live, though every gesture, every flutter of wings and frantic beat of the heart suggests a struggle: the memory of life beating upon the swan – the unique joy of feeling the wind in her feathers, and to feed and quench her thirst in sappy green water.

It is the loss of her young that hurts, the knowledge she must leave them. They are her babies! Her cygnets! Her Children! Her daughter and her sons! It is saying goodbye, the last look over a pure white shoulder, the look of love and regret, and then the decision not to stay – to surrender.

All this Sophie tried to convey to the audience. She didn't think about dancing or worry about steps. No need! She wasn't a ballerina. She is a swan.

At some point in the dance she began to weep. Perhaps that's it, perhaps her tears formed a pathway to the past thus allowing a kindred soul to seek her out and once more mingle with flesh. Maybe the spirit of Pavlova used the pathway to momentarily share the life and the art she adored.

Soul reaching out, Sophie danced as never before. 'Goodbye, Mummy and Daddy,' she whispered, tears falling. 'I love you.'

And somewhere in that hushed darkness – no more than a whisper of a bow drawn across a cello string – the answer came back… 'We love you too.'

Chapter Five
Little Trick

Aunt Sarah was furious. 'What do you mean you can't live here? This is your home. America has taken care of you. America has loved you and kept you from harm. Why would you want to live anywhere else?'

Fourteen days of staring at grey English rain falling from grey London skies Sophie is asking the same. It's a strange life, aimless, with plenty time and money to spend but no idea of what to do and what to spend it on. Most of the time she's sight-seeing or reading the Evening Standard sits-vac. There's no going back to Vermont. She misses America, misses the open-hearted people, but not the house – without Mom and Dad it is only a house.

It's eighteen months since she danced at the Gala. Nothing is the same. Tim was the first to go, offered a choice of staying or boarding at college he chose college. His departure was followed by Joshua prepping at Harrow.

'I've got to go, Sis. I can't live here, too many echoes.'

I'll move in with you,' said Granma. 'Two girls together, we'll get along fine.' Sophie is also conscious of echoes bouncing off walls but unlike the boys, who're neither blessed nor cursed with eidetic memory, she remembers every moment spent within the walls. It's bad enough living with that without Granma's endless questioning of the tragedy.

London overtook her mind, an apartment of her own and freedom to do as she pleased. Aunt Sarah couldn't accept it. 'I understand Joshua needs to be where he is. We were none of us blind to what went on between Adelia and that man Templar. Timothy at the Academy, that too makes sense. But you, Sophie, you don't have the ballet so why leave? Don't you love us anymore?'

Of course she loves them. There are days when sh is physically sick with the memory of how it used to be, Tim shooting baskets in the yard, and Mother (who could never walk anywhere, always on the run) and Dad, the sound of his briefcase smacking the hall table: 'Okay folks, I'm home!' Then there'd be Joshua teasing the cat, poor Willow, who, riddled with arthritis and ever faithful to Dad, crept away to die the day after the cable-car. That's the home she misses, not two women rattling about in an empty box.

So it's London now, Bayswater, top floor of a rambling Georgian terrace all high ceilings and stucco walls. No garden but a balcony and six flights up, it overlooks houses all similarly divided mostly occupied by sun-tanned Aussies who sit on the stoop and smoke into the early hours. Top floor suits Sophie, the silence of early hours, the waking of other apartments, pottery chinking and kettles whistling. A communal post-box in the entrance hall, mail sorted into pigeon holes every morning by Mr Morris, the old gentleman in the basement, taking his poodle out for a toilet break.

Alone and with no particular plan Sophie wanders the British Museum. Tuesdays she studies the Pre-Raphaelites and every Thursday takes a flamenco class: 'Good hands, Senorita, but stiff neck!'

Stiff-necked is what Becky thinks. They quarrelled at the Gala, Becky accusing Sophie of flirting with Johnny. There was no flirting. There was a kiss.

A beginning and then the audience exploding is all she recalls of her solo. Too many flowers for one performer at graduation is frowned upon. Flowers did arrive, lilies from Granma Ellen and Aunt Sarah, roses from Tim and Josh, and white-lilac from an anonymous well-wisher. A posy of Sweet-Peas laid her low: '*To our beloved daughter. We knew you wouldn't let this one go by, Mom and Dad*.' Arranged with Aunt Sarah before Switzerland, it suggests Mother doubted neither she nor Dad would be able to send them.

The flowers, the scent! Sophie was undone. But for Rudolph Nureyev she might've knelt on the stage forever – the audience weeping with her. He was with the party in the Royal Box, and gauging the situation – and showman that he is – climbed down onto the stage.

A cloak appropriated from *Romeo and Juliet* wardrobe flung about his shoulders he drew Sophie to her feet. 'Come, Mamselle. We do this together.'

That she should party after was absurd. She did go backstage but only for the US naval officer who stood throughout the applause with his hand pressed to his heart. She needed to know who he was. Weaving through goggling Mice she ran along the back-drafts. The first person through the crush was Johnny. Blocking all-comers, a glass of bubbly in one hand and handkerchief in the other, he polished her face. 'You don't need that gunk on your face.'

He kissed her, a crushing kiss that stung the lips. 'I've wanted to do that forever,' he said pocketing the handkerchief, 'but thought I'd better wait until the situation was less problematic.' He should've waited. The problem was behind him, Becky, a smile on her lips and fingernails cocked, and behind her – a frown on his handsome face – the naval officer. They never did get to meet.

~

Sophie was in Selfridges when she saw Sammy Warren, the elder of the twins who graduated in '62. Sammy was at the lingerie counter rifling sale items.

'Hello, Sammy.'

'Hi, Sophie! What you doing here? I thought you were back to the States.'

'I'm staying here awhile.'

'Where are you living?'

'Bayswater.'

'Hang on a minute!' Sammy dived into the rack and dragging out a pink satin Teddy held it against Sophie. 'What d'you reckon, a bit loud?'

'Screaming.'

'And this?' She held up a similarly bright garment.

'Depends if you want to sleep in it or stop the traffic.'

'Great! I'll have them and two pairs of mesh stockings.'

'The stockings have holes in the heels.'

'I know. It's why they're cheap.'

'What good is cheap if you can't wear them?'

Sammy grinned. 'We'll wear them alright, me and Milly, and with a bit of luck by the time we take 'em off they'll have more holes in them.'

'Of course!' Sophie got it. 'You're dancing at the Revue Bar.'

'We got the sack. We're a speciality act now at the Casino billed as 'The Warren Twins, Stripped to the buff and not a G-string in sight.''

'I hope it pays well.'

'Thirty rips per stocking at a fiver a rip, it's a doddle. If customers are willing to put up the fivers we'll put up with their fingernails. The greedy sods running the joint take their cut but we still come away with enough to send home.'

'That's good then.'

'I don't know about good. It's a far cry from White Lodge. You have to close your eyes and ears to a lot of filthy stuff. We don't plan on stripping forever, long enough to get a hairdressing salon back home. Talking of home I was sorry to hear about your mum and dad. As for the ballet, if you can't make it then the rest of us shouldn't bother to try. So, what you going to do now?'

'I have no idea.'

Head on one side, Sammy regarded Sophie. 'You should try the Revue.'

'Oh, I don't know. I'm not good at acting.'

'Acting?' Sammy sniggered. 'They couldn't care less if you can act. All they want is a gorgeous babe with a gorgeous body, in other words you.'

'Me?'

'Oh come on!' Sammy grinned. 'You were the best-looking girl in our set. Everyone said so. Sophie Hunter, the Body! You walk in and heads turn.'

Sophie blinked: best-looking girl? The Body? She can't be talking about me! Then she caught a glimpse of her reflection in the store window and of a man at the glove counter, mouth open, observing the same reflection.

'See what I mean?' Sammy grinned. 'If you don't believe me believe him.'

~

Sophie's had an upsetting experience. Tuesday morning she met the old gentleman from the basement. 'Good morning, young lady,' he said. 'And how are you this morning?' She was about to reply but was shocked into silence, the right side of his face dragging down in a crooked line. 'Mr Morris, are you alright!' she clutched his arm. 'I'm fine, thank you,' he replied. When she looked again there was nothing wrong. His face was as it always was.

An unpleasant incident made more so when later she heard he'd had a stroke and died. With no one willing to look after the dog Sophie took her. There's also a car, she learned about it from Mr Morris's daughter. 'Bloody thing, he spent every moment polishing it in a garage in Shepherds Bush. I don't know what I'm supposed to do with it,' she'd said. 'I live in a gated flat in Kew, no animals and minimum parking. Do you want it? It's yours for a tenner.'

A tenner changed hands. Now Sophie has a dog called Philomena and a Bentley Touring car called Phyllis.

Friday fortnight she had a call from Suffolk, an invitation to spend a weekend at the Abbey, dog and all. Foot down for an hour and a half and she's there.

'Thanks for letting me bring Mena,' she said. 'She's pining for Mr Morris.'

'No worries, Miss Sophie.' George took the leash. 'What's one more four-legged creature to the Abbey? I like the motor, very Hollywood gangsterish.'

Day after day, memory by memory, Sophie Hunter is crossing the Pond. As well as a dog and a car, she has a plane. Bobby Rourke's Beagle now roosts in a hangar not far from the Abbey. Johnny flew it over. 'Are you sure you're not making a mistake moving to London,' said Becky that evening at the dinner table. 'You'll find it lonely cutting yourself off from friends and family.'

Lord Beaufort smiled. 'I don't believe Sophie's in danger of being cut off from anybody, not while we are all here.'

'Of course not!' said Becky. 'I was thinking more of Mizz Ellen. She must be awful lonely now the boys are gone.'

Becky is hopping mad. The night of the Gala she dragged Sophie into the ladies loo, told her to keep her hands of Jay! They were engaged!

Charles Beaufort doesn't miss a thing. This morning when Sophie went for a swim he was raking leaves off the pool. 'Little annoyances will happen. They get in through the skylight. One must grin and bear it.' She might've thought him speaking of leaves but then he smiled over his specs. 'You used to call me Uncle. Being an Uncle is so much nicer than being a Lord.' When she didn't reply he took her hand. 'One mustn't allow other people's insecurities to become one's own. One must carry on as before.'

~

Sunday evening Sophie stood watching the gathering from the Minstrel's gallery. Nanny watched with her. 'I like your frock. Is it one of your mother's?'

Last year in Virginia Sophie determined to tackle mother's closet.

'Chuck it all,' Aunt Sarah said. 'I can't bear to look at any of it.'

Most of it went to the Sally Army. A couple of pieces found their way into Sophie's closet: a velvet evening gown, the grey dress she's wearing now, and the sable coat. Aunt Sarah was horrified. 'Don't take that. It's jinxed. It brought your mother nothing but bad luck. It'll do the same for you.'

Sophie wouldn't wear it but loved the feel of it. There are times holding it when she could hear Dad's voice and Mother's throaty laugh. The dress she wears was one of Mother's favourites. Palest of grey ankle-length chiffon shirtwaist, it is very pretty.

'Suits you,' said Nanny. 'I like the way it grips the shoulders and shows off your bosom and tiny waist. You're a real beauty, girlie, so stop hiding on the back row and learn to accept compliments because there'll be plenty.'

Sophie descended the stairs. She'd taken trouble with her hair, drawing it into a loose chignon, a Spanish comb in the back. Secretly, she is delighted with the way she looks. The Body for heaven's sake! Who'd have thought it!

Becky is gorgeous in rose-coloured satin pants and velvet jacket, her hair braided with a rose-coloured ribbon; she stands with Lady Beaufort and Gabriel's wife, Julia, a lovely woman, gentle and kind, and considering her husband's links with the past, incredibly generous.

'Sophie!' Julia held out a hand. 'Come and be with us!' She kissed her cheek and stepped back smiling. 'My word, aren't you beautiful!'

Lady Beaufort nodded, 'and with your father's heavenly eyes.'

'You know we were all in love with him,' said Julia, 'even Nanny.'

'Especially Nanny,' said Lady Beaufort.

Julia laughed. 'Yes, especially Nanny. He was a wonderful man. Do you remember when we did the 'Brain of Britain' quizzes? Talk about the Memory Man! America beat England every time! I didn't mind. I was on his team.'

Lady Beaufort chuckled 'So amusing and so naughty. I mind the time the camels got loose in the paddock. The General, Charles, and a couple of Japanese tourists chased after them. I never knew a man could curse in so many languages. Charles was quite in awe. I understand you've a similar gift.'

Sophie laughed. 'As yet not enough to curse but yes, a good memory.'

Their kindness was salve to her hurt. Later, however, the suggestion of following in father's eidetic footsteps took an unsettling turn.

The Great Hall was crowded, sponsors of Beaufort charities rubbing shoulders with local councillors. The guest of honour, the aging Russian ballerina, Tamara Karsavina, sat enthroned on a dais at the far end of the Hall, a rusticated tiara on her head. Sophie was making her way through the crush when she wagged an imperious fan. 'You there! Approach!'

She stared at Sophie from under heavily pencilled brows. 'I know you,' she said. 'You're the one that attempted the Saint Saens at the '63 Gala.'

Sophie curtseyed. It seemed the only thing to do.

Karsavina snorted. 'You might well hang your head! Dreadful mess you and the Tartar émigré made of it. Have you no regard for Fokine and his genius? Poor Anna must be spinning in her grave. Dancers of today!' She shuddered. 'Had I behaved so I would've been laughed off the stage. The pity of it is until then you had executed the dance with a degree of skill.'

'Thank you, Madame.'

'Do not presume to thank me. I'm offering an observation not my approval. You are no longer with the Company? A little on the willowy side perhaps.'

'It seems so.'

'No matter.' Karsavina shrugged. 'You were never meant for ballet. You are meant for other dance. It's why you were given the length of neck and the breasts. It is a body built for passion. You were born to drive men wild.'

A rouged tortoise emerging from a shell, she wagged her fan. 'This was once my ticket to freedom. Had I your beauty I would not be constrained by whalebone and petty rules. I'd be free to do what I wanted. Understand?'

'I think so, Madame.'

'Good! Now go away!' She snapped the fan shut. 'And grow a backbone to support that body.'

~

A quartet played in the Wedgwood Room and a soprano sang. Midway through the aria *Visi D'arte* from *Tosca* Johnny squeezed on the bench.

'I hope you're not another Tosca livin' and dyin' for your art.'

'Since I no longer have an art it's likely l shan't die from it.'

'Glad to hear it. Dedication to one particular thing is incredibly borin'.'

'You're not dedicated to the Great Park?'

'I'm dedicated to me.'

'Why do I find that hard to believe?'

'Probably in the way I find it hard to believe you're done with dancin'. You can't look the way you do and not dance.' He gestured. 'I love bare shoulders. You look like a relapsed nun, the spirit willing and the flesh more so.'

She twitched away. He leant against the wall playing with a lock of her hair. 'I love your hair. I like the way it corkscrews around my finger. It makes me wonder whether you corkscrew in other places.'

Sophie stared. 'What's the matter with you? Are you drunk?'

'Yeah, drunk with your beauty.'

'Behave!'

'I am behavin'. I'm just makin' an observation.'

'Yes you and the whole world.'

'You'd make a great Tiller Girl. My man, the TV producer, could get you a spot on the Palladium. You can stand on the turntable along with all the others and smile as you go round-and-round. What a way to spend your life.'

'People do what they can to get by.'

His hand was shaking, ash falling from his cigarette. 'Life shouldn't be about gettin' by. It should be about grabbin' fate by the scruff of the neck and givin' it a bloody good kickin'.'

Sophie rolled her eyes.

He giggled. 'Did I just mumble some bollocks about fate?'

'You did.'

'Jeez! It's me wants kickin'. I've been tootin' the flute when I shouldn't.' He grasped her hand. 'Stay with me, Sophie! Keep me on the straight and narrow.'

'That's asking too much of anyone, especially a relapsed nun.' When she went to leave he pulled her down. 'Then keep me company, if only for a couple of minutes. If Pa sees me like this he'll chuck me out.'

Legs outstretched, he babbled on about the Park and his plans for a new enclosure. Words slurred and icy skin, whatever he'd taken didn't suit. His fingers closed about hers and Sophie had a reprise of the 'Mr Morris' moment.

She aware of Johnny and another settling over him with bloodied tiger's claws embedded in his chest. Then it was gone and Johnny frowning.

'Why you starin'? Am I bein' an awful ass?'

'No,' she said trying to recoup. 'I was thinking of the new Tiger.'

'There is no new tiger. It died. It's why I'm so low. Strike that!' he laughed bitterly. 'It's why I'm so high. I should've got it out earlier but hadn't the cash.'

'I'm sorry.'

'Me too. It's a bit off when a Viscount has to prance about before a camera to earn his bread. I'm not crazy about doin' TV but if it pays I might be able to save somethin.' He carried her hand to his lips. 'Even you, Sophie.'

'Am I in need of saving?'

'Not now maybe.' He gazed at her. 'But one day.'

'Oh, there you are!' Becky pushed along the bench. 'You got to come with me! The designer, Pierre Cardin, is here. He wants you to model his gear.'

Johnny sighed. 'Becky, I told you I'm not doin' that. I'm makin' a big enough fool of myself as it is.'

'He's talking big money.'

'How big?'

'Major!'

~

Sophie made her way to the Orchid House. Uncle Charles was already there. 'Ah-hah!' He turned. 'I wondered how long before you paid us a visit.'

It was cool in the greenhouse, moist air turning the grey of Sophie's dress to pewter. They were talking of orchids when the doors creaked open. Simon and Sebastian Farrell stood at the door. 'I hope we're not disturbing you?'

'Not at all!' Charles beamed. 'Come in, gentlemen, and meet Sophie.'

'Hello Sophie,' said Simon. 'It's good to see you again.'

'You know one another?'

'We do, my Lord, though it is some time since we've spoken.'

'Fourteen years last month,' said Sophie.

Charles sighed. 'What it is to have a memory like yours, Sophie. I have trouble recalling fourteen minutes ago never mind fourteen years.'

'Me too,' said Sebastian. 'Yet where Sophie's concerned I believe a man would have to be blind not to remember.'

It is as Simon said, 'been awhile.' She last saw the Farrell twins at their father's funeral. Major Tom Farrell was a friend of Dad's. He was killed during the Korean War. Now the wheel has turned full circle.

'Sorry I couldn't make the funeral,' said Sebastian. 'I was serving abroad. I wanted to come. Your folks were good to us. Mom went through a bad patch when Pa was killed. Your mother would call and chat. Then there was your Pa sponsoring me to Annapolis and Simon to Law School.'

'I didn't know that.'

'Nor did we,' said Simon. 'We heard on our twenty-first. Blown away I can tell you. But for the General our lives would be very different. It's why we're here. He made provision, passed the sponsorship on should anything happen. We've been in Oxfordshire getting to know Mr Gabriel Templar, our new backer.'

'My dear dad!' Sophie's eyes filled with tears. 'I learn about him all the time.'

'As do we all.' Charles put his arm round her. 'Your father was a man of great foresight. He leaves a massive hole to fill.'

Perhaps word association prompts the 'Morris effect', a word linked to an image. One moment she's thinking of Dad, the next a shape settles over Sebastian Farrell, another Sebastian pausing in the act of crawling through a tunnel. 'Do you go caving, Sebastian?' It was out before she could stop it.

He shook his head. 'Nuh-huh. Why do you ask?'

'Sorry!' She floundered. 'I was thinking of Dad. How he used to go pot-holing. I somehow imagined your father doing the same.'

'It is possible,' said Simon. 'They both went undercover in Special Ops.'

That's it, thought Sophie. It's not so much a tunnel as undercover.

'And you, Sebastian?' she said recognising the insignia on his naval uniform. 'Do you follow in your father's Special Ops footsteps? An evasive smile and a change of subject supported her suggestion rather than denied.

'We enjoyed the Gala concert.'

'You were at the ballet?'

'It was all of a rush. We managed to get tickets but had to get back to Connecticut so couldn't stop to say hi.' Conversation turned then to music and ballet. Sophie chatted but shaken by the visions wanted the day over.

~

That night, unable to sleep, she sat at the bedroom window, Mena, the poodle, at her feet. What was it Dad said about the hours he spent locked away in the study? '*I look at things that are some way off and try bringing them closer. It's a little trick I learned that the Army finds useful.*'

Remote viewing he called it. Sophie wondered if the 'little trick' had been passed on to her or was it more her will-o-the-wisp companion, Bobby Rourke. Twenty minutes later, curls fizzing and temper to match, it was flesh and blood that bounced through the door. 'I thought we agreed Jay Beaufort is mine?'

'Must we go into this, Becky? It's late and I'm tired.'

'Yes we must. Why are you getting between us?'

'Can anyone get between you? I thought you were engaged.'

'We are engaged. Why, has he said different?'

'The subject didn't arise. God's sake, Becky, leave it will you!'

Sophie went into the bathroom, Becky on her heels, she was sorry she was being paranoid. It's Johnny! She had a chance of understudying *Viola* in *Twelfth Night* at the RSC but can't concentrate on her lines. 'He is such a flirt!'

Sophie stood brushing her teeth. There was a ripple in the air, an invisible door creaked open and Becky's face reflected in the mirror replaced by an older Becky who hugged an Oscar to her chest.

Flick, the image was gone. Sophie spat out toothpaste. 'Why are we fighting? We don't have to. We have our own lives. No need to quarrel.'

'I don't want to either. It's just Jay. He drives me crazy.'

'Forget Jay. Tell me about the navy chap at the Gala? Could he be anything to do with Sebastian Farrell here with his brother?'

'What?'

'I mean, did they wear similar uniforms?'

'How should I know.' Becky flung away. 'Ask Sebastian. I've enough to do without chasing another of your admirers.'

Early morning, Sophie woke to find Johnny sitting on the bed.

She sat up 'What are you doing?'

'I'm taking off my shoes.' Poodle scuttling, he flung his shoes across the room and began to unbutton his shirt.

'You shouldn't be here.' Sophie leapt off the bed.

'Don't be silly.' He shucked off his shirt. 'Of course I should. Where else would I be at three in the morning other than with the beautiful Sophie.' He scooted across the bed and hung out of the open window, his back a broad expanse of muscle. 'What a fabulous night! See that big old moon out riding high in the sky! He's a spoony-moon, the one that makes magical things happen.'

The moon wasn't the only thing riding high. Johnny was in Coke paradise. Fool that he is, he went looking for that guy. Didn't want anything but this is Toby from Harrow generous with his shit. A quick line, a sniff, and Yazoo, his fingers are twitching and his feet moving in one direction.

There was one place to go and one person to be with, delicate, luscious, right-on-the-edge Sophie, she of the white skin and wild hair you want to dig your hands into. And the breasts! Man, those breasts! All you want is to plug one of them into your mouth, slide between her thighs and go home to Jesus.

'So come on, Miss Goody Two Shoes,' he drawled, the spoony-moon reflected in his eyes. 'Let me be the first to show you how it's done.'

Sophie bunched her fist wanting to hit him, to smash his arrogant face, to make his eyes water and then kick him in the balls. But this is Uncle Charles's home, there are people staying here, important people, and Charles doesn't deserve this. One mustn't make a fuss. One must deal with it quietly.

It didn't go quietly. Johnny wouldn't go quietly. It was a knock down dirty thing. He didn't seem to realise she was saying no. His mouth was on hers, his lips hard and teeth sharp. Then he was pulling her pants, trying to drag them down while entangled in his own so that he fell and Sophie with him.

They fought quietly. Even then, though his weight bruised, she didn't really think it would happen. This is the man who mourned with her, who stood beside her throughout the funeral. This is Johnny, friend of many years, the one who said, 'my word as an Englishman.' She's known him practically all her life. He wouldn't hurt her. Sooner or later he'll come to his senses.

Wrong! His hand went over her mouth cutting off air.

It was over in a moment but the longest moment of her life. A crowbar boring into her it hurt. It was disgusting and dirty and she hated it and him.

Oh the disappointment! The betrayal! This is not how it was supposed to be! Something inside her broke, a dream punctured along with a hymen. Had it not been for a gust of air and a window slamming things might've been worse.

The window slammed against the casement. Glass shattered.

Johnny pulled back semen gushing onto her leg.

A dog paddling in the sea, he shook himself. 'Jesus, Sophie,' he said, gazing down, his face puzzled. 'What the fuck am I doing?'

'Me, I think.'

'What?'

'Me, you useless bastard!' She rolled from under him. 'You were fucking me.'

Uncomprehending, he gazed at her. The bewilderment on his face made her crazy. She slapped him. His head rebounded. She slapped him again.

'Out!' she cried. 'Get out of my room!'

A dribbling spout for a penis, he shuffled backward. 'God, Sophie, I am so sorry. Really I am. I don't know what I thought I was doin'.'

'Out!' Dragging a sheet over her body she scrambled to her feet.

'Sophie, forgive me! It's this stuff! It made me crazy.'

'This stuff? Is this an excuse your offering?'

'No, no, not an excuse I just... just...'

'Is it your word as an Englishman? That special thing you have, your lineage, honour and duty? Is that it?'

'I'm so sorry. Believe me, I am as shocked as you.'

'Shocked as me! Get out of this room! Don't touch me! Don't even look at me. Go, and don't ever come near me again!'

Weeping, she shoved him out of the door and locked it.

She was packed and out in no time. She left a note for Charles Beaufort. 'Sorry I couldn't stay. Something came up.'

Something came up? Yes, waves of nausea every time she thought of it. So much for heroes! For God's sake! All you hopeful souls out there, don't make idols of the people you admire! They are bound to fall.

Chapter Six
Shared Line

Sophie got a job on the perfume counter at *Galleries Lafeyette* in Regent Street. All was fine for a couple of weeks but then there was a problem with Mena. Mondays and Wednesdays the dog stays at the Greek restaurant on the corner of the road. Tuesdays and Fridays she's with Mrs Evans on the third floor. Saturdays and Thursdays with no one to take her Sophie comes home to a messy kitchen and complaints about barking.

Niarchos, the proprietor of the restaurant, offered a job waiting on tables with Mena in the yard. It's not ideal but being busy helps to stop her brooding on what happened. Time being a supposed healer you'd think she'd hurt less about losing her parents. But no, Jay Beaufort put paid to that.

All things considered the name suits him. It brings to mind a carrion bird that steals from the nest and maims the young. One good thing, he's off the market and hopefully won't be hurting anyone else. They are engaged. Becky from the boondocks can relax, she has the ring, and one day the ermine, but she lost a friend in the process. Not that Becky cares, the gossip columns full of her cat-got-the-cream face.

Is Sophie envious? Yes, but only of admittance to Suffolk and Charles and Lady Beaufort. She can't visit with Johnny there. She will never tell of that spoony-moony night when their son raped her. It would hurt too many people and those that need-to-know seem to know.

Gabriel called at the apartment. Coincidentally, she had been speaking to Josh about him. She calls the boys every week. Caught up in West Point affiliations Tim is managing okay but Joshua is not so good

'Hi Sis!'

'How did you know it was me?'

'You mean apart from the fact you call every Monday at the same time?'

'What's wrong? You sound upset. Are you unhappy living in Oxford?'

'No. Where else should I be but with my father.'

'Josh!'

'It's okay, Sophie. I've always known I had two dads.'

'And is that okay with you?'

'It would be if Dad Mark One was still alive.'

'You think of Daddy as mark one. Does that mean you think less of Gabriel?'

'I love Gabriel but Dad will always be Mark One. You see, he loved me enough to love me – if you get my meaning.'

'Oh I get it! And I think it is so big of you and grown! Mum would be incredibly proud of you. I know I am.'

'Aw, don't get mushy on me.'

'I'm allowed to be mushy. It's a sister's prerogative.'

It was then the intercom buzzed, Dad Mark 2 at the door.

Gabriel Templar is not as he was. When Mother died a light went out that will never return. He looks sad and will fade away if something doesn't happen.

Ever prescient, he smiled. 'I'm okay,' he said, his voice so like Dad it made her blink. 'While you and the boys keep runnin' into brick walls I'll stick around.'

Sophie didn't ask how he read her thoughts. This is Gabriel. It is always this way with him, a telephone line to the heart. 'Were you like this with Mother?'

He nodded. 'And your pa. We share a party-line.'

'That must have made life difficult.'

He shrugged. 'I didn't ask for easy.'

A question tickled her tongue but thinking it insensitive she kept quiet.

'Sophie,' he said. 'I know what went on that night with John Beaufort.'

'What?' She burned red. 'Don't tell me the line extends to my bedroom!'

'Don't be crazy! What you do with your life is what you do. I know what happened because he said. I didn't beat it out of him though I sure wanted to.'

What he didn't say (the truth being more than she can handle) is that he knew about it as it was happening, Gabriel tossed out of bed, a voice thundering in his head that continued to rage when face-to-face with John.

He caught up with him in the Elephant House at the Abbey. Sophie is Gabriel's ward. He loves her but it wasn't a guardian's rage he felt when he had him by the throat. 'What did you do to my girl?'

John said he'd called Sophie a million times trying to explain. Gabriel said he couldn't explain – there aren't the words to do it. The voice thundered on, the grip about the throat tightening. 'Hurt my girl again and I will kill you.'

Now Gabriel's come to see how she is. 'How are you managin', honey?'

Seeing she didn't know where to look he took her hand. 'Ain't no need for you to be ashamed. I ain't here to plead forgiveness for him. John will have to earn that hisself. I'm here to ask you not to stay away from the Abbey. Your brother is tuned to the unknown. Stay away and he'll start asking questions.'

Sophie thought about her visions, the 'Mr Morris effect', Johnny with tiger's claws in his chest, and Sebastian Farrell crawling underground.

'What do you mean by tuned to the unknown?'

'Joshua is sensitive to things. It's a family trait.'

'What kind of things?'

Head on one side, Gabriel regarded her. 'You tell me.'

'Oh, I don't know.' She hesitated, thinking her experiences that of a crazy woman. 'Seeing things that aren't necessarily real or that haven't yet happened? You know, flashes of the past and glimpses of the future?'

Gabriel nodded. 'Sounds about right.'

'The family trait, can it be passed on to everyone?'

'It goes where it's goes. It ain't for understandin'. It's for testin' and tryin' but not thinkin' to save the world. You can't save the world. Believe me I know! And if you or your brothers figure you can, you got a lot of heartache comin'.'

'So what do we do?'

'You take whatever it is by the seat of the pants and you fly.'

'You sounded like Daddy Bobby then.'

Gabriel grunted. 'If anyone knew about the seat of his pants it's that guy. Anyhow, Charles ain't too well. Don't stay away. I'll let you know when the coast is clear.' He paused. 'One other thing, go ahead with the plan.'

'Plan?'

'The one with the feathers?'

Sophie frowned. 'What feathers?'

'You didn't get that far? Okay, forget feathers! Just carry on with the plan.'

Sophie wanted to ask more about feathers and plans and family traits but the poodle was fawning over Gabriel's shoes. Animals do that, creep on their bellies toward him as though he's more like his Holy namesake than a man.

'I'll be makin' tracks,' he said. 'Ma frets when I'm not nearby.'

'I heard she wasn't well. Do you think she might like a visit?'

'I'm sure she would. You was always a favourite.'

'Perhaps I could come this weekend and bring Mena with me.'

'Bring whoever you like, honey, yourself, the dog, and maybe that tall UDT guy who seems set on being mysterious.'

'UDT?' Sophie frowned. Then she remembered something Ethan said about underwater demolition training. 'Are you talking about my pen-friend?'

'Pen-friend, huh?' Gabriel smiled, light flickering in his face. 'Is that what kids are callin' passion these days?'

'There's no passion. He's a mate.'

'Sure, he's a mate. It's what swans do for life.'

'Is that what you and Mother did?' she said, then wished she hadn't, Gabriel gazed out over the rooftops as though lost.

'That kinda love is a runaway train,' he said. 'Once you're on it you can't get off and innocent folk get hurt in the process.' Sophie didn't need to inquire of the innocent; her mind offered the face of Julia Templar.' But I can never give it up,' he continued. 'It's burned into me. You'll know what I'm talkin' about when it happens to you.'

'It won't happen to me!' Sophie was adamant. 'I won't let it.'

She walked him to the street. Gabriel looked about him. 'I like it here. I like the way the houses run into the other, the stories they could tell. I could live here but only for a while before longin' for my own country.'

'You miss the States?'

'I miss bein' in the past. I miss the tangle of the Mill, Baby Rourke and his bitter humour, your father's straight-talkin', you a kiddie helpin' Ma with the hogs, and your mother's hand upon my heart. That is my country.'

'You have two grand little boys.' Sophie couldn't help saying it.

'Yes, and a grand wife – but no shared line.' He strode away leaving an aside that was to stay with Sophie forever. 'You wanted to ask a question.'

'I do, though I'm not sure I should.'

'Ask away.'

'Do you still share a party line?'

'Sure. How d'you think I know about the feathers?'

~

It seems there is a plan and it involves auditioning for the Revue Bar in Soho.

Monday she dithered at the stage door.

A doorman stuck his head out. 'You an arteeste, Miss?'

'Er…I haven't actually done this kind of dancing before but I…'

'First door right and straight through.'

The first door on the right led to a corridor which led to a postage-stamp stage and bright lights. A voice called out. 'You here to audition?'

'I haven't done this sort of dancing before.'

'Do you know what sort of dancers we want?'

'I have friends who worked here, the Warren Twins.'

'Oh another escapee from the Royal Ballet! Okay, hike up your skirts!'

She hiked.

'Turn round.'

She turned.

'Smile.'

She bared her teeth.

'What is it balloons, snakes, or sword-swallowing? Your speciality. What do you use, balloons, fire-eating, ventriloquist dummy? You know, gimmicks!'

'I don't have one. It's just me.'

'Okay, just you, rehearsal tomorrow morning 10-30 side door.'

It seems the moment you have one job another is offered – if indeed a job is what the General is offering. The phone rang. 'Afternoon, ma'am. Am I speaking with Mizz Sophie Emma Hunter?'

'You are.'

'Commander Clyde St John Forrester speaking, US Navy, aide to General Samuel Jentzen. Will you hold the line please?' The line crackled and then a familiar gravelly voice spoke. 'Hello there, Sophie. How're you?'

'Hello General Jentzen.'

'I hear you quit school and are between jobs.'

'I might have something lined up.'

'Uh-huh. I was at a staff meeting yesterday discussing the late President's inaugural address. "Ask not what your country can do for you…"' et cetera.'

'Ah yes! My brother Tim quotes it on a regular basis.'

'Uh-huh. We were speaking of your pa and his proactive memory and wondering how you'd feel about taking part in a little experiment.'

Beyond an invitation to the US Embassy and car to collect her that was the gist of his call. 'I won't be there,' he said, 'my guy, Clyde, will. He'll be looking at your Box Brownie seeing if you and your pa work a similar wave-length.'

A week later a car came to collect Sophie. When they arrived at Grosvenor Square it was to pickets and people with placards. 'What's happening?'

'Protesters, miss.'

'What are they protesting?'

'The war in Vietnam.'

Sophie knew very little about the war. Ethan mentioned it. '*If you don't hear from me it's because I'm locked-out on Cissy or heading toward the Ho Chi Minh Trail. Either way I'll have known better times.*'

Ethan is sparing of words. What he sends is more notes from a diary than letters. I mean what is Cissy? A while back he sent a photo of what looked like a giant double-ended swing, a mathematical equation on the back: '*F=(mv2) r', Cissy, EH the Third, and a couple of other guys having our guts rearranged.*'

Cissy turned out to be an anti-gravity simulator where would-be test pilots and astronaut nominee gauge ability to withstand G-force. They sit in a horizontal egg-beater and whizz round until they throw up or pass out.

Why would you do that? Sophie wrote querying the point. Ethan's reply was terse and to the point. '*It's everyman's right to dream. I was born wanting to walk on the moon. One dream ends I needed another.*'

Sophie can't imagine Ethan a dreamer. He sent a photograph of men grouped about the machine, their backs to the camera. One man – medium height, thinning hair, EW3, according to initials beneath – pats the Centrifuge as one might pat a dragon. Gabriel talked of passion and swans mating for life. EW3's appearance might not inspire passion yet he is capable of sensitivity. The night before the funeral he sent a recorded message. '*I want you to know you won't be alone at the funeral. You may not see me but I'm there cradling your poor heart in my hands keeping it from breaking, yours always, Ethan.*'

~

Sophie is at the Embassy taking part in an experiment: '*Does sustained concentration on subliminal images encourage the subconscious to promote useful information.*' It's her third visit to the room top of the stairs. A pen clicker and a doodler, it's always the same two men. It's hot, the room airless, the men are bored and so is she. A projector throws images onto a screen.

Today she's looking at a bald-headed man in a wrinkled suit.

'So Sophie,' said the pen-clicker. 'What can you tell me about this guy?'

'Nothing! I don't know him.'

'You don't need to know him. Just tell me what you see.'

'I see he ought to have his suit cleaned.'

'You think he should have his suit dry-cleaned. Why d'you think that?'

'Because it looks as if it's been slept in.' She sighed. 'I have no idea why I'm here. I don't know what I supposed to be seeing.'

'You're not *supposed* to see anything.'

'Good because by now you realise there'll be no magical rabbit out of a hat from this girl.' She returned to the screen and the man in the rumpled suit who for some reason reminded her of the movie director Alfred Hitchcock.

The pen clicker yawned. 'Why Alfred Hitchcock?'

'I don't know. It has to do with film. Is he an animal lover?'

The doodler snickered. 'Animal lover!'

With that laugh the Morris Effect came into force. A door in Sophie's head opened and a dog crept into the room. She couldn't see it but heard it and felt its panting breath on her hand. Then she knew the man in the wrinkled was a scientist. 'He works with animals testing responses to pain.'

The pen ceased to click.

Sophie was aware of the dog leaning against her, whining and trembling, her body trembling in sympathy. 'Poor creature,' she whispered. 'Can you hear it?'

'Hear what?'

'That awful whining.' Suddenly, horribly, the whining ceased. Not a sound from the dog, only a body pressing against her knee and pain and silence.

She sprang to her feet. 'I'm not doing this!'

The pen clicker stood up. 'Okay, take a rest.'

'No!' Sophie cried. 'I'm not doing it!'

A door opened back of the room. Lights were switched on. A man in a uniform strode into the room. 'Sophie,' he held out a hand. 'We finally get to meet.'

'Commander Forrester. We've spoken on the phone.'

'You recognised my voice? Outstanding! You are your father's daughter.'

'You knew my father?'

'I served with him but only for a short while I'm sorry to say.'

Later in life, older and wiser, Sophie grew to recognise a weakness of hers: mention her father and you had a friend for life. Commander Clyde St John Forrester knew that. 'I worked with your father on a scanning program. He had the same brilliant memory. Get into a game of poker and you could kiss your annuity goodbye.'

'My Dad played poker!'

'We used to fool about a bit, play a couple of hands, test one another, who could see a card though metal casing sort of trick, but nobody cared to seriously take him on. What about you, Sophie? You play cards?'

Coffee was poured and she was offered cookies. Yes, she thought, they are trying to pacify me. 'Who is that man on the film and why do I feel so bad?'

'He was in research at Stanford, Behavioural Response. He went through a pack of hounds before we got to him. We had to put every last one down.'

A picture slithered into Sophie's head. She slapped her hands over her ears. 'Don't tell me!' she begged, not sure who she was begging, the man or the recorder in her brain. 'I know what he did to keep them quiet.'

'I'm sorry.'

'So you should be! Not just for leading me into it but for treating the whole thing in a casual manner. That man,' she pointed to the doodler, 'thought it a joke. But I get it! You expected nothing of me and so nothing mattered.'

Desperate to get out she grabbed her jacket. 'Today I learned a lot about this programme, how it can be cruel and casual. I learned a lot about the programme, and Commander Forrester, I learned a lot about you.'

She was halfway across the Square when he caught her up.

'Hold on!' he said, grey eyes glinting. 'You've no call jumping to conclusions. You're right the guy was a sonofabitch with no moral compass. He shouldn't have got into the country let alone a research centre but it was funded by tobacco and they pay megabucks for Intel only helpless animals can supply.'

Sophie snatched her arm away. 'I asked you not to talk about it. I'm having memory issues. The more you say on the matter the more I'm forced to see.'

'I'm sorry but I can't let you walk away with the wrong idea. It was one of our guys that smoked that particular rat from his hole. Right now the rat is someplace else trying to set up a similar deal. He's known to us now and can never rest easy. That's all I have to say. I had hoped you might understand us.'

'Who is us, Commander Forrester?'

'We're a branch of the military service whose aim is to serve the people of the United States of America.'

'What does that mean?'

'Exactly what I said! I'm sorry. Working with your father, knowing what he could do and thinking it might be in your genes I made the call. Now I regret it.'

He took a card from his pocket and held it out. Sophie shied away.

'It's okay. The Remote Viewing is dead in the water. Maybe you might have dinner with me some time.' Back he strode across the Square, female heads turning and placard-carrying students scattering to let him through.

~

Sophie plucked up courage to try the Revue Bar once more. She tiptoed in via the stage door. The director looked up. 'Well, if it isn't Just Me! You gonna stay long enough to learn the routine *and* come back the following night to dance?'

Cheeks scarlet, she scuttled in. She deserved his rebuke. Three times she'd attended rehearsal and three times lost her nerve before the show.

'Back again for another dose?' a dancer smiled.

'Hello Lola,' Sophie whispered. 'Sorry for being a pain.'

Lola shrugged. 'It was a year before I felt able to strut my stuff.'

'But can we call it dancing? I mean is it?'

'Don't be silly! What we do is sod all to do with dancing.'

Sophie was almost out the door again when stopped by a shout.

'Oy you!' another dancer yelled. 'Make up your mind will you! I got my kid to pick up, two fillings and a brace, a tenner or quick blow job. I'm not 'anging about while you and the snake-charmer discuss the finer points of baring all.'

'Piss off, Thelma, you and your bratty kid,' drawled Lola. 'You're always moaning about something.'

A spat developed, no real angst, an opportunity for a quick fag, a gossip, and to see if the fake tan had taken. Then for an hour they did their stuff, practised walking up and down the stairs and then left.

'You gonna turn up tonight?' said Lola. 'The boss ain't usually so easy-going.'

'So why is he?'

Lola laughed. 'Ain't you got mirrors at home? The boss looks at you and sees what punters will see, gorgeous face and best pair of tits this side of Tower Bridge. Have a cup of tea with me and Joe and I'll let you know how it works.'

Sophie lunched with Lola and Joe, head waiter at a nearby cafe. After lunch she was taken on a tour. Though small the house was a gem, Lola the do-it-all. 'I do the heavy stuff and Joe the cooking. It's arse-about-face but we like it.'

Sophie liked it too but wasn't sure of the snakes in the outhouse.

'This is Boris my first partner.' Lola wound the snake lovingly about her body. 'One year we did a Salome spot at the Alhambra in Granada. Best day's work ever. Ten minutes and my knickers stuffed with fivers.'

'He's certainly big, Lola.'

'He's old and cranky so I don't risk him. Rocky's my partner now. Besides the Revue we have a stint at Sally's in Soho and bi-monthly at Great Ormond Street. Kids love 'em. And forget the Lola business. I'm Karen to my friends.'

~

The friendship of Mr and Mrs Walker was the high spot of London in the Swinging Sixties – the Revue Bar the lowest. Becky is right, Sophie is a Mouse. The night at the Gala Sophie told Becky she risked heartbreak loving Johnny Beaufort. Becky was scornful. 'You offering me advice? Don't make me laugh! What do you know about anything? We call the other students Mice. We giggle at their pink-and-white worlds but who could be more a Mouse than you?'

Ten o'clock that evening, clothed in random sequins and smiling brightly, the Mouse descended a staircase to a band playing, 'Jezebel.' There were no smiles on the way back up, not from Sophie or the boss.

'It's a wonder some mouthy git didn't feed you to the wolves,' he said. 'The punters behaved. One more chance and you're gone.'

She was given three chances. The second night was as bad. The third and final night she made every move to total silence, not a sound from the audience, not a word or a whisper, until in desperation she made a curtsey. Then someone blew a very long, very loud, and very wet raspberry.

Mortified, she ran to the dressing room. The girls clustered about. Even Thelma was sympathetic. 'Don't worry, kid. You've either got it or you ain't.'

Karen, aka Lola, stood apart from the rest. She listened to sympathetic cooing and then stepped forward. 'I'll tell you what went wrong,' she said. 'She's ashamed of being here. She wants to pretend it's all a nasty dream and so pitterpats across the stage hoping to teach us and the punters better ways.'

'That's a bit harsh, Lola!' said one of the girls. 'After all she's never done it before and you know how that feels first time.'

'I know how it feels,' said Karen. 'I remember every second, Joe breaking his back in a restaurant working a sixteen hour shift and paid a pittance. I couldn't afford to be picky, neither could he. We had to pay our rent somehow.'

'Same with my bloke,' said another. 'He don't like me doing it but we got to buy food.'

'It's not about money with Sophie,' said Karen. 'She's got plenty.'

'But I need to pay my way as well as any of you,' said Sophie.

'Yeah but why strip when you've money?'

'It's not about stripping or money. It's about dancing!'

'Is that what you did out there, dance?'

'I couldn't move. It was their faces, the way they looked at me. They're disgusting. Don't you see that?'

'I don't. To me they're patrons. They pay, I dance! And if you think that about us and the people out there go shake your posh little bum elsewhere!'

'Yeah!' said Thelma. 'Toffee nosed cow!'

It was developing into a full-scale row when the manager stuck his head round the door. 'You lot! Out! Someone wants to speak to Sophie.'

The skeletal figure of Tamara Karsavina stood in the doorway.

The manager produced a stool. Karsavina perched, mottled hands folded over a silver-topped cane. Sophie waited for the tongue-lashing that was sure to come. Minutes passed. When she did speak Karsavina's tone was mild.

'You do not remember me.'

'Yes, I do, Madame, the Abbey. We talked of the Gala.'

'I speak of previous encounters. Four times I've watched you dance, yesterday in this place, tonight, at His Lordship's home in Suffolk, and some years ago in Vermont. You were a little girl then with a large head and magnetic eyes.'

'I'm sorry I don't remember.'

'I met your mama at Bennington. We lunched.'

'I didn't know.'

'There are many things you do not know, however if you have any hope of continuing in this branch of the arts then you need to understand the first rule of dance – if you do not believe in the dance it will not believe in you.'

'Yes, Madame.'

Karsavina's composure slipped. 'Do not yes Madame me! I cannot tell you my feelings when I saw you here. I was with friends. We come occasionally to rescue the odd refugee, to drink champagne and mourn the passing of an age. Tell me, Miss Hunter, late of the Royal Ballet, what happened that you need dip your toes in the dregs? Are you in financial trouble? You can't be impoverished. Your mama would never leave you without resources.'

'I'm not in financial difficulties.'

'Then why do this?'

'I wanted to dance. It seemed as good a way as any.'

'Dance! Do you refer to what you did earlier as dancing?'

'No, I don't. It was awful. *I* was awful!'

'Awful is not how I would describe your performance. Awe implies a state of wonderment. One might apply the term to the Gala solo but not this. One does not dance in such place neither can one earn a living, unless by extracurricular activity. So why? Is it a romantic disappointment?'

Sophie was silent.

'I see it is so. And yet you still want to dance?' Karsavina regarded her. 'Then do so and by all means choose Burlesque. It has a rightful place in history. No need to cower in the corner ashamed of what God gave you.

Find your craft but choose rightly. Your mama would want the best for you.'

'She would want the best *of* me.'

'Indeed. Your mother was a woman of my heart, fearless and forward thinking. She told me of her own choices and knowing how much she loved you, and how she'd hate to see you less than you are, I come with a gift.'

She laid a box on Sophie's knee. 'The last time we spoke I talked of my own disappointments. Do not become a disappointment to yourself. Take what is in the box and use it well.'

~

Unable to sleep Sophie put on her running shoes. It is a beautiful morning, raindrops glittering in the trees. She ran alongside the track, shup-shup, her shoes slapping wet sand. Her mind is filled with Ostrich feathers. That's what was in the box, a pair of exquisite feather fans. '*Magicians make the visible invisible,*' said a note. '*Do the same with your body and all will desire you.*'

Early hours of the morning she stood naked before the mirror adopting poses. The fans are beautiful, the names of legendary lovers *Eloise and Abelard* engraved on the handles. Gazing into the mirror Sophie caught a glimpse of what they meant to Karsavina and was staggered by the generosity. The fans were precious to the old lady, yet she gave them away to a stranger.

'Thank you, Madame,' she curtseyed. 'I promise to make them live again.'

Now, she runs in the Park feeling happier than she's felt in months. Shup-shup, she ran. In her mind another pair of shoes ran alongside. She is happy to hear them. She hasn't been out since Johnny's attempt at love. But was that love? She prayed not! Passion has to be more than grope and groan.

She thinks of passion and the elegant figure of Clyde Forrester strides into her head. A fabulous man! Good-looking, mature, a burst of lines about his eyes, he would know how to make a girl happy!

Sophie has his card. Maybe she'll give him a call and take him up on the invitation to dinner and whatever desert he might suggest to follow.

Heart beating a little faster, a laugh tickling the back of her throat and a Jodie song in her head, she began to sing under her breath,

Jodie cannot dance ballet
She's too tall to make it pay.

Then another voice, a companion, began to sing, softly at first and then louder, until, laughing, Sophie was singing along with it.

'Sophie need not dance ballet
She's too fine to stay that way
Look up to the skies and say
Tomorrow, baby, is another day
Sound off, 1- 2, Sound off, 3- 4,
Sound off, 1 -2- 3- 4, 1-2 ---3-4!'

Chapter Seven
Friends

'*Mankind seeks the things he cannot have,*' said Madame. '*You must become a magician! Sleight of hand! Now you see me, now you don't.*'

At the time of saying, Sophie dismissed the notion as the ramblings of an old woman. Now she works every day to perfect the art, Karen Walker, aka Lola, perched on the bed painting her toenails and making rude comments.

'Well that isn't very magical! Stop waving your arms about! You're dancing not drowning. And for Chrissakes loosen up! You look like a waxwork dummy.'

'The fans are heavy!'

'They're nothing on Boris.'

'Snakes are mobile. You can bend them.'

'Yes and get crunched for your pains. I don't know what you're moaning about. Move over let me have a go!' Head up and bosom like the prow of a ship, the fans trailing after, Karen prowled the bedroom. 'You got to take your time, titillate the punters. Don't be in a hurry to cover up.'

'I don't feel comfortable.'

'That's because you're thinking like a twelve-year-old – "snowflakes on kittens and woolly mittens". Kill that image.

You're not mummy's little sweetheart when you pick up these bad-boys. You're the hottest property in Soho.'

'What image do you have with the snakes?'

'Fivers stuffed down my knickers.'

'You do go on about money. I've not forgotten what you said in the Revue. I told you about the Trust in strictest confidence.'

'Friends are there to speak their mind not to stay quiet when a mate is acting like an idiot.' Karen grabbed Sophie, scraped her hair from her face and shoved her before the mirror. 'Is that who you think blokes see when you're on stage, a flesh-and-blood human being?'

'What else?'

'They don't see you. Tits and arse is all they see. They don't care what your name is. They don't care about your period pains or if you take sugar in your tea. They come to ogle a beautiful girl and then go home and screw their spotty girlfriend on the carpet while hanging your face over hers.'

'And that is supposed to make me feel better?'

'Yes, you silly moo, because the face they see isn't one you'd recognise. It's Marilyn Monroe, Audrey Hepburn and the first fumble behind the bike sheds, nothing to do with Sophie, ex-ballerina and all-round sensitive soul!'

'You think you know everything, Karen Walker. '

'I know a bit more than you. Okay, so what are you going to call yourself? I'm thinking Princess something or other.'

'How about Madame?'

'Chrissakes don't call yourself that! Not unless you want lots of whispering on your phone late at night and men hovering outside your door.'

'Then Mamselle?'

'Okay and a name, not your real name, something made up. You don't want people making life difficult. What would your dad think of you doing this?'

Sophie knew exactly what he'd think, *if it's honest why ask me?*

'Is what we do honest, Karen?'

'That depends on you. I believe in giving value for money. Now try the routine again and instead of thinking, 'I'm naked quick cover me up,' see the feathers as hands belonging to that gorgeous sailor currently wining and dining you.'

'Oh, Clyde.'

'Yes, Clyde. Has anything happened yet?'

'Not yet.'

'Then you've got to make it happen. Got to get down and dirty .The minute you do and Clyde's worked his brand of magic you'll have your own.'

'You sound like a sex-manual.'

'It's what you need. I mean, how old are you, twenty-something and still a virgin? And I'm not talking about the one who messed with your head! I mean mentally and emotionally you're a virgin. When you seeing Clyde again?'

'Friday. We're going to *Annabelle's*.'

'Don't go there! It's too crowded. You need small and sexy. Plenty of good food and wine and then of you go to his place and get properly sorted.'

Friday, Sophie chose her outfit with being 'properly sorted' in mind. A black silk Caftan from the Kings Road, black patent heels and black lace underwear, it looked more like *Bride of Dracula* than *Breakfast at Tiffany's* and so to bolster courage she had a couple of glasses of wine before leaving.

'You look different,' Clyde took her coat.

'Good different or bad?'

'Interesting different. Dined here before have you, Sophie?'

'No, what about you?'

A waiter approached 'Good evening, Commander. The usual table, sir?'

'Ah! I see that you have.'

It was a good meal, *al dente* pasta served with a very good wine. 'Nice,' said Sophie draining the glass. 'It doesn't burn the back of the throat.'

Clyde upended another empty bottle. 'It didn't get a chance.'

More wine and dulling of the nerves and Sophie's ready to leave. They arrived at his apartment in Camden. Quite how they got there she didn't know but thought it involved a taxi and lots of giggling on her part.

'You sure you wouldn't sooner go home?' asked Clyde.

'I want to see where you live and if it's as organised as you.'

Cool tiles underfoot, electronic surveillance and incense, it was his apartment.

'It's grounded like you, Clyde.'

'Yeah, grounded, that's me,' he said resetting the alarm.

'If you're worried 'bout burglars you might try a penthouse.'

'I don't worry about burglars. Can I get you anything?' He hung up her coat. 'A coffee and aspirin for the headache you'll have tomorrow.'

'I'm okay, thank you. Where is it?'

'The bathroom? Through there.'

'The bedroom.'

'You want the bedroom?'

'Yes I think I do.'

'You think you do?'

'Yes.'

'You need to be certain.'

Sophie stepped out of the Caftan. 'I am.'

~

'Well that was a surprise,' she said, gazing at the ceiling. Clyde was sitting on the bed knotting his tie. 'Good surprise or bad?'

'I can't say different,' she said, turning the bracelet about her wrist, a gift given earlier along with multiple orgasms. 'I've nothing to measure it against.'

'Nothing?' His eyebrows quirked.

'No.' She glanced at him through her lashes. 'Truly nothing.'

'Then more fool him.' He picked up his jacket and from a cabinet took what looked like a shoulder holster. 'I have to go – trouble at the Embassy.'

'And you're going to restore peace with a pistol? That is a shoulder holster I see, Commander?'

'I'm surprised you can actually see anything.'

'So am I. '

'Okay then, Sophie, take your time, leave when you want, stay if you want.'

'I have to get back. I promised Niarchos I'd be early shift.'

'Niarchos? That would be the guy from the Greek restaurant. You left the dog with them last night? I guess you came prepared for this little adventure.'

'I guess I did.'

'Okay.' He slipped a couple of bills under the alarm clock. Sophie looked at him. 'You may need to get a cab. It's no small distance back to your place.'

'I can pay for my own cab.'

The notes back in his pocket he leant down kissing her cheek. 'As you wish.'

'Thank you,' she said, 'and thanks for the bracelet.'

'You're welcome. I was someplace, saw the lapis lazuli and your eyes.'

Handsome face devoid of expression, he paused at the door. 'The Nothing? He wouldn't be the Viscount Nothing who resides in a rundown castle in Suffolk and likes to climb mountains and cage lions?'

Sophie declined to answer.

He nodded. 'As you wish, Sophie,' he said again. 'It will always be as you wish.'

On the bus home she wondered if it was as she wished. No matter how random the contact, no matter when and where they met, she always felt managed. The restaurant, Niarchos and Jay Beaufort, Clyde knew so much about her. Perhaps she ought to be worried, but then she recalled the

fabulous sex – the way her body became slithering liquid –
and thought to risk it.

It was as she'd said, she had no way of comparing. You
can't compare ripping hands to a practised touch.

Even so, it was awkward at first, not sure what to do or
where to put her hands. Clyde said, 'forget your head.
Switch off and let me do the rest.' And being a good girl,
and doing as she was told, she switched off.

'Oh!' She scuffed down in the seat. Enough of that! A
date with Commander Clyde St John Forrester is too rich
for the six am bus from Camden Town.

Throughout the next day, thighs sore and breasts
tender, she kept coming back to it. If asked to describe his
technique she would say well-versed. It's obvious he's had
bags of practice, a string of lovers over the world.

For sure he'll be able to converse with them as well as
drive them crazy. A well-travelled man, the phone rang
several times while she was there, service kicking in and
callers leaving cryptic messages in various languages.

She wondered about his work. One thing is certain the
room at the top of the Embassy and Remote Viewing is a
side issue. You don't need a gun for that.

The bracelet is lovely and so charmingly presented. 'I
see you don't wear jewellery,' he said. 'Is that a personal
choice?'

'I have Mother's things but can't wear any of it.'

'I know what you mean,' he'd nodded. 'When my
father died he left me his books. Old books, rare copies of
maps, valuable, I gave them to a local library. Pa was a
tough guy. He died at home in bed with his boots on and so
I'd no cause to mourn other than never seeing his craggy

face again. It was the stillness. The way the books sat closed tight like the lid of his coffin.'

This about his father, she later realised, was a gift, a rare glimpse into Clyde's personal life. He never discussed his situation. No hint of wife or children, past or present. The apartment is purely a bachelor pad, no photographs dotted about, indeed very little in the way of personal items.

'You could have given the maps to your sons,' she did a little fishing.

'The same applies to you,' was his reply. 'One day you'll get a kick out of seeing your daughter wearing her grandmother's stuff.'

It was then he fastened the bracelet about her wrist. 'Anyway,' he said. 'I hope you won't be offended if I offer this trinket by way of friendship.'

She'd touched his hand. 'Thank you, friend.'

It's likely the bracelet is a token of sexual conquest, the Commander's version of a scalp tied to his belt. There may well be many such mementos scattered about the Globe. It's none of her concern. It was an experiment Sophie is happy to repeat but not too often. Too many meetings and she might imagine the friendship more than it is and she is never going to do that again.

~

Mena's gone to live at the restaurant. Sophie was sorry to see her go but relieved. May Templar, long time friend and surrogate grandmother, is ill. Sophie wants to spend time with her. The Bentley broke down on the way to Oxford. It was late when she finally pulled into the drive. Tim was sitting on the fence waiting, so tall and so grown. 'How long have you been here?'

'I got in yesterday. You should take lessons in auto-repair, Sis,' said Tim examining the car. 'You can't drive a motor like this without knowing how it works. It's the same with the Beagle. You got to be in control. By the way, did you hear I was taking flying lessons?'

'Yes, dear brother, I did, but you've a year yet before you can apply for a licence.' Tim is always trying to steal the plane. 'Grandma okay?'

'Yeah and Aunt Sarah! They send their love.'

'So what brought you here?'

'Nana May. I wasn't gonna miss out again on saying goodbye.'

'You think it is goodbye.'

'Josh thinks so.'

Sophie went along to May's room, a sunny room on the ground floor with a wide expanse of glass overlooking the garden. May Templar was a shrunken carcase on a quilted cover. Sophie tried to hug her but May shied away.

'I can't stand to be hugged no more. Every bit of my body hurts.'

'So sorry.'

'It's okay.' May shrugged. 'I've been on this blessed planet too long. It's time to move on. Seen my boy anyplace?'

'Would you like me to go and look for him?'

'Will yer, honey. Pain lessens when he's around.'

'I've brought you a little present.'

'That's good of yer. Leave it on the side. I'll look later.'

Sophie met Gabriel on the stairs. 'I'm sorry,' she said. 'I hadn't realised.'

'She's old and tired. Did you say goodbye?'

A tear slipped down Sophie's cheek. 'In my heart I did.'

'Good. That's the place she'll find it.'

'I brought her a bed jacket. I thought she might like it.'

Gabriel smiled. 'I'll make sure she sees it. If it's anythin' like the blanket you and your ma made for Bobby to rest in it'll be fine.'

~

Jay was at the Templars on Saturday evening. Sophie saw the truck pull into the drive. He still calls her every evening, same thing every time, 'Sophie, speak to me.' She picks up the phone, hears his voice, and disconnects.

The truck stayed outside, the engine running and Jay staring ahead.

'Why doesn't he come inside?' said Julia.

'He's waitin' on Tim and Josh,' said Gabriel. 'He's taking them to the Abbey. There's a Rhino calf due and they want to be there.'

'I could've taken them,' said Sophie loath to see her brothers anywhere near and frankly surprised Gabriel didn't feel the same. Picking up on her feelings he followed from the room. 'I would've taken them but couldn't leave Ma.'

'Yes of course.'

'You need to be kinder to yourself, Sophie. Keep a pot simmerin' on a stove too long and you're likely to damage the pot and stove.'

'Are you suggesting I forget what happened?'

'No not forget. Maybe turn down the heat a little. Over time things have a habit of softenin'.'

'Yes and no doubt I'll soften. Life's too short, *carpe diem*, and all that.'

Gabriel sucked in his breath. Ashen-faced he stood holding his chest.

'What?' said Sophie.

'Your ma. For a minute there you was her. She said that to me once, *carpe diem*. At the time me bein' me I didn't know what she meant and took it wrong. Got myself all screwed up. That was then. I know what it means now and have to tell you don't waste your time bein' angry. It gets you nowhere. Do what them words say – grab the moment and never let go.'

Chapter Eight
Bluebell Girls

Sophie's been seeing Clyde for over a year. They meet
when he's in London, a trip to the theatre or the ballet.
They dine and then go back to his apartment. The US
heavily involved in Vietnam his visits are rare. With the
war in mind he persuaded Sophie to help the RV
Programme and in view of their intimacy she felt she
couldn't refuse. Once a week she calls now at a house in
Bruton Street. Same procedure, a room set up as a cinema,
her mandate not to think about what's happening only to
say what comes into her head.

Clyde says something similar during sex: 'What are you
feeling? No, don't think about it! Just tell me.' So far she
hasn't got beyond 'lovely' to which he rolls his eyes. 'Is
that the best you can do? You're an English woman raised
on Shakespeare. Surely you can do better than that.'

Lately he's been insistent. Then she gets angry. 'What
d'you want me to say? You want compliments or dirty
words? Shall I be Little Red Riding Hood? Oh Grandpapa,
what a big dick you have? Is that what you want?'

'No, ma-am!' Taut belly rippling, he laughed. 'That
would make me a pervert and you a tease. I want you to say
what's in your heart.'

Sophie thinks it best he doesn't know. There is affection but also growing unease and awareness that he wants more than she can give.

The RV meetings are conducted in a safe-room, the heavy insulation on the walls thought to cut out interference. Clyde says the experiments are important. Sophie is wary. She's beginning to think Remote Viewing heightens the Morris-Effect. The more she sits staring at a screen the wider the door opens in her head – yesterday on the Tube she caught a glimpse of the Past.

A bag lady sat eating fish and chips. She offered a chip. Sophie leaned forward to accept, there was a ripple in the air, and the old lady was no longer old, a smart tweed suit settled over a shabby jacket and a snakeskin purse over the bag of chips. The end product, a pert blonde, smiled at Sophie and said, 'they taste better out of newspaper, don't they, love?'

Sophie told Clyde. 'One moment I was looking at a bag lady the next a pretty blonde. What happened, do you think, that she should end up a tramp?'

'I've no idea. Life, I guess. Do you see much like that?'

'No and I wouldn't want to. I gave her a tenner and she looked at me like I was the bag-lady.'

'How did it happen? What are the mechanics?'

'It needs a trigger, a word or deed, but what word or deed I don't know. I don't actually see anything. It's more an image in my head, the person I'm with plus another.'

'You mean like a doppelganger?'

'I don't know what I mean. Has anything like that happened to you?'

'Mine is more a bloodhound tracking device. I find if I concentrate on where a person has been I can track him down to where he is now.'

'My brother Tim finds things people have lost. He calls it dowsing.'

'I don't dowse for objects. I dowse for flesh and blood.'

'That sounds like a scene in a Hammer Horror.'

He shrugged. 'Every viewer works differently.'

'There are others who see like this?'

'There are several known to me. You work with two of them.'

'What the doodler and the pen-clicker?'

'The doodler, as you call him, nailed the Stanford guy. Anti-vivisectionist, he spent hours on it, came close to a breakdown. Is your stuff like your pa's?'

'My *pa* said very little about his stuff and now I know why.'

'In any event, Sophie, you need to work on a jamming device. Wrong place at the wrong time a situation like yours could be dangerous.'

Sophie already has a jamming device. Dad taught her how. On her seventh birthday she woke screaming from a nightmare. 'See this?' He pointed to his watch. 'There's a red button inside. If I'm chased by a dragon I press it and the dragon explodes. I'll get you a watch, Sweet-Pea, then you can do the same.'

Now, if she's driving the Bentley or crossing a busy thoroughfare and the Morris-Effect comes on she remembers the watch.

~

In Bruton Street, images on the screen have changed to hexagonal shapes.

'It's a Rorschach test. I think you're trying to psyche me out.'

'Nah,' the doodler carried on doodling – a rose with what looked like Sophie's face appearing under his pen. 'That's already been done.'

'You mean the usual security check?'

He snickered. 'More than usual: names and addresses of former and current lovers, past and present history, Alma mater, political affiliation, hobbies, what kind of car they drive, what shoe and shirt-collar size.'

'What!'

'Oops!' He swung his feet down. 'I shouldn't have said that.'

'Does anybody really want to know such things?'

'Of course not! Why would they?' he said. 'I was only joshing.'

This is typical of the military. It drove Dad crazy. He'd say it's not enough to know how often you take a dump, they want colour, texture, and smell.

Sighing, she returned to the screen and what looked and felt like otters swimming in a lake. There was intensity to the image, a sense of danger.

'I see otters swimming.'

'Otters?'

'Yes, otters.' Outside, CND protesters were marching, singing and shouting rising up through the window. 'These Otters?' The doodler made a joke. 'Do they wear red bandannas and sing Bob Dylan's songs?'

'Very funny.' What a waste of time, thought Sophie. I could be home packing.

This weekend she's off to Paris to see Mariel Bellaton, ex-ballet chum, who dances at the Moulin Rouge. It clashes with Clyde's visit but can't be helped.

It is warm in the room. Sophie yawned and middle yawn an Otter saluted.

'Oh, a man's face.'

The doodler sat up. 'Describe him.'

'It was just a flash.'

'You have eidetic memory. Describe the flash.'

An Otter with a man's face! Sophie was in a rush to leave and so began improvising. 'Er… short dark hair slicked to his head. A curly mouth, always smiling, eyes the colour of wet leaves in the rain and a scar under his left eyebrow shaped like an icicle.'

'Very poetic. What else?'

'What else? He loves messing about in boats.'

The doodler's pencil was racing. 'Age and possible ethnic background?'

'Thirty and American.'

'How do you know that?'

Sophie knew because information was pouring into her head, height, 6-3, weight, 200lbs, Welsh/American background, born January 20th 1938, but then because it was improv – and she didn't trust it – she hit the red button.

All week she worried, what had she done, had she brought some poor innocent male to the attention of the US military intelligence.

She phoned Karen. 'I mean, who is Clyde and the pen clicker and doodler?'

'Who do you think they are?'

'My dad had links with the Central Intelligence Agency. I was brought into this via one of his connections and so assumed it was the same.'

Karen laughed. 'And what does the CIA want with a Fan-dancer?'

'You can laugh but all the time I'm in Bruton Street someone is listening in.'

'To what, to you talking rubbish? I'm sure they've better things to do.'

'I hope you're right. I'd hate to think I've interfered with someone's life.'

'Was it a bit of Clyde maybe?'

'No, not Clyde. It was someone I would've liked to know.'

'Who?'

'Oh, just someone I once saw, a stranger.'

It was a game Mother played. If they had a job they didn't like, say mucking out the pigs or clearing thistles, she would suggest a game. 'Look there goes Mr Rabbit,' she'd say. 'I wonder what Mrs Rabbit looks like?'

Sophie's part was to describe Mrs Rabbit from the feather in her hat to her pink suede bootees. It was a kiddie's game. The man Sophie described was real, the naval officer at the Gala. She remembers him as tall and good-looking, the rest – the colour of his eyes, scar on his eyebrow, age and family background – is pure imagination, or so she hopes.

~

Sophie is in Paris. Clyde brought them over. She'd wanted to take a ferry but he insisted. 'Why when I've Chrysalis ready and waiting?'

Chrysalis is his yacht. A member of the US America's Cup Team, he's crazy about sailing. It's the one subject he talks about. 'We got a new baby coming soon, Sophie, wait until you see her.'

Lately he does that, weaves her into future plans. The other night he opened a drawer in his bedroom and pulled out a diary. 'See this?' he said indicating names and telephone numbers. 'This is the Little Black Book every guy claims to own.' He dropped it in a waste bin. 'I hope you're suitably gratified.'

There's been a change of plans. Sophie didn't get to spend time with Mariel, a coffee and chat at Charles De Gaulle airport was all they managed before Mariel jetted off to New York and a chance of dancing with a new company.

Mariel left the key to her apartment. 'The lease is up next month if you're interested.' She suggested the Moulin Rouge as an opportunity but Sophie's seen an ad in *Paris Match* for solo spots at the Lido with the *Bluebell Girls*, and bearing in mind Gabriel Templar's advice, carpe diem, arranged an audition. She is anxious about that yet more so about meeting Ethan Winter.

He is coming to London! They are finally to meet! Thursday he left a message on her service: 'London first two weeks of June. Meet?' Sophie wrote back suggesting the 6th and Peter Pan's statue at the Serpentine. Now she thinks it was a mistake. They might not like one another and the friendship spoiled.

Sophie and Clyde quarrelled. He said she should stay aboard at the mooring rather than Mariel's apartment. 'Chrysalis is big enough and cheaper.'

'Mariel has a bathroom.'

'So do we.'

'Yes but very little room. I want to look at the apartment. I'm thinking if I get a solo spot at the Lido I might take up the lease.'

'You'll get the spot. They know a good thing when seen.'

'I hope so. It'll help make up for fifteen years wasted.'

'Fifteen years! Is that when you started out in ballet? Hell!' He hung his handsome head. 'You make me feel old.'

'How old are you?'

'Thirty-three.'

'How can thirty-three be old?'

'Compared to you it's ancient.'

'What were you doing fifteen years ago?'

'Pretty much what I'm doing now.'

'And what is that?'

'Best you don't know.'

'Your life worries me. It sounds like a spy movie.'

'It is a spy movie complete with mad scientists and special codes. What's the matter, honey?' He rolled onto his back pulling her astride. Lips firm and sweet he kissed her. They never used to kiss. Now he kisses all the time. It's nice but doesn't offer the fireworks one is supposed to feel.

'Why Paris?' he said. 'Are you done with England as well as the States? See yourself more a Parisian Mamselle than a Brit or a Yankee gal?'

'I don't plan to live here. I just want to dance. And though I love Virginia I was born in Suffolk and couldn't be more English. But you didn't answer my question. What were you doing fifteen years ago?'

'Like I said, same as I'm doing now.'

'CIA mad scientists and sexy girls with secret codes?'

'Sexy my ass! People have Hollywood's idea of intelligence gathering. They think microdots and Humphrey Bogart in a raincoat. They don't realise we have to go with the domestic view. Fifteen years ago me and every other American male was counting the cost of the Korean War. The Agency didn't see it coming. They thought it would be Russia and so busy concentrating on Europe they missed Hanoi and got caught with their thumb up their ass.'

Sophie was surprised by his reply. Clyde is so private, no professional or personal detail ever offered. When they meet, conversation is limited to life in London. Over the year a pattern has formed of good manners and discreet sex. At times when they dine in the same discreet club with the same discreet waiter drinking the same discreet wine Sophie wants to leap on a table and do a strip, napkins for fans and a whisky drinker's nose for a spotlight.

Karen has definite views about the set-up. 'You feel safe with Clyde. You think you won't get your heart broken.'

Sophie didn't feel safe that weekend in Paris. For twenty-five scary minutes Clyde stepped outside his perfectly pressed persona and allowed another man to come through – a man whose temper was hot but whose eyes were cold.

'Fifteen years ago I was a shave-tail,' he was saying, 'nothing to recommend me but my heart on my sleeve.'

'You do have a heart then?'

'Yes and one easily broken.'

'You'd never know.'

'I keep it under wraps. Talking of hearts and Suffolk, as indeed we were, have you heard lately from Viscount Nobody?'

Clyde has a thing about the Beauforts, especially Johnny.

'Don't start that again.'

'I'm starting nothing.' He pushed her skirt up her hips and his hand between her legs. 'I'm all alone on this boat. I'm cold and thinking to warm myself up.'

Eyes closed, he began to stroke outside her pants and then inside. 'Lift up, sugar.' She lifted. Pulling her pants aside he pushed his fingers inside her, moving them slowly back and forth Sophie leaning back against his knees. 'Speak to me,' he whispered. 'Tell me what you're feeling.'

A blush swamped her cheek. Sophie finds the situation awkward. Sex should be about love and the things you dreamed about as a girl. It shouldn't be about being a mistress. 'Are you happy with me as your mistress?'

'Hah!' He laughed out loud. 'Is that what you are?'

'I don't know,' she retorted, stung by his laughter. 'You tell me!'

He kissed her nose. 'Sorry, honey, I didn't mean to bug you.'

'You didn't bug me. I was trying to figure out what I am in your life.'

'You want to know what you are in my life? I'll tell you.' A kiss on her breast for every comment he told her. 'You're a gorgeous piece of unclaimed territory, a resting place in the desert of my life, my private Sanctuary. And in keeping with rules of Sanctuary, you must stop asking questions, and lay back and let me find peace.'

What could she do but relax and enjoy the feeling spreading through her body. It was so good. Then he spoiled it. 'Come on then,' he said, huskily, his fingers slippery and moving deeper. 'Tell me all about it. Is this how the Nobody makes you feel, all dripping wet and hungry for his prick?'

'Don't talk like that. You're spoiling it.'

'I'm spoiling nothing.' Buttons popping, he dragged her shirt open. 'I'm asking if what I do makes you want to unzip his lordly plus-fours and suck him off.'

Sophie pulled away. 'I'm not doing this.' Furious, she stalked out the bedroom and into the washroom. Clyde followed. She bent over the sink to rinse her hands and he pushed her skirt up her hips. She turned and he was on his knees his face between her legs, licking the front of her pants.

'Don't,' she moaned.

'Why not? Every woman likes a man's tongue inside her. Poor bastard on his knees worshipping the all-powerful pussy. It's a real winner. I'll bet the Beaufort heir is past master at cunt lapping. He'll have been given private lessons on the art by the Health Minister's wife.'

'Health Minister's wife! What are you talking about?'

He shrugged. 'He gets around.'

'God's sake! Do you check up on everyone I know?'

The washroom is small. Clyde is not. She tried to get by but he blocked the way, leaning her against the sink refusing to let her by.

'Sorry,' he said. 'I didn't mean to get fired up.'

'Then why do it and always about Johnny.'

'He hurt you. I don't like the idea of anyone hurting you.'

'Other than you, you mean?'

'No, I don't mean that.'

'Then stop bringing him up. It was nothing. It's over and done.'

'He still calls you.'

'How do you know that? Is this you prying again?'

'I know because it's what I'd do if I'd hurt you. Call until I was forgiven.'

The sink was pressing Sophie's spine. She was uncomfortable with the sink and with Clyde. Suddenly he was very tall, very dark, and very unsafe.

'Can I get by?'

'I will let you by if you tell me what's going on with you and the Navy SEAL.'

'Navy seal?'

'You don't know what a Navy SEAL is?'

'What is it?'

Eyes glinting, he observed her. 'You've never heard of a SEAL yet you have a date with one on the 6th of June.'

'The 6th of…? You're referring to Ethan.'

'I believe that is his name, Lieutenant Ethan Winter the Third.'

'Ethan Winter is my pen friend. Why are you asking about him?'

'I'm not. I'm querying the set-up. You told me he's your pen-pal…case closed.'

'It is not case closed! Why do such things? Do I do this of you, pry into your secrets? When was the last time I asked of your private life? I extend you the courtesy of privacy. Why can't you do the same with me?'

'I need to know you're safe.'

'And I wouldn't be with Ethan Winter?'

'Sure. By all accounts he's a regular guy. Even so, I am concerned.'

'You don't need to be. I'm a strong person beneath the tutu.'

'Maybe and maybe not.'

'So now can I get by?'

'Sure you can.' He was on his knees again. 'But not until I've paid penance.'

~

Early for her audition with the Bluebells Sophie settled in a cafe with a cup of chocolate. Cecile Brune, top model of the day, stopped by the table. 'I know you,' she said, 'you're the girl from Sadlers Wells. I saw the graduation concert. You danced the Swan. You were brilliant. What brings you to Paris?'

'I'm hoping for a spot at the Lido.'

'*C'est vrais*!' Cecile was silent for a while. Then she opened her purse and offered a card. 'When you're tired of that call this number. Chloe is my Agency. I have a branch in New York and in London.'

Sophie put the card in her pocket. 'Thank you.'

Cecile adjusted her wrap. 'I can definitely do something for you and none of it will require you to bare body and soul to the world.'

They talked awhile until Sophie left for the Lido where she was brought into the Long Salon and Miss Bluebell staring over her spectacles. 'And you are?'

'Sophie Hunter, Madame,' she said, automatically bobbing a courtesy.

'Goodness me! Yet another refugee from the Royal Ballet! Too tall I imagine? And you can drop the Madame. It smacks of Left Bank nightlife. You may call me Miss Bluebell or Miss Kelly. And what are you going to do for us today?'

'I dance with fans.'

'Really? Do you have decent fans?'

She undid the box. 'I think so.'

'Show me!' Bluebell carried the fans to the window. 'I know these. I've seen them in action. Did Tamara Karsavina give you these?'

Sophie nodded.

'Really? Then you must have struck a chord in that ancient lady's heart.'

The fans were passed back. 'See to the moth infestation and be at the Champs Elysée Saturday for rehearsal and the evening performance. Do you have your own costumes? I find most solo artists prefer to use their own.'

'I don't have them yet but I know what I want.'

'Everything must be in the best possible taste in line with the Lido thinking. We do not require you to dance naked. It will be for you to decide how far to challenge your own artistic thoughts on the matter. If you know anything of Sally Rand's work you'll know she keeps a sense of mystery, that which is permissible in the shadow of dusk is abhorrent in the stark light of day.'

'Thank you, I do understand.'

'Then that will be all. Pop in to see my assistant for dress fittings and to know dressing room etiquette and the keeping of our good name here at the Lido. Good day, Miss Hunter. I look forward to watching you perform.'

'But the audition? Don't you want me to dance for you?'

Miss Bluebell shook her head. 'If Tamara Karsavina thought you good enough to work with her treasured fans who am I to doubt your ability?'

Chapter Nine
Perfidia

Sophie phoned Mrs Evans, third floor flat, Bayswater, saying she'd be staying awhile in Paris and was told a man called at the house asking for her.

'Navy bloke, a Yank,' said Mrs Evans, 'Ian, I think he said. Nice feller. Very polite with family in Pontypridd. He says forget June. He won't be here.'

Ethan. Once again like opposite points of the compass they swerve by. Sophie is disappointed and relieved. The Otter nonsense, plus Clyde's ambivalence toward Ethan muddied the water – if it's meant to be they'll meet one day.

Today, she is in the Latin Quarter searching for dance outfits and thinking of Sammy Warren. Sammy was buying lingerie for her spot at the Casino. With only hours to go Sophie has a couple of bits but none of the delicate lingerie she'd envisaged. In desperation she is seeking old fashioned underwear.

She told Clyde. 'I thought it will add a little something.'

Clyde rolled his eyes 'Sure, an extra layer to hide behind.'

'Don't you think it's a good idea?'

'I think it's a lollapalooza but be real choosy, anything less than perfect will kill the act stone dead.'

Everything so far is ultra modern, Day-Glo nylon and really rather nasty.

Then she wandered into a side street and what looked like a Bedouin tent.

'*Vous venez, Mamselle*? 'A dwarf with wizened monkey face and execrable French accent beckoned. '*Je vous montre beaucoup de jolies choses!*'

Sophie didn't think she'd find anything pretty inside but followed the woman and found to her delight hand-sewn scarves of exquisite material and colours.

She told of the Lido and the need for lingerie. The woman held up a hand.

'I know what you want, ducks,' she said in a Cockney accent. 'You want old-fashioned passion killers.'

'You're English?'

'You bet yer life I am. Born and raised in 'Ackney. Me and my old man 'ave lived in Paree these ten years. What is it you're looking for?'

'I was thinking French knickers rather than heavy bloomers.'

'Of course you were! You want Chantilly lace, crepe de chine and slippery satin, bags of lace and wide legs.' The woman grinned. 'You know what they used to call them in the old days? Mother trusts me knickers!'

Sophie laughed. It was as if tender-hearted May Templar slipped her ailing body and zipping across the Channel took up residence in the dwarf.

'Abe!' A little man armed with note-book and pencil scuttled from the shop, Sophie's hazy thoughts translated into measurements. This done the woman turned to Sophie. 'When do you need 'em?'

'Maybe early next week?'

'Never mind next week! Give me your address and the cab fare and they'll be ready for you at…? She turned. 'What d'you reckon, Abe, four-o-clock?'

Abe nodded. 'Four o' clock.'

Late afternoon, carriages packed and people sighing, there couldn't be a worse time to ride the Metro. Sandwiched between a fat man and his copy of *Le Figaro*, and a man eating garlic sausage, Sophie sighed with the rest.

A skinny girl sat on one seat, a begging bowl between her boots, *J'ai faim* chalked on the side. Sophie stooped to drop coins in the bowl and the girl grabbed her hand. 'Beautiful lady, I tell your fortune.'

'No thank you.'

The girl held on. 'I tell fortune. You marry rich man and have many children.'

Sophie tried to pull away but the grip on her wrist tightened. 'I have message for you,' whispered the girl, her eyes sudden opaque glass. 'Your maman says to tell you it did not hurt when we fell. We landed among angels.'

'What?' Sophie could only gape. Heart pounding, she wanted to know how anyone could say such a thing but people were pushing to get off the train. There was nothing she could do but go with them and then stand helplessly on the platform as the train, and the girl, slid away.

~

Abe was as good as his nod, a better part of the assignment arriving at quarter to four. Sophie peeled away layers of tissue paper. The lingerie was exquisite, the stitches so neat one could imagine the work carried out by elves.

She agonised over colour and style until in deference to Karsavina chose a silver lace camisole with knickers so fine she could see her hand through them.

A stylist in a local salon looped seed-pearls through Sophie's hair so that when she moved they sparkled. The fans are perfect, the rhinestones polished and moth damage repaired. Four-inch satin heels and flashing earrings – success is now dependent on keeping her nerve and the right choice of music.

Yesterday she went to the Lido to practice the routine. They discussed music, a song called *Perfidia* suggested. 'Don't worry, Mamselle,' the musical director smiled. 'Trust me, it will be okay.'

Trust is all she can do.

Clyde is in the kitchen looking devastatingly handsome in naval uniform.

She told him of the girl on the Metro. 'I should've taken her name.'

'No need,' he said brushing his cap. 'She's a con artist. A couple of days and she'll have yours.'

'How could she know about my parents?'

'She doesn't. She'll have read about you or seen your face in the paper.'

'I don't see how. My face has never been in the paper.'

'Say that again same time tomorrow.'

'I'm so nervous.'

'Don't be. You'll be great.'

Sophie touched his hand. 'Please don't come tonight.
'What?'

'I'll mess up.'

'You won't mess up. I told you, you'll be great.'

'Oh I hope so!' Sophie screwed her hands together. 'Even so, please don't come. I'll be better if you're not there.'

'As you wish.'

Not a flicker on his face when he left, yet he was hurt. Sophie didn't want to hurt him but couldn't bear the thought of anyone she knew watching. If she is to mess up she'd sooner it was before strangers.

It seems Miss Bluebell feels the same, Sophie's number late and slotted between trapeze acts. Still, seventeen nude girls hanging in the air will take the patron's mind of any flop.

Nerves shredded, she paced the apartment. Suddenly Daddy Bobby was leaning against the wall. *Why so worked up? You're going to be okay.*

'I don't know that I will,' she whispered. 'I was terrible at the Revue Bar.'

The place was a whore-house. You should never have gone there.

'I had to start somewhere.'

Not there you didn't! Your ma would've had a fit.

'Bobby, there was a girl in the Metro who…!'

Forget it! He cut across her. *People like that don't care who they bleed dry.*

'Clyde said she's a fake.'

Well, if anyone knows about fakes it's that guy.

Sophie sighed. 'I wish I hadn't sent him away.'

'*Let him go! You want a buddy with you now not a puppet master.*'

'Clyde is my buddy.'

'*Monsoor Pierrepoint is nobody's buddy! He's a landmine waiting to be stepped on. Take my advice, Sophie, run away as fast as you can but run on real dainty feet!*'

The apartment intercom buzzed. Bobby flitted away. It was Karen.

'Open the door, Soph, it's chucking it down and I've had my hair done.'

~

They took a cab. Karen was miffed. 'Did you think I wouldn't find out?'

'I didn't want anybody to know.'

'I'm not anybody. I'm your friend and friends stick together.'

'I'm going to be awful and didn't want you to see it.'

'Bollocks! You'll be fabulous and I'm here to help you look fabulous.'

'The Lido has its own dressers. They might not let you in.'

'I'll get in. The guy on the door used to be a bouncer at the Windmill. Now have you got your stuff, towel, make-up box and two pairs of shoes?'

'Why two pairs?'

'Spindly heels can snap.'

'Damn! I never thought of that.'

'That's okay,' said Karen serenely. 'When you were yet again visiting the loo I packed another pair and that cream outfit for your encore. Mark my words tonight is the start of something big for Miss Sophie Hunter.'

'You sounded like Nanny then.'

'After tonight you won't need a nanny or a Commander Gorgeous.'

'You don't like Clyde.'

'I don't trust him.'

'I don't know why. He's been incredibly supportive.'

'I still don't trust him. For a start he's married.' Karen held up her hand. 'And before you ask, a couple of years working in the Lido and you'll be able to spot a married man before he comes through the door.'

'You think he is married?'

'Practically every bloke that comes to a strip joint is spoken for. It's why they come, to drool over the delicious fruit that hangs from forbidden trees.'

'You're such a cynic.'

'I'm as dewy eyed as the next but where men are concerned I have my eyes wide open. Didn't you think he might be married?'

'It crossed my mind but I thought he must be unhappy to be with me.'

'He and his missus could be happy as pigs in muck but that doesn't mean he'll give up the opportunity to stoke your fire.'

'Hang on a minute! Wasn't it you encouraged me to get my fires stoked by that particular poker?'

'Don't remind me. It was a bad choice! He's totally wrong for you, consequently you're not even smouldering.' The taxi-cab pulled into the Champs Elysée. Karen collected the bags. 'What time are you on?'

'Midnight.'

'Wow! That's the top slot. She must think they're on to a real winner.'

Sophie's stomach churned. 'I thought I was a fill in.'

'Nope! Folks get sleepy around midnight and want to go home. A doll like you prowling the stage and champagne corks will pop again.'

~

The dressing room was heaving. Dancers fighting for space before a communal mirror, backsides in the air and bare light bulbs highlighting bare breasts Sophie might have been at Sadlers Wells.

'I don't look like the other girls,' said Sophie.

'You're not supposed to. You're supposed to look untouched.'

'I'm going to be a complete and utter flop.'

'Shut up and put your shoes on!' Karen shoved her down on a stool. She slipped elastic bands round the shoe and over Sophie's instep. 'These will hurt but they'll stop you slipping. Now remember what I said. You're a great dancer, the best, concentrate on that thought. Head up, look straight ahead and…!'

'*Et bien*…! An ebony-skinned giant in a towering headdress elbowed in. A scarlet lipstick in her hand she turned Sophie toward her and began painting her lips. She grinned widely. '*Ma petite, smile, smile, smile!*'

The Lido dressers were everywhere pinning and fixing. Hands on the clock moved slowly and just as Sophie was thinking it would never happen a messenger poked his head round the door. '*Cinq minutes, Mamselle Sophie!*'

Karen walked with her down the passage. 'Head up and a smile on your face. Yes, the dirty old men of the Macintosh brigade are there but a lot of decent people too. Get beyond what you imagine and you'll be okay.'

Girls brushed by, sweat shining on their torsos. It was noisy in the auditorium, the band having to play above chatter and clinking glasses.

Miss Bluebell stood in the wings. 'Are you ready?'

'I think so, Madame,' said Sophie her teeth chattering.

'I'm never going to cure you of that, am I?'

'Sorry, I am just so nervous.'

'Maybe this will make you feel better. It was left at the stage door. ' White lilac, the posy that found its way to the Gala, Miss Bluebell wove a sprig into Sophie's hair. 'Someone loves you,' she said. 'Dance for that someone.'

The band played introductory chords to *Perfidia*. A crooner began to sing.

'*To you my heart cries out, Perfidia, for I have found you,
the love of my life, in somebody else's arms.
Your eyes are echoing, Perfidia, forgetful of our
promise of love you're sharing another's charms.*'

A spotlight centred the curtain. Trembling, the fans trembling in sympathy, Sophie stepped into the light. The crooner's voice was sweet. Words slithered about in the darkness, a single spot followed creating a pattern of light and sound. With the fans high above her head Sophie flowed into the pattern.

The melody wove in and out. With every slow and graceful turn about the floor a sense of stillness grew in her head, a feeling of being above the stage and looking down on a doll that twirled in every direction.

Suddenly the fans were an extension of her body. Flash, flash, super-sensitive, her skin purred as the tiniest feather frond slid over her body. It was all so acutely felt. Rhinestones flashing, she twirled the fans above her head and then wrapping them about her, circled the floor in a series of low *jetés*.

The room grew silent, champagne glasses set aside, every eye following the beautiful girl who, to languorous music, danced in the centre of the room.

~

John Beaufort was among the diners. He learned this morning she was to debut at the Lido and phoned the booking office. This poky booth with a couple of overweight Germans is all that's left. It's a fair distance from the stage yet along with every other man he sucked in his gut when she appeared.

Head up and sapphire eyes blasting out she strolled onto the stage as if she did it every day of her life. Creamy flesh glowing through flimsy underwear and fans above like canopied wings, the audience is spellbound – the German guys who hadn't stopped chucking food down their throats with open mouths.

Who is this girl? She's not the kid who blushed if he spoke to her. Sophie Hunter is a ravishing mystery and the kick of it – the heartbreak and shame – a mystery that, but for his stupidity, he might've had the privilege to unravel.

Even now he doesn't believe what he did. Images fill his head, torn underwear, red blood on white flesh and moonlight glittering on tears. He is ashamed and other than he was out of his head, has no excuse.

Years he's watched her grow, admiring the blue-blood quality of her father and mother, years secretly loving and waiting for the day she might become more than a dream. Then in one night – one stupid night – he spoils it.

It was his brother-in-law that came looking, Julia's husband, and (as everyone knows) Joshua's father. 'What did you do to my girl?' he'd roared. John could only shake his head. 'I don't know.'

He knows. Yes, it was the coke but also the set-apart look that drew him on, a natural innocence seen in rare animals. He saw it and wanted it for his own. Rape – he hated the word – was his unsubtle way of trying to pin her down.

The memory haunts him. He daren't tell Father, he'd be driven from the house and no return for this Prodigal Son. But then Father would never guess. Possessed of the same rare innocence Charles Beaufort wouldn't suspect his son a rapist. Who would? Why would anyone hurt the thing he loves?

In hurting Sophie he hurt himself and continues to hurt. His heart aches with a physical pain, a tiger's claws sunk in his gut he could not hurt more. He shouldn't be here, should be on that ridiculous TV show raising funds for a trek to Asia in search of the Snow Leopard. The BBC is interested but doesn't have the cash. The Wild Life Centre in Virginia is interested but won't proceed without a nod from their major shareholder.

Once upon a time it would've been easy persuading his mighty brother-in-law to finance the trek. Now there's a wall between the Abbey and Gabriel's house. Julia knows nothing and so continues to visit whereas Gabriel – and Joshua, who looks at a former friend now with wounded eyes, never calls.

Sick to his stomach, John has moved out of the Abbey, his leaving made easier by the National Trust brokering a deal where much of the Estate is under their management. It's likely he'll end up a fusty old bachelor grilling a chop in the South Wing but for now is staying with a pal in Knightsbridge.

No more tooting flutes. Never a heavy user he was more taken with the idea than the reality. That night blew the shit out of his head. He kicked the coke -but not the Sophie habit. That habit verges on paranoia, almost provoking a pissing contest the other night with a Yank outside her flat in Bayswater.

The guy was checking names on the intercom. It was dark but John recognised him from the ballet Gala when Becky threw a fit.

Becky, his fiancée! There is no formal engagement. He wouldn't do that, not to her or Father. She knows he doesn't want her, and when not going through his pockets, is checking his diary. Serves him right! You get what you deserve.

The Yank sailor that was outside her building is here at the Lido. Tall and well built, he should stand out in a crowd but has a way of being invisible.

What is it about sailors and Sophie? There's another here with similar camouflage: her lover, Commander St

John Forrester. Last year John got a friend in Washington to check him out. The friend came back with zip.

'Couldn't get anything,' he said. 'The CIA have a lock-down on the guy.'

John echoed another's words. 'What would CIA want with a dancer?'

Now watching her move about the stage the question seems dumb. Is there a man alive who wouldn't want her?

Forrester is a smooth character, glossy as a photograph in a Movie Magazine. What does he think when he sees Sophie on stage? Does he approve of her showing her body? John would hate it and figures the Commander to feel the same, not that you can tell what he feels. A brick wall is all you get from him. But walls can fall, and fall hard, as John can testify.

~

'Vite ! Vite ! Venez avec vous! Vite!'
Wringing wet, hair in corkscrews, Sophie races back to change. Karen is waiting. 'Don't talk,' she strips the camisole. 'Sip water and breathe.'

'C'est bien, Madame! Vous faites la robe et je farai les chevaux!' A Lido dresser drags Sophie's hair on top of her head, curls spilling from the top of a pearl coronet. Then, scowling at Karen and muttering of amateurs, she applies more lipstick to Sophie's lips and mascara until her lashes are like the fans.

Sophie pulls away. *'Ne me faites pas ressembler un clown, Madame!'*

'*Mamselle on ne peut jamais ressembler un clown!* ' The dresser shakes her head. '*Vous etes une ange! Vous etes Mamselle Perfidia!*'

'You could never be a clown. You are an angel. You are Mamselle Perfidia!'

Words ringing in her head Sophie hurries along the backdraughts.

Un, deux, trois the orchestra starts up. This time as she steps into the light the applause is a thunderclap. The diners are on their feet. Sophie gazes into the light, searching for a friendly face, a dancer or maybe a waiter.

A face zooms out of the crowd!

John Beaufort is here! Her heart stops. She stumbles and almost falls.

Shame turns her limbs to stone and she's back in the Abbey fighting and weeping. In desperation she mentally punches the red button. If a loving father's advice can blot out fire-breathing dragons, it can blot out a man.

~

Clyde saw the colour drain from her face and sick with rage wanted to put a bullet through Beaufort's head.

It was a mistake to come. She said stay away. He should've listened. It's not about guys drooling over her. He can handle that. That's not Sophie out there nor ever will be, that is the artist and so okay. It's the sense of helplessness that comes with loving. He hates it! He loves Sophie and it scares him.

Earlier this evening he came ready to offer all that goes with a thirty-six year old man with no roots to speak of, a dangerous job and short-life expectancy. He planned to dump Joan, his wife of fifteen years and her billion dollars, her house in Massachusetts, ranch in Maine, and the rest of the costly doodads.

He would've done it years ago but had collateral damage to consider, step-daughter, Bryony, and her kid, Jamie, who he won't see again if Joan waves a cheque book under Bryony's dependent nose.

Sophie asked if he had a heart. Until today he didn't believe he had. The band is playing *Perfidia*. Webster's dictionary defines Perfidia thus: '*Latin from perfidus, the quality or state of being faithless or disloyal.*' Clyde's had more women than he cares to remember. He was nineteen and a spoiled kid when Mom died, and so when newly-divorced Joanie Cabot flashed her baby blues he was ready to swap one momma for another. He didn't get a second Momma, he got a billionaire social-climbing cunt who loved nothing so much as mounting the Whitehouse Society Ladder.

'If you want it earn it,' she'd say. 'Go talk to Senator Grey. His wife lunches at the White House with Ladybird. Get me an intro.' A couple of years pimping her program and then he found a better use for a social calendar.

First on the list was Abby Ames with double F bra. Then Alison Beale, a girl with a foot fetish, after that was Anne Carteris, a chubby woman who loved to wear a Stetson during sex. Now there's Sophie and the diary is forfeit.

He lied when he said thirty-three. Thirty-six isn't old but compared to Sophie he's ancient. Though she won't remember, being too upset at the time, they met at her folk's funeral. It's a year since she let him into her body, but her heart stays closed – the cause of that laid at Beaufort's door.

John Beaufort, The Honourable John, as he is known, is everything Clyde despises. Born into a lineage so old no one knows who murdered who to bring it about, he inherits a name that causes a tug of the forelock. '*Charley Beaufort? Great guy! We play golf together.*' Lord Beaufort's file suggests early homosexuality yet in the main is seen as a loving father and faithful husband. So what went wrong that Junior became a despoiler of little girls?

She won't tell but her body shrinking from contact says all. Normally, that wouldn't bother him but this is the girl he plans to marry, ergo Beaufort blotted a hitherto pure landscape and must pay. That she doesn't love Clyde is Beaufort's fault *and* hers – she should stop crying rose-tinted tears and see a better man.

Talking of better men, the SEAL is here. Special Ops, Intel says the guy is due to ship out soon. Hooyah! A bunch of gung-ho Generals sending a bunch of kids Christ knows where against Christ knows who to do Christ knows what – which is okay except this is Nam and Christ don't live there anymore.

Hot-shot pilot, multi-lingual and sharp as a tack, he was spotted years ago by the Company and left to brew. Force majeure in his class, he was detailed Space Cadet but his dream was destined to fall apart. Now he's a SEAL Underwater Demolition Expert – a guy who likes to mess about in boats.

Otters? SEALs? Clyde wasn't there when she made the connection but reading the transcript his scalp prickled. Map co-ordinates were her father's trick. Don't ask how he did it just accept that given time Alex Hunter could, with above average degree of accuracy, pinpoint any target. You could say radar does as much, yet on a good day Hunter could tell you who was on what plane over what land and at what time. For good measure he might throw in the colour of the pilot's jockey shorts. That's why when SEAL insignia was flashed on the screen, and Otters suggested, Langley nerves began to twitch.

If a twenty-something dancer could make the link to a newly devised Counterinsurgency Task Force, who else could do the same.

Ash Hunter got results by way of eidetic memory and the knowledge of men. Sophie has her father's genes plus a subtle sixth sense. Clyde has a trick of his own, if asked to describe said trick he'd say, 'I'm a bloodhound. I sniff 'em out.'

It does seem to work that way. He needs a geographical landmark when seeking a quarry, last known address — even a public urinal — if the target's been there he's left a unique trace. One sniff and Tidy Man is on the case.

General Hunter was one of the Golden People. If his light fell on you in a kindly way you felt blessed. If he passed you by you felt like shit. For sure he wouldn't care to see his daughter with a married man, though if he knew the state of the marriage he might understand the need for a mistress.

Mistress? When she said that he laughed! Anyone less like a mistress he couldn't imagine. Sure, they have sex, but it's school-girl sex, lots of blushing and hiding behind doors when changing. He keeps a verbal lid on his feelings. On the issue of Beaufort he came close to scaring them both the other day, Clyde getting a glimpse of his life without her. It's pathetic and he hates it!

He should never have got involved. Jentzen went ape-shit when he found out. *'Her pa was my pal. It's not the first time you've let me down. You better hope it's the last because hurt that girl and I'll queer your pitch forever.'*

Jentzen is a powerful man with fingers in many political pies, with a threat like that Clyde should regret setting eyes on Sophie. Clyde doesn't do regret. Sooner or later he'll be left alone and crying. A sensible man would run. Clyde doesn't do sensible. He does what's required. Right now he's required to deal with a couple of minor issues, namely John Beaufort and Ethan Winter.

Sophie is leaving the stage. The crowd are stamping and whistling. He feels a surge of pride. Beautiful babe, he'd love to stay but has an appointment with a Navy SEAL — nothing dramatic, not yet, just a friendly word in the guy's ear.

Pausing only to offer a not-so-friendly word to the Viscount, Clyde St John Forrester strode out of the Lido. Sophie is his one chance of Le Grand Passion, a last flaming arrow fired over the moon and a reason to be alive.

Lose her to a Rugby schoolboy or a pen-pal? I don't think so.

Chapter Ten
Versailles

'*Venez, Mamselle Perfidia! Vite! Vite* !' They were calling for a fourth encore.

'Oh you must be kidding!' Sophie wrenched off the headdress. 'They surely don't want me out there again! I can't do anything different.'

'They don't want different,' said Karen wearily. 'They want you. Here! Put this on.' She offered a scarlet lace bra and G-string.

'I'm not wearing that. It's horrible.'

'There's the grey silk again but that's soaking. '

'I don't care. I'm not wearing that. And I'm not wearing those!' Sophie kicked off her shoes. 'The elastic cuts into my skin.'

The noise out in the club was deafening, people calling her name.

'What's the matter with them? Don't they ever go home?'

'Try this.' Arms filled with pink chiffon, Miss Bluebell pushed through the throng. 'It's a robe I keep in my private bathroom.'

'You can see through it,' said Karen. 'I thought you said she needn't strip.'

'Sophie's an artist who happens to work with fans. A stripper is a dancer who removes her clothes. One has nothing to do with the other.'

'They seem one and the same to me.'

'Then it's down to Sophie.' Both women turned to look. 'Well?' said Miss Bluebell. 'It's your choice but make it quickly. They won't applaud forever.'

Hair undone, feet bare and chiffon ruffling her ankles, Sophie walked into the light. The crooner began to sing again. Earlier he tried switching to another but was booed and had to switch back. Now borne on a wave of boozy hysteria the diners press forward hands outstretched inviting Sophie to touch.

'*Ici, Sophie*! *Venez a moi, Mamselle Perfidia*!'

Aware of Johnny, she hesitated. Then damn it she thought! Why should I be ashamed! This is my night. It belongs to me and the Lido.

She crouched down and chiffon clutched about her knees shuffled along the stage gently stroking the reaching hands with feathers, the patrons smiling and whispering. '*Merci, Sophie. Merci beaucoup, Mamselle Perfidia.*'

Exhausted, she stared out into the mass. Faces like melting wax it seemed every man and woman on the earth clustered about the stage. Then a man stepped forward. Dark cropped hair, eyes like wet palm leaves and a scar beneath his left eyebrow shaped like an icicle, he smiled.

'Hello Sophie.'

If Ethan could've captured the moment and had it sealed in gold it could not have been more precious. That fabulous face only a touch away and those electric eyes processing information: 'Oh, this is the guy from the Opera House!

Then the EW3 in the photograph he sent must be a mistake.'

Sure, he's the guy from the Opera House. He's in the photograph too, third plebe on the left upchucking his breakfast. The slip of the pen is the result of Cissy the Centrifuge, his initials scrawled beneath Doc Farmer, the Cambridge physicist, who in the moment the shot was taken pats the machine saying, 'sorry about that, Cissy. They don't make Star men the way they used to.'

Just thinking of Cissy makes him want to vomit. Unless you've ridden the machine you've no idea how tough it is. 17 Gs and he was out for the count. He tried describing it to Granpa Powell. As usual Granma added her ten cents. 'If we was meant to go to the moon we'd be there.'

A SEAL, he gets his ass kicked on a permanent basis but is not likely to suffer Cissy again. It's been hard letting go. His dream was to be the first man in space. Every move, mental and physical, was made with that in mind and he was doing okay with the Space Program, or so he thought until he realised it was never going to happen - that some guy with an ear to the Pentagon hotline had decided Ethan Winter the Third was meant for other things.

It had to be so, why else are his attempts to advance consistently thwarted. Take the latest excuse for non-selection: too tall, the same excuse handed to Sophie. Total BS! Successful Mercury candidates tend to be on the short side thus able to adapt to cramped conditions. Restrictions are set at 75 inches. At 6 '3 he's inside. It was bull-shit. Until then he'd adjusted his sights at every set-back. It was one denial too many, especially when that same week a guy with OSS background paid a visit.

'If it's not working for you, son, lay that dream aside and take up mine.'

Did chance bring a four-star General to the door? Sam Jentzen isn't saying, though he did mention President Kennedy's latest project, a Sea, Air, and Land training programme with a need for men with language skills. It meant letting go of the only life he knew to join up with a bunch of water-wading mavericks. What kind of a dumbass does that? And what is a Navy SEAL anyway? Now he's proud to be part of the men with Green-Faces. One dream down, now another (once as equally remote and precious) stares him in the face.

'Ethan!' He is still holding her hand. 'I have to get changed.'

'Sure.' He nods and holds on.

'Meet me at the stage door?'

~

Two in the morning and the Champs Elysée is jumping; bars are open and people spilling onto the sidewalk. Traffic dashes about, beat-up jalopies and those dinky scooters with pop-pop horns that made Mom smile when she was here. She reckoned Italians are tricky motorist, but Parisians are plumb crazy.

Mom enjoyed touring Europe that last summer. She said she wanted to be the one Swallow that made a summer. Shame it had to be her last. His Mom loved Sophie. They exchanged letters through a MASH unit in Korea and then back home until the last. Heart failure the doc called it.

Granma says Momma's heart hasn't been right since pa was killed at Guadalcanal.

Ethan would have liked to have been with Sophie when her folks died. He read about it: '*MOH hero of Anzio and wife die in cable-car tragedy.*' Painful to her, but to the world at large, the US in turmoil, a President assassinated, race riots and an escalating war, it was one more tragedy to add to the many.

He remembers the headline leaping out of the week old newspaper. Sophie's name was not among the survivors yet he knew she lived, felt it in his bones. Granma sent flowers on his behalf. On stand-by to shunt up the Mekong River there was nothing he could do. Since then he's made several attempts to meet with her but without success, the recital in '64 a case in point.

The plan was to go back stage, say hi to Sophie, and haul ass back to San Diego. Not a ticket to be had, Ethan was walking away when approached by a TV producer and offered a seat in a Box - the dancer, Rudolph Nureyev's idea, how Ethan had a pretty face and would look good on film.

The pretty face was happy to oblige. Time-wise he was on a tight rein and after the show went backstage hoping to meet Sophie. It didn't work out; her friend had some kind of hissy fit and Ethan unable to wait. Later, when no mention was made of the visit via letters he assumed the friend didn't tell. Then there was the aborted trip to London - one way or another if he were a gambling man he'd think the odds stacked against them ever getting together.

In London he spoke with a Mrs Evans, a neighbour, and recognising the accent happened to mention Gran was born in Wales. Now he has a pair of eyes promising to look out for Sophie.

Ensign Farrell is another link to Sophie, his late father a friend of General Hunter's. Seb and his brother were at the Ballet Gala in '63, Ethan recognising the blond hair over the crowd. He did think he might see him here but Sophie involved with an Agency man Seb probably though it best he stayed away.

If ever a guy has Blue Chip need-to-know it is Commander Clyde St John Forrester. 'You don't want to know about him,' was the response when mentioning the name. 'Mess with him and you mess with trouble.'

Ethan didn't want to mess with anybody yet the guy seems to want to mess with him. Six months ago Ethan was called front and centre, 'why is an Agency operative enquiring about an itty bitty SEAL?' He didn't know then but does now with those K-Bar eyes piercing his skin. And the other guy, the TV wildlife star, Beaufort, he's another pot about to boil over.

Something happened there, something amiss. Sophie's letters used to be peppered with his name. Now there's a lock-down at the Abbey and all who live there. She doesn't say why and he doesn't ask. A girl like that has plenty admirers. A SEAL Team relies one upon the other, a clash of interest is the worst possible scenario, yet Ethan can't dismiss the fact that when she walks through that door his heart will suffer more than anything Cissy could offer.

~

A ripple of applause greeted them as they entered the bar.

'Do you suppose that's for me?' said Sophie.

'Well it isn't for me.'

The waiter came with a bottle of champagne. Sophie didn't want champagne. Exhausted, she wanted to curl up and sleep. 'How long are you in Paris?'

'48 hours.'

'That's a pity. It hardly gives us time to chat.'

'It could be worse I might have missed you as I did at Covent Garden. I did tell your friend who I was.'

'I guessed as much.'

'If you don't fancy champagne how about an *aperitif*?'

'I don't really want anything. I hope you weren't bored with the show.'

'I've had worse evenings.'

'Oh right.'

'I'm joking, Sophie.'

'Of course you are.' Ridiculous! Years she's been writing to this man and now she has nothing to say. Ethan Winter is not as expected. What happened to Stumpy, the little guy with the pointed head?

'You thinking of living in Paris now?' he said, his voice as Mrs Evans described, warm buttery purr, vowels long and drawn-out and the consonants soft.

'Until I know what I'm doing.'

'You went down a storm.'

'So it would seem. Look! There's Karen and Joe!' The Walkers were across the square getting into a cab. Sophie offered use of the flat but Joe wanted the hotel. 'Perhaps we should we ask them to join us…but on second thoughts they'd probably sooner rest.'

'Would you sooner rest?'

'I'm fine. This is early for me,' she fibbed. 'I'm quite the night bird really.'

Nerves jangling, she played with a salt cellar. Calm down, she urged, it's the sudden switch from all the noise to this man, who is so contained and handsome in a chiselled way. Oh, and there is scar, except it's more a dagger than an icicle. 'You were injured?' she gestured to his eyebrow.

'A hockey puck.'

'I thought it might be a war wound.'

He smiled. 'I've got 'em but none I can show.'

'You play hockey?'

'Used to.'

'What do you do now?' she said thinking of Otters. 'I believe you were meant for a space programme, fly me to the moon and all that?'

He shook his head. 'DOR, washed out.'

'I'm sorry. I know that was important to you.'

He shrugged the elegant bespoke naval jacket remaining smooth across his broad shoulders. 'There'll be other opportunities.'

'I suppose.' Sighing she went back to the salt cellar, salt littering the table. She took a napkin and wiped the table. It's as well Dad wasn't here. He couldn't bear fidgets. She was about to pick it up again when Ethan forestalled her.

'It's okay, Sophie.' He set it aside. 'You're allowed to be disappointed. Pen-pals, kids writing, what do we know?' He picked up her bag. 'I'll get you a cab.'

~

They sat opposite ends of the seat, Ethan a dark profile and Sophie gazing out of the window at mascara smudged eyes. Whir, whir, a hamster on a wheel, she went over the last few hours. She's a success, Bluebell talking contracts and top billing. But was it real? Did it happen to Sophie or some other person?

It was warm in the cab, the air sweet with perfume. *Shocking* by Schiaparelli Sophie recognised it from *Galleries Lafeyette*. She always thought it too heavy for the English climate yet in a Parisian cab it's just right. I'll get a bottle, she thought, a large crystal bottle with a stopper. I'll use it in the act, slide the robe back over my shoulders and dab the perfume between my breasts.

Whir, whir, another turn of the wheel brought the inevitable, Johnny Beaufort, and what he thought of her performance. It was raining. A raindrop slid down the glass showing Johnny with tiger's claws embedded in his chest.

The raindrop slid on and her thoughts turned to Clyde. More rain pattered against the window but not a drop carried an image of his alter-ego. Maybe he's learned to hide his other selves. Now there's this green-eyed friend and confidante of years. Is he hiding his darker self too?

The cab pulled up outside the building. Sophie got out. 'I live above the archway. Won't you come up and take coffee?'

'I should be on my way.'

'Where are you staying?'

'I haven't found a place yet.'

She noticed he carried a duffle bag. 'You came straight from the airport? Come up! The couch opens to a bed and you're welcome to stay.'

'I don't think so.'

'Oh please come!' Suddenly it was important that he stayed. 'Good hotels are costly and I feel bad you coming all this way and me so unappreciative.'

~

Ethan turned over again. He should've held out for a hotel. In skivvies, jacket on a hangar and pants over a chair, it's 0600, every nerve in his body is screaming, a cat outside is yowling, and now Sophie's having a nightmare.

A SEAL these last few years he should to be able to sleep on a rail. The couch is comfortable. Okay, his feet hang over the end but even so, no excuses.

'Who am I kidding?' he turned over again. There is an excuse, a gorgeous excuse a finger tip away - an excuse every guy in the Team would understand.

There she goes again making that pitiful mewing sound. Is she ill?

Sighing, he got up and tapped on her door, 'Sophie, you're dreaming.'

Door ajar, he padded in. He opened his mouth to speak but was dumb. On stage she wears theatrical make up, peacock eyes and vivid mouth. Incredible as she looks then it is nothing compared to this pale loveliness.

He moved closer. Some kids have imaginary friends. Siddy Boscombe in first grade had *Captain Flash*. Siddy reckoned Flash's radiation suit kept ghosts away. Fred Lyle - Ethan's roommate in Annapolis - had an eagle called Mike who promised that before the decade was out he and Fred would board a lunar module. Well, a month ago they got aboard, Astronaut Candidate Frederick Lyle dying when a fire broke out in a simulation module.

Some guys have invisible eagles, others comic book characters. Ethan has a swan, a photo Mom kept of Sophie in a ballet dress with feathers in her hair.

Psychologists say invisible friends are born of loneliness. Ethan was five when Pa was killed and twenty when Mom died. Mom in the military and deployed to Korea he lived with his grandparents, consequently, he spent a lot of time alone. At the Academy he was all about the space programme, any spare time getting his tongue around Mandarin Chinese and darker Russian tones. He is good with languages. If he hadn't gone for the Space programme he'd have chosen linguistics as a career. He would pound the pool late at night translating Russian into Mandarin The instructor thought him a lonesome geek. He wasn't lonely - he had *Brothers Karamazov* and Sophie for company.

Lately she was with him on the Ho Chi Minh Trail.

Buds (Basic Underwater trainees) meet themselves face-to-face during 'Hell Week.' Ethan had his hell from day one. SEALs work as a team. Stick by your swim buddy, never leave him – Hooyah is the Holy Word!! A loner, he has problems being part of anything and for that Instructors made him pay.

School of Hard Knocks, make 'em or waste 'em, shit, they would assign him the shortest guy in class. Tall/short isn't easy. He had to win with the buddy or fail. A battle of wills developed. Whether rolling logs, or hands and feet tied together and thrown in the pool, he was put through the fire. The word got out that Ice-Man, his nickname, was a greedy sonofabitch who needed to win.

It wasn't that he needed to win so much as he found it impossible to lose. Soon it was Drop out or Die. Then, salve to a wound, a swan whispered in his ear. 'Don't be a smart arse. Be a member of a Team as well as a single unit.'

Psychologists would say he attached a face to a solution - that changed on the night of the Gala. On stage the fluffy tutu kept the kid-sister image alive yet when Beaufort swept her up in his arms the real Sophie was born.

Now, skin of velvet and lips like pale roses, a woman is all he sees.

He patted the pillow. 'Wake up, Sophie.'

Eyes filled with alarm, she reared up in bed.

'It's me, Ethan.' He sat back on his heels. 'You were having a nightmare.'

Heart pounding, Sophie gazed at him. 'I was?'

'Uh-huh. You were crying.'

She scrubbed her cheeks. 'Sorry for waking you.'

'It wasn't you so much as that cat outside your window.'

Embarrassed by her baggy t-shirt and him in underpants she shuffled to the window. There it was, a skinny creature clinging for life.

She fetched a stool. 'I'll do it,' said Ethan. 'I've a longer reach. It's caught in telephone cable. If I can just…!'He leaned further and the stool wobbled.

'Careful!' Sophie grabbed his legs. 'You might fall!'

Aware of the heat of his body and intense masculinity and her cheek pressed against his thigh and a muscular backside sitting on her head, Sophie began to laugh. She couldn't help it. It was so silly and like nothing ever imagined, and Ethan, even with the cat ripping his hand to pieces, was laughing too.

The cat hid under the bed. 'Look what it's done!' said Sophie seeing the scratches on Ethan's arm. 'Ungrateful devil! I wish we'd left it hanging.'

'Me too,' said Ethan grinning.

'Those scratches look painful.'

'They are,' he replied still grinning.

'Then why are you smiling?'

'Because… I'm thinking what a way to meet, me hanging out a window and you holding onto my ass!'

They laughed again and then in sudden silence gazed at one another.

'Do you have to rush away? Can't you stay a little longer?'

'I have tomorrow.','

'Then stay.'

~

A tin of sardines inside the wash basket and quick slam of the lid, they caught the cat, and then, a shower apiece, changed and went out into the morning air.

Sophie was aware of her heart swelling like a balloon. Something was happening, something so overwhelmingly lovely she thought to burst.

Every nerve drew her to him. With Ethan carrying the linen basket, and the need to be close, they continually collided. 'I wasn't, you know,' said Sophie.

'Wasn't what?'

'Disappointed.'

'That's good to know.'

'I wasn't sure who you were. I always thought EW3 was Stumpy, the little chap in the photograph.'

'I guess you're referring to the Cambridge man. The pen slipped and I scribbled wrongly. I didn't change it. I thought you'd know me. '

'I know you now.'

His gaze focussed on her face. 'Yeah and I know you.'

They dropped the cat off at the vet and then breakfasted at a local cafe, Ethan ordering everything in perfect, if rather particular, French. Sophie toyed with scrambled eggs. She should be hungry but a glance from him took her appetite away. He on the other hand was ravenous, plates of bacon and egg wolfed away. He grinned. 'Eat and eat some more is what SEALs are taught, you never know when the next meal is coming.'

'Sensible.'

He talked of the Navy but gave nothing away, the same reticence when writing letters in evidence. What he did say was short and to the point, suggestive of giving orders and having them obeyed.

'And so where will you be going next?'

'I won't know until I get there.'

'Will it be a war zone?'

'It won't be a pleasure palace.'

Remembering that her father said Ethan was bound by official secrets, she changed the subject. 'What would you like to see now you are in Paris?'

'The Louvre and the Château de Versailles. My Mom enjoyed them.'

'I think that's more the work of a month than a day, especially the Louvre.'

'Then you choose.'

'No you!'

'Versailles!'

'Versailles!'

Ethan grinned. 'We seem to be in one another's heads.'

Sophie nodded. 'And not for the first time.' Then, hesitantly and constantly editing, she told of the Jodie songs, how she'd hear him in her head.

He stared. 'In your head, huh?'

Sophie flapped her hands. 'Forget it. I don't want you thinking me crazy.'

'I don't think you crazy, because if hearing voices makes you crazy I'm just as crazy.' Then he told her how he thought of her as an imaginary buddy.

'You were my lucky charm, so to speak, my keep-safe.'

'A keep-safe?'

'I guess, I mean keepsake.'

'No, don't change it!' Sophie took hold of his sleeve. 'I prefer keep-safe. It's what I would want for you, to keep you safe.'

Eyes soft and gentle he smiled. 'Sophie,' he said, and her heart rolled.

~

It was in the Hall of Mirrors, light making darting arrows of his eyebrows, that he took her hand. 'I'll steer us around we won't get in each other's way.'

His fingers closed about hers. It felt right, so perfectly right it was all she could do not to dissolve into tears. 'It's okay,' he said gruffly. 'I feel it too.'

'What is it? What's happening?'

'I think it's called falling in love.'

Looking and staring and wondering they followed other tourists yet it was not to the splendour of Versailles they looked. Children clinging together, luminous faces replicated in sparkling glass, they looked into the future and wondered at the gift they'd been given and if there was a price to be paid.

'I shouldn't be doing this,' said Ethan.

'No, nor me.'

'There are others to consider.'

'Yes, others.'

'I told myself I shouldn't.'

'Did you?'

'Yes because of the others.'

'But you couldn't help yourself?'

'No.'

The guide talked of a stairway Louis XV1 installed for his lover, Madame de Pompadour, how she'd sweep through the galleries, petticoats swishing and diamonds in her ears and about her throat flashing like tongues of flame. Ethan listened but could only hear his heart pounding and only see Sophie's eyes.

'Could you love me?' he asked.

'Yes.'

'Without knowing who or what I am?'

'Yes.'

'Shall we go back to your place? I mean will you?'

'Yes.'

~

They stood in the bedroom. 'I want to undress you.'

Sophie raised her arms. He undid her jacket. Slipping the sleeves down over her arms took time but that's what he wanted - time to see and time to remember. Her tight Capri pants pulled at her underpants.

'Hold onto them please,' he said, a note of almost panic in his voice. 'I want to take every single thing away. I want nothing between you and me.'

Down to her brassiere and pants he stopped. 'Now me,' he said.

Part of him, and therefore sacred, she was careful with his uniform, hanging the jacket in the closet and folding his shirt. Unbuckling the belt on his pants she was seized with fear she'd never see him again. 'May I keep this?'

'Sure,' he nodded. 'Everything I have is yours.'

'Everything?'

'Everything.'

'Your heart?'

'My heart, my body, my soul.'

A ragged scar puckered the skin on his chest. 'What is this?'

'The sharp end of an assault rifle.'

Wishing it away she pressed her lips to the scar. 'Is that better?'

'Much,' he said.

On her knees she pulled the zip on his trousers, easing them down his thighs. Laying her head on his underpants she breathed him in. In that moment, her arms about his waist and face pressed to his stomach, she understood Becky Ryland's fear of losing John Beaufort. It is the kiss. The touch of lips unlocked her heart. From now on there is only this, Ethan's kiss.

~

Two hands clasped together, he wore an unusual ring.

'What is this?' Sophie held his hand up to the light.

'It was Granpa's. I don't wear it too often. It gets caught on things. See?' He took it off. 'Three rings joined at the base. Pull the rings apart and the hands unlock to a heart underneath. Granma had it specially made.'

'Your Granma?'

'Uh-huh. Granpa was a fisherman. She said the heart was hers and while he wore it he was safe. Married sixty years, I guess it worked. Now it's yours.'

'No!' She pushed it back. 'You must wear it and keep safe for me.'

'But I want my best girl to wear it.'

She rolled over. 'Am I your best girl?'

'You're my only girl.'

'What does that mean, only girl?'

'You fishing too, Miss Sophie? Trying to find out who came before you? If so, be at peace Fisher-Girl. No one came before and sure as God made little green apples, no one is coming after.'

'Little green apples?' Is that one of Granma's sayings?'

'Uh-huh. She got a million of 'em, one for every occasion.'

'Would I like your Granma?'

'You'll love my Granma. She's a firecracker, tough and testy, but with a heart as big as a bucket. She knows all about you. I tell her everything.'

'Until yesterday there was nothing to tell.'

He scooped her beneath him. 'There's been plenty.'

'Like what?'

'How I felt about you.'

'And how do you feel?'

'How do I feel about you?' He stared at her. 'I need you to remember me.'

Sophie shrugged. 'That's easy. I have eidetic memory.'

Needing reassurance, he pulled her close and whispering in her ear quoted Granma's favourite poem. Sophie leaned against him and listened.

''*Remember me when I am gone away, gone faraway into a silent land,*

when you can no more hold my hand, nor turn to go yet turning stay.

Remember me when no more day by day you tell me of the future you planned. Only remember me. It will too late to counsel then or pray.

Yet if you should forget me for a while, and afterward remember, do not grieve, for if the darkness and corruption leave a vestige of the thoughts that once I had better by far you should forget and smile than you should remember and be sad.''

That night in the Lido, Sophie danced for one person. When she slid the robe from her shoulders and, taking a bottle of cologne dabbed perfumed between her breasts, it was Ethan's lips that caressed her. When whispering of passion feathered fans wrapped about her thighs, it was

Ethan's voice in her ear and his powerful body that slipped and slid between her legs.

All and everything was his and always would be. As for Ethan Winter, he sat at the same table seeing nothing and no one but Sophie. All around people called for Perfidia. They shouted and applauded but he didn't hear. He counted the seconds on his watch and when it was time to leave got up, emptied the glass of champagne, walked to the apron of the stage and waited.

Eyes wide with love, she knelt before him. The Lido grew silent. Conversation fell away. Even the band stopped playing. When he placed her hand over his heart Sophie leaned forward, pressing her lips to his hand.

Words hovered on his tongue. 'Remember me.' Then he was gone.

Chapter Eleven
Dirty Deal

Karen phoned. 'How did it go?'

'Perfect.'

'Any details on the perfection?'

Details? Sophie closed her eyes and he was there, the smell of his skin in her nostrils and the touch of his hair on her fingertips. He was a revelation. Love is a revelation! Until Ethan she didn't know love. Whatever she feels for Clyde it isn't love. This is different. She is different! With him she felt awkward and under pressure to behave in a certain way, to kiss a certain way and move as he wanted. There is nothing awkward about loving Ethan and nothing that her body and sensibilities will not allow. In opening her heart he opened her body. His touch was a key and his kiss life-breath.

'Hey, Sophie!'

'What!'

'I said any details on the perfection.'

Sophie laughed. 'None.'

'Fair enough. When are you going to see him again?'

'Right now he's on his way back to the States. He'll call the moment he lands.'

'So what are you going to do today other than think on Mister Perfection?'

'I'm going to collect our cat. It was stuck in the ivy. Ethan rescued it.'

'Of course he did and now it will pee on your rug and cough up fur balls.'

'I don't care. It's our cat, mine and Ethan's.'

'And after that?'

'Miss Bluebell's called a meeting. They're taking a show to the States.'

'Are you going with it?'

'I'm not sure. I've just found Paris. It seems a shame to move on so quickly.'

'Okay, give me a call and we'll talk about it. I must dash. Got to check on Rocky and Co. Talking of snakes, what are you going to do about Clyde?'

Skies over Paris were suddenly cloudy. What is she to do about Clyde? She has to tell him. Ethan left with no plan of the future yet she is as sure of his love as of the breath in her lungs. There can be no going back to Clyde.

All morning she drifted about, checking the phone every other minute to make sure it was working. She collected the cat. A bath, a trim, and Voila! A very different cat sat in a carrier, who, according to a faded collar, is a Siamese Blue Point known by the name of Shima Von Chazanza of Oxey.

Sophie took Shima back to the apartment. There were messages on her service, Joshua warbling a Beatle song, Tim dropping hints about the Beagle and Granma Ellen asking about the Lido but nothing from Ethan.

It's okay. It's a long way to San Diego. Changing the bed she was tempted to save the pillow-case on which Ethan had laid his head—Mother used to do that when Dad was a POW, kept the pillows in a drawer until night-time. Then no, Sophie tossed the linen into the washing machine—why hold onto a memory when you can hold onto the man?

Alive to the magic of the day she walked to the Lido. Cars slowed alongside, drivers smiled and honked their horns, a woman calling out, '*Bonjour Mamselle Perfidia! Vous avez l'air heureax!*'

'I am happy!' Sophie called back. 'I am in love.'

The Lido was buzzing. They were taking a show to Las Vegas to a new hotel called Caesar's Palace. Dancers stood about talking excitedly.

'Ah Sophie.' Bluebell was waiting. 'Congratulations on your debut. You've created quite a following. I've had numerous phone calls about you.'

'Really?'

'You seem surprised. Could it be you don't know how good you are?'

'And not too tall?' Sophie twinkled.

Bluebell smiled. 'Far from it. Shall you be coming with us to Las Vegas?'

Sophie hesitated. Before today she'd only herself to consider. Now there is Ethan and all that he means. 'It sounds like fun,' she said noncommittal.

'More like hard work. It'll be a prestigious affair, the Mayor and guests. Marlene Dietrich is headlining and so I'd like to bring my best. We'll get together later and discuss it, perhaps a new routine if your fans will allow. '

Las Vegas with Marlene Dietrich! It's a shame Clyde isn't here. He'd know about such places.

Sophie shivered. A chink in her happiness arrived and a thought of Clyde's poker face, the mask slipped once and that in his hatred of Johnny. He never speaks of love. Will he mind how she feels about Ethan? But then she can't help it if he does. From now on she has one lover and one love.

~

Joshua is on the phone talking of May Templar. 'They say she's dying.'

'I'll book a flight. How's Uncle Gabriel managing?'

'He seems okay. You know how it is with him he never tells his feelings. Say, Sophie, we had a visitor last night, Johnny Beaufort.'

'Oh yes?' Her guard went up. 'And how is he?'

'Drunk and apologising to everyone, saying sorry he turned out such a jerk and could we forgive him. He said he saw you in Paris and that you were great.' A pause on the line, Sophie could almost see Joshua's brow furrowed.

'I felt sorry for the guy. Do you know what he meant about forgive?'

'Yes.'

'And have you forgiven him?'

'I'm trying.' Sophie's head and heart were so full of Ethan there was no room for anger, yet, a thorn beneath the surface of the skin, the memory of John and that night in the Abbey still hurt.

That evening there was a crowd at the stage door.

'*Qu'est-ce qui ce passé?*' she asked. The cabbie held up a copy of *Paris Match* and a picture of Sophie. '*Mamselle Perfidia, c'est vous!*'

The crowd was for her! People had brought gifts, flowers and autograph books to sign. Giggling students from a nearby school carried teddy bears tricked out in gorgeous underwear and tiny feathered fans, the bears suggesting Abe's nimble fingers and shrewd business sense.

The girls held out the teddy bears. '*Un baiser, Mamselle Perfidia, pleeze?*'

There was nothing for it. Sophie kissed furry chests until she could kiss no more. Then someone pushed a bunch of withered daisies into her hand.

'*From your maman.*'

It was the girl from the Metro.

'*Vite!*' The door-man rushed at her. '*Sale gitane, va-t'en!*'

She did look like a gypsy and the flowers were probably from a cemetery, even so Sophie had to speak. 'What do you want?'

'To tell of your mother.'

'My mother's dead. How can you tell me anything?'

'She tole me in dreams of you and your brothers.'

Sophie scribbled her address on a piece of paper. 'I'm at this address.'

'Non Mamselle!' The doorman shook his head. 'She steal from you.'

He and Daddy Bobby share the same opinion. They may be right but when offered a message from beyond the grave who will not listen.

The next day another crowd waited, Press cameras flashing. They were still waiting when she came out. The door-man loaded the flowers into the cab. Sophie smiled and waved. The cab pulled away and her smile died.

Another day and no call from Ethan – which is okay, she told herself, he's in the Navy and can't always get to a phone. But, it is worrying.

'But then he'll probably call tomorrow.'

~

Sophie stood gazing out of the window. Three days and still nothing, no calls from Clyde either which is odd since he normally phones every day.

A short while ago she stood here holding onto Ethan's legs, Shima yowling. She can still feel the tension in his muscles and smell musk cologne and man.

They had a wonderful day! She smiled and her reflection in the window smiled. They went to Versailles, walked the Hall of Mirrors, and then rode the cab home in silence, gazing at one another, no words only hearts beating.

Sighing she breathed on the glass and scrubbed at the condensation.

The M-effect rippled through the air. Whack! She hit the red button! 'Don't show me!' she closed her eyes. 'I'm afraid of what I might see.'

A struggle ensued, words and images trying to get through. The vision quivered, fragmented, and died, leaving the impression of hands covering Sophie's eyes, masculine hands with calluses on the palms. Hands she loved. Hands she'd kissed. Hands with a ring on the third finger! Ethan's hands!

Something is wrong. There is a reason why he hasn't
called and it isn't because he's en route to a battle zone.
'What's wrong, Ethan,' she leaned against the window.
'Why haven't you called? Didn't you really love me?'

~

It's a week since Ethan was in Paris. Seven long days and
seven longer nights, he tries not to think of it. Bound for
Saigon aboard the *USS Independence* he fiddles with his class
ring. The old one, Granma's hands-over-heart, he left back
home in Colorado. Couldn't bear to look at it!

He stares at the world through eyes as bleak as the sea,
and it isn't Sophie he remembers, not beautiful, gentle
Sophie – though his heart longs to retrieve the time spent
together, to hang over every precious second as a Philatelist
hangs over treasured stamps hardly daring to breathe. But
he can't allow himself to think on Sophie as the beloved,
nor remember her as a pen-pal. She must be scrubbed from
his life with all the energy Granma gives to the stoop.

It's another he remembers, it's Clyde Forrester he
wants to brood over, but not in the manner of love, more
in the way of firing an M16 rifle.

It happened on the airstrip in San Diego as he was
returning from Paris:

Coins jingling, Ethan was heading for a phone booth, his
head full of things he wanted to say, like, when are you
coming to the States, and did you dream of me last night? I
dreamt of you! And will you marry me?

A scene straight out of *Streetcar Named Desire*, Forrester
barred the way. 'A word with you, Lieutenant.' Sophie

never mentioned the guy. That she was involved with him was obvious – how involved Ethan was about to find out.

Conscious of an obligation, he followed the guy between rows of cars to the perimeter fence. Forrester lit a cigar. Searchlights criss-crossing his face and a glimpse of a holster beneath the pea-jacket added to a sense of drama.

Ethan smiled. 'What's going down, Commander Forrester? Are we auditioning for a part in the next Bond movie?'

'That's not such a bad idea.' Forrester snuffed the match. 'As extras we'd be better paid and I understand the bullets are made of rubber.'

'Do we need bullets for this particular scene?'

'You tell me.'

Trapped in jet-lag Ethan was only half awake. An uncomfortable flight from Paris, such turbulence it was a relief to sleep, and with the better part of heart and soul left behind in Paris -and Nam ahead – why would he want to wake?

Ethan shook himself. 'Back off, Commander! No need for guns.'

Forrester shrugged. 'Maybe not now but I dare say it will end that way.'

'Are you for real?'

'I'm not sure. Sometimes I look in the mirror and no one is looking back.'

That really riled Ethan. The rain was real. He was cold and wet. 'I can't do this. I need to phone my girl so cut to the chase and say what you gotta.'

'Okay then, how about this? If you value your life don't phone.'

Ethan was silent.

'What?' Forrester queried.

'I'm waiting for my cue. I didn't know if the next line is mine or yours.'

'Oh, it's yours, definitely yours.'

'Well in that case, are threatening me?'

'No. I'm threatening Sophie.'

At that point the breath left Ethan's lungs and with it any trace of humour. 'Sophie?' He knew he'd heard right from this coldly smiling man but had to ask. 'You would hurt Sophie Hunter rather than her be with me?'

'Rather than her be with anyone.'

'I should kill you.'

'Go ahead but bear in mind tomorrow's headlines will make fascinating reading: '*Medal winner's daughter embroiled in sex-slaying.*' Great publicity for a young dancer! It will knock the Profumo case right off the front pages.'

Ethan was ready to kill him. To hell with notoriety, he thought, dead, this guy can't hurt anyone. Forrester read his eyes and held up a warning hand.

'Wrong choice and it won't be me hurting Sophie it will be you.'

'How d'you make that out?'

'I'm a careful man. I believe in being prepared. If I'm not around to do my job I always make sure someone can do it for me.'

'You have got to be kidding!'

'No, I'm not kidding. Until you breezed along she was mine. Clear the decks and she'll be mine again. You look surprised. I don't know why. It's a dirty world filled with dirty people who, given the key to the right door, are only too happy to pay a call on such a delectable young person.'

'You amoral sonofabitch!'

'Now hold on!' Forrester tossed the cigar. 'Don't talk to me of morality. You moved in on her without a thought of the cost to me. And don't say you didn't know we were involved. You knew when you went to her apartment. And you knew before that, or if you didn't you should've – I left enough markers.'

'You mean poking around in my service files?'

'I needed to know who you were and to give fair warning which is more than you did for me. I may be an amoral sonofabitch but I'm here face-to-face letting you know how it is, not sliding round the back door. And another thing!'

He was real ramped up. 'When you put your mark on her did you count the cost to Sophie? Right now in terms of survival – me as you say an amoral sonofabitch and you a civilised man about to be dropped into harm's way – my chances of looking after her are infinitely better than yours.'

Ethan nodded. 'Maybe, but you shouldn't make guesses as to the kind of man I am. I stopped being civilised the moment you threatened Sophie.'

'Indeed we all have limits. She is mine.'

'You're full of it.'

'She doesn't think so, to her I'm one of the good guys and I have been good to Sophie. I was there taking care of her and loving her while you were still scribbling love-letters. And before you ask what kind of man threatens the creature he loves I'll tell you; my love's not wrapped in pretty words yet it's as real as yours. You have choices, stay away and she remains her exquisite self, keep on coming and take chances on me being as you say – full of shit.'

It was cold, rain dripping into Ethan's eyes blinding him. Instinct said the guy's bluffing but he daren't risk it. Gauging his thoughts, Forrester nodded. 'A threat is only as good as the action behind it. Leave and Sophie is safe.'

'How can she be safe if she's with you?'

'She is safe. This is a double sacrifice, yours and mine. I've only ever been a shoulder for her to lean on. When she hears you've skipped town I doubt there's a man alive to comfort her.'

That last comment was enough. Closing his eyes, Ethan made a vow, every atom of his being drilled into the reality of the vow. 'Okay,' he said. 'I'll go because, though I doubt the threat, you believe it and that's enough. I won't contact her. But if I hear you've done anything to give her pain I'll be back. Doesn't matter when, this year, next year, I'll look for you and I will kill you.'

'Well said, sir! Spoken like an officer and a gentleman. But you still don't get it. Sophie is a romantic of the worse kind. She believes in King Arthur and Knights of the Round Table. If she loves you, and by her reaction we can only suppose she does, she'll make a hero of you.'

'What are you saying?'

'I'm saying this has to be more than a manly stroll into the sunset. You must make her angry. You need to do something that burns the female psyche, a dirty deed rather than a noble sacrifice.'

'What do you mean by dirty?'

'I don't know.' Forrester walked away. 'You're a bright boy, top of your class in every subject. You speak many languages. I guess you'll work it out.'

~

Sophie woke in the early hours knowing May Templar, her old friend and nurse, had died. In a dream she saw Gabriel carry May to the window so that they might watch the sunrise together.

'You ready to go, Ma,' Gabriel said.

May nodded. 'Yeah I'm ready.'

'No worries to keep you landlocked?'

'Nothin' that matters. Will you be okay now, son? I don't want you rushing over here. You gotta be patient and live and think on your boys.'

At that Gabriel kissed his mother. 'I know and I'll be patient. I can't do nothin' else. Just give Adelia a message for me, will you? Tell her I'm holdin' the line.'

Sophie woke weeping for May and Gabriel and for Mother and Dad and all who die loving another. She mourned one death while fearing another, whose she doesn't know – yet thinks it might be her own.

Chapter Twelve
The Gate

'What a funny looking coffin,' said Nanny. 'It looks like a laundry basket.'

Her remarks dropped into the hushed chapel like stones into a well. These days Nanny Foster follows a path of her own with many tributaries. Few seek to challenge the things she says. They've learned she's best left alone.

Sophie sat contemplating the basket-weave coffin. It isn't what you'd expect of a famous sculptor but then Gabriel Templar doesn't seek public favour. Like Nanny, he steers a path of his own, less convoluted but more isolated.

Conservation of trees the priority, it will have been decided long ago. 'Why do I need a fancy box to meet my Maker,' May would've said. 'He knows who I am. Put me on the fire and divide the remains, a shaking of dust here for my grandsons and the rest to go home. If I'm to gather at a river it'll be the Rappahannock not the Thames.'

I shall miss her, thought Sophie. She was more a grandmother to me than Bobby's mother.

In response to the thought a sickly toffee-smell slid through the door. Sophie shuddered. Unable to love her own son, never mind a bastard child, Ruby Rourke was no one's Nana. 'Spare the rod and spoil the child' was her maxim. Cherries on her hat and liquorish-flavoured hellfire from her mouth, she was a cruel woman. May died cradled in the arms of a loving son – Ruby died alone.

Daddy Bobby is quiet, no diaphanous drunks lounging back of her mind, neither is she troubled by the M-effect. 'What do you mean you can't see anything?' said the pen-clicker Monday after offering reams of pictures.

'I have a mental block.'

'What kind of block?'

'A gate.'

'Well open it, can't you? You put it there.'

Sophie doesn't think she put it there, no matter, she can't get beyond it.

She came via Hammersmith for the funeral, Karen enquiring of Ethan.

'I wouldn't know.'

'He hasn't called?'

'No.'

'There's a reason. A bloke like that doesn't make promises and not keep them.'

'I'm not sure he made a promise.'

'He said he loved you, didn't he? What other promise do you need? He's in the Navy, probably in the thick of it and can't phone.'

Clyde said similar when ringing to say sorry he hadn't been in touch, he'd been away but had read news of her Lido triumph. Sophie attempted to explain. 'I'm sorry to do this on the phone. It's a horrid thing, cowardly, but I can't lie. You've been good to me and I am fond of you but I've met…!'

'You don't need to explain.' He cut her short. 'I saw the photo in *Paris Match*, as they say, a picture tells a thousand words and yours told plenty.'

'Thank you for taking it so well.'

'How else should I take it?'

'Well, thank you anyway…though having not heard from the man in question I might well be counting my chickens well before they're hatched.'

'Going by the uniform I'm guessing the guy's under deployment. I imagine he'll be in touch… sooner or later.'

~

It's peaceful in the chapel, the organ playing Mozart's *Ave Verum* and sunlight pouring through the stained glass windows. She sits holding Michael, the younger of the Templar twins.

'Are you okay with him?' Julia leaned across. 'He's an awful wriggler.'

Sophie liked holding him. She liked the blond curls at the nape of his neck and the way his bright glance flickered about the room. 'I'm fine.'

'You'll come back to the house afterward for a bite to eat?'

Sophie nodded. She would but with Johnny around she wouldn't stay. That he is at the funeral is a surprise, he and May never really got along but then Joshua did say he's not the same man.

Head and shoulders almost level with his father, Joshua sits with Gabriel.

Halo-like, his hair catches the light. It's the same with the twins. Courtesy of Alabama stock a whole flight of Yankee angels abide in England.

It's rumoured Gabriel has been granted an honorary knighthood. It's also said but for Julia he would've turned it down. Sophie hopes May knew before she died. How proud she would have been. And Mother! It was she who taught Gabriel to read. It's all so long ago yet Sophie can see them in the kitchen, leaning together. Maybe one day Ethan and I will sit like that.

Still no word, but every night – his belt wrapped about her hand- she kneels by the bed praying via a soul party-line. 'Darling Mummy, you will have seen the newsreel on Vietnam and soldiers coming home in metal boxes. Please keep an eye on Ethan for me. Don't let him do anything silly.'

If anyone knows about sharing soul-lines it's Gabriel. That evening, sitting in the parlour of Julia's pretty Queen Anne house, Sophie wanted to ask about Ethan but Gabriel looking so alone she hadn't the heart.

'Lovely service, Uncle Gabriel.'

'It's what she wanted it, no fuss.'

'Will you be taking May back to the house in Fredericksburg?'

'Uh-huh. I hung on to the old place. I couldn't see anyone buyin' it.'

'Will you be flying there?'

'Why, you offering to get me up in that paper-flivver of yours?'

'I don't think it would stand it. There's hardly room for me never mind a giant.'

'You know your mother used to kick hell out of Bobby takin' you in that. She reckoned it was held together by spit and string.'

'I remember.'

'You okay out there alone in that big sky, slip of a gal that you are.'

Sophie raised her eyebrows. 'Mam'selle Perfidia, a slip of a gal?'

'I know who you are. I see your beauty and your style. I know you're grown yet in my heart you're the same kiddie that flung her arms about me in '46. I was your caretaker in them days, drove you back and forth to school. Nothin's changed. You're still my little gal.'

'Oh don't be kind!' Tears rushed into her eyes. 'I don't think I can bear it.'

'It's okay, honey, I understand,' he said gruffly. 'I'm just as lonely. It's a sin to say that with my boys lookin' on. I know I'll be punished for bein' ungrateful but can't help it. I told you, ride that train and you can't get off.'

'Am I riding it?'

'Do you need to ask?'

'No. I'm on it heart and soul.'

'Then you got to trust your heart and soul to show the way.'

Sophie blew her nose. 'So will you be going home soon?'

'I got an exhibition first at the Louvre and talks on Rodin. Not that Ma will mind. She was never one for rushin'. Why? D'you wanna come with me?'

'Could I? I'll speak with Miss Bluebell, ask for compassionate leave.'

'Compassionate leave?' His see-all grey eyes rested on her. 'You grievin' for Ma or for that male swan of yours?'

'Both.'

Gabriel moved away, his place taken by Simon Farrell.

'It's good of you to come,' said Sophie.

'I should be here. You-all have been so kind to Seb and me.'

'How is Sebastian?'

'I haven't heard and am not likely to.' He bent and whispered in her ear. 'Same with you! Be patient if you're hoping to hear from your Lieutenant.'

'You saw the picture in Paris Match?'

'Could hardly miss it! Ethan Winter is a lucky guy. He and Sebastian are in the same unit so from the point of view of communication it's a wait-and-see.'

'If you do hear, you'll let me know.' She held his gaze. 'Good news and bad.'

~

On her way out Sophie stopped by Julia's sitting-room. She was at her easel painting. 'May I look?' said Sophie.

'Of course!'

'Oh, it's Archie!' The painting was of the black Labrador that used to greet them at the Abbey. 'Look at his dear old face. He was always smiling.'

'Archie was a happy dog,' said Julia. 'I was sorry when he went.'

'It's hard parting with pets. I've just found myself a cat, which now when it looks like I might be doing a fair bit of travelling, isn't exactly convenient.'

'Can't you take it with you? There are quarantine laws to think about but flying a plane it might trickle through. You could go via Johnny! What with the TV Show animals he has all manner of dispensation.'

Sophie was silent.

Julia set down the brush. 'Is anyone ever going to tell me what happened between you two… and don't say nothing did!'

'I don't think you'd want to hear.'

'Then I'm sorry. He must have really hurt you.'

Sophie turned to go. 'Thank you for your hospitality. It's always good coming here. This house is so happy.'

'The twins were born happy.'

'And you, Julia, are you happy?' It may have been the wrong thing to say but there was an undertow to the lovely face that begged the question.

She wiped her hands on a piece of rag. 'I get kisses from my children and kindness from my husband. If there's more to be gained from being a wife, a natural entitlement I'm in some way missing, I've learned not to search for it.'

Sophie kissed her and moved on. She was at the door when Julia called out. 'Beware! Nanny's on the prowl! I'm afraid she's quite cantankerous these days and says things she really oughtn't. Mrs Allen says Nanny knows exactly what she's saying and to whom. It's true she can be brutal. Last night she thought to inform me my marriage is a lost cause, there would never be anyone but the blonde beauty for my husband and the sooner I knew it the better.'

'Julia!'

'Yes, she quite drew blood. Silly, Nanny, as if I haven't known for years. My boys' love offers shelter but then there are those who having led a narrow life would strip me of that. Be warned, Sophie, hang on to your illusions. You need them. Don't let anyone try to take them away.'

As if proof were needed of the warning Sophie turned a corner on the stairs and there she was. An ancient battle cruiser she launched straight in.

'Hello, Clare. How you finding life among the Chinkies?'

'It's not Clare, Nanny. It's me Sophie.'

Nanny tossed her head. 'Don't mention that girl to me! Look at the way she turned out! Dancing in Gay Paree in her undies, I'm quite ashamed of her.'

'Oh Nanny!' Sophie reeled from the blow.

'It's a thousand pities her father isn't here. He'd sort her out. Lovely man, the General…and his wife. See her portrait in the gallery? Not a bit like her. I said to Lady Joanna you need a Rubens to catch that golden glow. Same with Sophie, you can't paint it. They'll be tears though for all her beauty. Young Johnny is in deep. Have a word with him, Clare. It's no good setting his sights on Sophie or Rebecca…of course, they're not together now, you know?'

'Really?' Sophie went with the tide – it was all she could do.

'Johnny gave her the sack. She's gone to London to be an actress but then she was always an actress. Neither of them will do for the Abbey, too nervy. I said to him choose a girl with grit in her bones none of your theatre folk.'

'I must be going.'

'Must you?' Eyes like dried garden ponds, Nanny had one more arrow left in the quiver though not to fire at Sophie. 'You didn't do so well in the marrying stakes Clare. You could've had that nice Jamieson boy but no, you would have a churchman. Now you've got a hermaphrodite for husband and no babies.'

With that Nanny trundled up the stairs. Sophie staggered down. 'Poor Clare,' she muttered. 'Thank God she didn't have to hear that.'

'Yes and I'm sorry you did.' Johnny stood in the hall.

Stuck in the narrow passage, a tricycle blocking the door and dogs clammering to get out, she could hardly ignore him. 'She has her opinions.'

'But not entitled to share them in so cruel a manner.'

'Excuse me, I have to get back.'

'Sophie,' he touched her hand. 'Please speak to me.'

'I am speaking.'

'You're not! You're killing me!'

'Killing you?' she said. 'Aren't you exaggerating a little?'

'Maybe, but that's how it feels. You won't pick up the phone or answer the door. How much longer are you going to hold out? I'm not asking you to forgive me just a chance to explain the incident.'

'Incident?'

'I didn't mean that. It's the wrong word. I need a moment of your time.'

'Okay, here's your moment.'

'What here on the stairs?'

'Sure why not? Since when did location bother you?'

'Sophie please! I need to say I'm sorry.'

'There! You've said it. No need to say anything again.'
She pushed by him. 'I need to get back to Paris.'

~

She did need to get back, if only to see how her lodger is
coping. Emilia Zwolski – the girl from the Metro – arrived
last week, her belongings in a baby-buggy. 'I am hungry.'

'This is a gated apartment building. How did you get
in?' said Sophie.

'I press the buttons until a door open.'

If anything sums up Emilia's philosophy of life it's that,
press the buttons and eventually a door will open. Karen
thinks Sophie's crazy. 'You left her alone in your flat?
You're out of your mind!'

'It'll be alright.'

'And you know that how?'

Sophie didn't know. Consequently, when outside the
apartment her hand shook so she couldn't turn the key. The
door opened to Shima purring and a delicious smell. Emilia
waved a spoon. 'I make beetroot soup.'

Apart from wearing Sophie's favourite sweater and
smelling of her favourite perfume there's no obvious
damage. The apartment is as she left it and not too much of
a phone bill. A fortnight later and hospitality begins to pall.
Emilia is everywhere. She has the radio on too loud and the
balcony window too wide. The bathroom's grimy. There's
a noticeable depletion of Sophie's wardrobe with
corresponding increase in Emilia's. Money disappears!

Friday, Sophie meets with Gabriel for the flight to Virginia, meantime she plans to speak with Miss Bluebell and organise help.

'Where are your family, Emilia?'

'I have no family. They all dead.'

'I'm sorry. How did that happen?'

Emilia snorted derisively. 'My country at war. How you think?'

'I think you need to find a job.'

'I have job. I keep apartment for you and Shima.'

'While I'm in Virginia perhaps but after that you must look for somewhere.'

'I no money. Where I live?'

'Where did you live before?'

Emilia contemplated handmade snakeskin boots. 'I stay with friend. She good to me. She never make me look for work.'

'Okay, I'll speak with Miss Bluebell. She might be able to help.'

Emilia grabbed the baby-buggy and made for the door. 'You no speak to anyone. They bring *le flic* and Emilia kicked out of France.'

Clyde called, Sophie said as she would be in the States for a week or two, would he care to meet. He said thanks, but he was on the move.

At least she offered. She'd hate Clyde to feel abandoned.

~

Abandoned is how Gabriel looked on the plane. Lost in his own impenetrable world he gazed out of the window, the loneliest man on earth. Pity poor Gabriel! Love of her sons affords Julia Templar shelter. He has no such cover.

They drove to the old house. 'It's had a tidy up since you were last here,' said Gabriel. 'You might say it's almost habitable.'

'Can I stay here with you rather than fly on to Vermont.'

'I shan't be stayin' here, honey. As usual I'm on the hoof. One night in town hereabouts and then I'm gone.'

'Don't you get tired?'

His shoulders rose in a huge sigh. 'I'm bone weary but I gotta keep movin' because I if stop and ask why I'd never take another step.'

'Would it be okay for me to stay?'

'Sure. The house would like you here and it is okay. I never knew whether Ma would visit so I made sure of it.'

Sophie stared at the pink oleander spilling over the porch. 'I could sleep here.'

'Okay.' He nodded. 'I'll come by this evenin' and set Ma to rest, meanwhile, the house is yours.

Anxious to know what was happening, Sophie called Paris.

The phone was picked up. 'Allo?'

'Emilia, where have you been? I've been calling on and off for two hours.'

'It not my fault. Cat piss on rug. It stink. I tell Shima no piss or I rub in nose.'

'Don't do that! She's probably scared. Forget the rug. We can get another.'

'I run out of money so I go see Bluebell lady.

'What already!'

'I buy cleaning things.'

'Fine, but just take it easy.'

'I go now. Me and cat watch TV, Rolling Stones singing.'

Click. She's gone.

Sophie sighed, Karen was right. More of this and Sophie will be lucky if she's a door left never mind an apartment.

~

Gabriel held the flask in his hands. All this time living on this planet yet he's never been so alone. In the beginning he had his Other Self clinging to his heart. She's gone. Now-and-then he gets the rare flash of her beauty and knows she is waiting and that when it's his time to cross over she'll be there.

Even if he wanted he can't follow because in '63 he promised to stay.

He made that promise in a private cemetery alongside Arlington.

Arlington! Field-after-field of white military crosses moving out into the distance! Static corn raised by the Reaper.

Thinking of it now a feeling of awe grows upon him. Gold braid, Medal of Honour or British Honorary Knighthood – it makes no difference, in that place you are the same rank above and below ground.

It wasn't Adelia that day seeking a promise. It was the blue-eyed man, Ash Hunter, steadfast unto death. 'Look after my children will you, Templar. You were best man for the job before. Nothing's changed.'

Though thinking 'you don't want much,' he couldn't refuse. Ash Hunter was doing what every man does to protect his family. Gabriel does his best to get between Sophie, the boys, and their knocks but there's only so much he can do. You can't get between them and freedom. How they love and live is down to them. They must learn as Gabe had to learn

And who is he anyway, the man with a head full of silence. He knows he cuts an odd figure in the Swinging Sixties. But what's to swing? This time, this waiting, is no more than a mirage. Now Ma's gone and he's that bit more alone. He has the boys, Mickey and Charley, and he has Julia and would die for them but always another Gabriel leads the way. No Savile Row suit and Hermes tie on this man, the old Gabe, lover of Adelia and father to Joshua, wears a black frockcoat and walks beside a hearse.

Joshua, my boy! When King David heard his son had died he couldn't stand to live. '*Oh, Absalom my son, my son, if only I had died in your place.*' That wail of grief is known throughout time. Anyone losing through death sings that song.

Knowing Adelia was dead split him in two. He fell, knees buckling, atria and ventricles exploding, blood poured into his chest cavity. He was dead. Then he heard it, a cry through time and space, 'Darling, don't do it! Please not yet! I need you to be alive for them!'

Zip! An angel shoved a hand through his chest sealing Gabriel up again; the twins helped get him back yet it is Joshua who maintains his father's heart.

'My boy, Joshua, and your grandson, Ma.'

'I got three grandsons. You need to remember that.'

'I will.'

'Don't forget they need a father as Julia needs a husband. I know you wed to give her babies and me comfort in my old age but don't let her be lonely.'

'I'm doin' the best I can to share what I have.'

'Yeah, well, I ain't talkin' Sue Ryland's bodily wants. She was ever hangin' on your coattails.'

'Folks have needs.'

'That don't mean you have to fulfil 'em.'

'Time you was goin', Ma.'

'Alright then, let me loose among the oleander and the bones of my old cat.'

'Okay, but if you're thinkin' of bidin' remember there are other bones here that are young and still carry flesh and in need of rest.'

'No need to worry. I'll be a quiet old spook. There won't be no weepin' and wailin'. As for bones, there ain't none as precious to me as yours, my boy, so do your best to get through this life and I'll see you on the other side.'

Gabriel emptied the flask. A breeze caught the ash sweeping it up and all about the grounds, moonlight making a sparkling shawl of the dust that once was a woman called Martha May.

Chapter Thirteen
Right Hon.

More strays! A brindled terrier and her pups, Sophie found them in the woodshed. A bowl of water and food scraps, someone's been feeding them. They could use a bath. A tub from the outhouse, and one of May's voluminous aprons, Sophie bathed them all. That evening she had a visitor and learned who it was tended the pups and kept the house clean.

Around seven the pups began to bark and the bitch to wag her tail. Sue Ryland strolled into view. 'Hi Sophie.' She settled on the step, her beautiful if a little time-ravaged face catching the rays of the setting sun. 'Gone has he?'

'Just after lunch! So busy!'

'He spreads hisself far and wide does Gabe.'

'I don't know how he keeps up. Can I offer you a glass of something, Sue?'

'No thank you, honey. I had me a couple of beers in the Hawaiian Bar.' She gave a wry grin. 'I guess you're surprised to see me back in my old haunts.'

'A nice surprise! Do you live close by?'

'I got a place up aways. I heard you was here and thought to say hi. I take it May is resting some place close by. Gabe knew she'd want to settle here. It's why he axed me to keep the place tidy. D'you think he'll sell it?'

'It's possible though he did say no one would buy it.'

'I'd buy it.'

'Perhaps you should mention that to him when you see him again.'

'Noh! I'm beholdin' enough to the man as it is. Sure is a beautiful evenin'.' Collar undone and benevolent bosom to the sun, she leaned against the stoop. There was a ripple in the air, the Gate swinging open and the M-effect offering a peep-hole in time, Sue naked and sweating astride Gabriel.

Sophie stifled a gasp. So that's where he was last night. She knew they were lovers in the past but hadn't thought it continued. Permutations of passion, Julia Templar and Sue Ryland passengers aboard the same express train!

Sue pushed back her hair. 'So what d'you reckon about your life, Sophie, you struttin' your stuff in Paris and Becky in New York?'

'Becky's in New York?'

'She's rehearsing some off-Broadway show that seems to involve kids protesting the draft while shakin' a whole lot of naked flesh.'

Still dealing with Sue's naked flesh Sophie refrained from comment.

'I don't get modern music,' said Sue. 'I sat in on a rehearsal. Nothin' you could hum. Whatever happened to love songs?'

'Gone the same way as love I suspect.'

'Oh-la-la! That sounded like pain. You been bitten by a mean love-bug?'

'It's okay…I'm okay, at least I hope so.'

Sue continued to stare. 'You are so like your mother. Was it right to love or was it wrong, she was always checkin' her conscience. By the time she'd made up her mind more often than not love had passed her by.'

Sophie's hackles stirred. It was a poke at Mother and not the first. 'My mother was a very giving person. I doubt I'll ever be as generous.'

'I ain't criticisin'. I'm sayin' conscience can get in the way.'

'Of what?'

'Kindness.'

Triggered by the words, the M-effect opened up again to offer another steamy scene from Love in the Afternoon, Sue's mouth plastered to Gabriel's flesh – her manic grip and his blank surrender shocking to witness.

'And that is kindness!' said Sophie.

'I have my own idea of kindness and that is to love and be loved without troublin' the bitch judge-and-jury in my head. Right now I'm questionin' my battered heart askin' if it's right to feed off pity when love is what I'm askin'.'

'Are pity and love so very different?'

'Depends who's dishing it out. You and Becky made up your quarrel yet? '

'It wasn't a quarrel so much as difference of opinion.'

'I don't care what it was. It's gone on long enough. Trot along to her show and kiss and make up. The other thing, the milord and his country pile, is over.'

'I'm sorry. Becky was awfully keen on him.'

'Keen?' Sue blew out her cheeks. 'You British and your understatements! Becky wasn't keen. She was crazy for him

as he is crazy for you and as the love of my life was and still
is crazy for your ma.'

When Sophie made no comment Sue got to her feet.
'Don't be mistaken about pity and don't settle for it! It
gives a bitter taste to a lover's kiss. Love is what we
deserve, nothin' less. And mend your broken bridges!
When the one you're angry with has passed over it's too
late to mend anythin'!

~

Clyde phoned. When she told him about Emilia he laughed.
'Crazy girl! There are other ways of helping without
renting your bed to a whore. Don't worry. I'm heading
that way in a day or so. I'll drop by to see what's going on.'

'Don't be harsh. Emilia is rather fragile.'

'Sure, fragile as bulletproof steel. I've met her kind all
over the world – opportunists ready to relieve you of all
you hold dear.'

'Well, thank you for the call, Commander. You've
cheered me up no end.'

'Sorry honey. I was born with misanthrope tendencies.
And why do you need cheering up? Have you been dipping
your toes into the psychic pool again?'

'No, apart from the odd X-rated movie that particular
pool has dried up.'

'So what is it then?'

'I know why Ethan hasn't called.'

'Do you indeed?' There was a pause the other end of the
line. A match struck, Clyde lighting a cigar. 'And why
hasn't he?'

'He's part of a special ops unit and can't call anyone. But why am I telling you? If anyone knows about undercover it's you.'

'Me undercover?' he scoffed. 'I don't do danger, sweetheart. I'm about as bland a guy as you can get.'

~

Sophie has been to Vermont visiting Grandma Ellen and is now in New York lunching with her uncle, Professor Maurice Parker.

'And how is your Aunt Sarah?' he asked. 'Is she keeping well?'

Aunt Sarah split from Maurice and married to a sexy test pilot and out swinging every night, Sophie was careful with her reply. 'How are you?'

'I get along. I see the boys. Davy's at the Johns Hopkins and as you no doubt heard Peter's wife presenting us with a cute little gal we're grandparents now. Apart from that I have friends, girlfriends even, though hardly girls as I'm hardly a boy. What about you? You got a regular or like me playing the field.'

'I don't know about regular but I do have someone.'

Maurice nodded. 'I guessed as much. All through our lunch date guys have been watching you but you didn't seem to know they were there.'

Sophie's smile was dazzling. 'Why would I see anyone else when I'm here with the brightest star in the hallowed skies of neuroscience?'

'Ooh Sophie!' he grinned. 'There goes your mother!'

'You and Mother really did get on.'

'We were our own support team. I supported her loving relationships. She supported me in the absence of mine.'

'Surely there was love with you and Aunt Sarah? You always seemed happy.'

'Seeming ain't the same as being, but sure, there was love at the start or an emotion passing for it.' He shrugged. 'You can't make a person love you. You're plugging a leaky dam, sooner or later the walls come tumbling down.'

'You know the ruling on the cable car has been adjudged and the Observatory found negligent. Mr Culpepper says we should seek damages.'

Maurice Parker nodded. 'I'm surprised it's still standing. Daniel Culpepper was crazy about your mom. With him at the helm I don't see the judgement could have gone any other way. What have you decided?'

'Tim could care less about damages but wants the place closed down.'

'And the big guy, Templar, what does he say?'

'No! Gabriel died on the mountain with Mother. Nothing will bring him back.'

'I guess not.'

'Uncle Maurice, can I ask you, if Mother had survived the cable car would she be here today?'

'You mean would she still be alive?'

'Yes.'

'Medicine being what it is that's not an easy question to answer. Your mom was a sick lady – also a determined lady. If she could've got better she would.'

The truth of the words hit Sophie. 'Did Dad know?'

'Can you see your pa not knowing about anything to do with your mom?'

'Of course he knew. So she stayed on that cable car for one reason and one reason only – she couldn't leave Dad.'

'That's some love. I wish to God I had known such.'

Sophie leaned across and kissed him. 'You might still.'

'Nah, it's too late for me.'

'With regard to love *je suis étudiante!*' said Sophie recalling Sue Ryland and her passions. 'Love is complex yet even I know but never too late.'

~

Sue got Sophie a ticket for the opening night of *Shout*. They are to share a meal afterward, Sophie instructed to wear best bib-and-tucker. Not wanting to disappoint she's gone with a velvet sheath, the back open to the elements, killer heels, diamond earrings and sable swinging from her shoulders – if that isn't the best b-and-t she doesn't know what is.

Clyde is in Paris. He phoned the hotel earlier. 'Your free-loading guest was out when I called,' he said. 'I went back later and caught her in.'

'I hope you weren't unkind. Emilia is wary of strangers.'

'More likely wary of cops.'

'Don't be so suspicious. Not everyone in the world is out to rip you off.'

'I'll remind you of that when you come home to an empty closet. Anyway, I had a word. I knew what to say. When it comes to her type I'm multi-lingual.'

'Poor Emilia,' said Sophie. 'She must wonder what she's gotten into.'

'Poor Emilia nothing! She knows exactly what she's gotten into. It's you that was born yesterday.'

Sophie took a cab to the theatre. Becky was at the stage door. She looks wonderful! A gold-lame mini-dress sprayed over her body, she's all flashing thighs and tossing hair. There's quite a crowd, people spilling over the sidewalk and police controlling the crowd.

'TV newsreel here,' said the cabby. 'I guess they're waiting on someone.'

He hit the horn trying to avoid jaywalkers.

Becky turned, pointed, and a whole phalanx of cameramen turned.

'Oh no, please don't tell me she's…!'

Being the 'lovey' she is Becky has seen the visit as a photo-op. People have teddy-bears in one hand and a lipstick in the other. A microphone is shoved in Sophie's face, 'how does Mamselle Perfidia feel about appearing on the Ed Sullivan Show with the star of tonight's revue, Rebecca Royal?

~

After the show they sat in the dressing-room, Becky removing her make-up.

'Rebecca Royal?'

'It trips off the tongue.'

'And the Ed Sullivan show?'

'Who knows?' Becky shrugged. 'Maybe some time in the future.'

'And the Cockney accent!'

She laughed. 'Good ain't it? Forget Queen's English Stick with Michael Caine and Terence Stamp and the good old Cockney! It's the London Way.'

'And is embarrassing your friend the London Way?'

'Aw come on, Sophie! It was just a couple of cameras, no circus parade.'

'Then you missed an opportunity.'

'You're right! Maybe next time you can wire ahead and give me time to arrange things!' Becky was pissed off. What's the matter with the woman? You'd think she'd be pleased with the publicity. She's not exactly setting the world on fire. Okay, she's big news in Paris and did hit the East Coast show-biz columns, which ain't bubble-gum, but that's Paris. This is New York.

'You need to loosen up and understand how it works. It won't happen if you sit on your ass. Gotta go for it; grasp the opportunity when it comes.'

'You mean *carpe diem*?' Sophie was beginning to see the funny side.

'Yeah that. Anyway, why the long face? Aren't you pleased to see me?'

'I am pleased. I'd forgotten what a buzz I get from being with you.

'Me too.' Becky raised her eyebrows. 'What did you think of the show?'

'Well…?'

'Well is right. It's crap! Give it six weeks and I'll be back in Earl's Court.'

'Is that where you live now?'

'I share with the Warren twins. Actually, you could do them a favour. Sammy is looking for work. They've had a rough time. They got the sack from the Casino and their apartment was broken into, plus Millie's pregnant. I've been putting them up but I've only one bedroom and you know how sharing can be.'

'I do! Give me your number and I'll give Sammy a call.'

'Give me yours. We share a line and the nosy cow next door listens in.' Becky stared at Sophie in the mirror. 'You were at May's funeral? Was he there?'

'Yes.'

'With a girl?'

'Not that I know of.'

'He dumped me. Bastard thought he was Rhett Butler, "Becky, go find someone who gives a damn." What about you? Did you nail that Navy guy?'

Sophie sighed. ''*Toutes les jolies filles aiment un Marin.*''

'Oh yeah, "all the nice girls love a sailor." I saw that headline. So do you? I mean, are you and him a number?'

'I'm beginning to wonder.'

'Are you? Shame! They're all bastards! Not a good one among 'em! Come on!' Becky flung a cloak about her. 'There's a bar nearby. Let's get pissed.'

~

They sat in the bar sipping champagne. 'I seem to recognise that cloak,' said Sophie. 'Didn't Nureyev wear it?'

'He did.' Becky emptied the bottle. 'He stole it from the Royal Ballet wardrobe and so I stole it back.'

'You and he were...?'

'Nah! His interest lies in another direction.'

'Ladies?' The waiter arrived. 'Champagne from the gentleman at the bar.'

'What gentleman?' Becky swivelled. 'Oh that gentleman, the groovy looking guy giving me an eyeful. Know him do you, Soph.'

Sophie turned to look. 'Yes and so do you. It's David Parker.'

'David Parker?' Becky's jaw dropped. 'That gorgeous hunk is Davy Parker?'

'Yes and the man with him is Simon Farrell, the lawyer.'

'God, he ain't bad either! Say buddy!' Cockney accent shot to pieces, Becky grabbed the waiter's sleeve. 'Go thank the gentleman and say we'd be pleased if he and his friend would share the champagne with us.'

The 'gentlemen' arrived, handshakes and kisses all-round, Becky particularly generous when offering Davy his share.

'Well, Sophie,' said Simon. 'Twice in one year? How lucky can a guy get?'

Champagne poured, and Becky batting her ridiculous lashes, they settled in a booth, or tried, their table a stopping point – menu cards to be signed and napkins to be kissed by Mamselle Perfidia.

'Jeez!' Becky stared. 'Who'd have thought a pic in *Paris Match* would bring this amount of publicity? Remind to try your tactics when I'm at the National.'

'You're at the National Theatre?' said Simon.

'Not yet but I'm gonna be.' She turned to David. 'And you'll come see me, won't you David, when I'm a star?'

'Sure if I can ever get away from catheters and heart monitors.'

'Of course, you're a doctor now!' She patted his cheek. 'But that's okay. I'll come see you when you're famous.'

'You'll have a long wait.'

'Oh, not that long,' said Sophie, booze and the M-effect tripping her tongue. 'You'll be a world famous surgeon majoring in heart and liver transplants and people queuing to offer you the Nobel Prize.'

David got to his feet. 'I think maybe we'll make that the last bottle. It seems to me you-all have had enough.'

'You're right,' Becky clutched his arm. 'The champagne has left me dizzy. It's not easy treading the boards, you know. So tiring! Do you think you could escort me to my hotel?'

They left, Becky leaning heavily on David's arm.

'Exit stage left vamping all the way,' drawled Simon. 'Do you think there'll be anything left of Dave after she spits out the pieces?'

'She's not like that. She's a very loving person who was been badly let down.'

'I didn't know.'

'Of course you didn't.' Sophie struggled to her feet. 'Even so, you shouldn't make snap judgements, especially when a person is in her cups.'

~

They didn't bother with a cab, Sophie preferring to walk.

'You okay in those shoes?'

'I'm okay for a couple of blocks after that it'll be a fireman's lift.'

'That's okay.' Simon flexed his muscles. 'I've had my daily dose of spirolina.'

Sophie took his arm. It was a fine evening, the odd star visible through concrete turrets. It was nice but it wasn't Versailles and Simon isn't Ethan.

'How is the law business these days?'

'Dark and devilish. What about you, are you enjoying your successes?'

'It's not Sadlers Wells but I need to dance and so no complaints.'

'The ballet meant a great deal to you.'

'Everything!'

'I guess the plans we make as kids are for kids.'

'Did you not intend to take on the dark and devilish?'

'The army was always dad's wish for me but I inherited Mom's tricky muscular system so I never would have passed a medical. Seb's made of tougher stuff. He fights for the military while I battle corporate law. As yet neither of us can decide which is the more devilish. Speaking of the devil…'

He paused, his hand covering hers. 'You said to tell you if I heard anything.'

'Oh God!' Fear leapt upon her. 'Please tell me he's not dead!'

'He's not dead.'

'What then?'

'He is married.'

It was so unexpected. Eyes wide, she stared at Simon.

'Married?' Such a silly word, who would believe that to be true?

'It was the week they lit out for Saigon, a shotgun affair, the girl pregnant.'

'Married?'

'Yes.'

'And his wife is pregnant?'

'That's the word.'

'Okay then. Thank you for telling me.'

'Sebastian was anxious and with the guy not playing a straight bat, he, I, thought you needed to know.'

'Not playing a straight bat. I can hear your English mother in that Simon?'

'She was a cricket fan. So was Dad.'

'Here's the hotel. Thank you so much for keeping me company.'

'You okay, Sophie?'

'Absolutely fine! I shall be even better when I've slept.' She reached up and kissed his cheek. 'Give my love to Sebastian when next you see him.'

'I will. And Sophie,' he held onto her hand. 'I'm real sorry. I can only think the guy made a mistake and then tried to do the decent thing.'

~

Sophie doesn't know how she got back to Virginia. She remembers packing a bag and, still dressed in velvet and sable, taking a cab to the airport. It was late afternoon when she got to the house. The dogs were waiting on the stoop. She fed them and then, her gown a dusky puddle on the floor, crept into bed.

The first impulse was to return to Paris, anywhere but here where she learned he was married. But then she's so weary and who cares about Paris? Emilia can strip it bare! Same with Bayswater, the Warren Twins can have it. She'll stay here wrapped in a cocoon of aging timber. If it's good enough for May's ghost it is good enough for her.

No dreams, silence on all fronts, she sleeps. She gets up, lets the dogs out, replaces the phone on the hook, showers, feeds the dogs, drinks a glass of water, goes for a walk, takes the phone off the hook and returns to bed.

During that time she had twenty phone calls, ten from Clyde, 'What's the matter? You got a cold?' Three from Josh, 'hang in there, Sis.' Two from Karen, 'sounds like a cold. Go back to bed.' Two from Miss Bluebell: 'Oh, you aren't well.' And three from Jay Beaufort, 'Don't hang up...!' Click!

Between naps she walks the woods, weaving a figure-eight detour to avoid the Mill and the Eyrie –thank you, today's memories are enough.

A litany runs through her brain, 'Ethan Winter married and his wife pregnant.' A ping-pong ball smashing back and forth about her brain, she tries shoving the words aside and a memory slides in, Ethan kissing her and stroking her ear.

Silly memories, lovely memories, hideous memories! 'How can he be married?' she asks the dogs. 'I'm his best girl – no one before me, and as God made green apples, none after.'

The dogs look away: 'People? Who knows why they do anything?'

She dreamed of dancing the Saint Saens, as a child, a cygnet, as Sophie, the ballerina, and as Sophie, a beaten and bloodied swan.

Early Sunday morning the dream changed. She was a swan flying over a lake, a solitary boat seen through the clouds. Somehow she knew the boat was an answer to all the world's mysteries. Waves scudding beneath, she flew down and was about to land, when a man appeared on deck

Face muffled by a scarf, he produced a rifle, aimed it and fired.

Crack went the rifle!

He fired again and again.

Crack! Crack! Crack!

She woke to the sound of gunfire and the dogs barking. Johnny Beaufort was outside! He knelt, stripped to the waist, flailing his chest with a whip.

God, what an awful sight and sound! Crack, crack, back and forth, right and left, the whip slashed thought the air, blood running.

'No!' She ran down the steps. 'Stop!'

'No!' She ran at him.

He held her off with one hand and cracked the whip, a scarlet wheal scoring his shoulder. 'I shall do it,' he panted, 'I shall stay here paying penance until you forgive me.'

'I forgive you!' she cried.

'No you don't,' he said. 'You're only saying it so your neighbours won't come and take me away as crazy.'

Crack! The whip again!

'Oh don't!'

'Then forgive me. Take me back into your heart and learn to like me again.'

'I do like you. I do!' she cried.

Moonlight glittering on his tears, he tried to smile. 'Say it again. This grass is awful wet and I'm not such a masochist I enjoy doing this.'

She fell on her knees beside him. 'I do like you, Johnny! I do!'

'Then kiss me, dearest Sophie,' he wept. 'Not on the lips if you don't want to. Any old kiss will do. I'm nobody special – just a silly bloody Judas.'

Chapter Fourteen
Sacred Promise

A week Johnny's been in Fredericksburg, eating, sleeping, and on his part loving, waiting for an answer as to where they go from here. At the moment, geographically speaking, they're outside a Mill, Sophie with her arms about her chest defending her heart. 'You used to live here?'

'Mom and I came in '46.'

'How old were you then?'

'Three.'

'Do you remember much about it?'

Stupid ass! Of course she remembers! She is the original Memory Girl. He'd like to ask if she'll remember anything of this last week but won't. He looks back at the time spent together in a mix of joy and shame – joy that he got to hold her in his arms, and shame that it came about in such a manner.

He never meant it to be an Honourable John Exhibition but suddenly standing outside, months of feeling bad overcame him and he was on his knees.

The Honourable John Beaufort indeed! As his father said at May Templar's funeral there's nothing honourable about him. That day Johnny tried talking to Sophie. She left, he turned away and there was father.

'What happened between you two?'

John had hung his head. 'Please Dad, don't ask! It will hurt me to tell and you to hear. Let me make peace with Sophie. That way one of us is saved pain.'

His father had frowned. 'Is that sophistry, John? Are you trying to soothe the savage breast or is it possible you believe you can make amends?'

'I can't make amends, sir.' He didn't fudge it. 'There is no reparation for what I did. I can only beg her forgiveness.'

How Father stared. 'Sophie's a good girl,' then he said. 'She takes after her mother in kindness. She may in time forgive you. I doubt I ever shall.'

Such a reduction in pride these days; ratings for the TV show have never been higher but his confidence is in the dirt. People think him a tough guy, these days wild creatures seem to know better, the sabre tiger last month a case in point. It was doped, should have been out for the count. He leaned into the crate checking its heart and wham! It flashed upward, knife-sharp claws in his chest. They were dynamiting a landslide that day and so he wore a flak jacket, had he not, it's likely he wouldn't be here.

'I want to love you,' he said the first night. 'You're so unhappy. Will you at least let me hold you and comfort you?' She stepped out of her nightclothes. 'Let *me* comfort *you*,' she said. There was no artifice or desire to tease, she might've been alone. Today, a week on, he sees that it is he who is alone.

~

Clyde is at the bus station seeing Bryony back to Portland; they've been staying at the cabin. The train hooted. 'Give Gramps a kiss.' Jamie offered a wet mouth. As usual Bryony's in tears, 'I don't know when we'll see you again. Ma went crazy when she knew we were coming to see you.'

'Don't worry about it. Come when you can.'

'But filing for divorce and citing the Senator? She is gonna kill you. Why couldn't you wait and let her divorce you?'

'Because she never would! She prefers me hog-tied to her cheque book.'

'She'll get you, Pa. If she can blacken your name she will.'

Clyde shrugged. 'Whatever she does it's worth getting out. Your mother and me were never right. You and Jamie are the best thing about that situation. Here!' He thrust a wad of notes into her hand. 'Get the truck he wanted.'

'Jamie doesn't need any trucks. He's more trucks than Western Union.'

'Then get yourself something.' Clyde slammed the door. 'Get your hair done and buy a dress you like. It'll save you asking your mother. As for blackening my name she'll need to get on the end of a very long queue.'

The bus pulled out and he's on the move. First stop, Langley and details of the next house cleaning then Fredericksburg. Yeah he cited Joanie and Senator Grey. She's been messing with that old fart for years. Well she won't get it into the Whitehouse now – not with her brave Naval officer husband telling all.

Bryony is right; the bitch will take every cent he has. Shame about Bryony, she got screwed by a sleazy Phys Ed teacher and wouldn't abort when he told her so. 'He loves me, Pa, but his wife won't leave him.' His wife's alone now, the Phys Ed falling under the wheels of the 7-45 to Union Station – Joanie needs to back off now or she might end up the same.

1400 hours and he's at the airport thinking of Sophie. What to do? He can't just say, 'okay, Cinders, you've lost Prince Charming but you may still go to the ball.' He needs to be subtle. There was no subtlety with the Navy SEAL. Clyde went to the airfield that night expecting to shoot or be shot. It didn't occur to him the guy might love enough to let go.

Clyde admits to a sneaking admiration for Ethan Winter, the guy suggesting he was romancing Sophie while getting another woman pregnant. SEALs are supposed to be a band of brothers, screwing a buddy's wife ain't brotherly.

Sophie's too trusting, witness the whore now sharing the Paris apartment. Hasty scuffling out back, she had a guy at the apartment when Clyde called. 'Who you?' she'd said opening the door a crack. He'd pushed by. 'Never mind who I am, what you doing bringing guys back to Mamselle's place?'

The place was clean, the floor scrubbed and towels out to dry. 'What are you, the maid?' She'd nodded. 'Emilia Zwolski, I keep clean and mind cat.'

Since the loss of Ice Man Sophie has been in a state of
Purdah, no sex for Clyde. He went into the bedroom. 'You
service guys in here?' he said.

The girl was horrified. 'I make rule, no one in
Mamselle's room.'

The whore had wrists like chicken bones, one twist and
crack. She was alone and scared and the bed where not long
ago the SEAL had laid his head was a magnet. 'Okay, Miss
Whoever you are,' Clyde had removed his jacket. 'I dare
say we can make an exception to that particular rule.'

~

Sophie slid out of the bed and into the bathroom. Locking
the door she turned on the tap and sat with her head in her
hands. A short time ago life was filled with options. Even
with her parents gone she had her brothers, and friends,
and a job at the Lido – so many blessings – and for a brief
moment shining over every blessing the impossibly bright
star of Ethan.

The blessings remain but the star has blinked out. How
could he do it? How could he hold her so tenderly and hand
on heart say, 'everything I have is yours.' Does that mean
his wife and child are hers? Should she call, wherever they
are, and say, 'hi, it's me. I'll be along shortly to collect
you.'

'Hello?' Johnny taps on the door. 'You okay, Sophie?'

'Yes, thank you, just running a bath.'

'I thought I'd make tea. Can I get you a cup?'

Johnny worries about where they might be going. He
needn't. They aren't going anywhere. Sue Ryland said sex

doesn't have to be about love. It can be about pity. Right now it is pity that moves John Beaufort, pity for her.

Water lapped her chin. I wonder what it's like to drown. Must be horrible that sense of choking. Choking is how she feels most days. Nothing is real.

What is real, or she suspects to be real, is too terrible to bear. If gossips are to be believed John Beaufort's had lots of affairs. It seems Ethan's the same. Clyde has also been busy, witness his diary of conquests. The M-effect suggests another diary in his head and this filled with the names of people he's killed.

It happened when speaking on the phone, Sophie suggesting Clyde's work was dangerous. 'I don't do danger,' he said. 'I'm about as bland a guy as you can get.' Then he'd laughed, and with that laugh so a 'diary' opened containing the names of men and women killed in service of the CIA.

Introduced as attaché to General Jentzen she never questioned his work. One time she did ask what ship he served. He said there was more to the US Navy than ships. 'You might call me a trouble-shooter. If I find trouble I shoot it.'

'*Monsoor Pierrepoint is nobody's buddy!*' Daddy Bobby tried to warn her, Pierrepoint being a reference to a public executioner. It's said there's 'none so blind as those that do not want to see. Nowadays instinct works overtime to correct blindness, witness earlier today when he phoned from a station. 'Hi,' he said, 'how are you?' A train hooted, the M-effect rippled, and a man fell under a train, the hand that pushed him belonging to Clyde.

Oh for silence, nothing in your head, no questions to answer, only the relief of silence. When did all the joy in life disappear? What happened to ballet slippers and Prom dresses? This is not how it was meant to be. Yet even in darkness there is light to be found and comfort in Ethan's betrayal in that married to another woman he is saved from Clyde's jealous rage.

~

Bluebell is on the telephone. 'I understand you feel in need of a break?'

'I did wonder if I might take a few months out.'

'You've only just arrived. A break now would harm your career and you don't have to be a regular at the Lido, just the occasional performance.'

John Beaufort overheard the call. 'You're chucking the fans, Sophie?'

'Not chucking so much as doing the odd show. What time is your flight?'

'There's a two o'clock flight and a four. I think I'll go for the later.'

'Will that get you home in time for the broadcast?'

'It'll have to do.' John has a date with the BBC, an interview about his forthcoming trip hunting the Snow Leopard. 'I'm trying to raise funds.'

'Oh well, please count me in.'

He laughed. 'As if I could take a penny of your money!'

'Why not?' she said. 'It's of no use in the bank.'

'Because…!' Suddenly he had to get away. He had hoped that, though battered, love existed between them, but no, he is seen as a cause and she a benefactor. 'Second thoughts I'll take the earlier flight. Pa's not well. The doctors think he's had a stroke.'

'A stroke?'

'Yah! It's not the first. He's been having a problem off and on for years.'

'I didn't know it was that serious.'

'You know Pa. He only shows the good side.'

'Should I visit? Do you think he'd want to see me?'

'Are you kidding? Of course he'd want to see you. We all would.'

'Then I'll try to get over in the next week or so.'

'Great. I'll settle for that.' He prodded his satchel. 'If you and the dogs want to come now I'll willingly carry you. The place isn't the same without you.'

She smiled. 'I miss the Abbey but need to settle the flat in Paris.'

'You're definitely quitting?'

'I'm thinking it's not for me.'

'What is for you?'

'I don't know.' She gestured to the puppies, 'perhaps these little chaps! You have Snow Leopards and Rhinos. I could care for more home-grown varieties.'

'Here in Virginia?'

'Actually I was thinking of buying the Mill.'

He frowned. 'Back with childhood ghosts?'

'Would it be such a bad thing?' She closed her eyes. 'These days backward seems infinitely preferable to forward.'

John winced. 'I guess that takes care of me and my hopes.' He paused at the door. 'This chap Forrester, what exactly is he to you?'

She was a while answering and then she said, 'a friend.'

The taxi pulled away, her face a pale oval at the door. John recalled Paris and Forrester's whispered threat: 'A word in your ear Viscount, two strikes and you're out.' Furious, he had leapt to his feet. 'Don't threaten me! I'm not afraid of you. I've faced bigger beasts with much sharper teeth.'

'Yeah, I get that in you Beauforts,' Forrester sneered. 'Explorer and champion of causes, it's ingrained. But that was yesterday, my friend. You and your kind are relics of the past.'

'Do not presume to know me, sir.' John wouldn't be threatened. 'My title might be a relic of the past but I am not.' He left Paris that night thinking he'd brushed shoulders with the devil.

~

Clyde means to propose and is in the airport Duty Free buying flowers for Sophie and a Tonka-truck Jamie might like. If he has a weakness it is Jamie. Medics reckon he shoots blanks so he'll not have kids of his own. A child with Sophie would be the ideal, a tiny ballerina to love and protect. He'd like to protect Sophie but people are their own worst enemy. You can show them a safe path but will they walk it – will they hell!

It was at that precise moment he saw the Viscount. It was him, John Beaufort passing within a fingertip length, a flight to London being called.

It was a bitter blow. He had thought the Suffolk connection broken. Here's Clyde worrying about her, running around checking the apartment in Paris and buying flowers, and here she is – seeing an old flame.

Knuckles white, he hung onto the Tonka Toy. Goddamn it! You can't trust people to do right. The minute his back's turned she's out of line – Beaufort's been with her, eating with her, sleeping with her, and laughing with her!

Crack, the truck came apart in his hand.

He tossed it in the trash can and the flowers with it.

It was three in the morning when he got to the house. The dogs heard him, a growl turning to a whine. He hadn't a key but got in anyway and when Sophie went down was in the kitchen drinking juice.

Framed against a whitewashed wall he seemed very dark.

The dogs had fled. Sophie saw them through the window huddled together under the stoop. It came to her that she must do something about Clyde.

She pulled out a chair and sat down. 'Are you all right?'

He nodded and carried on drinking. Then wiped his mouth and stood gazing about the kitchen, his glance settling on a line of china mugs. The mugs hung from hooks on the dresser. If glances had been bullets, and the rage fizzing through his body a trigger, not a single mug would be whole.

'You had a visitor.'

'I did.'

'Any particular reason?'

'Just passing through.'

'Is he likely to be passing back?'

Sophie sat with her arms folded. 'What is it you want, Clyde?'

He was a while answering. 'I did think I wanted marriage.'

'Aren't you already married?'

'Divorced... or soon to be.'

'Children?'

'Step-daughter.'

'Do you keep in touch?'

'That's where I've been this weekend. I got a cabin. She comes there sometimes, her and her boy.'

'That must have been nice.'

'Uh-huh.' He took the juice from the fridge again, drank, crushed the container and dropped it into the bin. 'What did Beaufort want?'

'To say hello and to apologise.'

'For what?'

Sophie bit back the word; Clyde must never know what happened at the Abbey, must never be given food to feed the jealousy eating up his mind.

'I think he was looking for backing for the Snow Leopard trek.'

'And did you give him anything?'

'I offered.'

'And did he take what you offered?'

Sophie stared at him. 'What do you want?'

'You already asked me that.' He undid his tie and loosened his collar. He seemed more relaxed but the choking in Sophie's chest remained.

'Well, what do you want?'

'Maybe I want to settle down. Get a little comfort in my life, a little normality.'

'And what constitutes normality?'

'I want freedom and a home to come to at the end of the day. I want money of my own! A little humanity would go a long way, no more grovelling for cash from some tight-ass bitch. Let's face it, none of us are getting younger.' His gaze flicked over her, the scrubbed face, baggy sweater and leg-warmers. 'Well some of us aren't.'

'And what do you want from me?'

'I did think you might be special.'

'You mean Mrs Clyde Forrester special?'

'The thought had crossed my mind.'

'Okay.'

'What do you mean okay?'

'I mean, okay I will marry you.'

That night Sophie soaks in the bath again. Always feeling so incredibly soiled it is the only place that offers comfort. As the warmth settled in she denied doubt. Marrying Clyde would be about safety and the protection of delicate things like mugs on a dresser and puppies that won't come indoors. Puppies and people need protecting. John is a tough guy. He climbs mountains and hunts wild beasts. He is able to take care of himself. But you never know. Even tough guys have accidents, they fall under trains or get shot.

There is Clyde too to consider, now sprawled on the bed, lashes on his cheek and mouth soft in repose, he needs protecting from the anger inside. They talked of rules or rather deals into the early hours. When Mom came to the States Sophie was only a child and though recalling much of the early years can't know all that passed between them. Now she is reminded of Bobby, a man that at even the slightest shift of the day would lose control.

She put it to him. 'I have to have my own place, Clyde.'

'To do what?'

'I don't know yet, maybe work with animals.'

'You mean his Lordship's animals?'

'I thought more domesticated animals, cats and dogs.'

'And where will you do this?'

'The Mill. It's empty now. I put an offer in.'

'What about Paris?'

'I promised Bluebell the odd spot. I also thought I might get in touch with Cecile Brune. She has offices in New York.'

'Why would you want to do that? You got of plenty money.'

'Even so I can't sit about doing nothing. I must earn my way.'

'You are your mother's daughter.'

'What do you know of my mother?'

'Enough to know her daughter needs to be free to live as she chooses.'

'Yes and being free means not being afraid. Will you let me be free?'

'Depends what you mean by free. If you mean taking up with Beaufort and the other guy, the SEAL, at the drop of a hat, that ain't gonna wash.'

'Why would I take up with them? John knows how it stands between us and Ethan Winter is married.'

'Okay.'

'And what does that mean?'

'It means okay. I said it once. I'll say it again; it will always be as you wish.'

'As I wish?'

'Yes. You want to make a wish then today's the day. Ask and I shall give. Go on name it, your heart's desire. Think of it as the groom's gift to his bride.'

'All right, since we are talking gifts, my wedding gift to you is every cent I own.'

'What?'

She nodded. 'I mean it, shares, property, everything. An end to tight-assed bitches, I'm willing to go with you tomorrow and sign it over.'

'In return for what?'

'In return for your sacred promise never to hurt the things I love.'

'Define things.'

'Things I care for – people, animals, anything!'

For the longest while he stared. Then he nodded. 'Okay.'

'Then say it, a sacred promise.'

'I will never hurt anyone you love.'

'Or anything!' Sophie insisted, shades of Bobby and Biffer's mysterious disappearance nudging her memory.

'Or anything.'

'Cross your heart so help you God?'

He sketched the sign of the cross on his chest. 'So help me God.'

Chapter Fifteen
Family

Sophie's appearing at the Waldorf this evening. Mom and Dad brought her to New York on her thirteenth birthday. They did the usual tourist thing and then went to the Guggenheim Museum to see Uncle Gabriel's piece, the statue art critics are calling 'The Second Coming.'

Several feet high – an angel clambering from the bole of a tree dragging a man behind her – it was more a glorification of wood and woman than a statue and utterly dominated the gallery. 'But that's Mom.' Sophie had stared at the angel's face. Dad had nodded. 'Yes but don't tell her.' He said that they made the trip at least once a year, he'd wait for her to recognise herself but she never did. A teenager and tactless, Sophie asked if it was Dad she dragged from the tree?' He'd shrugged. 'Take more than an angel to save my soul.'

It's in the New Guggenheim now and even more impressive against the stark white walls. Gabriel has pieces in the Louvre and the Tate but nothing compared to this. The Angel is reviewed as '*early Gabriel Templar and more of the heart than the mind.*' People gather about the statue. 'Is she an angel?' asks a woman. 'She looks more like a devil to me.' And Sophie thinks yes, love does that, splits you down the middle – half saint and half crazy person.

She shouldn't be here in New York. She should be in Virginia knee-deep in wedding preparations. It's what brides are supposed to do.

A year has passed since making a pact. She's raised the topic a million times suggesting dates. Til now Clyde's always backed away. 'If you're not happy with a formal wedding,' she'd say, 'we can do the quick thing in Reno.'

Friday he returned from Saigon flinging a piece of paper on the table. 'The church is booked 1400 hours Saturday fortnight. Go ring them bells.'

Thinking him joking she smiled. He'd nodded. 'Go! It's now or never.'

She didn't argue. His eyes warned against it, a wrong word and the wedding, and all promises, however sacred, null and void.

Gabriel was the first person she called. 'I know this is short notice but…'

'Sure. I'd be proud to walk you down the aisle.'

'How did you know I was going to ask?'

'Let's just say I knew. Do you want me to tell Joshua? You know Charles can't come, him bein' ill. And John definitely won't.'

'I know.'

'Then go ahead. Do what you gotta do.'

Telling Aunt Sarah and Granma wasn't easy. Fortunately they appreciated she was pressed for time and kept their complaints brief. 'We could've had more notice,' said Aunt Sarah. 'But never mind that – are you sure about this man?'

Least said soonest mended Sophie kept quiet.

Now she's in the Guggenheim staring at a masterpiece and so miserable she could weep. One good bit of news: Karen is to be Matron-of-Honour. As yet Sophie hasn't told Clyde. He doesn't care for the Walkers. Becky won't like it either but too bad, Karen is a good friend, it's right she has first place.

A last glance at the statue and Sophie rushed away to rehearsal. Clyde is coming later. She's has a surprise for him.

~

The rehearsal didn't go well. The show is called *Animal Crackers*, the revolving stage tricked out as a Zoo and resident dancers dressed as lions and tigers. Sophie's lucky; apart from a gilded tiger's mask she has her signature underwear and fans. The Bluebell Girls have two numbers *Daddy Wouldn't Buy Me a Bow-wow* and *The Good Ship Lollipop* and for both are dressed in satin rompers and accompanied by *Ellie-May Pierce and her Pantomime Pekes*!!

Nervous, the Pekes are peeing everywhere, and there's a problem with hydraulics, the revolving stage throwing dancers about. Marlene Dietrich refused to step onto it. 'I prefer to leave this life with both legs intact.'

Sophie waits in the wings. She's nervous and as always misses the ballet, yet appreciates the freedom found in her role as Perfidia. There is no right way or wrong way to dance with fans. As with the costume she's not fighting to breathe in a rigid bodice, her breasts confined like a

Carmelite nun, nor are her feet encased in cotton padding with the toes bruised and swollen.

The star of the show watches from the wings while sharing a cigarette with her dresser. She stares at Sophie. 'I know you. We have worked together.'

'I did back-up at Caesar's Palace last August.'

'Ah yes, I remember. One does not forget such a face.'

Sophie smiled. 'There are those that can and do.'

'Ah!' Magnetic eyes peered through cigarette smoke. 'Did you love him?'

'I did.'

'And now?'

Sophie shrugged. 'I'll recover.'

The orchestra are playing the introductory chords of La Vie En Rose. The crowd roar in anticipation. Marlene jostles an ermine stole about narrow ivory shoulders. 'I have loved many times but have only been in love once.' She touched Sophie's hand. 'Alas, Mamselle Perfidia, we do not recover.'

~

The show is over. People crowd the dressing-room doorway talking and laughing. 'Twenty-four curtain calls, Sophie? The show went really well!'

It did go well but a glimpse of the white lilac in the dressing room, and Ethan Winter the suspected giver, Sophie tore off the mask and sank into the chair.

'Okay then ladies and gents!' Clyde herded well-wishers out. 'Let's give the girl some peace.' He shut the door. 'What's the matter?'

She leaned against is chest. 'Tired, I suppose.'

'Come on!' He pulled her upright. 'I've a cab waiting.' She got in the cab. He went back inside returning with arms full of flowers, the posy among them. 'You should take a couple. You've earned them. Now where are we going?'

She gave the driver the address. 'It's an apartment I got for the weekend.'

The cab rolled through the brightly lit square stopping at a Brownstone.

Clyde peered out. 'Is this the place?'

'Yes. Top floor loft.' She took the keys from her purse. 'It's yours.'

~

Later, in bed, he said he liked the loft. 'It's great.'

'I thought as the modelling agency is here, and I visit two or three times a year, it would be nice to share time together.'

'You mean when I'm not wasting time in Saigon.'

'You really hate that job.'

He nodded. 'It's not why I signed up.'

'What did you sign up for?'

'I can't remember. It sure as hell ain't this.'

'Why don't you give it up?'

'And do what?'

'And be happy.' The kiss that followed was sweet. For a moment Sophie almost forgot the past, thinking – I could love this man. Then he ruined it. 'What a shame we've to go back,' she said. 'We could have stayed longer.'

'We can still.'

'No, I've to collect Karen from the airport. She's Matron-of-Honour.'

'Wouldn't a friend from the ballet be a better choice?'

'Karen is my friend.'

'She's a stripper.'

'She's still my friend. She's Matron of Honour and Gabriel is giving me away.'

Clyde laughed. 'A stripper for attendant and an ex con to give you away, it gets better. What happened to the old Milord? Didn't he offer?'

'I didn't ask. He's ill.' Sophie was angry. He springs a last minute wedding and then dislikes her choices. 'Anyway, I thought you wouldn't want him. Aren't you against aristocracy? Didn't you say they suck the country dry?'

'So they do.' He got off the bed and started pulling on his pants. 'No one at Langley believes anything that comes out of Whitehall these days. People like that, the old boy and his son, are always covering each other's ass. It's why they make mistakes. Look at Burgess and Maclean! And Philby for Chrissakes! The Agency's still picking pieces out of its ass for that one!'

'What has that to do with my wedding?'

'It's germane. I'm pointing out you can do better than a whore for a female supporter and a murderer leading you down the aisle.'

'Karen has been a good friend to me. I wouldn't want anyone else. As for Gabriel, he was always first choice. Before going to Korea my father, whose judgement you say you trust, placed Mother and me in his care. He wrote a will to that effect. When they were killed it was Gabriel who cared for me and my brothers. A lot of people have a cause to be grateful to that murdering ex-con and even if that were not the case he is, in his own right, a renowned sculptor and lately conferred Knight of the British Realm.'

'He's still a murderer and she's still a stripper. What will your real British Bluebloods think when they see those two tripping down the aisle?'

Sophie laughed. 'What do you think they see when I trip down the aisle, the Madonna of the Lilies? I take my clothes off for money. I may be paid thousands of dollars to do it but I am still a stripper. As for being a whore, and a woman paid for sexual services, only you can answer that!'

Fist balled, he lurched forward! Such a look in his eyes, neither knowing what would follow. Then he went into the bathroom and closed the door.

~

Marriage sits uneasy on Clyde. Years of Joanie and her crap have made him wary, plus the fact as his wife Sophie becomes a 'business target' and thus a weakness. He doesn't do weakness as he doesn't do meeting the 'family'.

They arrived in separate cars. A chip off the old block, Tim, the older boy gets out. Army greens and heavy boots, a dressing bag slung over his shoulder, he can't be more than eighteen yet belly ripped with iron breathes confidence. Barrelling over a beachhead, a M16 in his hand and tin hat on his head, you're looking at a future General Patton or President of the United States.

The younger kid, Joshua, wears a uniform but not bought of Brooks Brothers or Savile Row. You can't buy this in any store. Born into class, educated at Harvard or in Joshua's case Harrow, it's an inheritance. County pile and town-house, perfect teeth and shining hair, boating at Cannes and wintering at Kitzbuhel, they own the World. Then to shake the tree a third man slides from a car, Gabriel Templar, Honorary Knighthood by way of Alabama boondocks and the State Pen begging the question   how do you define blue-blood.

He took his time going down. We ain't buddies. They won't carouse together. When a bachelor night was suggested he cried off saying the Navy had organised a wingding. No wingding, Clyde and a buddy in a hotel for the night.

Palms sweaty, he goes down. Sophie turns, her eyes shining. 'My brothers, Timothy and Joshua, and my guardian and friend, Gabriel Templar.'

A triple whammy three men turn toward him and shake hands. Templar has a workman's hand with calluses on the palm. It touches Clyde and burns.

Waking from a nightmare that night he tapped on her bedroom door.

She pulled back the cover. Shivering, he got in beside her. She pulled him close. 'Why so cold,' she said. 'Did you have the window wide open?'

'I always sleep with the windows open.'

'Why when it's cold?'

'In case I need to get out.'

'In case you need to get out!' She shook her head. 'I really don't know anything about you or your work, do I?'

'No one should know what is done in the name of freedom.'

Her touch tender, she smoothed down his hair. 'Would you like to make love,' she whispered. 'Would it make you feel easier?'

He shrugged. 'I don't care. I just want to know you're here.'

It felt good in her arms. He slept for a while and then paranoia took over. Even in sleep he felt it, a terrible yearning for the fragile bag of flesh and bone next to him. Unable to handle it he got out of bed. She was beautiful in sleep, a marble figurine, he bent and kissed her. She whispered his name. In that moment he'd have given anything not to be Clyde St John Forrester.

~

'Gorgeous!' Aunt Sarah tugged at Sophie's gown, fanning the skirts so that they formed a teardrop on the carpet. 'I do love this creamy shade but still think with your hair and complexion a truer colour would be white.'

Sophie pulled the brim of her chiffon cartwheel further down over her face.

'I think a truer colour would be black.'

'You okay, dear?' Sarah Parker-Manners gazed at her niece. 'You're very pale.'

'I didn't sleep well last night, nerves I expect.'

'Oh how delicious!' Sarah picked up the bouquet. 'I'm not sure I'd have put white roses and white lilac together, yet today with everything so misty and fragile, especially the bride, it does seem to work.'

Sarah's fishing again. The wedding so sudden, it's enough to make anyone wonder. 'Is there a reason for this scurried affair, anything to tell me?'

'Like what?'

'Like you're pregnant?'

'I'm not pregnant.'

'Then is the Commander about to be posted overseas?'

Sophie rolled the soft white leather gloves up her arms. 'Clyde is back and forth to Vietnam all the time. His posting has nothing to do with the wedding.'

'Then why so hideaway?'

'Is St Jude's hideaway? I thought it a popular church.'

'St Jude's is a popular church but it's not Caxton Hall where all the celebs go to get married.'

'I'm not a celebrity.'

'You are if the crowds are anything to go by and London would've been better for your Lord de Beaufort. Not so far to travel.'

Sophie gritted her teeth. 'Uncle Gabriel is giving me away.'

'You mean *Sir* Gabriel don't you, Alabama Yankee in the Court of Queen Elizabeth? Wowee! Who would have thought it?'

'He wanted to turn it down but May wouldn't let him. And why should he after all the work he's done for children and wildlife over the years.'

'I'm not criticising! I think it's great – I really do. You forget I knew him before when he was a gravedigger and could barely string two sentences together. Now look at him. It was your mother did that, the Challoner touch.'

'Maybe. I'm glad Nana May knew before she died.'

'I said I'm not criticising. His meteoric rise proves American gospel: if you have grit and talent you can succeed whoever you are. You don't have to be born swallowing a silver spoon like your old Lord.'

'My "old Lord", as you call him, has had another stroke.'

'Oh dear! That doesn't bode well for the Abbey. I imagine the Hon John won't be coming… not that he would with you turning him down.'

'How do you know I turned him down?'

'Are you saying you didn't?'

'I'm not saying anything.'

'The Lady Sophie de Beaufort.' Sarah stood before the mirror adjusting her hat. 'That would be a wedding worthy of a hat and you wouldn't have needed Caxton Hall. You'd have been married in the…"*tiny jewel of a private chapel among the fluted columns of Gaudi design and where a statue of Perseus carrying the head of Medusa gazes down upon the hallowed tombs.*" '

'You've been reading *The Tatler* again.'

'They do lay it on a bit thick. Are there fluted columns?'

'Yes and a two-foot high Cellini Perseus they use as a doorstop.'

'You sure you don't want to change your mind on that issue? It's not too late. The die is not yet cast. I could smuggle you out back and onto a plane.'

Sophie smiled grimly. 'No the die is cast.'

'Pity. I quite saw me in the role of Grand Dame dispensing tea in the Wedgwood Room. I did ask your pa to get me an invite but he laughed. I'm not so sure he'd laugh today. Not sure you are laughing.'

'Do I detect a note of disapproval?'

'I can't say I approve of what you do. Fan-dancing is not my idea of dance and I doubt it was your mother's.'

'Aunt Sarah, have you ever actually been to a performance?'

'I did think about the Waldorf with Marlene appearing but couldn't manage it.'

'Am I that much of a disgrace to the family?'

'No and don't get snitty with me! I'm as laid-back as the next but still couldn't watch in comfort. You're my flesh and blood. It's one thing to see a stranger dance in the nude, quite another to watch one's niece.'

'I don't dance in the nude. I wear beautiful lingerie and carry exquisite fans given to me by a Russian ballerina, which had you been to the Waldorf and witnessed twenty-four curtain calls, you would know.'

'It's a long way from Sadlers Wells.'

'You don't need to tell me that. No one ever needs tell me that.'

'Sorry, Sweetie.' Sarah patted her arm. 'I don't mean to belittle you. You are my brother's daughter. You couldn't be disgraceful if you tried.'

'I am also my mother's daughter and can tell you she would have supported me in all my choices, career and husband.'

'As do I! I'm concerned that my favourite niece is marrying the wrong man.'

'You only have one niece.'

'You'd be my favourite if I had none! Put our minds at rest and say you're marrying because you love and not because he's charming as all get-out.'

'He is charming.'

'I am aware of his charm as will be every woman in the church. He could be a thousand times more charming and it wouldn't be right.' Sarah gave another twitch to her hat and stalked out. 'I'm going to see if Petey and Callie and the kids have arrived. They may be all of a pickle but at least they married for love and not some hidden agenda.'

Sophie sighed. A mild form of the Spanish Inquisition, it started last year with purchase of the Mill. Sarah hates the place and said so. One morning out front clearing the yard of weeds a coupe swung into the drive. Jaunty cap perched on shiny russet hair, Sarah got out. Never one to mince words she lit in. 'It's bad news, Sophie! Old hurts live here and old ghosts haunt the rafters. Bobby Rourke made your mother's life hell. Have you forgotten how it was?'

Fists in the dark and empty beer bottles rolling down the stairs, Sophie hasn't forgotten, yet her recollection of those years goes beyond what others saw. There was love in this house as well as pain.

Sarah's not alone in doubting. The boys say little but what they do say hangs in the air. 'Is it Clyde you want,' said Tim, 'or a knee-jerk reaction to the other guy?' She wanted to say it's a reaction to fear and the hope that in marrying Clyde the old saying, 'out of sight and out of mind' becomes true.

~

Joshua and Tim are staying in the cottage attached to the Mill. Gabriel prefers Ma's old place. Looking through familiar windows gives him peace. Now the limo is here to collect Sophie, a short drive and then the chauffeur opened the door. Gabriel got out and stood looking at the Mill.

Lord, the memories swirling through his head, *Pathe Pictorial Newsreel*, the Old Mill, Fredericksburg, 1946. In those days the house was like the man that owned it – a broken down wreck. Time ran backwards and Gabriel saw again the old pick-up truck he used to drive, he heard the motor running and saw himself a Marine Sergeant with stripes on his sleeve and a chip on his shoulder.

Once again Adelia steps down onto the yard, her skirt creased and tendrils of hair working loose from a braid. Shadowed eyes and trembling lips, she stands at the door, hand raised to knock, his beloved and heart of his heart.

'Uncle Gabriel?'

Now another girl stands in the doorway. No creases in this gown, only yard-upon-yard of creamy silk. The eyes aren't green, they're deepest blue, but like her mother before her, she is afraid of the future.

Last night Adelia came to him in the Eyrie as she used to in the old days. Two in the morning he heard her call. He ran all the way. The Eyrie ever his friend, the door opened before his fingers touched the latch. Up the stairs he went. In '46 the staircase was broken. It isn't broken nowadays. Even so, it is his old, worn boots that run up the stairs as the banister he touches is thick with dust.

Moonlight turning her hair to silver she was in the attic wearing the red raincoat, the hood hanging back. Afraid to speak in case she'd vanish he took a pace forward. Her name broke from his lips like a sob: 'Adelia.'

She turned. Out went his hand, their fingertips no more than a breath away.

'Have I long to wait?' he couldn't stop the question.

For a moment her hand touched his. Then, 'no,' she said, 'no time at all.'

Then she was gone and he alone with a cobweb in his hand.

~

When Clyde looks back on his Wedding Day he sees a crazy patchwork quilt, lots of coloured thread cobbled together. It started at 0800 hours, Grizz Hamilton, his buddy from the Agency, hammering on the hotel door. 'Time to get up, Tidy Man!' The guy looking back from the mirror is one cool dude gussied up in dress uniform, gold braid and medals – the man inside wonders if she'll leave him waiting at the altar.

They drove through crowds. 'They waiting for you, Commander?' says Grizz.

'Anybody there with handcuffs and a stun-gun?'

'Negative.'

'Then they are not for me.'

Next he's in the church. Her family are in the left-front pews, the right are for his family and friends. It's as well Sophie has a fan-club otherwise his side would be empty. Conversation drops as they enter, everyone turning to look. It's likely the wave of abhorrence coming down the central nave is imaginary. Until yesterday he thought it might be nice having brothers. Two minutes in their company and all hope of family feeling vanished. The older of the two, West-Point plebe, offered civility. The younger kid smiled. Females of the Hunter clan are equally guarded. He's gained a wife but nothing more.

There's movement at the back of the church. A fanfare and people are getting to their feet. In slow motion he turns. Beside him Grizz sighs.

Clyde knows that sigh. She's on Templar's arm and the woman behind, what's-her-name, Karen, looks good. Stupid argument! He should've kept his mouth shut. Who cares who gives her away as long as the gift is his?

The organ plays and a choir sings. Words float upward. Latin, the sound chills his blood. Then suddenly he's in the nightmare -eyes watch him from every pew, eyes belonging to the dead. They care less who he weds. They exist only to stare back in wounded surprise. '*Why are you doing this? Why are you killing me? What harm did I ever do to you?*'

Other eyes, living eyes, may be watching. Who knows, Ethan Winter might be among the shadows, and that click back of the church may be the priming of a .38. Maybe Winter has a theatrical turn of mind and waits for the pause when the Minister says, '*if anyone can show just cause why these two should not be joined together let him speak now or forever hold your peace.*'

Does Clyde care about being shot? There are worse places to die than at the foot of an altar – and worse places to lie than in the arms of one's bride.

God, she is breathtaking! Yesterday she was up to her elbows in flea-ridden mutts. Now she's a Snow Queen, her gown of swansdown.

The music is dying away. The Minister speaks. 'Who giveth this woman to be married to this man?' Gabriel

Templar steps forward, places Sophie's hand upon Clyde's. Now there is only one pair of eyes.

The heady scent of the flowers, the church and those eyes, Clyde thought he would faint. Ever seen a worm wriggling on the end of a hook? Never so exposed he wanted to drop down to the ground, to dissolve and disappear. Templar's eyes stripped him to the bone, everything ever said and done laid bare before God. The eyes told Clyde what he's always known, doesn't matter that they stand before an altar, doesn't matter that they make vows, Sophie will never be his. She'll always be an Otter's bride.

Book Two

It Was Like This

Chapter Sixteen
The Dream Weaver

First light and the platoon are heading 10 kilometres south of Saigon. Swampland north of Rach Vuna Gam, the drop-zone is known to be heavily patrolled by NVA units. Orders are to trek southwest in search of target enemy camp and having located hunker-down until able to engage.

Good-to-go, tightly buttoned up with an M16, three hundred rounds of ammo, concussion grenades, Para flares and a scope, Ethan did what he always did before combat, took a moment to be with Sophie.

It's two years since he held her. He's tried his damnedest to erase her from his mind but for the good it did he might've tried erasing the sun from the sky. She is the blood in his veins, the sky above and the water beneath, hope is gone yet he takes a moment to look at the photograph.

Some guys carry lucky-charms, a photo of a kid in a ballet skirt is his keep-safe. It doesn't numb the pain but it helps stop dangerous thoughts building in his head, thoughts like, 'I love you and I don't know how I can keep away.'

The photograph sits in the top pocket of his BDU, keep it safe, this day and the intent behind it as far removed from childhood dreams as a man can get.

Seb Farrell rolled his eyes. 'Are you ever gonna give up?'

'Something bothering you?'

'No, Boss,' Seb turned away, adding sotto voce, 'only the fact you're alive.'

It's okay, Ethan would feel the same. A flash of anger burns! Dumb picture! He should chuck it down the latrine along with any former hope attached to it. Time has moved on. Sophie is married to Forrester and Ethan divorced.

Two years ago he did as promised, provided Forrester with a dirty deal. He took a cab to Fred Lyle's apartment and stood outside listening to the woman crying inside. Then he knocked on the door and asked her to marry him. 'Why would you want to do that?' said Meg Lyle. 'You don't really know me.'

Even now Ethan wonders at his nerve contacting Fred's widow. Forget pride and honour! Hoo-yah! The need to ensure Sophie's safety overrode all else. Best man at their wedding, a wedding closely followed by a funeral, Meg was more acquaintance than friend. Though big on love the Lyle's were always short of dough, Fred heavily in debt to the race-track. Ethan proposed but even with a child in her arms and another due to pop -and heavies knocking on the door wanting cash – Meg took some convincing. 'I'm not asking for a hand out.'

'No,' he said, 'I am.'

Hell, the mistakes we make and the mistakes we ask others to make with us!

Her face when he told of Forrester's threats. 'You can't let him get away with that! You must do something.' He'd nodded. 'I am doing something. I'm asking you to marry me.' He could tell she didn't know whether to kick him in the nuts or call the cops. She settled for weeping. 'Freddy said you'd do this. He came the night he died, stood where you are lit up like Mardi Gras. I thought it was all the gin I'd swallowed, Freddy, I said, how could you leave me like this? He said it wasn't his choice but not to worry a buddy would help.'

Ethan had stood gaping at her. 'Fred said that?'

'Yeah him and that stupid eagle Mike!'

An hour Ethan was trying to convince her. She dug in, her argument was that Ethan would be seen as a betrayer and herself a whore. 'I've never been unfaithful to Freddy. Even with his gambling I stayed true.'

Ethan told her it wouldn't be for long, a year and she could divorce him.

It was her dead husband that won through, ghostly visitations. The deal was Ethan would help her and the kids and not get in her way. Her reply mimicked Farrell. 'With Freddy dead you get in the way just by being alive.'

'Something dirty,' said Forrester, 'to rattle the female psyche.' An affair with a buddy's wife, a kid here and another on the way, that's dirty.

One problem resolved Ethan must face another. Aware of Seb's feelings for Sophie he requested transfer. It was denied. 'SEALs are meant to be a band of brothers. If you can't get beyond this you can't get beyond anything.'

Ethan dropped the first bomb telling the team of the marriage. 'I got hitched last furlough.' For a time there was lot of back-slapping, Sebastian first to congratulate: 'You're a fast mover but with a girl like Sophie I'd be the same.'

A count of ten and he dropped the second. 'My wife is called Margaret, or Meg, as I think of her.' A couple of minutes he gave them to swallow that then he offered the *coup de grace*, 'what's more I'm about to become a daddy.'

Silence was what he got. A copy of *Paris Match* had been doing the rounds, the picture of him and Sophie kissing. Suddenly a Team leader is declaring himself a two-timing cheat who's been messing with a hero's widow.

An iron curtain dropped between him and the rest. Two years on it's still there but not so dense or so obvious. That he brings them back alive helps – they can't afford to distrust him. Seb Farrell doubts the whole deal. He thinks there's more than Ethan is telling and a dog with a bone keeps coming back.

Jaw tight, he stares. 'She's married now so why do you hold onto the photograph? Don't seem the decent thing to do.'

'Sit down.' There's no point in arguing. He can't tell of Forrester's threats.

Seb tries again. 'If you're planning a rematch it's over my dead body.'

'I said sit down, Mister Farrell!'

Seb withdrew. They stick together or die together and since one of them desires to live they must at least try.

Meg had her baby and there's Tommy Lyle, a cousin on the scene who's the image of Fred. Ethan sends regular cheques but he won't visit, not after Meg trying to stick a bandage over a dirty wound.

The night they wed they went back to her place where she assumed sex to be part of the deal. He woke on the sofa to find her on her knees undoing his pants and taking him in her mouth, salt tears mixing with semen. His heart was disinclined but his body was okay, a man's dick offering allegiance to no one.

No way! He owes Fred Lyle more than that. Now Ethan's alone with no hope for the future. Does he want to kill Forrester? What d'you think?

~

Two dummy passes to confuse enemy radar and then the pilot brought the chopper in fast and low, Ethan dangling portside and Seb starboard like clay pigeons abseiling a metal nest.

They drop, Sebastian landing on his ass, thick ooze cushioning the impact. No sooner down then he's up aiming his weapon into the jungle. Shit before shovel, he is assigned point-man this time around, to go ahead of the Team searching out menace natural and man-made. Point duty is okay. While not in control of his own destiny he is at least in control of his eyes and feet. The noise Bristow makes! If the VC hasn't heard them by now it's a miracle.

An hour later he lifts his boot and jungle comes away with it. Earlier Hacker Thompson tossed him a Hershey bar. It landed in mud. Now he's eating mud. It's not only the terrain you're fighting it's the heat. It drains energy and if not heat then sudden squalls of rain. You can do nothing but stay put. There are mosquitoes and red ants. He's double ordnance-taped the top of his boots, even so, one little bastard got through and is currently chewing his calf.

A point man needs eyes in back of his head. The trail is heavy with debris and criss-crossed with vines. Each footfall is your last. There's a swamp close by which means crocodiles are a possibility as well as booby-traps. Last mission out, he nearly died: the Ice Man saved him.

This is his ninth mission under Lieutenant Winter. Whatever you feel of the man you can't fault him as a Leader. They were pushing through swampland in semi-darkness. Point man again, his was about to step forward when the guy grabbed his arm. 'Freeze!'

There it was a rusted tobacco tin and line tied to a grenade pin, death at half a pace. A trip wire! Christ, he can't think of it now without wanting to barf. 'How did you know it was there,' he says. Cool as an iceberg, and as unfathomable, Ethan Winter says, 'a little bird told me.'

~

Having located the camp and it seemingly abandoned, the platoon dug in. Seven hours and still no sign of the enemy! Ethan tugged on the cord that tied him to Farrell and Farrell to Thompson and Hacker to Bristow, and Bristow to Doc Wallis and so on – every man in contact with another. No reply suggested Seb was asleep. Let him sleep. They'll know when the enemy is coming. It's so quiet you could hear a fly fart never mind the splashing of a sampan.

Time passes and a sense of calm suffuses Ethan's mind, a feeling of looking at the world with new eyes. It started with a rustle in the undergrowth, a skinny rabbit hurrying home to his burrow, every whisker exuding life. Then a water moccasin slipped through the reeds, agate eyes and flickering tongue, it was as beautiful as it is lethal.

An ant, persistent little fucker, clambered over his boot, legs nine-to-the-dozen, it is a work of genius, a total wonder as is all creation.

Ethan's not a religious man nor was his pa. Mom was more dutiful than committed. It's Granma of Welsh Baptist stock that does church every Sunday and is always telling Ethan to 'wash his soul clean in the blood of the Lamb.'

Having lost count of the men he'd killed he thinks it will take more than holy water to wash him clean. The day they were due to lit-out, he along with the rest knelt down in a makeshift church, guys mumbling the Lord's Prayer.

'Our Father, who art in heaven, hallowed be Thy Name.' The words stuck in his throat. What kind of father is the Lord God? Is He like Cyrus Winter, Ethan's pa, a man who loved his wife enough to bring her parents across the ocean to his home, who laughed when his first son was born, and wept with the passing of the second, Little Ephraim, catching fever and dying at three days old.

Pa was a great guy, tough as leather yet soft as silk. November 15th, 1942 he died, shot to pieces in shallow seas, breaking Mom's heart so it never mended.

Is the Lord a father who wakes you in the morning with a kiss, his bristly chin giving you a friction burn, and who slaps you about the head for teasing a neighbour's cat? Or is He the father Ethan's likely to be now, a stepfather who pays the bills but stands aloof.

Ethan's not sure of God yet seems to think he has seen a kind of angel, a divine being, a giant swan who he calls the Dream Weaver.

Fred Lyle once said that Mike, the invisible eagle, showed him heaven, and that was the apartment where he and Meg lived minus the 'fucking bank loan!'

Ethan's version of heaven is a fishing boat on a lake. He doesn't know where, figures it somewhere in Colorado, yet has seen it from above riding the back of a swan. It's likely if he were to tell a shrink about that the guy would be harking to childhood, was he jealous of Pa's pecker or some such crap.

The Dream Weaver is a giant cob with a mighty wing-span. The night before the current mission he dreamt it carried him over the lake, saying, 'the boat down there is your hope of heaven. All you have to do is want it badly enough.'

A good dream, he woke sure of the mission. Optimism causes life to seem full-blown. Minute to minute whatever catches his eye is filled with singular grace, even Hacker who black as pitch is invisible in darkness but who sleeps with his mouth open, teeth glittering among the leaves.

Warriors throughout history have moments like this. When Mom was dying she embraced every moment. Strange, he should feel it. It's not the first time he's been close to death, the last was a trip wire, before that the Space Project – hitching a ride aboard a rocket with a million gallons of liquid propellant under your ass is not the safest way to travel. Fred Lyle will vouch for that.

Light fading, Ethan flicked the ant from his boot. It's said roaches are likely survivors of global catastrophe, able to survive minus body parts. Clyde St John Forrester is a roach minus a soul. It'll take a global catastrophe to unsettle him, his life and deeds the roots of the mangrove tree secreted in dirty water.

Think of Forrester and every peaceful feeling vanishes. I should've shot him. As it stands only Meg knows what happened. Not even Granma knows. For a time she questioned the marriage. 'How come I never see your wife?' she would say. He said that it was a mistake and that they'd parted.

He had to say something! Tiny, but packed with ferocious life, if she suspected trouble she'd be packing a .45. She asked of Sophie until she saw pictures in the paper. 'She's a stripper. You're better off without her.'

If he dies today Granma will come out financially sound. Mom left more than enough to pay off everybody's debts including Fred's bookies. What a loon! Even when losing Fred took it on the chin: 'At least I know where I'm going when I die.' It's important to believe in something if only invisible eagles. Pa believed in paying his dues. Mom believed love triumphs over all. Granma says, 'the Lord moves in mysterious ways. Have faith and you can move mountains.'

Ethan never wanted to move mountains. He wanted to be with his girl. He felt closest to this unknown God when making love with Sophie.

The weekend in Paris they moved from couch to bed and back again. It was a feast and boy was he hungry. Ever hear a woman laugh in the moment of orgasm, a laugh so rich in pleasure it makes you come the same time? It's what she did. He'd give his right arm to hear that laugh again.

Making love? What does it mean? When you slide between a woman's thighs and her eyes are locked into yours, and you not only desire her you'd die for her, do you in that moment spin a magical essence that swirls through time and space and is known thereafter by the world as Love? Is it useful to the Father God that supposedly looks after His children?

With men like Forrester calling the shots, the Lord has to be mysterious indeed to keep love alive. Last time out Ethan did wonder if He was already on the case since no one saw the trip wire. The photograph fell from his pocket. He bent to pick it up and there was death in a tobacco tin. How mysterious is that.

~

Eleven hours squatting in mud; with the enemy camp 100 metres away and the need to listen Sebastian daren't move. He's pissed through his pants twice. You can't get up to piss. You're a Man with a Green Face. You're not part of the scenery. You *are* the scenery and must go with the flow, momentary warmth and a soggy ass. Hoo-yah, the joys of being a SEAL!

Most of the team are dozing. Not the Ice Man. Sebastian can't see him but can feel his gaze raking terrain. That marriage situation plagues Seb's mind. A guy would have to be stupid to dump Sophie. Winter is not stupid. The Hunter family are known to the Farrells, the General a close friend of Dad's. When Sebastian and Simon were kids and Mom struggling in post-war Britain it was Alex Hunter who smoothed the path. Then when Dad was murdered in Korea the General supported again through college.

Dad never met Sophie. After he was killed Mom would visit Vermont. Seb would hang about the yard with her cousins, David and Pete Hunter hoping for a glimpse of the long-legged beauty. That such a girl could be tossed aside never entered his head especially not by Ethan. Seb remembers him at the Gala, the guy was head-over-ass in love! Not only that, can you fight alongside a man trusting him as Leader and not get inside is character?

Sophie's married now yet Sebastian can't it let go and he's not alone, he hears guys chewing it over, though with nothing to go by they all say the same, that woman, Meg, is a two-timing bitch who suckered him in. It's the only rational explanation. He's a SEAL for Chrissakes! The only time a SEAL turns his back on all he holds dear is to draw fire from the homestead – to lose in order to win.

Hold on! Something is up! Whup! The line on Seb's finger is tugged. There are voices and the splash of a sampan. Guys are on their feet, locked and loaded, waiting for the signal. Forget theories. It's time for action. When this is over and boats coming in to extract the platoon then Sebastian is going to ask him straight, 'so, what's the real deal.'

~

It was a fuck-up. Hacker panicked. The sampan came out of the shadows. No big deal, an ancient mama-san, a girl, and a couple of kids.

Ethan Winter motioned to Sebastian 'Kids and women, Mister Farrell,' he whispered. 'Eyes open and shot ready but wait for the real target.'

He was letting them go, which, Copy-That, is okay by Sebastian. He didn't relish the idea of firing on kids. The sampan drifted by. Then the line tied about Seb's finger tugged again, Doc Wallis spotting another sampan.

The second sampan drifted into view, two guys in NVA uniforms, one of them pissing over the side. Things were suddenly dangerous. The first boat was still within firing range and with itchy fingers on triggers and no need for a blood bath Ethan made a decision.

He stepped out the shadows. '*Lai dai*! Come here!' he shouted. '*Lai dai*!'

A moment of stunned silence, then both NVAs put their hands in the air.

'*Lai dai*!' Ethan waved them forward. 'Keep coming.'

They were coming. He was talking in their language and they were listening. There was no problem. Then the younger NVA dropped his hands. Probably trying to button his flies, no man likes his pecker hanging out.

Hacker fired a round.

The NVAs dove overboard. The old mama-san was screaming. The kids from the first boat jumped into the ditch swimming for the opposite bank. The shouting and splashing was too much for Hacker. He let loose again and this time Bristow with him, bullets spraying the water.

Then, Chrissakes, Doc Wallis charges up from the rear and lobs a 40mm grenade at the boys, blood and flesh raining down. He follows that with a M30 strafing the far bank. The noise was horrendous, nobody could think.

'Don't shoot at the boat!' Ethan yelled. No one else seemed to see what he could see, the girl in the first boat crouched over a bundle.

Nobody hears him. The girl is hit. She sags sideways and a baby revealed.

Ethan took off splashing through the ditch. 'Quit firing!' he shouted again. 'There's a baby!' Suddenly it was important to get the child to safety. It is why Ethan was born; he couldn't save himself or Sophie but he could save the baby.

The NV guys were food for crocs still Hacker kept on firing. Only Seb Farrell had his wits about him and got on the radio calling in the boats. The girl was dead, her head blown away. The baby hugged to his chest like a pot of gold at the end of the rainbow, Ethan turned for the bank, it was as Hacker said afterward, 'sure, it was a baby, but a VC baby, fuck's sake, not one of ours.'

Thump! Ethan took a round in his chest. He felt his legs going and pushed the baby toward Seb. 'Take it, Seb!'

He didn't seem to want to. 'Boss,' he said shaking his head.

'Come on!' Ethan pushed the bundle at him again.

Seb leaned down to take it and Ethan knew the baby was dead, saw it in Seb's eyes, a little hand wide open, the fingers like tiny blood-stained petals.

That's when Ethan gave up. To hell with this, he thought. I'm going to my Lake. If they need me they can come get me.

Things were fractured from then on. He tried giving orders, saying they need gunships in and not to leave a stick standing. Words came out of his mouth, whether anyone heard he didn't know. Sounds mixed and mingled, the flick-flack of helirotors merging with the buzz of mosquitoes.

Faces loomed over him, Doc Wallis spattered with blood, and the medivac people. All the time this was going on a stranger stood watching, a blond guy, who for some reason Ethan associated with the Dream Weaver.

Time fused and time passed, he slipped in and out of consciousness, different faces every time he opened his eyes yet the blond guy always there.

'Who is that?' he asked Farrell.

'Who is what, Lieutenant?'

'The big guy standing next to Wallis, the one with wings.'

Hacker started to cry, silly bastard. 'Stow it, Hacker. It's not your fault.'

Farrell had his mouth to Ethan's ear. 'Sophie?' he says. 'What's the real deal?'

Ethan got scared. Until that moment he wasn't afraid. Who can be afraid with the Dream Weaver on your side? But with thoughts of Sophie he remembered a cockroach and didn't want to die without someone knowing the truth.

'I had to do it!' He grabbed Seb. 'I had to keep her safe.' He pulled him closer whispering in his ear. Blood staining his lips he talked until he was hoarse. 'S...so do you get it?' he stammered. 'Do you get why I did it?'

Seb nodded. 'Sure I get it. But you gotta clear your name, got to tell Sophie.'

'Can't. He might hurt her.'

'The guy's a psycho. He needs putting down.'

'Maybe but you g...got to promise not to tell.'

'I promise.'

'Sacred promise.'

'Hoo-yah!'

Ethan let go. Nothing else he could do. It was hard to breathe. His lungs were very empty while at the same time very heavy. His strength was fading and the blond angel coming nearer. There was a woman with him. Eyes of emeralds and hair of spun gold if he looked at her and kept looking breathing got easier.

She knelt beside him. 'Hello Ethan,' she said, a Britisher.

'Hiya.'

'You are in a bit of a state.'

'I sure am.'

'Let me help you.' She leaned down and stroked his hair.

'Are you a nurse?'

'I used to be.'

'Are you an angel?'

She laughed. 'No, nothing like.'

'Are you the Dream Weaver?'

'No, sorry.'

Ethan hooked a thumb and whispered. 'Is the big guy a Weaver?'

'That is possible.'

'Why are you here?'

'I've come to return a favour.'

'Favour?' It was dark. There was a hell of a fuss, medics shouting, paddles being waved and his shirt being ripped aside. Busy drowning in emerald kindness he couldn't worry about it. 'What favour did I ever do for you?'

'The biggest favour anyone could do for a mother. You kept my baby safe.'

'I didn't save anybody's baby. I tried but was washed out.'

'Yes that poor little baby did die but thanks to you mine didn't.'

'Oh! You're…?'

'Yes I am.'

'And I'm going to…?'

Green eyes flashed. 'No!' she said. 'Not if I can help it.'

Chapter Seventeen
Broken Toys

'No thanks.'

Culpepper frowned. 'What do you mean no thanks? Are you saying you don't want the transfer of property to go ahead?'

'I'm saying I never wanted it. These things are Sophie's. Why would I want them?'

'Your wife seemed to think you might.'

'My wife is wrong.'

'Is she indeed? Then might I ask you, sir? If after all this time and effort you do not want my client's beneficence why are we here?'

'Because until we are here and I am telling you face-to-face I don't want her goddamn trade-off, Sophie will continue to feel obliged to keep me sweet!'

'Trade off? Keep you sweet? I'm afraid I don't follow.'

Clyde smiled. 'I hope not. A lawyer like you, Daniel, a fine upstanding man committed to the paths of justice, you're the last person I'd want following me.'

'Commander Forrester, please.'

'It's okay. I'm just yanking your chain.'

'As I am only too aware, but can we please concentrate on the matter at hand!'

'Sorry, old chap. I had some good news the other day and can't help rejoicing.'

'Is that so?' Daniel Culpepper gazed at Clyde, and nostrils pinched as though detecting a bad odour began to read through the document.

Clyde tuned him out. Months they've been diddling with this. He doesn't want a bribe. It's Sophie he wants not her money. As her husband he's happy to share but won't be bought off. He'll do what he needs to do when he needs to do it. Happily the matter of dealing with her ex-lover is no longer of concern – the Ice-Man is dead.

Monday he heard it on the news. At the time he was taking a shower and nearly missed it: '*Navy Hero Loses Last Valiant Battle.*' At mention of the name of said hero there was a flash of intense joy but wary of Greeks bearing gifts he made enquiries, hearing of a military screw-up, women and children killed, and Ethan Winter wounded and dying of complications.

These days a couple of words are all a hero gets. No trumpet calls. US citizens are sick of Vietnam. Soldiers die. Who cares? Clyde cared. Needing to be sure he called the General. 'That right what I'm hearing, a bunch of Navy SEALs ran into trouble?'

'Navy SEALs don't run into trouble. They are trouble.'

'I heard one of them cashed in his chips, a guy with relative connections.'

'Then you know more than I do.'

It's a non-denial – Ethan Winter is dead. Clyde struck a pose: ''*Now is the winter of our discontent made glorious summer by this son of York and all the clouds that loured upon our house in the deep bosom of the earth buried.*''

Daniel Culpepper scowled 'Excuse me?'

'Act one, Richard the Third. I am eulogising the death of a friend.'

'A friend?'

Clyde grinned. 'Yes, sir, a friend. Can there be a more suitable occasion than the death of friends to quote dear old Wally Shakespeare?'

'I wouldn't know. I'm not a theatrical person.'

'No,' Clyde got to his feet. 'That's the difference between you and me, Daniel. You wear the oath of office on your sleeve. I have a little gypsy in my soul.'

Leaving Culpepper's office Clyde's sense of euphoria was replaced by frustration, the feeling of losing a favourite yo-yo down a drain and unable to pull the string. The more he thinks about it the more dissatisfied he becomes. Winter will still prove a winner. It's what happens when heroes die, the slate is wiped and dirty deals erased.

Some people are born winners. Look at Beaufort. You can't turn your head without seeing him on a billboard. Though meant to be a small affair their wedding was a stampede, a trickle of blue-blood from both sides of the Pond, sisters Lady Clare Beaufort and Julia, wife to Gabriel Templar, plus theatre folk from the Broadway hit *Shout*. Clyde was supported by Grizz and guys from the Yachting Team.

Approaching forty and counting friends on the fingers of one hand gives a man pause for thought. He can't blame Sophie for that – she's the goodwife in and out of bed. He asks and she gives including a raging orgasm when he's on form. He says 'I thought women only feel it when they're in love. Isn't that what you and your sisters preach in

Cosmopolitan?' She slides out of bed and under the shower.
'What can I tell you, Clyde,' she says, her eyes blank.
'You're an accomplished man.'

She won't concede on the Mill. Clyde hates the place,
Big Brother he gets from the Agency he doesn't need it at
home. He tried the Eyrie. When the key wouldn't turn he
smashed a window. Two minutes and aware of eyes
everywhere he's out again. Now he steers clear of Virginia
sharing his 'accomplishments' with golf widows. If he must
be home he chooses the turret room.

Being married to Sophie isn't easy. You gotta have
strong locks on the door if you want to keep a priceless
artefact but then you worry about provenance, is it real or
fake. Better to tear the heart from the body, that way you
lose nothing.

~

The phone rings with news from the Abbey, the old boy is
fading. Clyde promises to pass on the message but doesn't.
They're off to Paris next week to collect Emilia Zwolski. It
was him suggested it – Sophie can use the female company
and him the odd clandestine blow-job. If only he could
relax, after all, it's all happening, Ethan Winter a footnote
in the Greeley Gazette, Beaufort Senior about to meet his
ancestors, and if society columns are right the Viscount on
the brink of marriage.

He should quit the Agency and become Sophie's
manager, or maybe help with the animal sanctuary, sluicing
dog-shit down the drains instead of human.

Sophie was all for him giving up. 'Maybe it will stop your nightmares.'

The nightmares started with the wedding. Until then he slept sound. Now he's lucky if he gets an hour. Last time in Nam he was woken by Grizz shaking his shoulder. 'I've heebie-jeebies of my own without listening to yours.'

Same with booze! He used to be pretty much tee-total, now he drinks and it shows. He's had a call from the Olympic Team. They won't be using him in Munich. Up-and-coming hot-shots, there's no room for a drunk. Ask what the nightmares are about he couldn't tell you. Friday he woke backed up against the wall screaming.

Junior Mother Hen, arms outstretched, she bursts through the door. 'What is it?' she says. 'Eyes,' he whispers. She hugs him. 'Let's begin again.' He wants to believe it possible but sees a Black Hole where she sees rainbows. His code name is Tidy-Man, a broom sweeping away trash. Can there be a new beginning after that?

~

Sophie is on the phone to Emilia. 'Bring what you want. Don't worry about heavy stuff. Clyde will shift it.'

'Mister Clyde is coming here?'

'Yes. Is that a problem? I mean, would you sooner stay in Paris?'

'I come to USA. Mamselle need me. I keep devil away.'

Sophie replaced the phone. 'Emilia thinks you are a devil.'

'The devil, huh?' Clyde scooped her across the bed and pinning her arms to the pillow stared down. 'And what do you think?'

'I think she may be right.'

Sophie would've said more but his lips were on hers. It's not easy liking Clyde so she tries loving him. Today, sunlight highlighting their coupling she wants to scream. 'Don't,' she said against his mouth as he kneed her legs apart. 'I don't want to.'

His arm hit the small of her back curving her higher. 'Yes you do,' he whispers.

Closing her mind to love she wonders what the ghosts in the Mill hear when she cries out – passion or pain, to her they feel much the same.

Daniel Culpepper called to say Clyde refused the transfer. She's not surprised. He doesn't care about money; power is his thing, the same veil of secrecy that covered Dad's latter-day career, covers his. He has few possessions, the clothes in his closet expertly tailored yet not costly. The car he drives is old and weather-beaten. 'It's like me,' he says, 'eminently practical.'

There is practicality in Clyde that is terrifying – a place for everything and everything it its place. When offered deeds to the apartment in New York he quirked his elegant eyebrows. 'Gee thanks, Mrs Forrester. I guess this is your lucky day as well the realtor's.' He thinks she prefers him elsewhere. Near or far it doesn't matter. They are strangers walking the same path.

Clyde and his many lovers, his diary is again in use. Sophie doesn't complain. If her heart is closed to all men she can hardly demand fidelity of one. The deal was to be his wife. If being so keeps her loved ones safe she'll honour it.

But what a waste! He can be very considerate. That he stays away is as much for her as him. When he is home there are no demands. In the morning, a polite tap on her bedroom door, and showered and smelling of cologne, his dark hair a sleek cap, he smiles. 'Good morning, wife. Might I share your bed?'

Lately with the onset of night terrors she is an object to be tossed about in silence. In a room filled with thwack of headboard and bounce of a spring he remains mute. When asked why, he parodied something she once made:

'Is it dirty words you want? Shall I be the Big Bad Wolf and you Red Riding Hood? O, Little Girl what tits you have and what an ass!'

This morning he hurt her. 'Sorry,' he pulled away when she winced. 'I don't mean to hurt you.' She yelled at him. 'How in God's name did we get to this?'

He shrugged. 'I don't know. I can only work with the material given.'

~

Sophie is at the Rescue Centre, Judy, the brindle bitch, with her.

Helpers are already at work, hoses snaking between kennels. A patch of scrub close to Gabriel's Wild Life Reserve she acquired the land in '68. Between live shows and TV recordings this is where you'll find her, bare-faced and happy – no need to paint your face, it's all the same to abandoned pets.

Hokey, the Alsatian, arrived with dreadful cigarette burns. Up for a permanent home he looks pretty spiffy nowadays. She tried him at the Mill but he wouldn't stay. Only Judy stays, her pups re-homed months ago. Sue Ryland says it's because of ghosts in the greenhouse. Sophie knows it isn't Biffer's smiley little ghost that frightens Hokey. It is a man – or a devil, as Emilia thinks.

Clyde usually leaves after sex. Today he lounged against the pillows.

'Do you ever wonder,' he said, 'how we actually made it to the altar?'

'All the time.'

'And do you reach a conclusion?'

'A moment of madness is all I can think.'

On the subject of Clyde there is universal silence. Granma Ellen prefers Sophie's career successes to her personal catastrophes and sits front row at fashion shows. The boys pass no judgment, in sharing ghostly telephone lines they likely know more of her reasons for marrying than she. This morning Clyde said it was because he was in the wrong place at the wrong time. 'The SEAL broke your heart. I was dumb enough to try picking up the pieces.'

~

Sophie's spent the day painting. In '46 the cottage was the Challoner's bolt-hole, bright shutters and wisteria over the door; Emilia will be happy here.

'Don't you think you're layin' that on a bit thick?' Pop! Out of the blue Daddy Bobby sat on the stairs, his poor shattered face in evidence.

'What's wrong with it?' said Sophie. 'I thought I was doing a reasonable job.'

'I'm not talkin' about you paintin'! I'm talkin' your memories of this place.'

'I remember it as sanctuary.'

'It may have been so in '46. It ain't a sanctuary now, though, is it?'

'It's alright. It's still home-from-home.'

'Yeah that's right, Sophie Emma Challoner, keep tellin' yourself that.'

Miffed, Sophie bit back. 'Why is your face still wounded? I thought when you were in heaven you might have been healed.'

He grinned and was handsome again. 'This ain't my real face. This is my dog in the manger face I wear when reminding you what's real.'

'And what is real?'

Pop! Bobby was gone, his voice echoing. 'You'll find that out soon enough.'

~

General Jentzen phoned. 'Evenin', Mizz Sophie. I was wondering if you'd do me the honour of lunching with me in the not too distant future.'

'Of course! Perhaps when we get back from Paris we can arrange a time.'

'You're off to gay Paree then?'

'Yes, a stint at the Lido and then straight back.'

'Uh-huh. Well, perhaps you'd give me a call soon as you do. It's about the Commander and in your best interest to know.'

Best interest? Sophie decided she wouldn't be in a rush to return his call. Dad used to say old soldiers carry heavy back-packs. It's possible the General wants to offload his. No thanks, she's enough baggage of her own.

~

They arrived mid-afternoon at the hotel. Clyde said he'd go sort Emilia at the apartment. Sophie went for a walk. Paris is a beautiful city. If you're happy and in love it's the best – if you're lonely it is the worst.

This is her fourth visit since Ethan, the smell, the atmosphere, even the sound of traffic bringing back memories. Not that she needs reminding. He's always in her head. When exercising at the barre he's there and when she's scrubbing the kennels he's scrubbing alongside. At breakfast they share a bowl of cornflakes. He sings still in her head. Nothing has changed only the melody.

Four o'clock and lovers walk by the Seine. Hand-in-hand with Ethan she walked with them until she could walk no more. Then she hailed a cab.

Clyde having her keys, she rang the doorbell.

He was in his shirtsleeves. 'Been for a stroll?' he said.

'Yes, it's lovely out. Hi, Emilia, are you ready to go?'

Emilia stood on a chair opening the window. '*Salut, Mamselle!*'

Sophie was dumb. That window! She saw it again, Ethan rescuing the cat and being clawed for his pains, he's talking, smiling, '...*this is some way to spend a first night in Paris, me hanging out a window and you holding my ass.*'

'You okay?' said Clyde.

'Yes. Is Shima still with the vet?'

Emilia nodded. 'Shima having jabs.'

'And you,' said Sophie, 'anything you need to do before leaving, perhaps say goodbye to friends?'

'I no one to say goodbye to.'

'Is that true?' Clyde unrolled his shirt sleeves. 'There is someone, a woman you shared an apartment with?'

'No one.'

'Okay if you say so,' he shrugged. 'I must have got it wrong.'

Sophie's skin prickled. Clyde knows something and goads Emilia, using information to prod a helpless animal. She took Emilia's hand. 'Are you sure about coming to Virginia? It's not too late to change your mind.'

'I come.'

'But if there's a reason to stay in Paris,' Sophie persisted.

'No!' Emilia pulled away. 'I come to America! I stay with you and Mister Clyde and have apartment and car.'

'It's a cottage, actually,' said Sophie. 'I think you'll like it. I spent a lot of time there as a child. My mother and I used to…'

A look passed between Clyde and Emilia. Sophie saw it and remembered him opening the door in shirtsleeves and Emilia tucking her sweater into her jeans. 'Ah well.' She picked up her bag. Everything she needed to know is reflected in that look. 'Shima is with the vet you say?'

Emilia nodded. 'I go collect.'

'Don't bother,' Sophie walked out. 'I'll go. You two can finish up here.'

The smothered smile was no accident. Clyde's having an affair with Emilia and wants Sophie to know. Bobby is right. She thought she was bringing another lost soul to sanctuary but no, the only lost soul is Sophie.

Shima crated up and sent to the airport, Sophie is at the Lido. She rang Suffolk earlier and learning Uncle Charles is fast fading cancelled the homeward flight for a single ticket to England. 'What time do you think we'll be done? Only a friend of mine is ill and I'm going on to Suffolk.'

'I'm sorry to hear that,' said Miss Bluebell. 'Good friends are hard to replace.' Business as ever she produced a teddy-bear. 'Would you do the usual, though you're probably sick of it by now.'

Sophie took out a lipstick. 'I don't mind.' She kissed the teddy-bear. '…though if years ago someone had said my kiss would one day raise thousands of dollars I'd have thought them crazy.'

~

Clyde arrived as she was having her make-up adjusted. He leaned on the doorjamb. 'So why did you walk out like that?'

'Madame?' Sophie beckoned the dresser. 'Un plus rouge, peut-être?'

'Oui, Mamselle.' The dresser fluffed the brush about her cheeks.

She was still very pale. 'Et peut-être un peau de rouge a lèvres?'

'Oui, Mamselle.' The dresser applied more lipstick.

Clyde coughed. 'Did you hear what I said?'

'Yes.'

'So why aren't you answering?'

'Because I can't do this now. Ten minutes and I'm on stage.'

'When can you do it?'

'When I'm back from Suffolk.'

The door opened, dancers rushing through casting glances at Clyde.

Irritated, he straightened. 'I don't know why you're sharing a dressing-room. You should have star-billing.'

'Perhaps.'

'You would if I was your manager.'

'Would I?'

'So are you coming back to the hotel?'

'Probably.'

'Cinq minutes, Mamselle Perfidia!'

'Okay.' Clyde hovered. 'We'll talk then. Something I need to tell you.'

'Is it more news from Suffolk?'

'It's not Charles Beaufort.'

'What then?'

He made for the door. 'Let's just say it's in your best interest to know.'

~

The show over Sophie selects two posies, red-roses for Suffolk and the white lilac for her. Maybe Ethan sent it maybe not, no use worrying. There's a quick knock on the door. A beautiful face appears. Sophie is enveloped in Floris perfume.

'Becky! How lovely!'

'Is it lovely?'

'Of course it is. I'm always pleased to see you.'

Becky flopped in the chair. 'I'm in London and heard you were here so popped over the Channel. My God you look ravishing! Marriage seems to suit you.'

'You think so?'

'Well, it certainly hasn't aged you.'

'Pity. I was hoping for older and wiser.'

'Silly you. You'll never be older and wiser.' Becky stared about the room. 'So many flowers! Did you get mine?'

'Did you send flowers?' said Sophie knowing there were none.

Becky changed subjects. 'Isn't Miss Tucker fabulous and so young for her age?'

'Yes indeed and probably in her case a lot wiser.'

'Now look, Soph!' Becky tossed her hair. 'I know I haven't been in touch but I've been busy.'

'What? David Parker busy?'

'Oh Lord not! He's long gone! I'm seeing Simon Farrell now.'

'I didn't know that.'

'I bet you didn't. Incestuous little bugger, aren't I?'

Sophie laughed. She could never stay mad at Becky. 'I see the cockney accent went by the boards.'

'Absolutely! I am all Sybil Thorndike now, a wee stammer, drawn out vowels, and clipped consonants. It helped no end with *Hedda Gabler*.'

'Yes congratulations on that. I thought you were wonderful.'

'Oh my God.' Becky's smile was electric. 'You came to see me. I thought it was you up in the gods so silent and watchful.'

'You were worth watching.'

'So Larry Olivier thinks. It's why I'm in England! I'm to work at the National.'

'You must be thrilled.'

'I'm out of my mind!' Becky perched on the table. 'How's my ma doing?'

'I wouldn't know. She's in England.'

'Oh fuck it, of course she is! Yes, broke and battening off poor old Charley who was ever good for a sob-story.'

'Becky!'

'Well it's true. You know he was always willing to help out. I haven't been to the Abbey in ages. I couldn't. Jay there, it would kill me to see him.'

'You still feel the same?'

'Well, not quite the same. We mellow, don't we? Actually, on that subject I need to ask you a question. Did you ever sleep with him?'

Sophie was silent. Does rape constitute sleeping with a man? 'No.'

'I'm sorry. I know I shouldn't ask. It's just that he was always so weird about you. I always took it as guilt.'

'I feel guilty about many things, Becky, but not about John.' Needing to get out she gestured. 'Help yourself to flowers.'

'If you're going on to Suffolk you might give the lilies to Ma.'

'Alright.' Sophie switched off the lights. 'I'll give Uncle Charles your best.'

'Oh do. He is a good guy and I'd like to be there but…' She shook her head, diamonds flashing. 'He settled money on me, you know. Said it would help get me started. God bless him.'

'Yes, God bless him.'

'Sophie, do you miss the ballet, 'cos I do. I would've held on but was no Sophie Hunter. But you're not a Hunter anymore, are you? You're a Forrester, a wood cutter.' Feral smile in evidence Becky threw a scarf about her neck. 'I caught a glimpse of Clyde earlier. Did he stay for the performance?'

'I don't know. Better things to do I would imagine.'

'I must be hard watching the world drool over your wife. But then he's gorgeous and for every man drooling over you there's a woman drooling over him. When you see him tell him Becky says hi, will you? He came to see me in *Shout*. I was quite overwhelmed.' She picked up a bunch of roses. 'You seemed a little jaded tonight. Maybe it's time to do something new.'

~

Sophie sat in the hotel room brushing her hair.

Clyde was watching. 'You were good tonight.'

'You stayed? I didn't see you.'

'I was up back with the lighting guys. I hung on thinking you might need me.'

'That was kind.' Bristles crackling, she carried on brushing. 'Becky said I was jaded.'

'Becky can fuck off.'

'What was it you wanted to tell me?'

'In a minute.' Clyde slid off the bed. It's too hot. Air-conditioning in France is the pits even in the best hotels. 'Next time you have your own dressing room or you don't dance. Bunched in there with all those broads it's not right.'

He pushed open the balcony doors. Having arrived at this point he doesn't know if he wants to tell. There's a definite chill in the air. 'I just wanted you to love me,' he said. 'But you don't. Look at you! You're angry as hell but it's not jealousy you feel.'

'Do you want me to be jealous?'

'It would be something.'

'What was that about Emilia knowing someone here?'

'She does know someone, a woman she lived with, the last sucker, you might say, to give shelter. And she's no Zwolski! She's Emilia Sabri, Algerian, come over on a tanker and was living in Marseilles.'

'I don't care about her name. I know she needs a place to live and so until you've made arrangements she can stay but not in the cottage.'

'She doesn't have to come. She can stay here.'

'You can't do that, not now you've promised. It wouldn't be fair.'

'Do you think it fair marrying me and not loving me?'

'Did you give me a choice?'

'This is still about him, Ethan Winter.'

'Maybe.'

'You know he's dead.'

The brush stopped in midair.

Dismayed by the colour leaching from her face, he tried softening it and told of the news flash. 'He was wounded and died in hospital. The funeral is next week.'

The brush remained poised in the air. She didn't believe him and stared as though waiting for a punch line, her reflection in the glass white as the bed-sheet.

'Shame you booked the flight to London,' he hovered. 'If you leave now you'll make it. Greeley, Colorado, one horse town.'

Face momentarily stripped of beauty, she struggled to gain control.

'I'll take you,' he found himself saying. 'We could leave now, get a flight and attend, though you're likely to run into his widow.'

It was the word widow that did it! The brush jerked and continued on. 'While I'm in Suffolk feed Judy. I'm not sure about Shima and quarantine. You need to check.'

Clyde told her of the rumours filtering back – how the SEAL mission went badly, a woman and her baby shot. Winter taking a bullet and … and…!

He would have said more but was stopped by the look in her eyes.

'Sophie?

Eyes huge, she looked up.

'I'm sorry.'

She nodded. 'So am I.'

Chapter Eighteen
The Light

First stop was London and Karen and Joe Walker. Relationships between them are a little strained these days. Clyde disapproves of Karen and makes no attempt to hide it. Chill in the air or not they seemed pleased to see Sophie. She tried to be equally pleased to see them but her lips frozen and voice a croaking toad she could barely speak.

'What's wrong?' said Karen.

'Ethan's dead.'

'Oh my God! I am so sorry.'

'He was shot.'

'I'm so sorry.'

'So am I but I can't seem to cry.'

'Of course not! You cried enough when he left.'

'But that's it, I didn't! Not a tear, nothing. I must be a heartless bitch!'

'Bitch nothing! It might be better if you were, stop people stomping all over your life. You can't cry because you're too busy feeling it. I would be the same if it was Joe.'

Sophie collected the car from the garage and started out for the Abbey. The white lilac posy she left with Karen.

'What another one?' said Karen. 'Makes you wonder.'

'Doesn't it.'

~

George Allen was on the steps, his face worn with care. 'Ever-so glad to see you, Miss Sophie. His Lordship perked up when he knew you was coming.'

'How is he?'

'Poorly. He seemed to be gettin' over the first stroke but then 'ad another.'

'What do the doctors say?'

'What do doctors ever say, keep taking the pills…though what good pills are now I do not know! Truth is he's worn out.' George took a hanky and blew his nose. 'Right then, where's them feather 'ats of yours?'

Sophie hauled the Lido headdresses from the boot. 'Are you sure about this?'

'Sure I'm sure. It was me suggested it to Lady Joanne, tell Miss Sophie it'll help the wife if she could bring some of them feather 'ats to mend.'

'I could've left them in Paris but don't trust anyone but Mrs Allen.'

'Don't you worry.' George disappeared under clouds of feathers. 'Betty's lookin' forward to havin' a go. She says mendin' them will help keep her mind off other things.'

They climbed the stairs, an elegant dancer and multi-coloured duck. Sophie couldn't help smiling. 'You could always wear one rather than carry.'

'Not likely! They weigh a ton! I said to the missis I don't know how you girls walk with that lot on your head and flash-bulbs in your face.'

Neither do I, thought Sophie, especially with a hangover. During the flight from Orly she had a couple of drinks, now her head is aching fit to burst.

She sighed and George thought he understood.

'Bloomin' reporters! I caught one of them earlier 'anging about the Maze with his camera. Needless to say it was His Lordship they was after.'

'You'd think being ill they'd leave him alone.'

George dropped the headdresses, a tear trickling down his cheek.

'Oh George!' Sophie hugged him. 'You were referring to Johnny.'

'I don't want to jump, but the same time I'm ready to serve him – not that Johnny would keep me on, me and Betty will be put out to pasture.'

'Surely not.'

'I don't care if he does. Forty years I've been with His Lordship. I started out green as grass. He taught me everythin' I know right to coachin' me through the dinners when His Majesty King George was alive. He never let me make a fool of myself or him. A better man I shall never know.'

'I'm sure you've been a great help to Lord Beaufort. He relied in you so.'

'God knows it was a privilege. Truth is he don't fit in no more. Too much of a gent. It's for the Beatles and kids with long hair.' George gathered up the headdresses. 'He'll be in a better place soon, and if he ain't careful with his climbing and his animals Master Johnny will be up there with him.'

'He hasn't changed then, still flashing teeth and rattling sabres.'

'Him and that whip!' George snickered. 'Did you know Hollywood's after him, some cranky remake of Tarzan. Talking of cranky, a leak in the ceilin' has put paid to your suite. You're in your old room, the Violet Nursery.'

'I shall enjoy that. Can Nanny Foster still tuck me in?'

'Nanny 'as a job tucking herself in nowadays never mind anyone else. It's a fact we've all gone down terrible since you were last here.'

Gone down is true. Two minutes and Sophie knew things were a lot worse than imagined. Lady Joanna was in the Wedgwood Room with Miss Jakes, her companion, both underweight sparrows in Shetland twinsets.

'Sophie, my dear! So good to see you. Is the Commander with you? No? Never mind. All these wars, I'm sure he's a busy man. Charles sends his apologies. He wanted to meet you but didn't feel able to manage the stairs.'

Uncle Charles hasn't managed stairs for months, George and his valet bringing him down in the lift. Things must be bad if he can't get down at all.

Sophie was making her way along the corridor when Johnny rounded the corner. 'Hello John,' she said. 'I'm so sorry about Uncle Charles.'

'Uncle Charles?' he queried, eyes like flint. 'I'm not sure who you mean. Are you perhaps referring to Lord Beaufort?'

'I meant Lord Beaufort.'

'Then be so good as to say so.' He walked on.

My God! Thoroughly chastened, she hurried to the library and entering closed the door behind her. A rug over his knees, Charles Beaufort was asleep by the fire. Head back and mouth open he was gaunt. Whatever happened to the giant of a man who loved to live? So dear, so needed, and now so…so…!

It was too much for Sophie. She was turning to leave when he heard.

'Hello, my dear.'

Sophie burst into tears.

'Oh, my little girl!' He struggled to hold out his arms. 'Come give me a hug.'

She ran and falling on her knees laid her head on his lap. She cried and couldn't stop. 'He's dead, Uncle Charles. Ethan is dead!'

'Oh poor young man!' He wept with her. 'He's given his life for his country.'

Sophie clung to him. He stroked her hair with his good hand, so paper thin she could see firelight through it. 'Please don't you go!' she sobbed.

'I'm afraid I don't seem to have a choice.'

'But it's everyone I ever loved!'

'Not everyone. You still have many who love you.'

'I know,' she cried, 'and I'm sorry to be selfish but they aren't you, and they aren't Mummy and Daddy, and they aren't him!'

Charles sighed. 'No nor will they ever be.'

Afraid to move in case he too vanished she held on. The clock struck four and then five, the fire dimming to amber. Then Mrs Allen poked her head round the door. 'Excuse me, Milord, but Madame thinks you should be resting.'

'Yes, of course.' Sophie scrambled to her feet. 'I mustn't make you tired.'

'One moment please, Mrs Allen.' Charles Beaufort waited until the door closed. 'My dear, you too need to rest. You've had an awful shock.'

'I'm alright, really I am. It was finding out.'

'I'm sure. Better give me a kiss then and say goodbye.'

'No! Not goodbye! I'm staying a whole week. I shall see you later.'

He took her hand. 'No, Sophie, listen. It's best to say goodbye.'

'Goodbye?' She gazed at him.

'Yes. Gabriel is coming. He phoned earlier to say he would be here.'

'Oh.'

'Yes, oh.' Charles smiled and there was a ripple in the air. The Gate swung wide and another Charles Edward Cecil Henry de Beaufort shone through the smile, a face that burned with bright light, so pure and so kind Sophie for the first time in her life understood the meaning of the word good.

Sobbing she kissed him. 'Goodbye, Uncle Charles.'

'Goodbye, my dear, and God bless you.'

~

Sophie woke to headlights sweeping the drive. Doors slammed and boots crunched on the shale. Gabriel is here.

She lay watching the sky through the window. The moon is high, that same spoony-moon that brought childhood to an end. Tonight it is somehow softer.

How strange, she thought, sleepily, the world smiles when he is near. Clocks tick and stairs creak, a mix of dried lavender and mildew the same air rolls through these ancient corridors. Same damp sheets cover the bed, heat from her body causing steam to rise. The fire spits in the hearth and the nursery fireguard in place. Everything is as it should be, centuries of porous roofs and water leaking from rusty pipes creating a mythological zoo of the ceiling. Wild and wonderful creatures hover above, dragons, devils, and faeries flash and flicker in the whitewash. Faces of beloved pets smile through the cracks, Rosie the Golden Retriever by the armoire, and Biffer, the Airedale, at the cornice, and by the window the cat, Willow, who died the day Daddy died. Still-life, it remains the same year-after-year yet when Gabriel is near there is a softening and a rustling, the whole house reaching out to embrace him.

Gabriel gave her away at the wedding – so handsome in grey cutaway, no wonder Mother adored him. On the way to the church he asked if she felt she must do it. When she said yes he took her hand: 'Okay then do it,' he said, 'but when you can't live with it anymore call out and help will come.'

It was that promise that got her through the ceremony.

He's here! Footsteps on the landing! At her door to the nursery he paused, his shadow gilded and rippling like hovering wings. 'You awake?'

'Yes.'

'You said your goodbyes?'

'Yes.'

Silence and then softly: 'Go to sleep now, honey, and mind you don't believe all you are told. Love can never die. It lives on forever.'

Gabriel registered her response – a mixture of puzzled silence and muffled sobs. He waited until her breathing changed, smoothing out and when she slept he carried on to Charley's door.

He knocked. 'Okay to come in?'

Charles was awake, dark-rimmed owlet eyes staring through the gloom.

'Oh do please come in, dearest boy, and welcome.'

A narrow shape lying in the bed, other than old world courtesy there was not much left of him. Gabriel recollected a time in '48 when on a flight to Paris that same courtesy offered a bum a cup of Earl Grey tea and a new world.

There is nothing he would not do for this man, nothing he would not give. His life, Gabriel Templar's life? Sure, no need to ask. Alas, there's nothing he can give now – only share these last moments, sit with him, wait with him, and when the light comes help him to cross over into glory.

He sat by the bed repeating the phrase that commenced their friendship. 'I see you're readin' Captain Fordyce's book on the plight of the Bengal tiger.'

Charley smiled shyly. 'Your memory is extraordinary.'

'That was the first thing you said to me. I sat opposite you in that bucket. First time I'd ever flown… well, on metal wings, that is. You were kind to me.'

'I remember. You were a beautiful if rather lost soul.'

'I'm still lost.'

'Still beautiful.'

'Maybe. Have you said your goodbyes?'

'Yes, to those I can say it to.'

'Not to John?'

'No. He wouldn't hear me. Poor boy is overloaded with grief of his own. He did something very silly some years back. He hurt young Sophie. Now he wears sackcloth and ashes. It's not doing him any good. I fear for his health.'

'Don't. She'll make him well again one day.'

'You think so?'

'I do.'

'You will take care of him, won't you?'

'To the last.'

'Thank you.'

'Sophie's terribly distraught. Her young man died.'

Gabriel stretched out his legs. 'I heard a similar rumour.'

'Rumour?' Charles stared. 'Oh,' he whispered. 'Perhaps it isn't as we think.'

'Nothin' is ever as we think.'

They sat together, didn't talk much, Charles too weak and Gabriel waiting.

'I've had a good life and I hope I'll have a good death.'

'Uh-huh.'

'Will I meet him over there – the young man I once loved so very dearly?'

'I wouldn't count on it.'

'I suppose not. It was always one-sided and of course there was Lady Joanna. I had to give her what I could.'

'We must do our best by those as needs us.'

'Julia needs you.'

'I know and I'm still here.'

'Will I see you over there?'

'Not yet but in time.'

'You do know that I love you, don't you.'

'Yes.'

'I mean love you.'

'Yes.'

'And that I loved you the moment I saw you.'

'I do know that, Charles, and I appreciate it.'

'I just wanted you to know.' Charles groaned. 'I hurt so, Gabriel. Everything hurts from the top of my head to the soles of my feet.'

'I know.' Gabriel straightened. It was coming. He could hear it, that special sound. At first it was no more than a breath of wind on the horizon, a lark singing in a clear sky or a low note on the cello Julia plays.

Charley could hear it too and was afraid. 'Is it coming?'

'It's coming so be brave and embrace it 'cos it'll set you free.'

Gabriel took the old man in his arms. He loves Charles Beaufort as the father he never had. Everyone loves him, no one wants him to go, but who can stand before the Face of the Lord when it is time.

Whoosh! The trumpet call crashed out of the sky and down through the roof, piercing and rattling that poor frail frame like a hurricane.

'Oh,' gasped Charles. 'The light!'

'Yes.' Gabriel closed his eyes. 'The Light.'

Chapter Nineteen
A Funeral

'The funeral is on Monday.' Sophie was on the phone to Clyde. 'I'll be home straight after.'

'Why not now? The man is dead. No need for you to stay.'

'There's every need. Charles Beaufort was kind to me and to my family. I must show my love and respect for him, surely you can see that?'

'What about your love and respect for me?'

'As soon as the service is over I'll take the next flight back.'

'And what happens meanwhile? One milord down does the new incumbent get automatic *droit de seigneur* or has he already bitten that tasty little cherry.'

'I'm going to put the phone down. '

'Don't put the phone down.'

'Don't talk to me like that then.'

'Don't put the phone down! Don't ever put the phone down on me! I don't like people doing that. It is bad manners and I don't care for bad manners.'

'Then don't be cruel. You've no need to be. If I could be in two places at once I would. I owe Charles Beaufort and mean to pay the debt.'

'Thinking of debt you might consider what is owed to me, your husband.'

'If it's a question of love, honour, and forsaking all others until death I think you'll agree that particular debt is paid.'

'You are referring to Emilia.'

'Emilia's situation is difficult. There are others who aren't so compromised.'

'Compromised? What do you mean by that?'

'That little black book you once so gallantly threw away.'

There was a pause and then. 'You'd better go. We'll talk when you get back. You'll be pleased to know Emilia is well. In fact she's here.' Short conversation off phone. 'She says to say she can't sleep in the cottage. It smells of paint.'

Sophie didn't ask where Emilia slept. She didn't care.

'Tomorrow we're looking at cars,' said Clyde. 'As she works for you now, au pair to our unborn children, she'll need a runabout. I thought a Corvette. I saw one the other day, red with leather trim. What do you think?'

'Do what you think best.'

'We don't want her compromised. Can't have her tied to a kitchen sink. As employers we need be as Caesar's wife, above reproach, don't you think?'

Sophie replaced the phone. She has never felt so alone. Rootless, she doesn't know where to go or what to do. With Uncle Charles gone another anchor is withdrawn and hope of future visits to the Abbey dashed by the new Earl's icy demeanour. John Beaufort – one can't call him Johnny now – bears a heavy burden. He needs someone to stand by him. Gossip columns show him with Amanda Beresford, the show jumper. She seems nice. Let's hope it lasts.

~

The funeral is due to start any minute.

'Are you managing, Sophie?' said Julia.

'Just about. And you?'

'I shall be glad when it's over. He suffered a great deal toward the end and Mother because of it. I was going to ask if you would take care of Nanny. I'm not sure Mrs Allen can cope today. But you do look rather fragile.'

'I'm fine. I'm glad to help.' Sophie hasn't told anyone else about Ethan. No point. He is her grief. They have their own. Minding Nanny is a fulltime job. Just getting her to the right seat in the chapel takes all one's energy.

No sooner was she seated than Joshua down from Harrow squeezed in beside them. 'You look terrible, Sis.'

'Thank you very much.'

'You know what I mean, beautiful but frayed.'

'I've been rather busy. How are you?'

'I'm okay. Sad about Charley but I was prepared. Dad told me it would happen.'

'Of course he did. How's school?'

'It's fine. I have a couple of close buddies. They're coming down after the funeral. Needless to say they're both gagging to meet you.'

'I would love to stay to meet them but as usual dashing away.'

Grey eyes searching, Joshua nodded. 'You know, if you're not happy you can always come with us. Julia would be cool about it.'

'Thank you. It's good to know that.'

Joshua grinned. 'Is it true you're giving me the Bentley?'

'I don't know. Maybe you'd better ask your dad.'

'Well, you don't need it and it's no good in London rusting away.'

'There's no rust. It's in mint condition as you well know.'

Milly Warren's chap has a wedding-car business, the Bentley being the star of the show. When taking over the lease of the Bayswater flat he offered a deal – when Sophie is in London the car is hers, when not he uses it for weddings.

She will give it to Joshua. Tim has the Beagle. The girl that flew planes and drove a Bentley no longer exists.

'You okay?' Joshua's hand wrapped about hers.

She nodded. 'I see Tim didn't make it.'

'You know him, West Point before all else.' He got to his feet. 'Up you get, Sis,' he whispered. 'Charley's here.'

'*I am the resurrection and the Life* …'

The coffin was borne into the chapel on the shoulders of six men, John Beaufort up front with Gabriel, a pair of willowy cousins supporting the centre, and the twins, Simon and Sebastian Farrell, at the rear. The coffin on a trestle and service begun John Beaufort took up a position in the family pew with Gabriel and Julia. The Farrells squeezed into the pew behind Sophie.

Joshua likes the twins. He turned and with sad smile gave them thumbs up.

Seeing them here was a shock to Sophie. She hadn't known them to be pall-bearers. She had thought Sebastian to be in Colorado burying Ethan.

Mindful of Lady Joanna's frailty the service was brief, no eulogies or list of achievements. Charles wouldn't want it. He'd say if people didn't know him while he was alive why bother now he's dead. As the coffin lowered into the crypt they sang his favourite hymn. An old-fashioned tub-thumper it always seemed at odds with an urbane man, but he loved it. Sophie can see him now on Sundays his head thrown back and face alight with faith.

'Oh that old rugged cross, despised by the world,
has a wondrous attraction for me, for the dear
Lamb of God left his glory above to bear it to Calvary.'

She didn't mean to weep. Her tears were for Uncle Charles, yet also a flag-draped casket somewhere in Colorado.

~

After the service they gathered in the Sheraton Drawing Room. Sophie was anxious to leave but couldn't get a flight until later in the week. She slipped out to the orchid house. Opening the door she was hit by a wave of heat. Easy to see Charles hasn't been able to get around, the orchids are fine but the more fleshy plants dry. Taking a bottle she began to mist leaves.

Ten minutes and John pushed through the door. 'Deep in thought, Sophie?'

'Just considering the future.'

He took up another bottle and began spraying with her. They stood side-by-side, Sophie hunting for conversation. 'Amanda seems nice.'

'She is.'

'I hear she swims with dolphins as well as show jumping.'

'She does.'

'That must be fascinating. I understand they are very bright creatures, as much, if not more brain mass than men and women.'

'You don't need brain mass to be brighter than men and women.'

'I suppose. Have you known Amanda long?'

'Long enough.'

'Is it a serious relationship?'

'Is that any business of yours?' He carried on spraying. 'Well?' he said. 'Isn't this where you say no need to be rude, you were only making conversation?'

'There is no need and I was making conversation.'

'Well don't! Not if it's to do with relationships! You can ask how much money I stand to inherit and if I'm to play Tarzan in a new series. You can ask if the tear in my left shoulder is holding or will I need surgery. You can even ask if it's true Pa left a hole in my heart bigger than any overdraft, but you can't ask of my love-life, not since you made it clear you want no part in it.'

Sophie took a tray from the fridge, chipping ice for the orchids. She kept silent, nothing she could say.

'I waited for a call,' he continued. 'You didn't phone and when you did visit it was when I was filming. I'm thinking don't pressure, she'll make up her own mind. What happens? I pick up a paper and read – 'Virginia beauty to wed.''

'I don't think it was quite like that. I wrote and told you. As for my wedding you refused my invitation on account of your father being ill.'

'I would've refused anyway. I couldn't have borne to see you with that man. And don't nit-pick! You should've told me long before,'

'I chose not to.'

'Yes, because you are afraid of your husband.'

'Why would I be afraid of Clyde?'

'I don't know, maybe because he's a psychopath!'

'Don't be absurd.'

'I hope I am being absurd because if not then you're in trouble.' He spread his hands. 'How could you do it? We made love! I deserved an explanation if only to say it's payback? You had a legitimate axe to grind but I did think you'd forgiven me or least respected my feelings for you.'

'I did and I do.'

'That's not how it feels. Why him? And don't tell me it's love because it can't be and look the way you do. You were unhappy last time we met but now, you're empty.' He threw the spray aside. 'Empty as this bottle! I don't know what's going on but feels to me like you're submitting to blackmail.'

'What are you saying? Such arrogance! Do you really believe I'd marry a man I dislike because you misused me one night?'

'Wow, that's says it all. You don't love the guy or even like him!'

'That's enough John! I'm not discussing my marriage with you. I'm here to pay my respects to your father not to open old wounds.'

'Seems to me they were never closed.'

'Maybe not,' she snapped. 'That night did rather dent my soul.'

'What did I tell you? You haven't forgiven me.'

'I have forgiven you. You haven't forgiven yourself.' Fingers numb and heart even more so she carried on chipping the ice. 'I don't know why I'm listening to you. Good or bad my life is none of your concern.'

'That's it,' he hissed. 'Retreat behind secrets and your feathers and your furs. Stride the catwalk! Lie to your followers, tell them they worship a human being instead of a heartbreaking bitch lethal as any ice-pick!'

He snatched the ice-pick cutting her hand in the process and then slammed out, leaving her nursing a hand as well as her heart.

'Damn it,' she whispered. 'That hurts.'

Hand bleeding, she tried to unfold a hanky but couldn't manage.

'Hold on!' Sebastian wrapped a handkerchief about her hand. 'You'll get blood on your clothes.' Seeing he'd walked in on a private conversation Seb was turning away when Beaufort's hectoring tone stopped him. Fool of a guy; is that any way to tell a woman you're crazy about her?

'I don't know why I'm so upset,' said Sophie. 'It's only a tiny cut.'

'Yeah tiny,' said Sebastian softly, 'a mile deep and a mile wide.'

'I need to get out.' A blind creature she headed for the door.

'I'll come with you.' Tucking her hand through his arm they set out. They trudged through the snow. They were gone for a mile or so when he saw she needed to rest. 'We should go back. You're not dressed for this.'

The question was in her eyes. Sebastian rehearsed question and answer all the way from the airport to the Abbey. He's not good with lies. It's a family joke you always know when Seb was lying his lips were stuck together. He didn't want to lie to anyone but under promise has no choice.

'I thought you'd be in Colorado,' said Sophie.

'It was a private funeral, close family only.'

'Did Ethan have family? I thought there was only a Grandmother.'

Sebastian shrugged. 'These things are how people want them.'

Puzzled for the man she loved she shook her head. 'I hear horrible things about him, how he bungled a mission, and if not that then of him betraying his buddies. I don't understand any of it.'

Caught in the jet-stream of her eyes Sebastian held his ground. Chinese whispers growing to gossip and from gossip to myth, he's heard it all but has no defence to offer. What he did say was trite. 'The Lieutenant was a good man. He did the best he could under difficult circumstances.'

'How did he die?'

'He took a round in the chest. We got him out. Medivac did their best but…'

For a time she continued to stare and then abruptly switched topics.

'Are you going on this expedition in search of Snow Leopards?'

'Expedition?' It was so complete a switch Sebastian was taken aback.

'The trip I hear Joshua talking about?'

'Is it going to happen? Listening to John I got the feeling it was more a fund-raising gag than anything serious.'

'Is it dangerous? I don't like the idea of Joshua doing anything silly.'

'I'm sure he won't, not if Sir Gabriel is involved. I can't imagine him letting his boy do anything foolish.'

Hearing Joshua referred to as Gabriel's boy was a jolt. It was the first time outside the family Sophie had heard it said. Something of what she felt must have shown in her face because Sebastian apologised.

'I didn't mean to offend. I thought the relationship common knowledge.'

'It maybe knowledge but within my family hardly common.'

'I'm sorry.'

'No, Sebastian, it's me who should be sorry. People aren't blind. They know what their eyes tell them.' She took his arm. 'It's time we got back. Thank you for the comfort and your honesty.'

~

That night, unable to sleep, she went to the pool. The lights were on, Sue Ryland leisurely putting through the water.

'Hey!' Sue paddled toward her. 'How was my daughter when you saw her?'

'She seemed cheerful.'

'She should be! Did you ever think that trash *Shout* would be such a hit? I guess it got her noticed. What are you doin' these days?'

'Much of the same.'

'Maybe you should try for a change. You don't look so hot.'

'And how do I look?'

'Like you've no reason for livin'. You need to sort your life out, Sophie Hunter! Go home and get rid of your hangers-on.' Sue got out of the pool and strolled away. 'And if you can't let go of the past at least forgive it!'

Sick of people telling her how she looks, Sophie dove into the pool. Can't they see she's trying to do her best? Furious, she cut through the water, length after length, hitting the edge and flipping back. Up and down, burning with rage, until she saw she was not alone, an Otter swam alongside.

Head down, she kept going. Metre after metre and the Otter with her, ten, twenty, thirty lengths, his sleek form scything through the water, except the water in which he swam was sunny and salty not heavy in chlorine.

On-and-on, until unable to bear it, 'why are you here?' she cried, her voice bouncing off the walls. 'Why isn't it over and done and you buried in the ground? I mean, for God's sake, you're dead aren't you!'

The Otter melted away leaving an echo. '*…aren't you… aren't you?*'

Chapter Twenty
Headstones

It's a long way to Colorado but sick of airports, and in desperate need of closure, Sophie's driving there. She's taking Emilia's car. More Chinese dragon than automobile, the Corvette is scarlet paint and shiny bumpers, the same kind of bait Bobby used when trawling the waterfront.

Sophie needs to get to the Centre to settle the dozen feral cats brought in yesterday – and just like wild cat, with Clyde away, Emilia creeps softly following Sophie everywhere. It's a difficult situation for both women made more by him one moment treating Emilia as drudge and the next as his tart.

'You go Paws today, Mamselle?'

'Yes and I'm away tomorrow for the weekend so you'll be on your own.'

'What will I do?'

'Same as you have been doing I imagine. Emilia, I'd sooner you didn't run my bath or take up my clothes. You're not here to be my maid. You're here to find a job and a place to live and hopefully to be happy.'

'I stay with you and Mister Clyde and be happy.'

'No.'

'Why not?'

'You know why.'

Emilia stuck out her lip. 'Then I stay at Centre with dogs and live in kennel.'

Sophie shrugged. 'You could do worse. Anyway, from now on please stick with my name and not Mamselle.'

'But you are Mamselle Perfidia. My name is Emilia Kaina Sabri. I take oath soon and become Yankee.' She shot away returning with a copy of the Oath of Allegiance. 'Mister Clyde say practice.' Hands twisting together, every word a weight on her tongue she read, '*I hereby declare, on oath, that I absolutely and entirely renounce...?*' She paused. 'What mean renounce?'

'You need to see a lawyer.'

'No lawyers!' Emilia snatched the paper back. 'Mister Clyde fix it.'

'It's not a question of fixing things. You can't expect citizenship by right.'

'Mister Clyde fix it. He fix everything. He good man! No devil.'

Sophie set her jaw. 'Mister Clyde is away.'

'You all go and I alone!' wailed Emilia.

'I suppose you could come with me.'

Sophie has to go to Colorado. Remember me was the last thing Ethan said. If dreams and visions of Otters are witness to his words then she'll never forget. Clyde's not alone in night terrors – now they both tremble.

Clyde hates his job and it seems with good reason. After he left for Saigon she found a bundle of newspaper cuttings relating to a CIA Programme under investigation: '*Another Mai Lai?*' screamed the headlines. '*Villagers tortured. Women and children murdered. Nixon demands details.*' There was a page of the Greeley Tribune, Ethan's death sandwiched between the birth of a baby and an ad for a lawn-mower There was also a cutting from a San Diego newspaper featuring Ethan's widow, remarried, she and her two children smile into the camera under the heading, '*Time Heals.*'

Clyde never leaves papers lying about. Sophie was meant to find this. Thousands of miles away and yet he's still calling the shots

~

'Hello there, Mizz Sophie.'

She was knee-deep in pig poop when the General called.

'I'm afraid you've rather caught me in a mess.'

He shrugged. 'Not too fuss. It's like I say to Mrs J when any of our animals miss a cue, a critter has to do what a critter has to do.'

'Indeed. Wait while I wash my hands and we'll go into the house.'

'I'm okay here out in the open. No electronic ears to the wall.'

Sophie wiped her hands. 'Is this about Clyde?'

'It's more about you.' The General gazed around. 'I like what you're doing here. This is a good place you're runnin'. And that's a nice Alsatian. What's his name, Hokey? I wouldn't mind a mutt like that.'

They walked the compound. 'Your pa would've liked this place. Straight man, if I had a gripe I tell him straight and he tell me. I'd like to think we could do the same.' When Sophie didn't comment he continued. 'There was a time when I thought you might hook up with a young SEAL friend of mine called Winter.'

Sophie dropped the pail. 'You knew Ethan?'

'Uh-huh. His pa was a buddy.'

'I didn't know.'

'At the time it didn't seem important to tell because you was doin' okay, but then Winter up and married another gal.'

'There was that.'

'I was surprised when you married Forrester. I figured it a rebound thing. Dumped, it's natural to bite back and the Commander is a pin-up kinda guy.'

Anger snapped and words rushed out. 'I didn't marry on the rebound. I thought very carefully about it and I can tell you it has nothing to do with pin-ups! It was about being afraid for others and remembering what my mother went through. They say lightning doesn't strike in the same place twice but it does! It can strike on and on until you don't know whether you're coming or going. The things I could tell you! Things I've seen and I hated to see! And I have to say I blame you for it, General.'

'Me? What did I do?'

'You got me into the Remote Viewing Program. You opened doors that should've stayed shut.'

'Is that so?'

Afraid to say more she shook her head. A four star General, and a superb tactician, Sam Jentzen let the silence grow. He sighed. 'Your Pa was a whiz at Remote Viewing, night and day fetchin' intel out of nothin'. He reckoned everyone could do it but not everyone should. Do you think it genetic?'

'I hope not. I wouldn't want a child of mine worried by it.'

'I was your pa's buddy as well as his CO. I knew of your mom's situation, that she came to the States on a promise that turned out a pack of lies.'

'It wasn't all lies,' said Sophie. 'Looks are deceiving. Bobby Rourke may have been ill and unhappy but he did try to be a good man.'

'I never supposed it one sided. It takes two to tango. Me and Mrs J have battle scars. We lost one of our boys at Iwo Jima and another afore he was born. Tragedy makes you question things. She tosses stuff at me and I toss it back, reasons for goin' and reasons for stayin', but nothing about bein' afraid.'

'I didn't say I was afraid.'

'You said you were afraid for others. You intimated obligation. But you're right about looks being deceiving. Take a man like Clyde, savvy and super quick on the draw. Calm on the outside but what goes on beneath. Is it a case of still waters or do rivers run so deep anyone attemptin' to cross will drown?'

'I won't discuss Clyde. He's not here to defend himself.'

'Does he need defendin'?'

'I'll not be disloyal.'

'I should hope not. A wife should defend her man, gettin' between him and rumours, because you know there are rumours.'

'I know. I read some of it yesterday in the Washington Post.'

The General spat. 'That's Nixon and his yellow-belly cronies pullin' the rug from under honest warriors. It's bull-shit, if you'll pardon my French. It's some dirt-bag suggesting we appease enemies of United States! It's political wragglin', a pissin' contest, excuse my French again, between the NSC, FBI, the CIA, and every other goddamn acronym this side the Adirondacks, and it ain't the rumour I'm referrin' to.'

'What then?'

'Intimidation on the home-front is what I'm talkin' about -cave-man tactics as Mrs J calls it, keep 'em pregnant in the kitchen and a gal on the side. I met a young lady earlier when I called. Pretty gal, foreigner, says she's your maid.'

'I don't have a maid.'

'That's what I thought.'

'General? This investigation? Is Clyde in trouble?'

'Your husband signed up to a cause that takes no prisoners. If things go wrong, and it's a job where things are meant to go wrong, he'll get no back-up. What is right today is wrong tomorrow and those doing right out in the cold.'

'He is my husband. I shall do my best for him.'

'That's as well because whether we like it or not he lays his life on the line for his country every day of the week. No rest for what he does.'

'So I've noticed. Excuse me, I'm away this weekend and have a lot to do.'

'I'll be on my way. You dancin' some place?'

'I'm going to Colorado.'

'Colorado!' He frowned. 'Why there?'

'I feel I need to.'

He was gone. 'Thank you, Mizz Sophie. You've eased my mind.'

Lucky him! His visit did nothing for Sophie. She stooped to pick up a pail, the Gate opened, a train whistle blew and a man was pushed under a train – the hands that pushed were Clyde's and the man under the train was also Clyde.

~

The cemetery in Greeley was huge, moss-covered monuments toppling together like the ruins of Carthage. But for a gardener she wouldn't have found the grave. Even then she doubted it. Such a narrow slot! Ethan Winter took up so much of her world he surely occupies a similar space in preparation for the next. 'Are you sure this is his?' she asked the gardener.

'It has the number.'

'Lieutenant Ethan Winter the Third, Navy SEAL?'

'Don't know about no Navy SEAL. Nobody knows about them. But I know this is marked as another lady came looking.'

'An old lady?'

The gardener nodded. 'Older than most sleeping here.'

Mrs Powell it had to be. Poor Granny! What a shock to lose her grandson and find him here. But then Sophie realised that couldn't be so. His grandmother wouldn't need to ask of his grave, she would've been here for his burial.

It was in a corner against a hedge. Her parent's plot is always neat and with fresh flowers. This was abandoned before it was dug. Sophie brought a sprig of lilac from her bridal bouquet but there doesn't seem to be a flower holder.

'This any use?' The gardener offered a jam-jar.

'Thank you. I'd assumed a holder.'

'Where the dear departed are concerned it don't pay to assume anything. Them that love come again to mourn. The weepers and shriekers never come they pay their duty to the lawyers.'

'Did you dig this grave?' said Sophie.

'No or I'd have shored-up the edges. It shouldn't be here. It was nipped in on the quiet though it's not a bad spot. The hedge is hawthorn and will keep a body dry and gofers away. Dig that bit of lilac in and it may root.'

Sophie was doubtful. 'You think it might?'

'Plants are funny. If they like a place they take even when wilted.' He took the piece. 'Leave it with me I'll see to it.'

Sophie sat on the grass. The gardener is right. A warm day shaded by the hedge and a blackbird singing, it is peaceful. Emilia doesn't care for graveyards. Slot-machines in the hotel and twenty dollars in change, she's happy.

Daddy Bobby was right about hustlers. Sophie did think Emilia the helpless victim. How naive is that? Whose car is that in the parking lot? And who for the last year lived rent free in Paris and now does the same in Virginia?

Yesterday they started out at six in the morning. It was gone ten in the evening before they reached the hotel. Hundreds of miles of freeway and Emilia complaining all the way: 'I am thirsty. Give me dollars. I am hungry. I see Cowboy boots! You give me dollars and I buy!'

Helpless, hah! She'll outlive them all.

Sophie was about to leave when an elderly lady hurried down the path, a neat little body in polished shoes and hand-knitted cardigan, it can only be Granma Powell.

Out of breath from hurrying she came at Sophie. 'I know you. You're the girl my grandson wrote to.'

'That's right. I'm Sophie.'

'What you doing here?'

'I came to pay my respects. I wanted to tell you how sorry I…'

Mrs Powell cut across her. 'Go away!' she said.

'I beg your pardon?'

'Go away!' The old lady flapped her hands. 'Shoo! He wouldn't want you here!'

Shocked, Sophie stared. 'Why wouldn't he?'

'He just wouldn't.'

'How do you know that?'

'Because he told me! He said as much afore he died!'

Sophie ran to the car but was shaking so much she stalled the engine.

'Missy?' There was a rap on the window. The gardener poked a piece of paper through the gap. 'The old woman says sorry. She didn't mean to hurt you and would you call at this address after six.'

'I couldn't. Not after that.'

The gardener nodded. 'She probably didn't mean to be fussy. Some folks can't handle grief. Go, Missy. You need to know what it's about.'

So many unanswered questions she was unable to stay away and after six followed directions to Blue Farm, Mrs Powell waiting at the gate.

'That's some fancy car you got.'

'It keeps overheating.'

'Beauty is as beauty does.' They entered the kitchen. 'You caught me baking so must excuse the mess.' There was no mess. The farmhouse was like the woman, sharp and shiny. Mrs Powell offered tea and then began slapping dough around and Sophie with it. 'You married that navy chap then. I saw your picture in the paper. Does he treat you well?'

'Of course.'

'What's he doing now?'

'Serving in Vietnam.'

'Is he by Gar!' Mrs Powell nodded grimly. 'Well, he'll know all about it then won't he.'

More Assault Course than chat, for the next hour Mrs Powell offered opinions on everything but the man closest to their hearts, no mention either of his widow and child. Despite the many photographs on the mantle – Ethan smiling across the room – only once did his name come close to being spoken.

'We lost my man in '61 with a cold on his chest. Et…the boy loved his Granpa, there was no comforting him. Won't be that way for me! If I were to catch a cold I wouldn't fight not with no one here to weep for me.'

Every gesture suggested the old lady would sooner be alone. A plate of biscuits offered, Sophie reached out and the plate withdrawn.

She got to her feet. 'I'd like to buy a headstone.'

'You'll do no such thing! It's none of your business. You're not family.'

'But surely…?'

'Headstone indeed!' Mrs Powell's eyes snapped. 'D'you think I need reminding of my kin? Do I need some bit of concrete to keep 'em safe in my heart? My memories go deep. Don't matter where they are, heaven or hell, this world or the next, I know their names and am not ashamed.'

'No indeed. Why would you be?'

'There's some need reminding. I didn't see you shedding tears at the grave. You bought flowers and a pretty face but did you bring a broken heart?'

It was too much. Sophie was out the door when Mrs Powell called her back.

'Would you like to see his room?'

They climbed the stairs. The door opened. It was the boy and the man from the space-ship drapes at the window to a star-spangled bedcover.

Unable to breathe, Sophie crouched down. 'There now.' A rheumatic hand patted her shoulder. 'So you did care for my poor boy. He said you did.'

The door closed. Alone, Sophie lay on the bed. Where the sun shone through the window the cover was warm as though a living body lay here. This is where he is, not that cemetery. Other people are under that sod. He is here among the loose ends of childhood with movie posters on the walls and textbooks on the shelves. It's here she can grieve for herself and for his hopes.

It was then she saw the black shellac box. It sat on the dresser, had it been scarlet with a neon sign X marks the spot it couldn't have called louder.

It was full of letters, her letters, years of a girlish hopes and dreams. His are hidden away in the Mill-tower in a *Dairy Milk* chocolate box.

January 12, 1951 dates the first letter. It was addressed to Ethan's mother, Lieutenant Jane Winter, 4th MASH Field Unit, Korea. He was alive when Sophie wrote it, as were her parents, and May, and Uncle Charles, all alive!

The box back on the dresser she went downstairs.

Mrs Powell was in the kitchen still pounding dough.

'Did you see all you wanted?' she said.

'Yes, thank you.'

'Will you come back?'

'No.'

'And the grave?'

Ah, poor lady! There was fear in the question.

Sophie hugged her. 'Why would I worry about a grave when he's not there? It's as you said, he is in my heart safe and warm. It's where I'll keep him.'

Chapter Twenty-One
Bitty Bits

The Deputy Director smiled. 'I get your concerns, Commander. Being away from home puts a strain on any marriage. Our wives, God bless 'em, have to compensate for spouses on the end of a phone. It's difficult especially with children to consider. You and Mizz Forrester haven't been blessed.'

Clyde yawned. 'No, no blessings.'

'Statistics show the early years of a childless marriage prove problematic especially when one half of the partnership works away. Your wife travels too, doesn't she? Myself, I don't buy into that. If a marriage is strong, distance is no distance, equally, five years or fifty if it's rocky it's rocky.'

CA kid was kicking a dog against a wall. Clyde stuck his head out the window. 'Do that one more time and it's you hitting the wall! *Di-di mau*! Clyde tossed a coin. 'Get me a cold beer.' He turned back to the Director and his statistics. 'I'm not here to discuss my marriage. I want time out.'

'As I said, I'd like to oblige but the situation as it is, everyone trying to plug a hole, I can't afford one of my best men off-line.'

'I'm not going off-line. I need time out. I'm beat.'

'We're all beat but until there's an order to pull out we follow the program.'

'There is no program,' said Clyde wearily. 'There never was. People don't know who to trust. We can't rely on interpreters because we don't know who we're talking to. Officials are taking bribing factions to settle old scores, in consequence hoodlums knock on doors in the night, hold a gun to a guy's head, take turns with the wife and daughter before shooting him and setting fire to the village. If that's a program it's of mass murder and a disgrace.'

'The program has inbuilt weaknesses but has also had successes.'

'Do you have statistics on these successes, Deputy Director, I mean dates, times, facts and figures? Because if you do mail me a copy so that when I'm hauled up before the Senate and questioned about the *program* I can satisfy them, if not myself, that the last years of my life haven't been wasted.'

The DD shuffled papers. 'The 1970 End of the Year Report states the degree of success in the counter-insurgency effort is directly related to the Phoenix Program and that statistics...' Clyde switched him out. When a fool starts to believe his own lies walk away before you start believing yours.

As he said to Grizz Hamilton, 'his loyalties are to the Pentagon. We're just so much throwaway.'

Grizz sipped beer. 'Calm down, Clyde. You're letting it get to you.'

'Isn't it getting to you?'

'Sure! I hate every second I'm here.'

'Then why so cool?'

'I'm not cool, I'm broke! None of us will come out of this smelling good. I've a wife and baby back home and an overdraft and must look to myself.'

'Damn nerve of the guy!' grated Clyde. 'He has his own personal boom-boom girl and gets his rocks off every night yet gives me marital advice!'

'It's what he does to throw us off track, works on our weaknesses.'

'Since when did my marriage become my weakness?'

'Maybe weakness is the wrong word.'

'What is the right word?'

'Don't bite my ass!' snapped Grizz. 'You want a word? Try paranoid! Tapping wires and checking her every move! If I did that my wife would've booted me out years ago.'

'I'm not paranoid. I'm concerned. '

'Concerned, my ass! It's a wonder you haven't got her caged and a tray of food under the door. I don't know how she stands it.'

'You don't have to know. It's none of your business.'

'Sure, but you asked! For a smart man you do dumb things. You want her to love you yet bring a whore into the house. How dumb is that. You've given Sophie and her lawyer every which way out. But then maybe that's what you wanted. Sick of trying you'd sooner get out.'

'That's not what I want.'

'Then cut her and yourself some slack. Your marriage is not over and neither is this war. Both are highly volatile and the way you're going with your boozy kerb-crawls you're likely to get yourself, me, and Sophie, killed.'

Grizz tossed the beer can and walked.

This job is getting to them all. Almost everyone on the station is high on amphetamines or grass. It would be easy for Clyde to do that, sail through the remains of the war with a shit-eating grin on his face. He doesn't pop pills, smoke grass, or kerb-crawl. He drinks.

Sophie's step-father was a drunk who, according to local legend, hid out in the turret. At times that unhappy spirit settles over Clyde. Then he gets a drift of how the guy screwed up his life – it's like looking in a mirror.

~

Sophie was with Daniel Culpepper. 'I ought not to have married Clyde.'

Daniel looked over his spectacles. 'And have you said as much to him?'

'How can I? While he's away my hands are tied.'

'But for his pride your hands would be even more tied. Had he agreed to the transfer of property your marriage would still be a mistake and you'd be saying goodbye to a great deal of money.'

'I'm not concerned about the money.'

'Then you should be!' Daniel lost his temper. 'A lot of consideration went into the making and preserving of it. Your parents wanted you to live as you desired. It's why they drew up a trust fund. They loved you and your brothers and wanted you safe. It's not for you to cast that love aside. I told you passing the inheritance wouldn't do. You should be grateful for the Commander's pride. But for that you'd have nothing to care nothing about.'

~

Sophie's working out in the turret room. It's peaceful
there, one can see over the trees to the Eyrie chimney-pots.
The house is still empty. What is it about these two that no
one stays? She did think of buying the Eyrie but chose not
to spoil yesterday's memories with today's sorrows. Now
unloved it returns to a former state, cracked glass in the
orangery and wisteria rooting under the tiles.

The Mill holds onto memories. The turret room is all
Daddy Bobby. In the old days a sofa stood by the window
piled with copies of Rose Grower's Weekly, empty beer
bottles and a rubber duck brought from England.

The day she moved back to the Mill she found the duck
wedged under a radiator. Not wanting to be reminded of
the past she threw it into the bin. Yesterday she heard the
squeaker. She looked up and there reflected in the mirror
was the sofa and a figure materialising through early sun.

It was Clyde. Hands knotted together and lock of dark
hair on his forehead he sat as Bobby sat squeezing the duck.
Horrified, she watched until the figure wavered and
dissolved. It was gone but not before she felt his loneliness.

~

There's a fashion show in Richmond in aid of War
Widows. It's too close to home for comfort but
approached by General Jentzen's wife she could hardly
refuse. The Mall centre stairs and escalator are used as
walkways. The background music is deafening, Sophie can
barely think – not that thinking is required – Space Woman

from Venus, white leather bodice and thigh boots, hair in a thousand plaits wound with gold, a Ray Gun in one hand and a Borzoi hound in the other, she just needs to stay upright.

One more turn wearing an even more bizarre outfit and she's away. Pro bono work, all profits to the fund, Cecile Brune means to squeeze the last drop of blood from the stone. 'Hold that costume. We've time for a couple of shots!'

'Five minutes and then I must go,' said Sophie.

'Okay, then five minutes. Oh, and this is for you!' Cecile tossed a posy of white lilac through the air. 'I've been carrying it around since the last shoot.'

It is always the same florist, 'Forget-me-Knot'. Ethan Winter – supposing it is him – must have left a standing order. Back home she picked up the phone. But then afraid of what she might hear let it go – better flowers from the dead than none at all.

~

Joshua called. 'Hi, Sis.'

'Hello, Josh. This is a nice surprise.'

'You being sarcastic?'

'Why would I? It's good to hear from my brother if only once a blue moon.'

'I've been busy. How's Clyde?'

'How's Clyde!' Joshua never asks after Clyde. As far as he and Tim are concerned her husband doesn't exist. 'What do you mean?'

'He's in Vietnam, isn't he?'

'You know he is. Why are you asking?'

'No reason. I was thinking about him the other day and wondered if next time he's on R&R he might like to hook up with me and Dad. We could go fishing.'

'I'm sure he'd like that.'

'Okay good. See you then.'

'Josh, before you go! You don't send me flowers, do you?'

'What do you mean?'

'You or Tim, you don't send posies to the shows?'

'Why would we do that?'

'Indeed, why would you.'

Another call was from Simon Farrell's legal practice, Ethan's Granma died and left a bequest, 'could Sophie attend a reading of her Will.

'I can't,' she said to Clyde when he called. 'But I will go to the funeral.'

'Of course you will. You loved her grandson.'

She wouldn't deny it.

'They say he was a coward and led his men into a trap.'

'Who says?'

'It's the word among those who know.'

'Is it your word?'

'What makes you think I'm in a position to judge? I take people as I find.'

'And how did you find Ethan Winter?' Such a long silence, she could almost hear the wheels turning and information being processed, what to tell and what not. He switched into another gear.

'You went to see Culpepper today.'

For a moment Sophie thought him clairvoyant and then remembered General Jentzen's comment about wire tapping and knew that technology rather than the paranormal kept her husband abreast of the times.

'Emilia needed advice.'

'And what did Daniel advise?'

'He's drawn up a list of suitable employers.'

'And what would she be doing servicing grease monkeys off the oil rigs?'

'That was France. She doesn't have to do that now.'

'What else did Daniel suggest?'

'Oh, you know Daniel. He likes to be clear on everything.'

'Yes I know, Daniel. I seem to recall he wanted background checks on me but you told him not to bother. Why was that, dearest wife? Were you in a hurry to wed or concerned about what he might find?'

'I was concerned with you keeping your promise.'

'What promise is that?'

'Never to hurt anyone or anything of mine.'

'Oh, that promise!' He laughed. 'Hah!'

Sophie bit her lip. She should keep quiet. No point baiting. 'Josh sends his regards and says next time you're home maybe you-all could go fishing.'

'Say? My kid brother-in-law is offering a peace pipe?'

'It seems so. Will you accept it?'

'Sure why not. I've not so many friends I can turn one down.'

Clyde was pleased. She could tell. So what devil made her spoil the moment? Maybe the sight of Emilia swishing out the drive in the Corvette.

'And did you?'

'Did I what?'

'Keep your promise?'

A pause and then, 'will you ever know.'

~

The Deputy Director threw the pass at Clyde. 'You leave 0700 tomorrow.'

'I thought you said we were stretched.'

'And so we are.'

'So why suddenly am I let out the cage?'

The DD slammed the door. 'How should I know?'

Clyde packed a bag. 'So what do you reckon, Grizz?'

'I wouldn't get too excited. Five will get you ten it's an ex-filtration. A Company agent up the line is about to be busted. They need you to get him out.'

'You're probably right.' Clyde slung the bag over his shoulder and hustled before someone changed his mind. 'At least I'm out of here.'

'Yeah,' said Grizz, 'out the frying pan and into the fire.'

~

Another funeral! Is there no end to them? Life is so bitty!

Sophie took a plane – no way would she drive after the last effort. A hired car, she drove away. The service was the other side of town well away from the old cemetery. The church was full. She slipped inside and sat behind a pillar.

'You'll love, Granma,' Ethan had said. 'She's a bit like taffy, hard on the gums but sweet when you get to the root.'

It's certain the people of Greeley thought well of her. The vicar called her a pillar of the church, other mourners said she was the kindest woman, which made Sophie's experience the more inexplicable, that day being made to feel as though she'd offended Mrs Powell and the entire bloodstock line.

There was activity at the altar, Sebastian Farrell coming to the lectern.

Sophie was not surprised. She thought he might be standing in for Ethan.

He coughed and rattled a piece of paper. 'Good afternoon folks. My name is Sebastian Farrell. I'm here on behalf of my friend, Lieutenant Ja…!'

There was an odd moment when he paused, caught his breath, and started again. 'This is for my buddy Lieutenant Ethan Winter the Third. Since he can't be here to tell of his grandmother I thought you wouldn't mind if I did.'

He spoke of Ethan's love of his grandmother. The same build and rangy walk, same intensity of gaze, Sophie found it painful to watch and listen.

The service over, the cortege passed out of the church.

Sophie remained behind, head bent saying a prayer.

'You okay?' Sebastian was there.

She jumped. 'For a big man you make very little noise.'

He grinned. 'So my housekeeper keeps telling me. She says I need a bell about my neck then she'll know when I'm gonna pounce.'

'She is hoping you will pounce then.'

'It would seem so. Are you coming to the graveside?'

'Do you think I should?'

'I'm sure Ethan would like you there.' He offered his arm. They followed a pathway, the cortege stopping at a large plot.

Sophie stared. 'She's to be buried here!'

'Uh-huh. She was warden at this church.'

'Are his mother and father also here?'

'I reckon.'

'Why isn't Ethan with them?'

When Sebastian shrugged it was too much for Sophie. All eyes watching but she didn't care, and livid, turned on her heel. They were ashamed of him! Some damned piece of military bungling and they hide him away?

She tossed her flowers in a waste bin. She bought them for the old lady but she's not having them. She doesn't deserve them! What kind of person leaves her grandson alone like that?

'And she had the gall to question my loyalty!'

Sebastian caught her up. 'Don't leave like this.'

'I can't stay. It's too horrible.'

'No,' he held onto the door. 'Come back into the church.'

'How could they do it? Have you seen his grave?'

'I've seen it.'

'And do you think it right him tucked away among the weeds?'

'It's a grave, Sophie. It doesn't matter where it is.'

'Of course it matters! He shouldn't be among strangers. He should be here with his family and people who supposedly loved him.'

'Does he need that?'

'Maybe not but I do! His grandmother was horrible to me, Sebastian, really horrible. She accused me of not caring. And all the while… all the while…'

He pushed his hands in his pockets. 'I know it looks bad.'

'It's not about how it looks! It's about what's right!'

'Maybe, but it's done, and there's nothing you can do about it.'

'He doesn't have a headstone, a wooden stake with a number.'

'Do you need a stone to remind you of the man you loved?'

'That's what she said. "'Doesn't matter where they are, heaven or hell, this world or the next, I know them and won't be ashamed.''

'Are you ashamed of Ethan?'

'I didn't like him leaving me. No woman would. But that's nothing to do with this. I don't know what happened in Vietnam. I know what's being said but saying doesn't make it true.'

'No! It doesn't make this true either,' muttered Sebastian. 'Are you going to be okay? Would you like me to come home with you?'

'I'm alright.' She wiped her eyes. 'You don't need to bother.'

'It's no bother. I was coming to see you anyway. As you're here you'd better take this.' He offered a package. 'Simon gave me this. It's from Mrs Powell.'

'I don't want it.'

'Take it.' He put it in her hand. 'It was meant for you.'

'Is there a message?'

'Not that I know of but if there is I'm sure it would be along the lines of she hoped one day you'd understand.'

'I don't understand,' she wailed.

'I don't suppose you do. Go home, Sophie,' he slammed the car door. 'And don't come back! There's nothing here but heartache!'

She drove to the old cemetery. It was about to close, the same gardener locking the gates. 'You're closing?'

'There's time,' he said unlocking the gate 'Is it that same grave you want?'

'Yes, unloved and forgotten.'

'Don't know about unloved,' he said. 'There's many a soul strange to the world buried here but that don't mean they're unloved.' He walked with her. 'I'd better keep you company. It's late. I don't want you gettin' lost.'

'Do people get lost here?'

'All sorts of things get lost here. Folks lose their wallets and their jackets and keys to the front door.'

'Things,' said Sophie.

'And people, and memories, and lives too. See that?' He pointed to a stone-mausoleum. 'A couple of years back a lady got locked in.'

'Oh, poor thing! Was she found alright?'

'She didn't want to be found. They'd buried her husband in there. Fifty years they were together. She left a note, couldn't imagine life without him.'

'That is so sad.'

'They're together now. Ain't nobody keeping 'em apart.' The gardener hugged his chest. 'You won't stay long will you, Missy. It's not the place to hang about.'

'I'll be as quick as I can.'

He sniffed. 'Only there's no one alive in that grave, you know, just the cold clay. You do know that, don't you?'

'Yes, I do, thank you.'

Now she's here she didn't know why. Having tossed the flowers she's come empty-handed, offering nothing but regret.

It was cold and cloudy. She was chilled and hated this lonely place.

Then she saw the lilac.

'Oh!' The gardener had rooted the sprig. He'd made a cross of wooden stakes and bound the lilac about with raffia. He must have been watering it because though frail it was very much alive.

Sophie looked to thank him but couldn't find him. Such a kind and caring man! She shouldn't be afraid. Everyone here, including Ethan, is in good hands.

She left with a lighter heart. A tiny miracle, it meant so much seeing the lilac, like returning a living flower to a dead man.

Book Three.

This Is How It May Be.

Chapter Twenty-Two

The Ghost
Fort Belvoir, Virginia.

Sebastian shook his head. 'I don't care for the deception.'

'I'm not crazy about it myself,' said Jake. 'A new identity takes some getting used to. I'm still having trouble answering to another name.'

'I'm not talking about what's going on here!' snapped Sebastian. 'I'm talking Sophie. I get the initial cause, the dirty deal and all. You had to protect her against Forrester's psychotic itches. I was with you all the way on that, I still am, but looking her in the eye while denying you is making me a Judas!'

'I know and I'm sorry.' The locker emptied, Jake zipped the bag. He doesn't have much to pack – dead men don't have possessions. 'This probe into CIA activity in Vietnam has left a lot of guys twisting in the wind. Forrester's never been under so much scrutiny and doubly dangerous because of it.'

'I get that too but it still leaves me lying my ass off.'

Jake shrugged. 'A Navy Lieutenant by name of Jackson Frost can rotate to Virginia any time without drawing attention. Like his name he can vanish overnight. If Ethan Winter, a Navy SEAL with a score to settle deploys to a unit close by an ex-lover, then, according to general opinion the ex-lover's husband will see it a challenge. Right now a CIA hired gun sniffing out a covert operation is not what anyone wants. But show me another way and I'll do it.'

'When you say *general* opinion I guess you're referring to Jentzen.'

'The General was in deep with Pa. What brought him to the hospital I neither know nor care. Most folks had me on the way out, you included.'

'Hacker had you dead and buried before we dusted out.'

Jake smiled grimly. 'Oh ye of little faith!'

'You came through.'

'I'm grateful to whoever made that possible, including the General, who told me I could be of use to Special Ops *and* Sophie if the world thought me dead.'

'And so you died.'

'Don't tell me you wouldn't have done the same! Forrester thinks within his skin. On a clear night it's less than thirty minutes from Belvoir to the Mill. Do you really think he'd see my deployment as anything other than a threat?'

'He'd see it as he's meant to see it, the writing on the wall. Even so, I can't help thinking you're being set up.'

'I don't doubt it. To get what he wants Sam Jentzen will use whoever and whatever is available. Right now he's using me.'

'And you're okay with that?'

'I have no choice. I'm in Clyde Forrester's head. Dead or alive I'll always be a problem to him.'

'Do you plan to stay dead?'

'I am Jackson L Frost. The other guy is so dead he couldn't attend his grandmother's funeral.'

Sebastian smiled wryly. 'You know I almost slipped up in the church and called you by your new name.'

'Would anyone have known the difference?'

'Sophie would. Were you surprised she was at the funeral?'

'I would have understood if she stayed away. Gran was hard on her.'

'Yet she left Sophie a gift.'

'That wasn't Gran. That was me.'

'I guessed as much. I won't ask. I'm sure you know what you're doing, though I will ask how you know it's less than thirty minutes to the Mill.'

'Me and my best running shoes I timed it. Are you ready and packed?'

'Ready as I'll ever be. What's the ETA on the flight?'

'Fort Eglin at 1600 hours. After that it's sunny Hanoi. As far as I can tell the official rumour is the extraction of diplomats friendly to our cause. Though bullshit it's best we leave it that way. Look! They're rerunning Apollo 11.'

They stood watching TV footage of the moon landing. A maid shuffled in. She set a tray on the table and in so doing nudged the portable TV. 'Don't move the TV,' said Jake. She moved the TV whereupon he tossed it out the window.

'For a dead man you've a lively temper,' said Sebastian. 'What did you say to the poor woman?'

'I gave her a potted history of my life. I said, a US Space Cowboy is walking on the moon and but for the machinations of men I might've walked with him.'

'And all that in Yaqui Indian?'

'It was that maid that taught me. '

'And that's what brought Jentzen to the hospital, your usefulness to the cause, not your cute looks and preppy ways. You're a useful man to know, and sentiment, and friendship with your Pa, has damn all to do with it '

~

Jake went for a swim. The ocean is his refuge. Buoyancy eases aches and pains while allowing him to think. A marathon man, he runs for miles but with the identity change must stay close to the compound. At home in the Bay he thinks like Kingsley's Water Babies – one day he will die in water.

Three minutes and twenty-seven seconds flat line aboard the chopper, according to the medics he's dead already.

Yeah, he died, or rather Ethan Winter died. An NDE they call it, a near death experience. He remembers being shot, and evac'd out. He remembers the chopper beneath him and the drips attached to his veins, Medivac people, the smell of sweat and antiseptic, as real as the bullet in his chest.

There were others aboard the Huey that ought not to have been, Mom and Pa smiling fit to burst, and angels, so beautiful they might've stepped out of a Cathedral window.

He'd like to talk about that to someone but Navy SEALs don't speak of angels, not even to a best friend.

It took a bullet to recognise Seb Farrell's worth. Intel on the demise of EW3 is confined need-to-know. Seb was brought in as gofer navigating the hospital, Fort Belvoir, *and* Granma Powell. She had to be told. It was the one condition Jake made; not to go to her grave thinking her grandson preceded her.

Public info was minimal, two lines in the Greeley Gazette and a hole in a defunct cemetery, a formal service and military escort at the family grave rejected as too risky. Rumours were circulated, use made of the botched mission. Sam Jentzen was apologetic. 'I know this ain't right. That kind of mud on a man's name is enough to make him sink.'

The day Jentzen came to the hospital talking of multilingual skills and military counterintelligence Ethan Winter developed pneumonia. His battered body didn't give a shit for counterintelligence, Hacker's jittery finger killed off patriotism as well as flesh. That was when Jentzen, wily old goat, switched tactics, his words cutting through consciousness as a knife through flesh.

'I paid a visit to a friend of yours recently, Mizz Sophie Forrester. Hearin' rumours I was concerned for that lady. Seems the Commander is up to his old tricks, some foreign gal he imported to share the marital bed.'

Kaboom! The patient was alive and kicking. No need for CPR paddles!

'Rumour has it,' the General continued, 'when not dancing in her scanties Mizz Forrester is alone with a bunch of mutts in that wreck of a Mill. Shame you two didn't make it. I saw the picture in the paper and thought you hit gold. Then you married someone else. What were you thinkin' hitchin' your wagon to another when you could've had the classiest gal this side of heaven.'

Hours Jentzen played that line until the fish was dragged out of the Doldrums onto the bank. That's when he learned of the Dirty Deal.

'Why didn't you come to me?' he yelled. 'I'd have shot the asshole! No one would've cared. They'd have put it down to a KGB spook or a pissed-off husband.'

When asked if he thought Forrester would have carried out his threat Jentzen shrugged. 'Her life ain't exactly a bed of roses now. Best you die, son, and stay dead until you can settle the sonovabitch once and for all.'

So, Ethan Winter died, his body removed from the morgue to Fort Belvoir. A funeral of sorts took place at the old cemetery, a weighted box dug into the ground, three mourners in attendance, a four star General, a priest and a gardener. One man died another was born, Jackson L Frost, aka The Ghost.

~

Another day, another move, this time to USAF Fort Eglin in Florida; Jake met up with his new commanding officer who looked up from the notes. 'It's not so easy to shin over the wire here, Lieutenant. Save your energy for better use.'

'Yes, sir.'

'You knew it was expected of you?'

'I thought as much. It was a little too easy.'

'I see you started out as a space cadet. It must be hard coming to terms with this. All that early dreaming of flying to the moon, then the SEALs, now a bullet in the chest and you start again from nothing. Try to fit in. Speaking for myself I'm glad to have you aboard. I'm sure you'll prove invaluable.'

Ethan saluted and marched out. No! Jake Frost marched out. He mustn't even think his former name! If he's to survive he has to let go of FW3 heart and soul

Briefly panic gripped him. The suppression of self is harder than imagined. A polecat in a cage, it's okay when he's on exercise but when confined to barracks he feels he's going crazy.

Years of being his father's son and proud of it, this is difficult. Months pass and still he struggles. A shrink he sees on bi-weekly visits admits it isn't easy. 'You can leave your home,' he says, 'and burn family albums but the former man still remains. The only way to stay sane is to create a parallel self, a man who looks like you, thinks like you, but has another name and history.'

'And how am I supposed to do that?'

'Start by telling me about the dead man and what gave him pain.'

'I doubt you've the time or the Navy the dough for your fees.'

'Never mind my fees. That's not your concern.'

'Never mind your fees! What kind of shrink are you?'

'A well paid shrink. I found your case interesting. It has echoes of the past.'

'What some other poor sucker had to rebuild his life?'

'*Her* life actually. It was a lady I once had the honour of knowing.'

Other than to hint of personal involvement it's all he knows of Professor Jacob Feldstein. Cashmere sweater and butter-soft Italian loafers, the guy breezes into the hut, lights a cigarette, and smiles. 'How are you doing, Jake?'

'I'm angry.'

'You're angry?'

'Goddamn right I'm angry. I've been pissed upon every which way I turn.'

'You're angry with the wrong person.'

'Who should I be angry with?'

'Not your former self.'

'I thought you guys were into people taking responsibility for their actions.'

'So we are but blaming Ethan Winter won't help.'

'And calling me Jake will? Surely there's more to a man than a name.'

'Indeed Shakespeare said it, "a rose by any other name would smell as sweet."'

'And being Jackson L Frost will make me smell sweeter? Doc, seriously, isn't what you're telling me the biggest load of bullshit?'

'It may be bullshit but out there in the greater world there are people who only get by learning to adopt this bullshit.'

'Yes,' said Jake grimly. 'They're called the CIA.'

Feldstein smiled. 'You'll survive. You are aptly named.'

'Aptly named as in a kiddie's nursery book?'

'I must admit to being intrigued by the choice. It seems somewhat provocative. Why this name do you suppose?'

'I don't know. It's what I'm waiting to find out.'

As far as Special Warfare is concerned, his mission is to translate intercepted Chinese and Russian radio messages as to the whereabouts of American POWs in North Vietnam. Above and beyond that Jake's personal mission is to learn what's happening with Sophie and get her out. It's in the vow he made to Forrester: '…*give her pain I will look for you and I will kill you.*'

Twice now he's been within touching distance. The first time was at Belvoir. The camp was so close! He nipped over the wire and ran all the way. It was close to midnight when he got to the Mill. There she was, the radio playing a Beach Boys number and she painting an outhouse.

Green Man mode he'd crept to the door. Their weekend in Paris was full of magical moments; Sophie leaning over the balcony drying her hair, Sophie, skin like buttermilk adjusting the straps of her brassiere, Sophie eating cereal milk moustache along her lip, Sophie, eyes closed and languorous, her heart beating beneath his hand, and Sophie in lacy pants darkening her eyelashes. Absorbed in the task she leans into the mirror and then catching his eye, smiles. It is the smile you take to your grave yet compared to the living girl is nothing.

Now here she is splashing paint about! The need to take her in his arms was so strong he dug fingernails into his scars until, afraid to do more, he crept away.

The second time he saw her was in the old cemetery hiding behind a mausoleum. She was at his grave. Twenty minutes he crouched watching and was about to break cover when the Senior Citizen Cavalry headed up The Pass. 'I wanted her far away from you,' Granma said later. 'I knew you'd be here and was scared you'd do something foolish.'

It was he scribbled Granma's address and gave it to a gardener. 'Give it to that girl,' he said. 'Tell her to come and visit.' And it was Jentzen who called and said Sophie was coming to Colorado. At the time Jake was at Blue Farm, 48 hour undercover R&R. He checked hotel bookings and finding where she was staying watched and learned that she still cared for a dead man.

Knowing she cared made staying away more painful. As it was he did break cover, hiding a couple of items along with letters in a shellac box when Granma died. Sophie has the box. He prays one day she'll open it.

~

It's pedal to the metal this last month at Eglin. Night-after night they're out on live-fire training. Assault teams cram aboard HH-53 Jolly Green Giants. They wear the usual body armour and carry the usual Search and Rescue weaponry plus infra-red 'night-sights', Sears and Roebuck blow torches, bolt cutters and jars of baby food; the scuttlebutt is they're either about to rescue malnourished babies or unleash a herd of wildebeest.

They storm makeshift compounds and airlifted out are required to carry heavy equipment and/or another man, the intended target clearly considered too weak to carry themselves. There's lockdown on all Intel in and out. No one's saying it yet everyone is thinking it, the exercise is to rescue GI POWs.

Lieutenant J L Frost will be with them. Though uncomfortable with the name it's getting easier, he doesn't have quite so blank a stare these days when the roll is called. Jack Frost! Someone clearly thought they were being funny.

'A name like that,' he said to the General, 'you do realise guys will start calling me Ice-Man. That's a name associated with Ethan Winter. Don't you think Forrester will make the connection?'

The General had smiled. 'I'll be mighty disappointed if he don't.'

Everything Jentzen does has purpose. Jake's name, identity, papers, medical background and history all hand chosen yet if he was hoping for the Ice-Man tag he'll be disappointed, the Team have started calling him Ghost-Man.

His hair is white as any frost. It started going that way when he was shot. When he looks in the mirror he sees a stranger though the name-tag seems kinda fitting. It's what happens to a man when he dies.

~

Thursday, he got back from exercise around 2100 hours. A tough day, they had to run ten miles in combat gear and then swim a lake. By the time they hit base they were all exhausted. A mass of cuts and bruises Jake took a shower, stowed his equipment, fell on his bunk and slept. 11.59, he rolled out again and walked through a wall.

Yeah through a wall! It's called out-of-body travelling. That's an NDE and now walking through walls. Seb says it was a dream, that they were so beat up from the exercise they had no defences. If it was a dream it was like nothing ever dreamt before. Over he went, rolling on his left side, then up and out, punching a hole through a SEAL barrack room wall to a dog pen.

He'll never forget it! There he is suspended in a corner of a wire pen looking down. Sophie is in her pjs, a dog in her arms. Poor critter, it's shitting blood, poisoned, Jake seen something like when Mom's terrier ate snakeweed.

Sophie was upset and the dog howling in pain.

'Sophie!' Desperate to help he called her name, 'Sophie, I'm here!'

Though his voice echoed about the cage nobody heard…or so he thought, but then, as if walking through walls isn't weird enough an angel appeared.

It was the Dream Weaver from when he was shot, the big blond guy with wings, except he didn't have wings, he was wearing a tux and a black tie.

'No!' Sophie puts out a hand. 'Uncle Gabriel, don't come closer. There's nothing you can do and you'll get filthy.' The guy didn't give a damn for fine tailoring. He got on his knees and taking the Alsatian in his arms began to pray.

No words or hallelujahs only a dog whimpering and Sophie weeping.

The dog died and the man, angel -whoever or whatever he is – laid it down.

'Don't cry, honey,' he says, hanging his jacket about Sophie's shoulders. 'He ain't dead. He's born again and flyin'.'

The illuminated dial on the clock flashed 11.59- 1200 and Jake is back on his bunk sobbing. Okay, some aberration of the brain, the guy no more an angel than Jake, yet, the strangest thing, when he said that about reborn, he wasn't looking at Sophie! He was staring up; seeming to know Jake was there.

Those eyes held a message. As with all dreams the message was lost with the dawn yet Jake knows what he is meant to remember. Medics say it's natural to be depressed when wounded. That wasn't why he wept. He wept because of saying farewell to Mom, to Pa, and Gran and Gramps, and all memories of life at the farm. It was as the Dream Weaver said, from that day on Ethan Winter was truly dead and Jackson Frost reborn and flying.

Chapter Twenty-Three
A Poem

Sophie was breakfasting with Gabriel. He was speaking in Charlottesville yesterday and being late stayed over at the Mill. It's as well he did. Hokey died in the night of poisonous weed. 'Thank you for taking care of poor Hokey.'

'I laid him under the Spruce alongside Biffer.'

'Poor fellows had a lot in common. Both led miserable lives.'

Gabriel stirred his coffee. 'Thanks for lettin' me bunk down,' he said. 'I would've stayed at Ma's except it ain't mine no more.'

'You sold Nana May's house!'

'It was time.'

Sue's car pulled into the drive. 'I've come for the keys,' she says. The keys were passed, Sophie suspecting payment for the house was not of coin, no more sex in the sunlight, a promise has been made and a bond broken.

'I'd best be goin',' said Gabriel. He kissed Sophie, his lips warm. 'Take care, honey. Stay tight to that sanctuary of yours and it will take care of you. If the Commander calls tell him if he needs me I am bound to be close by.'

The car swung out of the drive and the sun with it leaving the women shivering. Emilia slid out of the shadows. 'Gabriel is gone.'

'Yes,' said Sophie. 'With the trek to India he's limited for time.'

'Gabe oughtn't to go,' said Sue. 'Johnny gets the bit between his teeth he don't care what danger he walks into or who walks with him.'

'Staying for breakfast, Sue?'

'No thanks.' Seeming at a loss she patted Sophie's hair. 'Pretty braid.'

'I do it better,' said Emilia. 'I learn in Paris.'

'Paris, huh?' Sue fumbled with the keys. 'You and me should set up shop. I got nothin' else to do these days.'

Tyres screaming, she took off.

Emilia stood watching. 'That angel,' she said.

'Sue is a very good person.'

'Not her! The Gabriel Knight.'

Emilia has an interview today for a nanny.

'Do you want me to go with you?'

'I go with Enrico the chauffeur.'

'If you don't like it there you don't have to take it. There's Mrs Ryland's offer.'

'Mrs Ryland offer me nothing. She want me out of Mill.'

Sophie felt a flash of anger. 'She's not the only one!'

'Maybe I go. It depends.'

'On what?'

'If Mister Clyde want me to stay.'

Sophie slammed the closet door. I should throw her out. It's not as if she contributes. Last night she locked herself in her room saying the Angel of Death is coming. Then Hokey got sick. It's a pity that other Angel of Death wasn't here to help. But then Hokey is afraid of Clyde.

'Animals smell blood on his hands,' said Emilia gauging Sophie's thought.

'And yet you don't mind taking what his hands are willing to give.'

'I earn every cent.'

'How do you?'

'I give sex. It is how I pay my way.'

'Get a job!' snarled Sophie, 'and you'll never have to pay that way again.'

~

Sophie's waiting for Clyde in the parking lot at Langley. When he came through the doors she offered a kiss but he held away. 'What's wrong?'

'Hokey died last night. Poison, Uncle Gabriel said.'

'Why was Templar with you and not his own place?'

'He gave Nana May's house to Sue Ryland.'

Clyde snorted. 'That makes sense. There was always something going on between those two. The scent of their sex is all over that house.'

'That's a strange thing you do, nose people out.'

'I don't nose anyone out. I recognize essence.' Eyes darkly solemn he said. 'I'd know you anywhere.'

Sophie changed topics. 'Uncle Gabriel sent his regards. He said if you should ever need him he's bound to be close by.'

'Bound to be? That's a very particular thing to say. What did he mean by it?'

'I don't know and you'll have to wait to ask. He and John Beaufort and the boys are going to Nepal on a photo-shoot.'

'And you're not happy about it.'

'From what I've heard it can be dangerous.'

'So can crossing a railway-track.'

'They are my kid brothers. I am allowed to worry.'

'Kid brothers! You seen the size of those guys lately?'

'Maybe you should go. Keep an eye on them for me.'

Clyde opened his mouth but thought better of it. He needs to make the most of this break, according to Langley he may never see another. 'You've more chance of finding men on Mars than GI POWs alive and well in that locale.'

He'd asked why mount a rescue operation?' The AD had scoffed. 'Some guy with an overactive imagination reckons he's spotted a prison compound with newly erected guard towers. Calls for help are spelled out in stones on the ground and NVA prisoners report seeing American GI POWs in that area.'

'You think it a possibility?' then said Clyde.

'Doesn't matter what we think. It has POTUS approval.'

'Why me?'

The Ad had shrugged. 'We've guys out in Laos. If the DOD mount this operation then Charley will be everywhere. We'll not smuggle a fart out never mind a man. You've worked that area. You speak the lingo and aren't afraid of things that go bang. Plus you wanted out. Think of this as your free pardon.'

~

Clyde was stripped to the buff showering Saigon shit from his veins when Emilia opened the door. 'Mamselle gone to Centre.'

'And so you are here.'

'I come to tell you I am offered job.'

'Is that so,' he carried on pulling soap suds between the cheeks of his ass.

'I am live in nanny. They give me room and car and dollars.'

'Good for you.'

'I want to be American citizen. You still help, Mister Clyde?'

'Sure why not. You earned your keep.'

'I want house of my own, husband and picket fence. I want American dream.'

'Is that all you want?'

She unbuttoned her dress and opening the glass door stepped under the shower with him. 'I want to fuck with you,' she said and grabbed his balls.

'Hey, take it easy!' he winced. 'They're the only two I got left.'

Water streaming over her shoulders, she went down on her knees and took him in her mouth. He didn't mind. What's one last suck between friends? It is over with Miss Sabri. If he makes it back from North Vietnam he'll make good; no more Tidy Man, no more Killing Fields, and no more Little Black Book.

Sharp teeth grazed his prick, nails dug into his skin, a soupcon away from pain it's easy coming into her mouth.

No barriers and nothing to worry about, it's shelling peas. Gently he bundled her out. 'You have to go now, Miss Sabri. Get to know your new employers.'

Wet hair clinging to her face, she stood looking at him. 'You want me to go?'

'You must do what's good for you.'

'You not want me to stay?'

'It's time to move on. What's the husband like? Make a good fuck will he?'

Momentarily her eyes registered hurt. Then she shrugged. 'I like chauffeur more. He drive nice car and has clean hands.'

~

There's to be an auction at the Rescue Centre. Things are good between Sophie and Clyde. In an effort to keep it so she is donating her theatre clothes to the sale. Clyde said he didn't have a problem with her dancing. 'The woman on the stage is Mamselle Perfidia, the girl here with me is my wife.'

'Thank you,' moved by his words Sophie kissed him, 'but if I don't get the closet sorted before Emilia gets back there'll be nothing left of either.'

'How old are these kids?'

'The girl is ten and the boy coming up thirteen.'

'She'll be good for their education. Entente cordiale will never be the same.

'I am relieved she's going.'

'I am sorry I brought her.' Clyde drew Sophie close, their images replicated in the mirror. 'Well, will you look at us, the happily married couple?'

Sophie smiled. 'How long are you home?'

'Long enough to make plenty pretend babies until we get us a real one.'

'You mean we should adopt?'

'We can't hang about. I'm an old man not some sprightly shave-tail. One thing, I'm not bringing a kid to this place. I don't mind living abroad if that's what you want, Paris or even Suffolk, but not here.'

'Not Suffolk with Charles gone.'

'And the new Milord getting married?'

'That has nothing to do with it. I am glad John's getting married.'

'How's your buddy Becky taking it? She was crazy about the guy.'

'She'll get over it. People do get over such things.'

It was on Clyde's tongue to say, 'but not you.' He kept his trap shut. Last night they had the best sex and stayed together 'til morning with her head on his shoulder. The Hon John married. The Ice-Man dead, why rock the boat?

~

It's settled; a last performance at Caesar's Palace. Sophie suggested the solo *Sugar Plum Fairy*. Miss Kelly prefers the Saint Saens. 'It was your debut piece. It should be your finale.' Pity Clyde will miss it. He has to return to Vietnam, one last job, he says, a last kick at the devil. The boys in Nepal will also miss out.

Sophie worries about them going. People go climbing all the time, but with Mum and Dad ever a reminder, she's naturally cautious.

Her worries must have connected, and the psychic line ever buzzing, Tim phoned. 'Johnny and the Sherpa guides are already out there going over the route. It's all very British and well organised.'

'I can't help remembering Mum and Dad.'

'Sis, I'm a plebe at West Point, I squat in Beast Barracks. If I can't manage a little old mountain trek then I'll eat my stripes.'

Sophie and Clyde spent the weekend in Portland looking at lots of spacious houses with lots of windows letting in lots of light. Back home one is constantly aware of gloom. Green slats don't cover the windows as they did in '46 yet the Mill is as blind to the light as ever.

Clyde is keen to move but there is the Rescue Centre to consider. It may not need Sophie but she surely needs it.

Goods for the auction packed and ready to go Emilia hovers to see what might come her way. She picked up the shellac box. 'This for sale?'

'No.' Sophie put the box with the sable. 'It has sentimental value. You can't auction sentiment.' Thinking about adoption she held up a cache of bracelets.

'Which of these would you keep for a daughter?'

Emilia crossed the room and placing her hand on Sophie's belly said, 'you no need bracelets. You have a son with grey eyes and hair like ink.'

Sophie sighed. 'That's a nice thought.'

'You not believe me?'

'No.'

'But I see the future.'

'I don't believe in the future.'

~

That evening, Clyde helping at the Centre, Sophie opened the shellac box. She did tell Sebastian Farrell she didn't want anything of Mrs Powell's but the need to open the package burned until she opened it and found the shellac box and her letters to Ethan and Granma Powell's ring What's more, hidden in the lining is a copy of the Rossetti poem he quoted.

Shocked, she sat on the bed. It wasn't in the box at Granma Powell's house so why here now? 'Remember me,' she read, ' when I am gone away, gone far away into a silent land, when you can no more hold me by the hand, nor I half turn to go yet turning stay. Remember me when no more day by day you tell me of our future that you had planned. Only remember me…!''

'What's that you've got?' Clyde was at the door.

'Oh!' Sophie crumpled the letter into her hand. 'You startled me.'

He came into the room. 'What is it?'

She slid the poem under the cover. 'Nothing much, just some old letters.'

'Letters to whom?'

'Ethan Winter, my pen-pal. It's nothing, just schoolgirl chatter about White Lodge. Old stuff! Defunct!'

'Where did they come from?'

'Sebastian Farrell delivered them as left to me in Mrs Powell's Will.'

'For what purpose?'

'I don't know.' Under the cover her hand closed about the poem. 'I was sorting through the closet, stuff to take, stuff to go, and I found this.'

'And is this to go?'

'I hadn't really thought.'

'Maybe you should. If we're to put right all that went wrong between us you should get rid of stuff like this.'

'Perhaps you're right. Are you finished at the Centre?'

'I got a bonfire going burning grass about the pens. I stink of smoke and did think to change my vest but if you've things to burn I can wait.'

'You mean the letters?'

'You said they were defunct.'

'They're still memories to keep.'

'You have eidetic memory. Since when did you need to keep anything?'

'Because I do! It's what people do, hold on to look and treasure.'

'And do you look and treasure these?'

'I treasure them certainly. Don't you have things you treasure?'

'I don't believe in holding onto the past. I move on.'

'Must I do the same, move on from things that are important to me?'

'A bunch of old letters is important to you?'

'In terms of the past yes!'

'More important than me?'

'I don't see one has anything to do with the other.'

'They are connected. Stuff like this gets in the way.'

Sophie proffered the box. 'Then take it if it means that much. As you say I have an eidetic memory. Every word is in my head and will stay so.'

'And the ring, the one you shoved in the drawer, is that to go?'

'Sure.' She shrugged. 'It can be auctioned along with the rest.'

'And what about the other thing you're trying to hide.'

'It's a poem.'

'You wrote your pen-pal a poem? How cute is that.'

Sophie didn't reply.

He grabbed her braid and tugged. 'Give it to me.'

'No.'

'Give it to me!'

'No!'

Clyde pulled her hair and kept pulling until she was horizontal, neck stretched out like an animal to the slaughter. Prising the poem from her hand he left, taking the box and the ring with him.

He went back to the bonfire. Dumb ass! He's screwed up again. It's that helpless feeling in his head, that suffocating sense on non-ownership. It overwhelms him. Sophie makes him vulnerable. Standing on the landing watching her read piffling notes made him crazy. The expression on her face! The softness of her mouth! It's all there to see, a love so real but not for him.

It's pathetic. She's pathetic! Where's her pride. The guy is dead, why can't she accept that? And for that matter why can't he, Clyde? Who cares what she did as a kid! It's now that matters!

It was as she said, schoolgirl stuff notes on life at ballet school. Even so, he fed them one-by-one to the flames, dead grass and dead dreams going up in smoke. The poem he kept. Winter's handwriting, what is that doing in the box?

'Chrissakes!'

It hit him then! A Company man, he recognised a drop when seen. This is no accident. The poem is a message to Sophie; 'hold on! I am alive.'

Why isn't he surprised? Maybe deep down he's always known the guy was alive. No matter the Intel, the funeral and notices of death, he's always suspected that somewhere in the world Ethan Winter lives and breathes.

Clyde sat back on his haunches, his world – the temporary make-believe world of happy families – collapsing under his feet. Ethan Winter is alive. Sophie hasn't made the connection yet but she will and she'll leave – although after his little show of temper in the Mill she's probably already packed and gone.

Well maybe he's something to say about that. Who the hell does she think she is? After all he's done for her! Carried her through, took care of her!

Ungrateful bitch! But then that's people. They are born ungrateful.

~

He took his anger to the turret room and a bottle of rye whisky. Sophie's in the cottage, cat in a carrier, dog on a leash and bag packed. She's been there a while, innate good manners keeping her there. Fuck it! She can wait. He'll go down and see her when he's good and ready.

The clock ticks. The day moves on. Strange, sitting here Clyde sees how when the light changes the room changes, the mirrored wall becoming an evening sky. Glass all around, the sun goes down forever, his face alters, and in the shifting *trompe l'oil* he is two men – Clyde St John Forrester, fine upstanding Naval Commander, and beer soaked pilot by name of Robert Rourke.

Hour after hour the guy sat here drinking and playing with a rubber duck. The duck is gone but here in this soupy twilight Clyde can hear it squawking.

'I am a ghost,' he whispered, 'keeping company with another ghost.'

Suddenly afraid, he tossed the bottle and went downstairs. She was still there waiting to say goodbye. 'Off then are you?' he said.

'Yes.'

'Where to?'

'I don't know, probably Paris for a while.'

'Didn't take you long to decide.'

'Is there any reason to stay?'

Sophie tried not to look at Clyde, an aura of unhappiness about him that if she looked too long she'd stay. Mum struggled to get away. She tried to leave so many times but every time Bobby talked her round. The two men are alike, the same rage seething under the skin and the need to crush and destroy.

'What are you thinking?' said Clyde.

'That you and my step-father are alike.'

'Hah!' He snorted. 'I was having the same thought or rather *we* were having the same thought, a hired gun and suicidal drunk.'

'My step-father may have been a drunk but I don't believe he meant to die. He crashed trying to avoid my dog.'

'Well, what d'you know, a drunken sop and yet still a hero. Will I go the same way, d'you suppose, crash and burn trying not to kill a pet of yours?'

'I hope not.'

'I burnt the letters. Not that they said much, kid's stuff.'

'I was a kid when I wrote them.'

'I guess so. 1958 how old were you, fifteen?'

'About that.'

'I seem to think we've had this conversation. You asked what I was doing fifteen years ago. Do you know what I did and still do?'

'I have a fair idea.'

'And does that fair idea bother you?'

'Of course!'

'The letters? Was that all the correspondence between you?'

'Those and the letters he wrote to me.'

'Where are they?'

'In the stove.'

'You burnt them sooner than me read them?'

'They were none of your business.'

'What about this?' he proffered the ring.

'It was his grandmother's.'

'And she left it to you? Doesn't that seem odd, the ring coming to you and not a relative? Doesn't it tell you something?'

'Like what?'

'Rings usually mean commitment.'

'I didn't have a commitment with Mrs Powell.'

'She seemed to think you did.'

'Why are we going through this when it's over?'

'Because I'm not sure it is over. I don't think it ever was. I think the guy is alive and you, or rather me, the victim of a hoax.'

'Absurd.' She picked up the bag. 'I'm going now.'

'What if I don't want you to?'

'Clyde, let's at least try to be civilised.'

'What's civility got to do with it? You're my wife. Wives don't leave their husbands, especially military wives.'

'I can't stay. I've tried but it doesn't work.'

'And why is that? Was it doomed to failure from the start or could it be you've been going through the motions waiting for the other shoe to drop.'

'I've tried as much as anyone could try. As for waiting for a shoe to drop I really don't know what you're talking about.'

'Don't you? So you're not in touch with anyone, not writing more letters?'

His voice had taken on a flat, empty, quality. It made Sophie afraid yet at the same time angry. 'Why would I write letters to anyone?'

'Perhaps you wanted another chair to sit on before giving up this, a chair your ass has been keeping warm all the time you've been with me.'

'As I've said, I don't know what you're talking about.' She stood and he shoved her down. 'Stop it,' she said. 'You're being stupid.' Again she stood up and again he shoved her down and this time held her down.

'You're not going until I know the deal.'

'What deal?'

'The deal! You, Winter, and the romantic reconciliation you've been planning.'

'God's sake!' Sophie was horrified. 'Ethan is dead. There can be no reconciliation romantic or otherwise.'

'If it's not Winter you're after then who? Maybe it's bigger bait. Maybe his Lordship getting married caused you to rethink your situation.'

'This is ridiculous! One minute I'm leaving you for a dead man the next for a man about to be married, I think you're losing it!'

'Sophie.' His fingers closed about her wrist. 'If I were you I wouldn't call a man crazy when his fingers are near your throat.'

'It doesn't matter what I say. You'll do what you want.'

'Then again maybe I'm waiting to hear more about secrets kept from me, the messages and cute little poems. And on the subject of secrets let's not forget his new Lordship, because if anyone ever sat on a secret it's you two.'

'Now what are you saying?'

'You know what I'm saying. '63 or '64, I'm not sure which, something happened between you and him.'

'Nothing happened.'

'Don't lie to me. Your face isn't made for lying. Something happened that caused you to turn sour and him to be on his knees begging mercy.'

'I tell you nothing happened.'

'Yes it did. Do you know what I think?' His took hold of her chin. 'I think he came on too strong one night, scared the pants off of your young ass so that you never wanted to see him again.'

'Oh do stop!' She tried to pull away but his fingers dug deep. 'So stupid! What did or didn't happen between me and John Beaufort is ancient history.'

'The flame may be out but the fire's still burning. All it needs is a glance from you and married or not he'll come running. Maybe it was a woman scorned kind of thing. You wanted the ermine cape and tiara and offered first dibs which he was pleased to accept but then didn't follow through.'

'I wanted nothing and offered the same.'

'But he took anyway.'

'Yes.'

'He raped you?'

'Yes.

'He really did?'

'Yes.'

'Oh Sophie, my poor girl.'

What happened next, what made him do what he did, Sophie will never understand. One moment his face was tight with anger, the next his mouth soft and his gaze filled with compassion. Drawing her into his arms he kissed her lips. 'I love you,' he said. 'I shall always love you.'

Then he hit her.

She fell. He hauled her up and punched again. Fingers curled into a tight fist he raised his hand for a third time. Muscles straining his fist hovered.

'No, Mister Clyde!' Lipstick smeared and hair mussed up, Emilia stood at the door. 'You not do it.'

'Mind your own business,' he said. 'This has to happen.'

'You not make murder! You go prison and gas-man murder you.'

'So what! We all have to die sooner or later.'

Talons extended and Cowboy boots clacking, Emilia flew at him. Punching and scratching she leapt on his back. Up and down the room they struggled until Clyde began to laugh. 'Get off, you dumb whore.'

Still they struggled until he threw her off. 'Silly bitch!' he said laughter turning to tears. 'Go pick on someone your own size.'

Hands shaking, he lit a cigar and wiping tears from his cheeks stumbled out.

Chapter Twenty-Four
Rescue Party

'Holy Cow! That's one hell of an eye.' Sue peeled the ice-pack from Sophie's eye. 'Sonofabitch! He's lucky I wasn't around.'

'And even luckier Emilia was around.'

Sue smiled grimly. 'Yeah but, honey, keep it in perspective. She didn't save your ass. She saved Clyde's. Where is she now?'

'With the chauffeur at his place. He came to collect her.'

'Let's hope she stays.'

'She won't be back. She's got most of my wardrobe including the sable. She wrapped herself in it, said she was suffering from shock.'

'And you let her!'

'I didn't care. She could have had it all. I just wanted out.'

'What about Clyde? All his stuff is there.'

'I dare say he'll clear it.'

'What flipped him over the edge?'

'I think his work is driving him crazy.'

'Enough to want to kill you?'

Sophie remembers leaving with Shima under one arm and Judy running alongside. She remembers heading into the woods for Nana May's house. What is not clear is how she arrived at the Eyrie.

She let herself in via the orangery, the door opening to the same elegant rooms and hand-painted ceilings, faded now, the colours befitting the original house. Built in mid 1800s, Dad tried researching. Few solid facts emerged the land hereabouts a Civil War battleground. Legend says the Mill and the Eyrie were built by twin brothers, a blood feud resulting in the death of both.

In the South, tales of Civil War feuds are not uncommon. Last night, alone in the sitting-room, Sophie knew she'd only to reach out to touch the past. It was there in the tinkling of a piano and flash of sword. One day, she'd thought, I'll learn the truth about the Eyrie. Then she saw her bruised face in the window and knew she'd best forget the past and deal with the present.

'So what will you do?' said Sue.

'I have a show in Las Vegas.'

'Can you dance with your face smashed up like that?'

'Stage make-up will cover most. If not I can always wear a mask.'

'You mean like the mask you're wearing now?'

Sophie stared. 'You think I hide behind a mask?'

'I think there's more to you than anyone knows. I used to wonder why you were with that man. Now I figure you married him to keep someone else from getting a beating.'

Tears welled up in Sophie's eyes. 'Can I stay?'

'Sure. It'll give me somethin' to occupy my mind.'

'Sue, how would you feel about working at the Centre? It will always be my concern but until I've resolved things I need someone. You'd have lots of helpers and I would pay you as manager.'

'I can't say I wouldn't be glad of the money. Gabe's left me the house but a girl has to live and there is no way now I can ever ask of him again. What about the Mill. You gonna sell?'

'Yes or burn it to the ground! Aunt Sarah says it's jinxed.'

'Aunt Sarah's talkin' out her fashionable butt! Ain't nothin' wrong with the Mill that the right family can't cure. Blamin' bricks and mortar for human disasters is plain dumb. Same with people! Round these parts my name is mud and that's okay, I earned it. Gabe never earned the stuff he got.'

'People were hard on him?'

'Hard ain't the word, folks callin' him a murderer.'

'They don't call him murderer now.'

'Damn right they don't! They call him Sir! Sir Gabriel Templar, Knight to Her Majesty the Queen of England. Suck on that sinners!'

'I'm sorry it didn't work out for you and him.'

Sue shrugged. 'It wasn't meant to work out. I was meant for booze and blues. Gabe was meant for God.'

~

Three days and Sophie went back to the Mill. It looks as it always looks, an afterthought inhabited by ghosts. She came bearing gifts, a vase of Morning Glories and a bag of

Doggobix. The flowers she set a vase in the window, the dog biscuits in the greenhouse. On a chilly morning like this, a blanket in his basket and the kerosene stove sending out heat this was Biffer's idea of heaven – God, Bobby and Biffer willing Hokey will find the same heaven.

No wind to rattle the sails, it was so quiet. There is nothing so sad and silent as an empty house. Climbing the tower stairs Sophie knew she was done with the place. Any last business would be handled by lawyers.

In the turret room sunbeams flash on Granma Powell's ring. It sits on the table along with a bracelet – a delicate thing made of coral it lies in the palm of her hand as an unfulfilled promise.

So many windows in this room, the Tall Ship in the glass fire-escape door sails away into the distance. Dad said the first time he slept here he dreamed he was aboard that ship. Now he and Mum are on that ship dreaming together.

Turning, she trod on the squeaker toy. Bobby called the rubber-duck his worry-bead and would sit for hours nursing it. Sophie would say, 'don't squeeze so hard, Daddy Bobby. You'll hurt it.' He'd shrug and say, 'it's the duck's neck, honey, or your ma's. You can't have it both ways.'

~

'Did you know a Snow Leopard can't roar?' An excited Joshua called. They'd arrived in Nepal and setting up base camp. 'Johnny says it's the larynx. They can hiss or chuff but can't roar. It's why they are called the Grey Ghosts.'

'Don't talk to me of ghosts.'

'Sis, the dead can't hurt you.'

'No but mountains can.'

'You worry too much. It's going to be a walk in the park, everything organised right down to a mess tent. Sophie, is everything okay with you?'

'I'm okay.' Bruises about her eyes may well be likened to the stripes of a Snow Leopard. 'We have an auction tomorrow raising funds for the Centre.'

'A pity I can't be with you helping out.'

Sophie smiled. 'You've become very English, Josh. Sharp consonants and short vowels I might be listening to John.'

'God, do I really? I can't have that. It's uncool. Where are you staying?'

'In New York with the rest of the Bluebells. One night and one performance, I couldn't be bothered to book a separate hotel.'

'That's not what I meant.'

'I know.'

~

Sophie phoned Simon Farrell. 'I need to return the ring.'

'Why? It was left to you as part of the Powell estate.'

'I know but it's become an issue.'

'What sort of issue?'

'I can't say other than I can't keep it.'

'Then you'd best give it away.'

'How about if I donate to charity? There's an auction on Friday at the Centre. I thought any money raised could buy bench seats in memory of Mrs Powell.'

'That's a nice idea. Go ahead if it pleases you. And Sophie, if you need help please say. I'd be offended if I thought you in trouble and me in the dark.'

Sophie and Sue are at the auction. The place is heaving, donations piled high. Bric-a-brac, garden produce, tools and implements, if they could get it through the door it was for sale, staff and volunteers collecting for weeks. Two o' clock a bunch of autographed teddy bears came up for sale. The bidding was frantic. It gave Sophie the shivers feeling as if the clothes were sheered from her back.

The General was there with his wife, and Emilia, glamorous in black Russian sable, jeans, and high-heeled Cowboy boot.

Sue rolled her eyes. 'Talk about nerve! If brass neck could be bottled she'd own a goddamn vineyard.'

'I suppose her money is as good as anyone else's.'

'Except it ain't hers. It's the guy with her.'

'That's Enrico, chauffeur to her new employer.'

'And her new meal ticket! She doesn't let the grass grow under her feet.'

'You sound not exactly unimpressed.'

'I've spent my life doing the same. Gabriel gave me the house but I'll still hustle. I don't know different. Becky's the same but I guess you know that.'

'Is she still seeing Simon?'

'Nah, he's a steady guy and she don't do steady.'

'Is the house entirely yours?'

'With certain provisos one of which was a kiss goodbye.'

'You think it was a parting gift?'

'Uh-huh. Gabe is another movin on.'

'To where?'

'I don't know. Wish I did. Oh look, there goes your maid and the meal-ticket with her. Look at him run! He knows he'd best make the most of this. That gal ain't cut-out to be a chauffeur's squeeze. She's after bigger game.'

'She was in love with Clyde.'

'Then it's best she does cut and run. Any woman fool enough to love that guy will be as the bible says castin' pearls before swine.'

Around four Granma Powell's ring came up for bidding.

'You sure you want this to go?' said Sue.

'I have no choice.'

'How much do you reckon it'll make?'

'The auctioneer put a reserve on it.'

'How do you think your guy would see his grandmother's ring payin' for dog kennels?'

'I hope he'd see it for how it's meant, a memorial to his grandparents.'

'Benches is a great idea. Maybe you'll do the same for me when I die. It would be nice to leave behind somethin' other than a bad impression.'

'Lot number 407,' the auctioneer tapped the gavel. 'Interest already shown in this piece, a bid of five hundred dollars. Who'll bid five hundred and twenty…?'

'Five hundred dollars!' Sue whistled. 'Is it worth that kind of money?'

'I wouldn't have said so.'

'Well whoever they are ain't willin' to take a chance.'

Sophie was surprised. She hadn't expected it to do anywhere near as well and judging by the absence of competition neither did anyone else.

The General was passing. 'Good day, Mizz Sophie. You got a plan in mind for all that cash?'

'I am as surprised as everyone else.'

'I bet. How are you keeping?'

'I'm well, thank you.'

He leaned closer. 'You got trouble with your eyes behind them dark glasses?'

'Nothing to worry about.'

'Are you sure?'

'Certain, thank you.'

'Well if'n you do need help don't hesitate to call. There's a lot of folks with a lot of love always looking in your direction. Now if you'll excuse me, ladies, I'll be marchin' along to pick up my prize.'

'You bought somethin' at the auction, General?' said Sue.

'I sure did. I got me a teddy bear with Mamselle Perfidia's kiss on his ass. My eldest boy is with us at present, some messy divorce. He said if I don't come back with one of them not to come back at all.'

~

Daniel Culpepper called to say the locks had been changed and for once ventured into personal remarks. 'I must say I am disappointed in the Commander. I never thought him a gentleman but didn't know him a brute. Your poor, dear mother! What would she think? "Take care of my daughter, Daniel," she said to me. "She will need you. "'

'You and mother got on well.'

'I like to think she trusted me. I would like to think you do the same.'

'I do.'

'Then take my advice and seek a restraining order. He's a dangerous man.'

'He isn't a danger to me, not now.'

'After what he did?'

'As I said it's not as bad as it sounds. I shan't see him again.'

'You seem very sure.'

'I am. An angel told me.'

'An angel? I wish I had your faith.'

It wasn't a question of faith. It was a telephone call. It happened early yesterday morning. The phone by the bed rang. Not wanting Sue to be disturbed she'd snatched it up. 'Hello.'

It was Uncle Gabriel. 'You okay?'

'Not too bad,' she croaked.

'It probably looks worse than it is.'

Oh, she thought, Sue must have told him. 'Probably.'

'Are you wounded, honey?'

'My heart aches, if that's what you mean.'

'Love does hurt.'

'Was that love?'

'I reckon. He never meant to do nothin' but scare you hopin' you'd leave afore he did somethin' worse.'

'Surely there are better ways.'

'Maybe, but when you ain't thinkin' straight them ways ain't so obvious.'

'Where are you?' The call was all clicks and whistles. 'You sound like you're in a lift or halfway up a mountain.'

'I ain't up there yet. Are you expectin' to see him again?'

'I don't know.'

'You won't. He's done what he meant to do.'

'And what was that?'

'Set you free.'

That's all he said. The line went dead. Sophie replaced the phone and slept. Next morning she apologised to Sue. 'Sorry about the call. It seems Uncle Gabriel's lived so long in England he's forgotten time differences.'

'Gabe phoned here?'

'Yes, this morning around four am.'

'I don't think so, honey.'

'He did. We spoke of Clyde.'

'And what did he tell you?'

'He said not to worry. He wouldn't be coming back.'

'Well, that's a comfort, though I reckon you dreamt it.'

'I didn't. He called.'

'No, honey, he never…leastways not on this phone. Listen!' Sue held the phone to Sophie's ear. 'It needs reconnecting. It hasn't worked in years.'

Chapter Twenty-Five
Grey Ghosts

'Get some sleep, Commander,' said the pilot. 'Until we see the coastline you can't do anything.' A hood about his head, Clyde hunkered down. 0220 it's pitch black outside, the hood is soft as a woman's breast and as comforting.

Sophie! Sophie! That last raised fist! While his heart fights to erase the memory another Clyde wants back in the cottage to finish the job.

'Don't do it, Mister Clyde,' says Emilia. 'You go gas-chamber.'

There won't be a gas-chamber: First Commandment of the Company Bible as follows, '*Thou shalt not get caught but if you are, make your own way home.*' He will either by a drop from a thirty-story window, a fast car into a slow wall, or a personal favourite, a deft handspring in front of the 7-45 to Union Station.

Knowing he needs to get a grip Clyde drew a shuddering breath. Orders are to link-up with a tactical force at Udorn airbase to collect an agent at the North Vietnamese border, thereafter, at the prescribed time to blow the station, and whoever's left in it, to hell and back.

Early 60s he worked this route. Getting in shouldn't be a problem, getting out is another issue, blowing C4 likely to bring every goon within a hundred miles.

Right now there's plenty of noise in his head, the after-effects of a boozy night slugging it out with the plane engine and thwack of a fist hitting a cheek.

What a pantomime, two skinny girls, a flick of his wrist and both would be dead, the thought of Winter being alive brought him very close

He went to Langley where questions regarding Ethan Winter drew blank stares. What is it they say – want a job doing, do it yourself? The only way he was ever going to know the truth was to do a little digging of his own, with that in mind he'd bummed a ride on a Company plane to Buckley Airbase.

A phone call, a borrowed jeep, and a torch and shovel, it was dusk before he arrived at the cemetery. Man! He thought he was fit but by the time he was down to the casket he was done. He was taking a leak by a hedge when a guy steps out of the darkness. Thinking there'd be at least one body in the grave Clyde hefted the shovel – no need, it was an old guy, a gardener, who, offering a quart of whisky, took the shovel and began filling in the grave.

Weary, a sprig of dried lilac in his hand, Clyde sat watching. Dead flowers for a dead man, he'd felt the need to explain and said robbing graves wasn't his style, that he was looking for someone. The gardener wasn't fazed. 'Folks are always losing things,' says he. 'They come looking for their wives, and sweetheart. They weep, asking where is he or she. I tell them what I'm telling you, no one here, they've gone to a better place.'

Taking that as a sign, Clyde flew back to Langley Air America. Boots thick with graveyard dung, other passengers thought him a nut-job. They are right. I mean, who does that, flies hundreds of miles to exhume a body. Only a crazy man sits by a grave sharing whisky with another crazy man.

Appearing out the shadows like Boris fucking Karloff, the gardener was either crazy or a ghost, the whisky was real as was the mud on Clyde's best Hampton brogues. Whoever or whatever, it comes down to this – Ethan Winter did not die. As the old guy said, there's no one there, he's gone to a better place.

'And we're not talking heaven!' Clyde slammed his fist into the seat. He must stay focussed, because if the SEAL is alive then this mission is a set-up.

The more he thinks, the more he suspects he was suckered on all sides and that only Sophie was telling the truth. The question is who's the Company Rabbi behind it? General Jentzen's ugly mug springs to mind, that old guy has a long memory and a bug up his ass ever since Clyde's fling with his wife.

~

Jake is in Thailand at a US Airbase. He's on the telephone, person-to-person with General Jentzen. 'Did you get the ring, sir?'

'I sure did.'

'And if worst comes to worst you'll tell her about me?'

'You can count on it. It's with your lawyer, Farrell.'

Jake breathed out. 'I am obliged to you.'

'Glad to be of service. I'm assuming you've arrived at a destination some place I'm supposed to know nothing about?'

'That's about the sum of it. We landed yesterday.'

'You've received final orders?'

'No sir, not yet. There's total shut-down on all calls coming in and out. It's only because you are you that we are talking now.'

'Rank hath privilege.'

'So it would seem. Sir, how did she look?'

'Probably best I don't tell you.'

Jake's heart froze. 'What do you mean?'

'Son, if I tell you she looked bruised, it's in the hope you'll use the info, and the way it makes you feel, to get back in one piece and kick the butt that did it.'

'Is she okay?'

'She'll be better when she knows you're alive. Forget that now! Concentrate on what you can do for your country and the guy who betrayed you. And Jake, one thing you do need to know, it wasn't me who picked you for this mission.'

'Sir?' Jake was puzzled.

'The OC chose you as man for the job. I did suggest a new identity and I did put pressure on folks to get a certain sonovabitch sent to a certain place hopin' another sonovabitch would put a bullet between his eyes. But I never wanted you caught in the crossfire. That whoreson guy messin' with women got me all fired up. I gave a shove here and there hopin' he'd never worry another woman but I didn't allow for you bein' in the same place at the same time.'

'Sorry, Sir, I'm afraid I don't…?'

'Forget it! You'll know what I'm sayin' soon enough. Maybe it's fate. What they call it, Kismet, the lap of the Gods. Anyway go to it, Jake, my boy. Do best for your country and your soul.'

The line went dead. Jake was left looking at the phone.

Seb Farrell glanced up. 'What was that about?'

'I have absolutely no idea.'

'Did he mention the ring?'

'Uh-huh. It's with Simon.'

'Anything more?'

'Nothing that makes sense.' The General hinted at a hidden agenda but that would have to wait. Jake was too busy assimilating the word bruised.

~

They're on stand-by. The main taskforce continues to arrive at the base. The nature of the mission is classified, yet every man involved suspects he's part of a Search and Rescue to free American POWs. From what Jake gathers, teams of men – mostly Green berets aboard H-H53 helicopters – will cross into North Vietnam and from there proceed to destinations unknown.

When Jake first transferred to Fort Belvoir he worked for IPWIC – the interrogation of prisoners of war committee, translating intercepted radio messages trying to figure the whereabouts of North Vietnam GI POW camps. Once relocated to Fort Eglin he managed night raids along with the rest. Two months ago he was called into a briefing room and told to head up a team.

The OC, a fussy little guy with pencil moustache, swagger stick, and British military affectation, quoted a Chinese War Historian. 'Sun Tzu said the secret lies in confusing the enemy. Lieutenant Frost, in order for this mission to work we need the enemy mightily confused. He must not suspect our true intent. The main assault force demands considerable sea and air support geared toward diversionary tactics. They'll be plenty noise. Your task will be to add a noise of your own, and while you're at it bring back a couple of lost lambs.'

He went on to say the mission was to extract agency operatives from a covert CIA station on the Laos border. 'We're none of us at the Company's bidding,' he said, 'yet in this instance, *quid pro quo*, we agreed to oblige. You're to get them out and then to remove the camp from the landscape in whatever way you can. However, since it's a balls-to-the-walls mission, you may regard it a volunteer situation, every man with the right to refuse.'

At first it didn't go down well with the Team. When it comes to distrusting Central Intelligence Jake's not alone. 'Why are we cleaning up their shit?' asked Pick Madsen. 'Ain't they got enough of their own to do the job?'

They argued. Jake listened and when they'd finished talking got to his feet. 'Okay, you heard it,' he said. 'You know the score. Do you want to do this?'

A grin spread throughout the room. 'Hooyah, Boss, fucking A.' Now, grim tomb raiders loaded down with weapons, they wait to board a Huey.

Jake has a headache.

'What the heck was up with you in the night?' says Sebastian. 'All that moaning? You sounded like you were dying.'

'Bad beer. My guts were giving me hell.'

It wasn't his guts. It was a dream; it started out okay, him fishing on the lake, the sun shining and birds singing. Then a phone rang from inside the cabin. A voice, Southern drawl with hint of menace demanded, 'Ethan Winter?'

'You got the wrong number,' said Jake, 'no one of that name here.'

'Okay, well whoever you are,' the voice continued. 'I got a message for you: "Vengeance is Mine saith The Lord".'

'That it?' says Jake in the dream. 'That's your message?'

At that the caller smiled, Jake can still hear the smile in that voice. 'I could add take it easy. Everythin' comes to he who waits.'

Vengeance is mine saith the Lord? Jake slammed down the phone. What kind of message is that when a guy is about to go behind the lines?

Still in the dream he goes fishing. Quick as a flash a storm breaks out, lightning flashing and winds howling. He's tossed into the lake. Water bubbling in his lungs he is drowning, when a giant hand plucks him out and the voice says, 'I told you take it easy. Everything comes to him who waits.'

Jake woke knowing it was the Dream Weaver, or rather Sophie's uncle, his human counterpart.

~

The Huey is reined back, rotors idling. Jake is called into the briefing room where he's told there's an addition to the Team, a Company guy who knows the area and who has offered assistance.

Assistance my ass, thought Jake, this is typical last minute add-on, some corner-cutting shit-for-brains officer killing two birds with one stone.

Then through the driving rain Jake saw him coming, a tall figure stooping under the rotors, the face momentarily caught in the glare of the lights.

'Oh my Lord!'

'What?' queried Sebastian.

'Kismet.'

'Kismet?'

'Uh-huh, in the shape of Clyde Forrester.'

What did Jake feel when he saw him? At first there was a pile-driver to the heart, every pain caused by this man rushing upon him, himself, Ethan Winter slighted as a feckless piece of shit, a man who pissed in his own mess-tin betraying one woman while screwing another. Then there were the blows to pride, rumours of incompetence in the field, the distrust of brother officers and shame to the family. Large as life and twice as hearty this smiling killer brought heartache to a beloved grandmother helping her to an early grave.

Blood pounding in his skull, Jake is on his feet.

'Don't do anything stupid,' hissed Sebastian.

'Stupid?' The need to leap down on the tarmac and fill Forrester full of holes was so strong it passed from man-to-man. Nostrils twitching, the scent of bad blood detected, heads turn in relay. Then like a cool rain dampening heat, a voice whispered in Jake's ear. 'Vengeance is mine saith the Lord!'

He sat down, information slotting into place. The General's rambling begin to make sense. This is nothing to do with Jake, he is a small pawn in a larger game, and how this age-old feud fits the magnitude of the occasion, the beating of rotors and screaming of jets, the good guys, the heroes, heading into war. All it needs is a villain to put in an appearance, a suave Savile Row Michelangelo-sculpted villain, who wears the same combat gear yet with a style none can gainsay.

~

Clyde strolled up the tarmac, threw a bag in through the door and climbed aboard. He sits, glances around, and smiling sketches a salute. The rest regard him in silence. Seven men plus two riding shot-gun on the doors, similar in height and build, bulging with armament and Close Quarter Combat gear, it's hard to tell them apart yet a sniff of the air and Ethan Winter is known.

It is Clyde's belief that every man, woman, and child on the planet has their own particular scent. Kids bring flowers, scabby knees and sunshine. Most men and women bring humdrum and a smear of shit and with a lot of prayer – and a deal of wishing – will come up clean. There are those who can never be washed clean. Doesn't matter how shiny the surface or polished the nails filth within seeps through. Good people tend to smell of grass and trees with an undertone of loneliness. Joanie walks into the room and Clyde gets *Chanel Number Five* and pig's trotters. Bryony is damp lavatory paper. Her boy, Jamie, bless him, is fruit loops and football. The Agency Director is spit, polish, and a Raven's claw. The late General Hunter brought a combo of open air, Cosmoline and true grit. His daughter, Sophie, is crystal glass with a soupcon of Rue.

Clyde has no idea what essence clings to his soul but thinks it can't be good.

When nightmares are upon him, the ever-present eyes, it's sex and sulphur, but that is probably Emilia's sucking lips and likening him to the devil.

A man dies and the scent dies with him. Two minutes and the trail is cold. Ethan Winter the Third is alive. Clyde knows because right now the scent of righteous fury is careening through the chopper, coming down in waves and homing in on Clyde with all the weight of a Force 10 gale.

He bent under the swell. Were he out sailing Chrysalis in this kind of storm he'd be baling for his life! The scent is a giveaway as are the eyes, cammo-blackened rimmed and staring through holes yet unmistakable.

'Well, what do you know?' Clyde acknowledges those eyes with a bow. 'The Ice Man Cometh.'

Chapter Twenty-Six
All or Nothing

Heavy cloud and strong winds have kept the crew locked down at Base Camp. It's cold, wind whipping tents into frantic bubbles.

Gabriel braved the storm to check on the boys. Wrapped tight in a sleeping bag Tim was asleep and snoring. Joshua was awake. 'You okay, son?'

'I've been better.'

'You'll acclimatise.'

'I doubt it. Mountains in the sky are not my natural habitat. I'm a lazy beast only truly happy when wallowing in California sun.'

'Then you picked the wrong country for your Alma Mater, England ain't nothin' whatsoever to do with sunshine.'

'Yup, grey skies, lumpy porridge and lumpier beds.' Joshua yawned. 'I don't like all this hanging about.'

'Is it hangin' about that bothers you or that you can't chat with the cute redhead you met at Base Camp.'

'It's not that. I've a lot of catching up to do, verbs I need to conjugate.'

'Oh you're missin' your Latin verbs! I get that. I was the same your age.'

Joshua laughed. 'She was cute wasn't she?'

'She was and you'll see her again so quit pushin'. You're your mother's son. She couldn't sit still. Your sister's the same.'

Joshua's smile died. 'Is this thing with Clyde ever going to be over?'

'That's their business.'

'But they're in trouble!'

'If they are it's their trouble.' Gabriel returned to the tent he shares with John Beaufort and shucked down inside a sleeping bag. 'Are we climbin' tomorrow?'

'The guides say it's clearing after dawn, John replied. 'Are the boys okay? I imagine they're wishing they were anywhere but here.'

'Right now Tim dreams of savin' the world and Josh a gal with lilac eyes.'

'Josh is in love? First love! I've forgotten how that feels.'

'Have you, John?'

'Thirty-something and in love with the same woman, I guess no one knows better. You and my dad were here in '57. How does it feel coming back?'

'Not good. I lost my enthusiasm for climbin' in '63.'

'The cable car! Forgive me. I'd forgotten you and the Hunters were close.'

'No problem. At least you didn't say me comin' will offer closure.'

John grimaced. 'Ridiculous expression! What do people mean by it? Closing the door on grief? You'd think it a wild beast to be penned in.'

'I can't say I've found it easy to handle.'

What happened in '63 will always be a problem to Gabriel. Closure suggests shutting a door. The day she died it wasn't a door that fell between them so much as another word associated with death. Moth's wing or cobweb lace, this veil is loosely woven yet as denying as steel. Weeks will go by and all is silence beyond the barrier. The earth turns, someone mentions her name, and she's a breath away. Padlocked or barred there's no closure against that.

'Do you think Sophie will stay with Clyde?' John's eyes were bleak. 'I'm not prying. I'm just concerned.'

'I know. You said it yourself, the same man loving the same woman.'

'Stupid! I should let go. Clinging to the past doesn't help either of us.'

'Is it the past?'

'It never got started. I put paid to that.'

'If you think it is past best leave it and deal with what you got.'

'Is that what marriage is about?'

'It's what most marriages are about.'

'Amanda and I are friends. Feeling the way I do I can't allow it to be anything else. It wouldn't be right.'

'That's a tough decision. Can you leave it like that? I mean, you bein' who you are and carryin' a line folks have expectations.'

'In the matter of loving Sophie expectation counts for nothing. I know my duty and like Dad I'll give my life to the Abbey but I won't give my soul.'

'That's a lonely way to go, John. Love is a risky business. When a train leaves a station it don't usually turn back. It carries on to the final destination.'

'And leaves the one left behind utterly alone.'
'Yeah, if he ain't willin' to bend.'
'Were you willin' to bend?'
Gabriel closed his eyes. 'It was that or break.'

~

'Ow!' Joshua winced. 'Take it easy, Dad, or you'll cut off circulation.'

'It needs to be tight.' Gabriel tugged the harness. 'No use tryin' to fasten it when you're fallin' head over ass.'

Check complete and stifling a sigh Gabriel moved on. Tough guy, a cadet at West Point, Tim thinks he can take care of himself and doesn't want anyone fussing. Tough! Today he'll be checked and double-checked with the rest.

Gabriel doesn't trust mountains. Having claimed one love they're not getting another. He taps Tim's knee. 'Show me your boots.' Grudging, Tim raises his right foot then the left. These days there's distance between them, it's born of Tim's loyalty to his pa and the fact that Joshua is Gabriel's boy.

John Beaufort is an experienced climber. Tim is part of the Army team. Gabriel is no slouch. In '57 he and Charles Beaufort climbed the North face of the Eiger. It's Joshua needs watching. Dreamer that he is he believes the Universe and everything in it was created for him. Most sports favour the young but the high altitude and lack of oxygen sucks on the inexperienced.

They're not doing the Eiger, yet lowers slopes can be dangerous. Josh is not mindful of danger. Look at him laughing with the cameramen! No one wants harm to come to him. Let's hope that on this day the mountain feels the same.

~

A clear bright dawn John makes last preparation. It's best to get started before sun warms the ice. So much time and effort invested, it's to be hoped one of the cats puts in an appearance. Snow leopards! What the hell was he thinking? He can't afford these pipe dreams not with so much riding on the outcome. But what a farce it's turning out to be! Journos and hangers-on, it's more a three-ring circus than the holy pilgrimage he envisaged.

5 am they gather for the Puja, asking a blessing from the goddess of the mountain. A Lama priest in tatty robes and Reeboks shakes rice water over juniper fire. Creaking knees, they kneel on frozen ground. The rituals go on forever but no one can move until the priest gives the sign.

Sharing a tent with Gabriel is a revelation. Artist and tough guy, accused of killing his father, he came into the family with a hell of a reputation. Pa loved him. Julia adores him as do the twins. Here the Nepalese bearers treat the man with respect bordering on awe – holy man or not he's human hence things back home are awkward. Julia is crazy for her famous husband but with him travelling so often, and mother frail, she spends most of her time at the Abbey or with Andrew Keen, owner of the gallery where she shows her paintings. A widower, and always keen on Julia, they lunch, play bridge and talk of art. It's likely nothing will come of it yet she is lonely.

Gabriel's not an easy man to know. He walks through life encased in steel. Julia would be first to say she is wife by default, a love triangle in America with Sophie's mother being Julia's, and Gabriel's, eternal cross.

Dad worried about it. 'Please don't worry,' she said. 'My portion of bread may well be meagre but I'm aware which side is buttered.'

Watching them suffer adds to John's conviction. He can't be like Gabriel and doesn't have a son to sustain him. Joshua was born out of passion. The twins, Lord bless them, are sweeties for Julia. It's not enough for John. All or nothing is what he's decided, and if it has to be nothing then at least it's his choice.

~

The Puja ceremony over the Lama priest claps his hands and everyone gets to their feet. Gabriel is still kneeling. The Lama shuffles over and whispers in his ear. Gabriel collapses, sliding sideways.

John ran to him. 'What's the matter?'

Gabriel staggered to his feet. 'I felt kinda faint.'

'Was it something he said?'

'He told me not to make selfish prayers.'

'And were you?'

'I guess I was askin' for a long and a happy life.'

'What's wrong with that? I see nothing selfish in that. It's what we all want.'

'Is it what you want?'

'Isn't it what everyone wants?'

Pale and shaky, Gabriel smiled. 'Well I hope you ain't plannin' on bein' an exception to the rule 'cos my prayers weren't for me. They were for you.'

That got to John. He had to rush away. A burden had been lifted, his tears sluicing the past down the mountainside. In Gabriel's prayer he had been forgiven for hurt to Sophie, and not only by Gabriel, but also by her father, Alex Hunter, and God help him, Charles Beaufort, his own father.

All or nothing, he wrote a note to be posted. 'Thanks for being a good friend, Amanda. I'm sorry it couldn't be more.' Amanda knows what ails him, the fever that until this day has drained them dry. She'll read the note and be free to start her own recovery. As for the climb there'll be no Snow Leopard today or any other. Dad said if you sniff an egg and it smells bad don't eat it. This egg is rotten. No team work, the cameramen losing interest, too many hidden agendas, you have to know when to throw in the towel.

~

John joined Gabriel in the tent, both thinking of the Lama priest. 'What do you suppose he meant by selfish prayer?'

Gabriel shrugged. 'You know these guys. They live to be inscrutable.'

'We were taught never to pray for ourselves, only for others. Nanny Foster drummed it into our heads.'

'That old lady can sure put a damper on any day.'

John smiled. 'There speaks the voice of experience.'

'We had a brief skirmish.'

'In which you were vanquished.'

'Totally. Say, John, what do you want most in the world?'

'You mean right now?'

'Uh-huh.'

'Well, right now I want to get this trek over and at some point see a blasted Snow Leopard to get it filmed and in the can!'

'And beyond that?'

'To be honest I'm sick of wantin'. My life has been about wantin'. It comes with the territory.'

'You mean inheritin' the title?'

'Yes. From birth one is always looking toward inheritance. It can't be any other way. As you said settling for the things would be the sensible way. Unfortunately, in terms of Sophie I'm conditioned to want one special thing and in a strange way that sets me free from wanting anything else.'

'You are a brave man.'

John grinned. 'I am a fool but a resigned fool and therefore in blinkers so try not to let me fall. What about you? What do you want most in the world?'

'Not to be here.'

~

An hour along the pass and Gabriel still puzzles the Lama. When that old man had leaned down, his breath a mix of raw onions and jasmine tea, Gabriel had wanted to take hold of his scrawny frame and toss him in the fire.

Such rage! He had thought he'd left that behind in the State Pen or the Marine Corp. Seems that part of him, a kid arraigned for murder, is very much alive. Twice lately he's felt it, today at the Puja and the last day in Suffolk.

He never wanted to do this trek. This last year he's been working on a new piece and wants to get back to it. Last February in China he was given a piece of black marble. The driver of the cart had beckoned Gabriel. 'You silent, Master,' he said. 'Take this and it teach you how to speak.' Now the marble is in his studio in Oxford. He's struggled with it, but then the week before the trek he got a glimpse of the creature enfolded within, saw hands clawing to get out and eyes begging release. Now the Lord God is biting his heels and he's stuck on a mountain with a priest laying a curse on him.

In Suffolk they got traditions in the Abbey going back centuries. One such tradition belongs to Charles's and his time as explorer and mountaineer. In the acting profession no one refers to the play Macbeth as anything other than the Scottish Play. Charles had a thing about saying goodbye when going on a climb.

It's a totem thing, a mojo, a spit-in-the-eye-of-the-devil. Any other word will do: so-long, cheerio, ta-ta, anything but goodbye. 'It's too final,' Charles would say. 'It puts a hex on things.'

Gabriel's not superstitious yet he humoured Charles's whimsical ways as did the family. That last day in Suffolk one of the household went against tradition.

It happened in the nursery. Gabriel was watching the twins as they slept. The door opened and Nanny Foster wandered in. Ma never liked her, said she was another

Ruby Rourke mischief-maker. Gabriel felt sorry for her. It's tough being old and dependent. That morning sympathy fled.

She slid up to the bed where Mickey and Chas were sleeping -those lads, you can't keep them apart; they start out in separate beds but end up together.

Up she comes smiling and winking. There and then Gabriel was seized by the desire to throw her out the window. 'Hello, Sir Gabriel,' she says. 'Saying ta-ta to the twins?' She went to wake the boys. 'Don't wake them,' he said. 'Let them sleep. She pouted. 'Nonsense! They can sleep anytime. You must say goodbye to your children. You're going up a mountain. You might never see them again.' She pulls the blanket away and nips Charley's cheek. 'Wake up, young Charley!' she shouts. 'Daddy's going away and you're to say goodbye!'

Just thinking about it Gabriel is sick with anger. Both boys were awake and holding on to him and crying, 'don't go, Daddy, don't say goodbye!'

The row brought Julia. Hair hanging down and a brush in her hand she stood in the doorway. Unmoved, she watched, grey in her hair and a question in her eyes. Then she walked away, not a word, only another echoing goodbye.

He left for the airport knowing he is a selfish son-of-a-bitch. Part time husband and father, he'd made a mess of their lives. Listening to John Beaufort struggling with love for Sophie and unwilling to compromise he was ashamed. If he'd said no when the need was pressed upon him Julia Beaufort would have found someone else and loved as she should be loved.

He never wanted to wed. Any feeling he had was for Joshua. But time goes on and Ma was lonely and Julia was there. He tried being honest. 'I don't want to short-change you,' he said. 'You deserve better.' But encouraged by Ma, and by Charles who liked having Gabriel nearby, Julia wouldn't give in. 'I know you can't give me all,' she said. 'I don't ask all, just a part of you.'

They wed, the twins came along, and Julia had part of something. There's a story about a Greek guy called Orpheus who followed his wife to hell trying to bring her back to life. The greater part of Gabriel died in '63 with Adelia on a mountain side. Divided, split in two, like Orpheus he is forever searching, and until he finds her again will never be whole.

It was the same when she was alive. In serving his need for her it seems he could be in two places at once, a mystery like that, the splitting of an egg can't be explained. Some people call it a gift. To be with Adelia is a gift. To be without her is a curse and not only his. It is Julia's curse, and little Mickey and Charley, and anyone else other than Joshua who seeks to love Gabriel.

Now there a Lama priest whispering in his ear suggesting it's too late for regret. 'I hope you said goodbye to your children, Master Archangel,' said the priest, his words echoing the Nanny. 'You're climbing a mountain. Do not be selfish and cling to tradition. You may never see them again.'

John Beaufort asked what Gabriel wanted most in the world. He replied, 'not to be here.' John probably thought him referring to the trek and the mountain. That's not what he meant. That's not it at all.

Chapter Twenty-Seven
Puppets

Doors slam shut, the chopper begins to lift. They're in the air, the landing strip receding below. Boots scrape the floor and rotors churn. No one speaks. Then as though challenging tension a SEAL – middle left, no name, no pack drill – nods toward Clyde. 'Shall I shoot him now, Boss? It'll save time later.'

Jake shook his head. 'Patience, my friend,' he said, calmly. 'No need to rush. I have it on good authority everything comes to him who waits.'

That was forty minutes ago. The drop-zone in sight they're on the alert.

'I guess this was always going to happen,' says Forrester.

'Written in the stars I'd say.'

'Believe in fate, do you?'

'No! Justice!'

'Justice? Isn't that another word for revenge?'

'Not in my book.'

'So who are you now?' asks Clyde. 'I mean what am I to call you?'

'What would you like to call me?'

'I'd like to call you deceased as in the ad in the Greeley Gazette.'

'That won't do. I've been there and didn't care for it.'

'I guess that grave really is empty.'

'Don't know about empty. There may be an incumbent but it isn't me.'

'Something of a miracle wouldn't you say?'

'I would.'

'So what *do* I call you?'

'You can call me Boss or Lieutenant, take your pick.'

'Maybe I'll settle for hey you.'

'Sure why not. It has a ring to it and I have been called worse.'

'Man that's true! Yellow-funk coward was what I heard.'

Teeth white against the mask, Jake grinned. 'Commander, you're way behind the times. It's gotten a whole lot richer since then and in several languages.'

'And that doesn't worry you?'

'Clearly not as much as it worries you.'

Jake made a decision. His grief with this man is personal. While there are others under his command it will remain so. Nothing gets in the way of the mission. If Forrester can't see it that way he's not getting off this Helo.

He leaned forward and every SEAL leant with him. Temperature and noise level drop. Hand on the holster of his sidearm, he stared at Forrester. 'As of this moment you've two choices. You're with us or you're against us.'

Forrester eyes are black stones. A minute ticks away.

Jake unclips the holster. Alongside him Sebastian Farrell shifts in his seat. He knows as does every man in the Huey once drawn the .45 will fire.

'Well Commander? Which is it to be?'

'Depends.'

'On what?'

'How long you intend the moment to last.'

'I can tell you how long it will last. While I am Team Leader it will last until every man, including you, is back on the Helo and lifting out. Think of me as Noah and this the Ark. I'm not leaving until all the animals are aboard.'

'That's a comforting thought.'

'Then be comforted.'

'And after that?'

'Anything goes.'

Forrester was silent. Then he nodded. 'Agreed.'

The holster is fastened. A light blinks red. Men get to their feet.

The Huey makes two dummy passes. The light blinks green/green, and one, two, three... eight black-widow spider abseil into the night and landing with a series of muted thumps they melt into the undergrowth.

Clyde followed into the darkness, the image of a primed .45 burned into his retina. That's okay, *Boss*, getting out of this alive means working as a unit. Just because I've screwed up my life doesn't mean I'm in a rush to end it. Ethan Winter, Jack Frost, whatever you're called, dodged one bullet. Odds are you can do it again.

Ah but he is so angry his chest aches from holding it in! It's one thing to suspect a set-up quite another to watch it roll out. Winter is bright but he's no Machiavelli. In hospital doped to the eyeballs and a bullet in your chest you're in no condition to figure a scheme like this. It's obvious whose hand is at the tiller. This is about Sam Jentzen's wife and a fumble behind a hatcheck stand. Clyde's here to atone for a long-standing sin. While the meatheads lumbering in the Boss's wake don't know the joke they recognise the clown.

The Director said it. 'You'll be supported by special ops. It's a tight operation, and not among friends, but from what I hear the guy leading the team is hot stuff, though the name, Frost, wouldn't suggest it.' At the time Clyde thought it a reference to being behind the lines. Not a chance! It's in the words 'not among friends.' The Director was giving the puppet a glimpse of the strings.

~

It begins to rain. As shadows they move as one.

They've covered plenty ground and already soaked to the skin. Jake keeps them moving. According to calculations they're within five clicks of the target. There's a shift among the Team, though still wary they see Forrester is familiar with the terrain and as fast and quiet as any man. No spare wheel, they're less antagonistic and ever witty, Forrester responds with the humorous gesture.

Jake's sends him up front where he can be seen. Don't be fooled by the grin, humour is his coverall. Underneath that smile is a hair trigger.

The Point Man signals. 'Target ahead.'

Binoculars trained on the site, Jake indicates a washing line. 'You sure you have a guy in there?' he says to

Forrester. 'Only it would be a lot easier to lay C4 down without disturbing the inmates.'

'I am assured of the agents. Why are you thinking of going ahead?'

'Negative. As I said we're not leaving until every man is back on the Huey and if he's here that includes your operative.'

The Team take up assigned positions. The plan is formed, no need for debate. Jake nods to his radio-man to maintain shut-down. 'Copy that, Boss.'

Jakes smiles bitterly. He knows about copies. Whatever else happens he'll keep the name Frost. Until yesterday this name didn't fit. Lack of self worth and Granma Powell's fretful voice in his ear, he felt he'd let the family down. Then he bumped into Hacker Thompson in the mess-tent, or rather Hacker concerned with an oversize burger bumped into him.

Burger poised and mouth open Hacker stared taking in Jake's white hair and worn face. There was a moment, a count of three, when wheels were turning. Then 'commonsense' prevailed – a bullet in the chest and a grave in Colorado rendering a familiar face unfamiliar. 'Sorry buddy.' Hacker bit into the burger and walked on. In that moment Jake understood what the General meant by die today and be free tomorrow. The pain of losing life as Ethan Winter remains, yet as Jake Frost – no fouled-up missions and pointing fingers – he is a free man.

It's the same with the words Vengeance is Mine. At the time they made no sense. Now with Forrester less than a hand clasp away they make sense. In the dream the voice on the phone was that of Sophie's uncle. Jake used to think a man couldn't be in two places at once. He doesn't think that now. There's more to man than the flesh, it's as Forrester said – some kind of miracle.

~

The main assault began at 0200 hours. When the OC said they'd be making noise he meant it! Planes launched from Aircraft Carriers in the Gulf of Tonkin began rolling across the skies, so many you couldn't keep track, A-7 light and A-6 medium attack flying in two waves of three tracks each wave three minutes apart, the A-6s coming in low altitude and the A-7s above at about 20,000 feet. Along with attack planes there are EB1s and EK8-3Bs with electronic countermeasure to block NV radio frequencies. Add to that, F4 Phantoms screaming across the skies and you get an idea.

The Phantoms were launched against Russian MIGs fighters except there wasn't any. It seemed the Armada of the Sky had taken North Korean air-waves by surprise.

'Jesus Christ,' whispered Seb.

'Yup and His Holy Mother.'

Jake and the Team were not the only ones watching the display. Two minutes of rolling thunder and they knew the station manned. Three guys ran out of the hut and climbing on a wall stood shouting and gesticulating. A trio of ducks in a row against the skyline waiting to be shot down it didn't go unnoticed. Aware of fingers on triggers Jake shook his head. He too would prefer picking them off there-and-then but without confirmation it couldn't be done.

'Your guys?' he whispered. 'Do you know who you're looking for?'

Forrester shook his head. 'Not from this distance.'

They needed to move. Soon the alarm will be raised in every village. At the moment – the three Stooges intent on the wall and so much noise above – they could have rolled Cissy out and no one would've heard.

The compound was on a hillock edged on three sides by a ditch. The left-hand ditch was filled with filthy water, human waste, and a dead rat. Breath tight and weapon high, Jake slid into the ditch. Seb and Forrester with him they climbed the bank until Jake was so close to the middle duck he could see the picture on the guy's T-shirt, Bugs Bunny chewing a carrot: '*That's All Folks.*'

Whoosh! A Surface to Air Missile streaked skyward over the Gulf. North Korean Air Space was finally awake. Two minutes and another SAM raced away and then another, flares floating through the navy-blue sky like Chinese lanterns, flares fell, illuminating three dirty tadpoles squirming on the bank.

The men on the wall turned, looked, aimed their weapons, and were blown away by Pick Madsen and his M30. 'Oh well,' said Forrester picking a piece of flesh from his vest. 'I guess you won't need my nose after all.'

The station was empty save for rats and a half starved dog. That there had been prisoners was apparent, shackles on the wall and traces of blood. A mound of earth out back suggested whoever was there had been killed.

Jake kicked the mound. 'Do you need to know what's under here?'

Forrester grinned. 'What and find another empty grave? I don't think so.'

'Listen asshole!' barked Jake, sick of the man and his smile. 'Is there any point digging? Would you know your guy if he's there?'

'Waste of time.' Forrester shook his head. 'Dead, the trail is washed out.'

'Bit like this mission,' said Sebastian.

'I wouldn't say that,' said Forrester. 'Old friends reunited? The chance to catch up on the news, whose doing what to whom?'

'Can the chat!' They backed up beyond the ditch into scrubland and waited. Much as Jake wanted to blow the station he had to wait until the Huey returned. Flares still dropping and planes overhead they had a degree of cover. Blow the C4 and the world would know where they are.

'So what do you think?' Seb whispered. 'Has the main assault party landed?'

'They're here and busy.'

'But why no retaliation? Where are the North Korean fighters?'

'I can only assume Sun Tzu was right. It is about the element of surprise.'

'Talking of surprises,' Seb thumbed toward Forrester. 'Who'd have seen that one coming? I don't trust the guy. He wants you dead.'

A report radioed, Jake left Seb to his ruminations; he doesn't trust Forrester either but needs to focus on here and now. That the CIA operatives aren't here is not his problem. Getting the Team back is. If Forrester wants a pissing contest he'll have to wait for a convenient wall.

~

There's a scrimmage going on, Pick Madsen and Spider Law squaring up.

'What's going on?'

'It's the fucking dog,' spat Law. 'Madsen wants to take it back with us.'

Frustration, the lack of a resolution to the mission, plus the racket from above, was getting to them. 'Forget the dog.'

'But Boss look at it! It's starving.'

'Leave it your ration.'

'And what happens when the C4 blows? Does the dog blow with it?'

'What can I say, Pick. It's a dog's life.'

'Let him take it.' Forrester tossed in his two cents.

'It's staying put. Madsen, drop that rope and get over here!'

Pick untied the dog where it fled to the edge of a clearing.

Forrester laughed. 'Lieutenant, I'm surprised at you. I would've thought after your former mischance, the woman and her baby and all that, you'd be leading the charge to take Bowser back home.'

'And why would you think that?'

'Family feeling! My wife is into animal rights. I felt sure a friend of the family would see a chance to redeem himself. You know, badge of honour? We didn't kill any goons or set prisoners free but we did save a cute little doggie.'

'Shut your mouth.' Red rag to a bull Sebastian stepped up.

'It's okay, Seb.'

'It is not okay! Who the fuck does he think he's talking to? How dare he talk of Sophie and the family as if he's part of it? He's nothing. Shit trodden in on a stranger's boot is all he is! And speaking as a close friend of the family the sooner someone scrapes him off the better.'

'Belay that, Seb!' Jake took his arm. 'Don't do this now.'

'It needs to come out. People need to know him for what he is, the dirt that's on his hands. They need to recognise evil and keep their distance.'

'Helo approaching, Boss!' said the radio man. 'New orders coming in!'

Jake listened in on the radio. 'Hold up! A secondary wave of the Main Task Force dropped on the wrong compound is taking fire. We're going in to help.'

Adding fire to fire the C4 blew as the HH-53 lumbered away. Up against a flesh and blood enemy and not their personal demons the Team is tight, sphincters and emotions in check they are charged with new meaning.

Radio silence broken Jake hears messages passing back and forth, details unclear yet it seems there's been a blunder. The main assault party hit the correct target but two compounds being of the same size and appearance a HH-3 drifted south and set the secondary wave down among hostiles.

'Drop Zone in sight.'

The chopper was dropping into the thick of the fight when an explosion lit up the area, multiple gasoline barrels on fire, the scene below floodlit.

'Holy shit!' Seb gasped. 'See what I see, Boss.'

'Affirmative.'

'See how tall those guys are and their clothes!'

Jake nodded. There were new faces down there. Lighter skinned, taller and wielding better equipment – they are not Vietnamese.

'What's your guess Russian?'

'I reckon.'

'What are they doing here?'

'A training camp is my guess,' said Jake.

It was more than a guess. Back at Fort Belvoir he heard Russian technicians were training the North Vietnamese in the use of interceptor equipment. If that's the case here then history may well prove the HH-53 'blunder' no blunder at all; dropping on this compound may turn out to be a lucky strike.

~

Jake's orders are to take out a machine gun nest south of the west wall and from there to blow a bridge north of the compound.

They're out the chopper and running. Talk about Armageddon, the sky so heavy with traffic, noise presses on the scull. For NV troops this must have been some alarm call, even now they have that stunned WTF look in their eyes.

Three minutes and the target fox-hole found and the machine gun silenced. While not exactly a walk in the park the team come through without a scrape. Next step would have been to get to the bridge and employ satchel charges. They never got to it. In the confusion some guy juggling too much data forgot there were foot soldiers in the area and sent Airborne in to dispose of the bridge by way of cluster bombs. Blown face down in the dirt Jake heard and felt the resulting explosions. Then a Skyraider is screaming in from the north strafing what's left of the bridge. 'Jesus Christ!' Forrester is alongside. 'I wish I'd remembered to bring my journal. This is turning out quite a day.'

The A-1E came in again bullets flying, and then seeming to recognise the poor bastards huddled in the grass, tips its wings and leaves.

'So what now, Ice Man?' said Forrester. 'Do we come out with our hands held high or do we call for mother?'

Jake didn't answer. Ears ringing, he was staring at the burnt out wreck of an armoured car. Overturned and stripped of useful parts it lay aslant of what was left of the bridge. There was a problem with that carrier.

'What? Forrester sniffed the air.

'I'm not sure.'

Jake sat up and suddenly Forrester's coming at him.

The barrel of a rifle poking through the armoured car turret, Clyde spotted the problem, and with the speed and force of a line-backer ran at Jake.

They hit the ground, the bullet parting Clyde's hair. He felt the burn as it removed a layer of skin from his cheek and scalp. There was the rap of a '45 and the shooter was sprawled over the carrier, half his head missing.

Blood trickling down his cheek he sat up. 'That was unexpected.'

'You can say that again,' muttered Seb Farrell.

Clyde wiped his face. 'Too close for comfort wouldn't you say?'

Jake Frost was staring at him as was the rest of the team.

Hand shaking, more surprised than anyone, Clyde continued to wipe blood from his face. 'Oh Mr De Mille!' he parodied hysteria. 'I'm ruined, aren't I? I'll never get another close-up again!'

'No, you goddamn hustler!' Seb Farrell tossed him a band aid. 'You got the one thing you were missing, a fencing scar.'

~

The Team are waiting extraction. The compound is a blazing ruin. F-4s continue to shoot-up-the-sky as do NV Surface to Air Missiles but with the message 'negative packages' picked up on the radio the feeling among the Team is that the station back there is empty of prisoners.

'I guess the VC moved the POWs,' said Pick Madsen.

'Looks that way.'

'Then all of this, the whole deal start to end, has been a waste of time.'

'Can the chat, Mister Madsen,' Jake Frost jumped on it. 'We don't know the facts so until we do maintain present order.'

Clyde said nothing. No point in offering an opinion. Whatever went down it'll only be men with need-to-know who learn the truth, all else will be whatever sweetened pill the world is thought best to swallow.

Exhausted, too weary to move, he sat cradling an M16. Open-warfare is not his bag. He prefers being alone and in control of his own destiny. That way, he decided, he wouldn't do anything dumb, like saving the life of a guy he loathes.

Would you fucking believe it? Empty-eyed he stared out. Ethan fucking Winter aka Jake Frost! I pulled him away from line of fire.

It wasn't a question of choice. It was a knee jerk reaction. No time to think, it's what you'd do for any guy in line of fire. There's no other explanation, at least none he can give credence. Okay, for a split second he did see Sophie's face, the way she looked the day he said Winter was dead, the emptying of life from her eyes, the sinking down from which she has never really recovered.

The Huey's taking the SEALs back to Udorn. Clyde's made his own arrangement bumming a lift aboard a sea plane with a CIA mucker.

No jolly SEAL camaraderie for him. It's Udorn, Papa Joe's Bar on Lilac Street, a large beer, and a juicy thigh sandwich – Jake Frost, the Company, Sam Jentzen, and for that matter, Sophie, can go to hell!

'A moment of your time, Commander.'

Here comes the office boy, Lieutenant Frost, and his notebook mentality needing to check me off the list. 'What do you want, my fine friend?'

'I understand you've made separate travel plans.'

'That is the case.'

Frost stuck out his jaw. 'We came as a team of eight. If it's all the same with you we go back as a team of eight.'

'No can do, Boss,' Clyde clipped his forehead. 'Me and my new babe magnet scar have an appointment with Papa Joe's. It won't wait.'

Frost stares. Clyde can read his bewilderment: 'What the fuck is it with you? Why mess with a whore when you could have Sophie?'

Sophie, Sophie, Sophie! The name gives Clyde such exquisite joy and pain. So much he would like to tell the lady – how he feels about the touch of her skin, the velvet of her lips and how it feels to hold her, but none of it to this guy.

Silence builds.

Frost shrugs. 'Have it your way.'

'I intend to.'

Frost continued to stare. 'I should say thank you.'

'Why?'

'I believe it is customary to do when someone saves your life.'

'As it is customary for the saviour to reply you're welcome, but don't bother because you're not welcome. I don't know why I did it. Given the same situation I'd leave the guy fill you full of holes.'

'Is that so?'

'It is. Best you keep your thanks to yourself and put the whole unfortunate business down to a mental aberration on my part.'

'As you wish.' Frost turned and walked away.

As you wish?

As you fucking wish!

Clyde raised the M16 to his shoulder. He had Frost in the crosshairs, the wide shoulders and swinging walk. There was silence. Planes passed over head, Helos chippering their lazy way across the horizon, but not a sound, only blood pounding in his ear. His finger hovered and in the heat haze a drop of sweat slid down his cheek onto his lips. It tasted salty like tears.

He lowered the weapon.

And behind him six men lowered theirs.

Chapter Twenty-Eight
Photo Stills

They've been climbing an hour. The air is thin; people were flagging until there was a shout, a Sherpa indicating pugmarks in the snow and a mangled carcase. They huddled about the remains.

'Is it a leopard kill?' said Tim.

'Looks that way.'

'Do you think he's still around?'

'I doubt it,' said Gabriel.

'He could still be close by. What do you say, John?'

John prodded the carcase. 'I say, we can wash this one out. Whatever made this kill will have gone to ground sleeping it off.'

'There might be another close by.'

'These are solitary animals,' said Gabriel. 'They don't usually hunt in pairs.'

Tim set his jaw. 'It's got to be worth a look! I mean, Jeez! It's the closest we've been to anything of value on four legs since we came. I for one don't want to have come all this way and go back empty handed.'

The discussion passed back and forth until it was suggested they drop down a level gaining better air and then go on to Camp Two.

Gabe knew they were wasting energy. In this thin air successful climbing, the kind that gets you to the top of Everest is a continual round of ascent and descent. You can't keep going up; starved of oxygen a man becomes confused and make mistakes. You must allow for dropping down to lower points and resting otherwise your body will give up. Charles used to say reaching the top of the North Face meant climbing three times over. 'Snakes and ladders, dear boy. You just hope to climb the ladder more times than you fall down.'

Stumbling and falling, Tim was first to feel it.

Gabriel helped him to his feet. 'You okay?'

'I'd be a lot better if people stopped asking if I'm okay.'

'You seem to be in trouble.'

'I'm not.'

'Maybe you need to rest awhile.'

'Maybe I need to get off this mountain.'

'I thought you were one for goin' on.'

'I've changed my mind.'

'Timothy Hunter changin' his mind! Now I know there's somethin' wrong. What is it, son, you missin' army fatigues?'

Tim tightened the pack on his back. 'I am not your son.'

'What?'

'I said I'm not your son. I am Alexander Hunter's son, grandson of William Hunter, and nothing whatsoever to do with you.'

'Okay.'

'Actually it's not okay. While a murdering ex-convict continues to be in close contact with my family it is anything but okay.'

'You need to rest.'

'And you need to drop the idea of being a guardian to me and Sophie after this climb. We're able to take care of ourselves. The whole notion of guardianship was wrong. We have Aunt Sarah and grandmother. Why would we need you?

'It wasn't my idea, Tim. It was your father's.'

'So you say.'

'No, it's what Alex Hunter and his lawyers said, not just once, three times. '

'I don't care how many Wills or how many lawyers it took to draw them up! Lawyers make mistakes. They are not infallible.'

'You sayin' your father was mistaken in wantin' me to care for you?'

'I'm saying my father was an honourable man. This guardianship came about because he felt in some way obliged to bring it about.'

'Believe that and you know nothin' about your father or me.'

'I know this much, no one can stand in for my pa. No one! I didn't need guarding in '63. I don't need it now. And if there had to be a death on that mountain why couldn't it have been yours.'

Tim blundered away.

Gabriel stared after him. What brought that on? This is completely out of character. Black and white of opinion he is his father's son yet like his father usually well-mannered. Gabriel gave him a moment then followed.

'Okay, what's the problem?'

Tim was weeping. 'I told you I don't want you calling me son.'

'We've established that. Now tell me what's really botherin' you.'

'It's the way they died.' Tim scrubbed his face with his sleeve. 'I can't get that out my head.'

'It was to be expected. Bein' here you're bound to feel that way.'

'I never expected it. If I had I wouldn't have joined the trek.'

'These things sneak up on a man,' said Gabriel. 'You think the darkness is past but then you find you're only marking time.'

'I'm sorry about what I said,' Tim struggled. 'I didn't mean it. It's just that I wasn't there when they died. All these years in my heart I've been waiting for them to come home. Today I realised they're never coming home.'

No more climbing after that, Gabriel told John they needed to return.

The route down is steep with heavy overhangs. Snow falling thick and fast, a Sherpa saying there were heavy landfalls overnight, they agreed for safety's sake to split into three teams, John leading the first pack, Sherpa Nasang the second, and Gabriel the anchor man on the third, roped together, and visibility decreasing, they were at least in touch.

They start down. Gabriel stayed in close to the boys. Contrary to former worries Josh came out of this well. A natural, he seems to know where best to put his hands and feet. Tim is all over the place. Almost ten years have passed since the cable-car tragedy. If that boy feels anywhere near the loss Gabriel feels then God help him. It's never over. There's only one cure for such a wound and it can't be found in this world.

~

Tim can't wait to get down and out of Nepal. Not being with his folks when they died has always been a problem. Sophie and Josh dealt with it first-hand, hard for them but real. For him what happened in Switzerland has over time become a series of long range photo stills.

In '63 tragedy was furthest from his mind. He was chatting to a girl in the Whitney's pool, laughing and wondering how long before he could kiss her. Then someone called his name. He'd turned. Diana Whitney stood cradling the phone, her face pale, her husband equally pale behind her.

As a species we treasure romantic notions. We think we're attuned to our nearest and dearest, being so close to Mom he'd always assumed he would know if anything happened to her and Dad. It turned out he knew nothing – his brain, or whatever passes for a brain, busy ogling a bikini top, water in the pool highlighting the girl's nipples. Next he knows he's throwing on his clothes and in back of a Buick. More phone calls follow more photo stills, a funeral parlour massed with flowers, the perfume so heavy it made him vomit. Then shoulders back, he's kitted out in best blues part of the West Point escort.

Click, click, then there's a row of pretty ladies weeping, Sophie a pale beauty in a black veil. The last photo is of a pair of caskets being lowered into a hole in the ground, a wreath of white daisies floating on top.

Rat-ta-tat, a gun salute, and silence.

Years go by and the same silence stops his ears. At night at Granma Ellen's he'll creep into the rumble room where Mom's clothes are stored. A blanket about his shoulders he'll sleep in the rocking chair. Sometimes she's there stroking his head and kissing him. 'Don't worry, darling,' she'll say, 'I'm here.'

When John Beaufort suggested Nepal an old friend of Mom's, a psychologist, said it might help. It doesn't help. Everywhere he looks rock surges to the sky, and he, Tim Hunter, is crushed under the weight of grandeur.

Then they find the remains of a dead goat and silence is broken. Feelings rush in, guilt at not being there to say goodbye. Sophie had the ballet and a complicated love life. Josh had Suffolk, the Brits, and Harrow. Tim had West Point and a guardian. This hard, cold rage isn't aimed at Mom and Gabriel. Things happen in wartime and Dad was missing for three years. Nor is he angry with Josh, the product of those three years.

It's Dad! Tim's anger is for Dad.

During the Korean War Mom suffered in silence. If she did speak of Dad it was within her heart. Gramps never stopped talking. 'My son! My boy, the Medal Winner!' Alex Hunter assumed mythic proportion. He was the distant Ideal, the man, the hero his young son hoped one day to be.

Then the war is over. Alexander Hunter marched through the door and what d'ya know the tales are true! Tim is the only son of a hero.

Years go by and life is good. Then one day childhood is done. Such a man shouldn't die on a mountainside. A hero should scorn mortal situations. He should defy a dumb mountain. He should have yelled, 'I am Ash Hunter, survivor of two wars, Holder of the Medal of Honour and father to a beloved son. I'm not dying. My boy Timothy is waiting back home.'

At and around this time a lesser known hero was ever in the background, Gabriel Templar, a man who could stare into the sun. When Tim was a kid he looked up to the man who worked with eagles, the man with wings. When Dad died he turned again to the hero. Too late! The hero was someone else's father – no seats vacant at the hearth.

Last night Joshua sat toasting his feet before a fire. Though yards apart father and son were joined together, their movements mirrored.

It hurt seeing that. Tim wanted to destroy the bond, to take a knife and slash the strings so that Josh and his living father would know how it felt to be alone.

What kind of brother thinks like that? Dad trusted Gabriel. At cost to himself he made his wife's lover guardian to his children. In wishing that guardian dead he denies his father's sacrifice. It's as well Joshua didn't hear the way Tim spoke to Gabriel. It would have hurt their friendship. Joshua is really bright! He got himself into Harrow. Bright and spooky he senses situations before they happen. Sophie's the same. The weird stuff links them together. Tim has his own intuitive map-reading thing but in the main is a hands-on guy.

West Point sees Tim as a typical army brat and that's okay, he is proud to follow in father's footstep, to be like

General Alexander Hunter is reason for living. Today on the plateau he was no hero.

It was the goat's carcase. Bloodied flesh was all it was, a hank of skin and bone. The light inside, the living creature was gone. It made Tim think – is this what life comes down to, people and things vanishing overnight, because if it is then the world is a terrible place and every footfall hazardous.

It rattled him. What are they doing on a mountain? Accidents happen on mountains. Anyone can fall and disappear.

Now he's questioning every move. Stumbling, losing momentum, he doesn't know where he is.

Maybe it was that loss of concentration that made him slow to act when the path fell from under Gabriel's feet.

'Oh shit!' Joshua felt it first and called out. 'Look out Dad! Look out Tim!'

There was a splintering crack and the sound of Gabriel's boots scrabbling for purchase on loose snow. Tim felt the rope whip through his harness and heard Joshua's cry of fear as he was dragged to the edge.

He hit out slamming his axe into a rock-face, a Sherpa ahead doing the same. There was a brief cessation of movement, all and everything held in stasis, and then the edge of the path crumbled.

Gabriel was falling and dragging Joshua and Tim after him.

A knife flashed. Tim saw it. He wanted to shout: 'Don't Gabriel! I didn't mean it! I don't want you to die!'

But his tongue stuck to the roof of his mouth.

Zip, the knife flashed again, a rope was severed.

Released from the dragging weight Joshua fell forward onto the path and Tim with him. The scraping sound of boots on stone was no more.

Chapter Twenty-Nine
Wasted Effort

'What say we toddle along to the concert?'

'Concert?' Clyde stared into the bottom of the glass.

'Yeah.' Hilliard pointed to a poster pinned over the bar. 'They're doing Messiah here at the Base. The choir's not overmuch but I'm giving it a go.'

Hilliard started singing, everybody in the bar turning to look.

'Nice voice, Pat,' said Clyde. 'Tuneful but rusty.'

'That comes of too many fags. My mammy warned me. She said I'd end up with lung cancer. But look at me.' He pounded his chest. 'Sound as a bell.'

'My mammy used to warn me against things.'

'Giving up fags?'

'No, married women.'

'And she was right. Stick with spinsters, Clyde, my boy. They're grateful for whatever they get. So are you coming to hear Messiah?'

'All that caterwauling, I think not.'

'Well I'm going. Bartender!' Hilliard slapped the counter. 'Slip me a bottle of your finest!'

'I thought we were going to Papa Joe's.'

'We went to Papa Joes.'

'We did?'

'Yes and got kicked out, you and your wandering hands.'

'Oh yeah, shame about that. She had great tits, lively.'

'Yes and a couple of lively brothers. We were lucky to get out alive.'

'How was I to know she was getting married? They should have said. If I'd known there was a bridal party I wouldn't have bothered going in.'

'I guess so. Bartender! Where's that bottle!' A bottle crossed the counter and was stuffed in his pocket. 'That's me sorted. Are you coming or not?'

'I've no ear for music.'

Hilliard slid off the stool. 'Then I shall see you later.'

'Not much later I hope,' muttered Clyde. 'This place is a dump. I don't want to be hanging about here all night.'

Hilliard consulted his watch. 'The concert finishes at 2200 hours. A nightcap in the Commissary and a couple of hours sleep? How does 0230 suit you?'

'0230? I wouldn't have thought you could see the plane never mind fly it.'

'Sure I will. This is Patrick Hilliard you're talking to, Connemara's answer to Eugene Esmonde. If I can't get you home nobody can.'

'Okay then, let's go to the concert.' Clyde lurched to his feet. 'I can hardly sit here drinking on my own.'

Hilliard swept the room with his arm. 'Why be alone when you can have all these gorgeous creatures just waiting to entertain you.'

Clyde looked about the bar. Twenty pairs of eyelashes batted, the usual hybrids, males passing as females, females pretending to be female, and an undertow of whatever pleases. 'I'll pass. Why chew on horsemeat when you've prime rib at home.'

~

They sat at back of the chapel, Hilliard sucking on a bottle and Clyde staring into nothing. What am I doing here? I could be halfway home.

They ran into the two FFs earlier out by the harbour wall. Strange, he ought to have registered some feeling seeing them but felt nothing. Other than a brief contretemps on the sidewalk – knee jerk machismo – they went their separate ways, a backward glance and then nothing, each dead to the other.

Dead is the way Clyde feels and has felt since digging the graveyard in Colorado, as though in searching for a dead man he left a living self behind.

This morning he visited the Company office relaying information, that there was nothing and no one to save at the outpost other than a mangy dog. They were too busy listening to messages coming across the wire. One guy was cracking his sides. 'Thousands of dollars and hundreds of man-hours figuring it out and the mission to rescue American POWs draws a big fat Zero.'

His partner was equally gleeful. 'Nixon's public relations guys must be working their balls off right now trying to figure a favourable spin on this.'

Clyde was not amused. 'Is that how you see it? Wasted effort?'

The guy had shrugged. 'Is there any other way? They're gonna need Harry Houdini to pull this one out the bag or another Winston Churchill. A guy who can turn Dunkirk into a triumph is the only one to get them out of this.'

Useless bastards! Had this been another day and another Clyde he'd have kicked their lazy asses. What do they know schlepping about in their air-conditioned room eating popcorn and drinking beer? Clyde's eyes are still buzzing from watching the Skyraider surf the bridge. The guts of the pilot! That didn't look like wasted effort. Being sent to pull a non-existent agent from the field is a waste of effort! Finding shackles and blood and a newly dug grave and some poor sucker buried beneath, that too is waste.

He put it to them. 'Since when was trying to save a man's life a waste of time.'

'It is if he'd never had a life to lose in the first place.'

Clyde knew that the Shit-for-brains was trying to be smart; still, he couldn't get the words out of his head. Never had a life to lose? Sitting in the barracks chapel listening to good music badly sung that sounded like an epitaph.

He's never been into heavy stuff. Classical music, fat sopranos rattling their tonsils, is not for him. The choir were not good. Bored as he was, weary unto his bones, ears still ringing from gunfire, for a time nothing got through, and then this girl, ugly looking broad with bat-wing ears began to sing.

If you asked him now what the aria was about he couldn't tell you – a shepherd carrying a lamb, Come unto Jesus all you who are heavy laden, who knew? Whatever, the purity of her voice and the idea of being carried home

to rest got to Clyde, and there in that scrappy building –
jarheads sweating like pigs – tears filled his eyes. It would
be good to be home, to wake in the morning with sunlight
streaming through the window and birds singing.

He'd get up, take a quick shower, brush his teeth, and
then knock on her door. 'Come on in,' she'd pull back the
bed-cover. 'I've been waiting for you.'

Stupid, he brushed tears away. You know what this is,
it's After Battle Blues. It's in the faces of guys all around
you.

Still fighting back tears he sat there. Next he knows
Pat's urging him to stand.

'Get up,' he's saying.' It's the Hallelujah chorus.'

'What!' Everyone is on their feet and singing, sweaty
jarheads and all. Fuck it, he didn't know a word, had to
stand there looking dumb.

Hilliard told him later it was a custom started by an
English king getting to his feet mid-concert thus forcing
courtiers and everyone else to stand with him.

The English! That's typical of their rules and
regulations. Tea and strawberry jam and scones, bearskins
and bowler hats, Simpson's in the Strand, Sophie's full of
it. She'll smile and say with lemon is the only way to drink
Earl Grey tea. And if you wanna eat fish and chips do it out
of newspaper. A bag lady once told her it's the English
way.

Clyde slumped down in the seat. Soon as he's back
Stateside he'll take up with someone new, maybe Emilia
again…though no, not her! Maybe that flautist there in the
orchestra? She looks pretty hot. He's got to do something.
Thinking of Sophie is gonna kill him.

~

It was cold on the airstrip and surreally calm after all the heavy metal.

Yawning, he climbed aboard. Hilliard was in the cockpit signalling A-okay to the flight deck. Clyde had a hangover. Pat, who'd consumed infinitely more booze, was full of pep. 'Shut the fuck up will you, Pat.'

'What's the matter, nasty head?'

'You could say that.'

'You should have stuck to whisky. Mixing drinks gives you a hangover.'

'Then again it could have been the choir.'

'They really weren't very good. But they tried, and isn't that all we can do.'

Christ! Clyde had forgotten that Pat is the male version of Pollyanna. Even in the darkest hour he'll find the silver lining, which if you didn't know his story you'd wonder why he drank so much.

Clyde doesn't wonder – he knows. Ten years ago Patrick Finlay Hilliard was married to his childhood sweetheart. They had three little daughters, 2, 3, 5, and a neat terraced house in Derry close by the industrial estate. Pat came home one morning to half the street blown away plus his little family.

It's how he became known to CIA. After the tragedy he moved to Boston to be with his sister. There is strong Irish American affiliation in Boston, maybe more than a few IRA sympathisers. In '69 when the bombing campaign started in Northern Ireland Langley got a call offering information on links back home.

It's how they met, Clyde acting as go-between. In the question of why a man would inform against his own and what would happen if they found out Pat's position is clear. 'They can do what they like with me. If what I tell you stops one man coming home to find his children in pieces and his wife's hand still wearing her wedding ring in the front yard then it's okay.'

This man has been brought so low and yet can enter a church, kneel and pray, and then sit humming a religious aria that speaks of 'a voice crying in the wilderness,' without acknowledging the terrible irony.

Clyde asked him. 'How can you believe in God after what you've been through? Where was He when your kids were dying?'

Pat looked at him. 'It's not the Lord's fault the gas-pipe split. It's the fucking eejit that laid it. And He was there when my little 'uns passed and caught them in His arms.'

Still baffled, Clyde pursued it. 'If you've that kind of faith why the need to get rat-assed?' Pat smiled. 'The Lord God is no tyrant. He has a kind heart and love of humanity. He knows I don't want to aim this plane into the ground or put a bullet in my brain. He knows I don't need to go to Hell. I have it here. So when in desperation I tilt the bottle His mighty hand tilts it with me.'

That kind of philosophy is beyond Clyde. He doesn't know what to do with it. All he can do is be there when God isn't enough and Pat calls in the early hours. 'Tidy-Man! I'm teetering on the edge. Come stop me!'

No call for help this morning. Pat is up and running. It's Clyde that's teetering. No sleep and too much booze he couldn't be further on the edge. Mission? If there was one

it's done now and he won't be taking it up with the
General. He had it coming. Leonora Jentzen is a good
woman and not used to loosening her corsets with a guy
half her age. She didn't like what they were doing but, as
with most women whose husbands are away, was prey to
Jackals.

It will be interesting to see if the Director keeps his
promise and lets Clyde leave the Company – not that it
matters. The marriage is over. Culpepper will get his
decree nisi. With nothing else to do Clyde might return to
Saigon. Whatever the day there are always messes to clear
up and Pipers to Pay.

~

When the needles flickered on empty and Pat began to
pray, Clyde was asleep and dreaming and thought the
muttered prayer part of the dream.

More memory than dream, he was in the Mill turret
room setting the shellac box on the table with a new
bracelet inside.

Last time in New York he bought it. Coral interwoven
with gold, he thought it a beautiful thing. A kiss before
leaving, the bracelets used to be his trade mark. Time
moving on there must be scores of them dangling from all
manner of wrists. Only the other day he was crossing
Times Square. A girl passed by, Haley is her name, a
receptionist at Brooks Brothers Midtown, great ass, apples
under a satin doily.

Recognising her and the bracelet he smiled. She cut him dead and in passing rattled the bracelet, 'drop dead, sonofabitch,' the message.

Bad habits are hard to break but he shouldn't have passed it on to Sophie. She's a gold band on the third finger situation not a Bibelot Babe.

In the dream he picked up the coral bracelet and hooked it about his own wrist whereupon like the jaws of a trap it sank into his flesh.

It hurt! He tried pulling it off but it wouldn't budge. In the end he was shouting. 'For Chrissakes let me go! I promise never to do it again.'

He woke to Hilliard praying and the plane dropping out of the sky.

'What the fuck?' Clyde started to his feet.

'Fuel gauge's on empty.'

'You have got to be kidding!'

'Nope. It's those thieving bastards back at the Base,' said Hilliard. 'They're always doing it, siphoning the tanks of one plane to feed another.'

'Why didn't you check?'

'I did. The gauge is faulty.'

The way they were dropping, the speed and angle, they were in trouble.

'Where are we exactly? Give me coordinates!' Clyde got on the blower putting out a May-Day. 'Chrissakes Pat, why didn't you wake me?'

He shrugged. 'And do what, have you stick your arms through the windows and flap! You couldn't have done anything. I figured I was better floating her down on my own rather than you up front panicking.'

'I'm not panicking.'

'You are and you need to shut up. I know what I'm doing. I've seen where we're going, that strip of beach coming up portside.'

'You talking crash-landing?'

'I ain't talking feather beds. Now back off,' said Pat adjusting the flaps. 'I know my plane. I know what it can do and what it can't. I need quiet to find my way through and you need to get back there with the crates making sure they're tied down. Don't want anything flying loose when we hit dirt.'

Clyde crouched among packing cases wedged between washing machine parts and Singer sewing machines. From a bird's eye view he could see the strip of beach rising up toward them as a strand of satin ribbon.

What a pilot! The Skyraider pilot had nothing on this old drunk. The plane was coming in soft and smooth nothing shaking. All Pat had to do was keep his fingers crossed and pray. 'Hail Mary full of Grace the Lord is with thee, blessed art thou among women and blessed is the fruit of thy womb, Jesus…'

They were almost there. He almost had them home! Then startled by the roar of the incoming plane a flock of gulls scattered and bounced against the cockpit window, feathers flying.

Pat looked up, lost concentration, and struck a reef.

On impact Clyde was catapulted over the crates into the fuselage. Steam hissed and metal splintered. Then there was darkness and a voice echoing.

'Holy Mary, Mother of God, pray for us sinners now and at the hour of our death.'

Chapter Thirty
Branches

Gabriel doesn't remember much about the fall. Afraid the boys might follow, slashing the rope was all he knew. There was darkness and then Light and then Adelia. He was back in Virginia in '46 outside the Eyrie and there is sunshine, birdsong and rose petals falling. The sun is warm on the back of his head and he's telling her she should get a hat because skin like hers burns easy.

She carries on dead-heading the wisteria. 'I don't have a hat.'

'They got 'em in the store,' he tells her. 'I could run you.'

'Alright if it will make you happy,' she says. 'But there's no rush.'

There was no rush. It wasn't a rushing day. It was a day for being glad to be alive and for her beautiful eyes. He's happy to see her even though she's someone else's girl. The house is run-down and the wisteria overgrown. She needs to keep at that climber or next thing it'll be lifting roof tiles.

Grabbing a pair of secateurs he props a ladder against the wall. 'This stuff is all well and good,' he says, 'but you gotta stay on top of it.'

She smiles. 'I know it's an awful fuss but it does smell so heavenly.'

That sun is making him sweat. Gold curls back of her neck like rosy question marks she looks to be burning up. He doffs his cap and pops it on her head.

'Attenhut!' She salutes. 'The Marines have landed.'

With that the wisteria melts away. It is still '46 but further back in time in the reception centre New York Harbor. Some pug-ugly immigration jerk is looking at her dirty. 'What's a girl like you doing on a tug like that?' he is saying. 'A guy who can afford sable can afford to buy airline tickets.'

Gabriel is furious. 'Knock it off.'

The immigration officer turns. 'What did you say to me?'

'I said knock it off!' Gabriel stands firm. 'That's a lady you're talkin' to.'

'I don't care who she is,' the guy's red faced. 'She's gotta abide by the rules.'

'Mizz Challoner's here at the invitation of an American citizen and should be treated right. Of course, if you'd sooner take it up with the Captain then go to it though how he'd take it – him a hero and a decorated man – I don't know.'

'Regulations are regulations,' says the guy, whereupon Gabriel punches him across the room. 'What regulation allows you to beat up on a woman? To amuse yourself pullin' wings off little things? Tell me 'cos I'd sure like to know!'

Then he's back on the ladder trimming wisteria. Adelia is smiling. 'You know that didn't happen, don't you?' she says. 'You never did hit him.'

'No, but I sure wanted to. Guys like that think they can say anythin'. Bad enough folks call me a murderer and a dummy without startin' in on you.'

'You are no dummy. You are Sir Gabriel Templar, world renowned sculptor and my very dear friend.'

'Sir Gabriel?' He grinned. 'I hear folks sayin' that and think they're talkin' of some other guy. It was you did that. You gave me schoolin', helped me learn to read and write. Til you came along I was a dummy.'

'You were no such thing. To me you were like the hymn, all things bright and beautiful. You still are. But Gabriel, all that belongs to the past. Bad-mannered Custom's officers aside there are rules that do matter.'

'I ain't never been one for rules and regulations.'

'I know, even so there are natural laws none of us can afford to break. '

'Such as?'

'Such as keeping the promises we make, seeing them through to the end.'

She starts telling about the rules. Seeing as he'll do anything to keep her there he listens but is finding a particular branch of wisteria a distraction. It's an old branch, been there years, and so heavy it drags the rest of the climber out of shape. He reaches up to trim it and the ladder wobbled.

'Careful, Angel Gabriel,' she says, 'reach too high and like Lucifer you'll fall.'

'That needs to come out and give light to younger shoots.'

'But what about those that wind about it?' said Adelia. 'Won't they die if the supporting branch dies?'

'Young plants shouldn't need to hang on to anythin'. If they wanna grow strong and tall they've gotta push out on their own.'

'Not when they're so very young. Little things need a hand to lead them.'

Gabriel frowned. 'Pa would say mollycoddlin' never did anyone any good.'

'Yes while reaching for a leather belt. Your father was a bully,' she says. 'Being strong isn't about muscle. It's about making the right choices.'

'Yes, ma'am,' said Gabriel suddenly overcome with need. 'And I'm choosin' to trim that branch.' He reached up, the ladder swung out, and he fell. Down he fell but where he landed there was no sunshine and no Adelia.

There was snow and cold and bitter pain.

'Oh my Lord!' The pain is so bad he bit through his tongue, his mouth filling with blood. Oh yeah, he remembered the path gave way, now his right arm hanging loose where muscles tore in the shoulder and he's a nasty looking green fracture below his knee. Pain is coming in waves and so insistent it carries him into darkness and from darkness to sunlight again.

Where else would he go but to the past and his beloved?

They're outside the Mill again and this time he's spiffed up in US Marine Corps uniform, razor buzz hair, stripes, spit and polish – unconscious, bleeding to death, hallucinating, yet in his heart still trying to impress her.

May '46 he brought them here from New York in an old pick-up truck, her and her little girl. They'd travelled from Britain aboard ship on a GI Bride ticket. Bobby Rourke was supposed to meet them but lost his nerve and hid out in the tower. Adelia is wearing a grey suit and a cute feathered hat on her head with her curls coming down. She is as she was in '46, waiting at the door, everything she owns in a suitcase and a kiddie's buggy.

She brushes petals from his hair. 'You've confetti in your hair.'

'Not from our weddin' I ain't.'

'I know and I'm sorry. It seems that was never meant to be.'

'I guess not.'

'You got married. A lovely girl, Julia, I met her several times. Is she kind to you?'

'Better than I deserve.'

'I'm sure that's not true.'

'She could have done better.'

'Then maybe you might take the chance to make it better.'

'Maybe.'

'Have you been happy?' she asks.

He sighs. 'Here and there. What about you?'

'Quite happy, thank you, though I worry about the children.'

'Kids are a worry.'

'You have children now.'

'Uh-huh, two boys, twins, Charley and Mickey.'

'Are they handsome like their father?'

'They got a lot of their mother in them, silver moonlight.'

'And of course there is Joshua.'

Gabriel smiles. 'Yeah Joshua.'

'He is beautiful, isn't he?'

'The spit of his mother.'

'Gabriel?' She pushes back her hair a sign she's anxious. 'What time it is?'

'No idea though I reckon it must be late.'

'I ought to be going,' she says. 'I feel like I've been here forever. Truth is I shouldn't be here at all. It's the Mill, it draws me back.'

'Me too. I spend a lot of my time thinkin' of the past.'

'Not too regretfully I hope.'

'Never! I wouldn't have missed it for the world!'

'No more would I but we mustn't spend our lives looking back. We must look forward, if not for ourselves then for our children.' She smiles. 'Well goodbye, Gabriel. I mustn't keep you. You have things to do.'

Gabriel wanted nothing more than to stay in that golden day. It's likely now he'll end up a ghost haunting the Mill but if she can drop by now and then that'll be okay – her and that sweet kiddie in the buggy, Sophie.

Vroom! With the memory of Sophie he's back on a mountain in Nepal wedged in a Juniper tree. Groaning, he looks about him. There's no way of telling how far he fell or if there's a likelihood of rescue. It's still daylight though the light is fading.

'Whoah!' Shifting about caused the Juniper roots to shred and it's them that stop him from falling to his death.

The tree is old dying in the cold. He's a heavy guy. Sooner or later it will go and nothing below but a long fall.

On the left there's a ledge. It's a six or seven foot drop but if he can roll onto that he'll be more secure but in order to do that he must sever the roots that maintain him.

Lord, he's tired. Half a century is enough for any man. The strong years, the years of passion, are behind, ahead is age and infirmity. There is Julia. She'll mourn but the truth is she'd be better off without him. No shortage of admirers she could start again, the boys will weep yet they're young and strong. With or without a father they will flourish.

There's not so much pain now. It's there harrowing away in the background but not for long, sub-zero temperatures already closing his body down.

Weary though he is it's not his nature to quit, *Semper Fideles* once a Marine always a Marine. The roots of this tree are no different to the ties that bound him as a boy: Pa's leather belt, Bobby Rourke's jibes, medics scorn in the draft queue and vicious screws in the Penitentiary, one time or another they've all tried to put him down.

'I'm tired of strugglin',' he whispered. Snow fell, pain receded, and with it the need to make any kind of choice. A crippled bird in a shaky eyrie he wants nothing more than to sleep under a mantle of snow.

Minutes tick by, time slows down and with it his heart. Then out of the curtain of white a shape arose bringing with it the smell of raw onions and Jasmine tea. The Lama priest grinned. 'Good day, Angel Man.'

Gabriel squints at him. 'What d'you want? If you've come to tell me not to forget my kids you're a bit too late.'

'I bring you a gift.' Leaning through the snow the Lama offers a hunk of black marble. The marble is unquiet, the centre a heaving mass of molten lava. Faces loom through the mass, gargoyles, demons and angels with glowing faces.

'What is this?' he says, not really caring.

'It is the unborn children of your craft waiting to be set free.'

Gabriel peers into the marble again and sees more faces, the twins, Charley and Mickey, Josh, Tim, and John Beaufort.

'And these kids?' he asks. 'What do they want?'

'They also wish to be free.'

'Fine! I'll leave them to it.'

'Can you leave them like this?'

'Why not? They're grown. They don't need me.'

'Neither do they need your death.'

Pop! The Lama vanishes.

Earlier, Tim wished Gabriel dead, now when that wish is about to be granted a spook appears and berates Gabriel for dying.

Some days you just can't win.

Tim's words hurt, they cut real deep. As if Gabriel had a choice! In '48 Alex Hunter and his lawyers came up with a Last Will and Testament that tied a man to the promise only an angel could keep. Not content with that he did it again in '63: *'Look after my children, Templar,'* he asked of him that day by the graveside. *'You were best man for the job before. Nothing has changed.'*

Ash Hunter was not alone in passing on burdens, the beloved asked for her children. Then another anxious

father, Charles Beaufort, white and frail on his death bed
begged a promise for his son. '*Promise you'll take care of him?*'

Promises like that bind the heart and soul, now a will-o-
the-wisp hallucination adds a chain to the door.

Gabriel sighed. There's no doubt his death would hurt
John Beaufort. His dreams of finding a Snow Leopard
turned to ash, the loss of Sophie, and now his brother-in-
law killed in the trek, that's a life-long burden. It's the
same for Tim; wishing a man dead and seeing it happen is
hard to manage. Joshua too, beloved boy, will mourn
thinking his mother left him on a mountainside and now his
pa is doing the same. Last but no means least there is
Sophie, his little honey, who Gabriel loves as his own. Her
life is complicated and likely to remain so. If anyone needs
guarding it is Sophie.

'But Dear Lord!' Gabriel reared up, shouting into the
void. 'What about my choices and my needs? Doesn't
anyone care what happens to me?'

Silence and the tender touch of snowflakes on his cheek.

Sighing, he blinked the snow away. Why is he shouting?
Is he seeking God's opinion? If so God is keeping quiet. He
knows as does Gabe it don't matter what anyone thinks.
When questioning the soul it comes down to the man.

The knife still in his hand he sawed at the harness
hacking lengths of rope. Gasping, he reached down and
looped the rope under and around the boot on his injured
leg. Both ends tight about his good arm, and back braced
against the tree, he hauled on the rope and screaming all
the way the bone realigned.

Rocks and dirt fell upon his head. The tree groaned. He
groaned with it. 'Hang on old feller,' he whispered tying a

ligature above the bleed. 'You and your kin were ever a friend to me. Stay a while longer and then when the bough breaks, and down comes Gabriel, baby and all, we'll both be free.'

There's nothing else he can do for his body. Now it's for the spirit to prevail. Years ago when life and love was flowing he came across a man, a Teacher, who taught Gabriel how to leave his body and travel among the stars. If he is to survive this cold and pain he must reach out again to the unknown.

It's a long time since he journeyed this way and must be careful. He's older and weaker and any other power he once thought to possess dulled with the loss of Adelia. She was and continues to be the great cause of his life. Knowing she is but a touch away on the Other Side is such a lure that once out and travelling he may not be able to return.

Closing his eyes Gabriel reached out to the Creator of All. A prayer on his lips, the same prayer he offered this morning, long life to those left behind, he slashed the remaining roots and flung his body out.

Down he dropped, one moment teetering on the edge the next face down on the ledge. Once again he's out and running through darkness. When he gets to the other side, alas, it is not to Adelia's smile and the sunshine of Virginia. It is to sea, and sand, and to another broken bird.

It is this day, and blue sea, and a plane beached in the shallows, and a man drowning.

Chapter Thirty-One
Rusty Water

'It isn't here.'

'What isn't here?'

'The white lilac.'

'White lilac?'

'The posy of white lilac. It's not here.'

Becky tossed her shawl on the chaise. 'I wouldn't worry about flowers. You've enough here to start a market garden. And if that little display out on the sidewalk is anything to go by you'll likely to get more.'

They'd tried for a pre-show drink on the Strip but despite wearing dark glasses found that like Mary's lamb everywhere Sophie went the crowd was sure to go. 'It's her! The Frenchy stripper!' Next there's a queue of men and women offering books and toys and anything else she is willing to sign.

So much for serious acting! Becky has never known that hysteria not even when *Shout* was the byword. She's in the wrong profession. Maybe she should switch to Burlesque, offer a little Greek tragedy stripping, purple veils and heavy eyebrows, Eurydice minus the flute.

It makes you wonder what people do want. They flutter about as if Sophie were a sacred object and they in need of blessing. They didn't seem to mind that their worship wasn't sought, that though smiling their idol was a million miles away. It was too much for Becky; twenty minutes of that and it was back to Caesar's and a palatial dressing room with a star above the door.

'Lord, Sophie! That was some stampede.'

'Yes,' said Sophie searching through the flowers. 'It was a bit manic.'

'All that screaming? Anyone would think you were Mick Jagger.'

'Yes, wouldn't they.' It wasn't there. No sign of the lilac. Oh well never mind. It is early. A couple of hours to go it might still arrive. Sophie donned a robe and began readying her make-up whereas Becky stretched out on the chaise sipping wine and popping candied strawberries. 'This is some dressing room. An ice box as well as a bar! All I get back home is a shared cubby hole.'

'You don't seem to mind.'

'I don't.'

'You see England as home now?'

'I guess so.' Becky yawned. 'Thanks to Charles Beaufort I have the flat in Holborn and a neat little pension in Florence. You should come out and stay awhile. You'll love it. It's warm. Not a bit like London. And gorgeous guys with bare chests and gleaming teeth, none of your bowler hat brigade!'

'What's happening work-wise?'

'I've a couple of things in the pipeline. My agent is in talks with Mary Tyler Moore. Then there are rumours of an Ibsen season next year off-Broadway.'

'And you're up for a part?'

Becky crossed her ankles. 'I'm hopeful.' Smiling, comfortable, she talked of life in the theatre, the push for work and the pressure to keep working.

'Are you seeing anyone?' said Sophie.

'There are two or three Italian marksmen but no one special. I'm in no rush. What about you? If what Ma says is right you'll be getting a divorce.'

'Possibly.'

'No possibly about it! This is the 70s! No woman needs to get beaten up and smile through it!'

'I'll work something out. Meanwhile like you I'm not in a rush to start again.'

Becky nodded. 'If I were you I'd make the most of being single. It won't last. What happened to that Farrell guy? You see anything of him?'

'I did hear Simon is seeing someone.'

'Not Simon, the other one, Sebastian. Love the name! So Brideshead Revisited. Now if Larry were to produce that I'd be champing at the bit. I love grace and favour stuff. By-the-by did I tell you I ran into Sammy Warren? Married now with twins of her own! Good luck to her! At least she's out of the rat-race.'

Sharp and savvy, Becky reminisced of life, love, and romance.

Sophie pursued a rat-race of her own, the enigma of the Rossetti poem. Can it be as Clyde said – a message? Surely it's no more than a few lines on a piece of paper, a woman's thoughts on love. Remember me is all it says.

Where Ethan Winter is concerned she needs no reminder. Omnipresent he is everywhere. Tonight he's not alone, that other male, mystery of mysteries, her husband, is here. Dark eyes impenetrable, he leans against the drinks cabinet, a whisky in one hand and that damned rubber duck in the other.

People offer advice. Sue Ryland says loving that kind of man is casting pearls before swine. Becky says make the most of being alone. How can you be alone when head and heart are rented out? Gone but not forgotten, these men leave concrete memories, gold signet rings, bruises and the odd complication.

Yellow bruises turning green, Sophie brushed shadow onto her eyelids. Mom went through a similar facial refit in a fight for freedom. Now she bears similar tokens. It's down to her. Stay away from that crazy Hall of Mirrors, the Mill, and she has a chance of freedom.

The Mill holds on. Hamsters on a wheel the inhabitants chase one another's tails. Sue says people bring their own luck with them, that a house is no more liable for the lives within than the moon for driving people crazy. Tell that to Captain Robert Rourke DFC and to Biffer and Hokey under the Spruce. To get away from such a magnet you have to be stronger than Lot's wife.

More flowers arrive, pink roses from Granma Ellen and Aunt Sarah, lilies from Tim and Josh, champagne from the Farrells but no white lilac.

Becky talks. Sophie listens, smiles, applies lipstick, and wrestles with the notion that the grave in Greeley, Colorado, is empty.

I know! It's a crazy idea fuelled by Clyde's paranoia yet the more she thinks the more she suspects Ethan Winter is underground but not under the sod.

Doubts about the grave arose a few days ago along with the complication and are gathering momentum. Granma Powell's ring rang a bell, a ring signifies commitment, but to what, or rather to who, a dead man?

Days pass and rusty water dripping from a faucet doubt muddies former certainty, suddenly Clyde's insistence that Ethan is alive is viewed alongside Sebastian Farrell's pained silence and the realisation that not once in conversation did Sebastian confirm Ethan's death – he avoided the word

Then there's the cemetery, Granny Powell's gnarled hands scaring vultures away: '*Go away! Shoo! He wouldn't want you here*!' And what about Mrs Powell's funeral and Sebastian slamming the car door? '*Go home, Sophie, and don't come back! There's nothing for you here but heartache*!'

The real mystery is why five hundred dollars for the ring. It isn't worth fifty yet a buyer wanted it so much he was willing to tack a nought on the end.

Drip, drip, more water and her head will overflow and she'll believe that if there is a casket and mortal remains they are none of Ethan and that strange unearthly man, the gardener, meant exactly what he said: 'He is not here.'

Becky fanned her face with a programme. 'I see you've two numbers, *Irma La Duce* first half and the Saint Saens in the second. A bit of a jump that, a hooker to a dying swan. That'll be Miss Kelly, one bite of the cherry not enough. Talking of hookers I see your British buddy out front.'

'What!'

'The stripper. The Soho gal, what's her name, Karen?'

'I don't know who you mean. I do have a friend out front and she is called Karen and she does work in burlesque but she's no hooker.'

'I guess I used the wrong word.'

'I guess you did.'

'I didn't mean anything by it.'

'You were insulting.'

Becky grinned. 'You're awful snitty today, darling. What is it nerves?'

'Hardly… darling.'

'Ouch! Okay, you need a break from the dance but a word of caution. Don't take too long. Out of sight in this business really is out of mind.'

'I'll take my chances.'

'What about the modelling biz?'

'I've kept that option open.'

'Good idea. You don't want to throw the baby out with the bath water. I *said*, you don't want to throw the baby out with the water!'

'I heard you.'

'Nothing to say?'

'About what?'

'Babies? Sprogs, the patter of tiny feet, horrid little beings that keep you broke and rip your body to pieces – is that the reason you're taking a break?'

'You're as bad as Aunt Sarah,' said Sophie. 'She's forever fishing for tiddlers.'

Becky laughed. 'I know. Ma's the same. Are your folks here tonight?'

'Gran and Aunt Sarah will be. The boys are away climbing, and, well, you know about Clyde.'

'Actually I don't know, only what Ma said and she's tight-lipped. Not that anyone need say anything. Your Mary

Quant eye-colouring speaks volumes. Your husband was the best looking man ever but a little combustible for me.'

'Why the past tense? I didn't kill him.'

'You were thinking on doing so?'

'There was a moment when a shellac box was within hand's grasp.'

'Oh, don't tell me the worm is turning.'

'I was never a worm. '

'No more of a cute furry bunny.'

'I was never that either.' She shed her robe. 'Becky I need to change.'

'Of course! Us single gals need to be out there earning a living. Not that you were ever married. You were always single in your heart.'

'I tried to be a good wife.'

'Did you?'

'Yes, I did!'

'Oh come on, Soph, don't tell me you were into the guy. Okay, you got married, but not for one minute did you believe in the love, honour, and forsaking all others bit.'

'I didn't?'

'Whatever you gave it wasn't love. Everybody knew it, especially Clyde. More than anyone he saw it a one-way traffic.'

'That's a horrible thing to say.'

'Is it? Well ignore me. Who the hell am I to criticise. I'm only saying there's no need for recrimination. It's over and done. Go to Reno! Get a quickie divorce. Good riddance and all that stuff.'

'Don't say that!' Sophie leapt to her feet. 'You have no idea what I felt for Clyde and no right to offer an opinion. Me and Clyde are none of your damn business but for your information, and to set *everybody* straight, it was as real as anything you'll ever feel and I resent you suggesting otherwise.'

'My goodness, you are fired up.'

'And with good reason! As you said who are you to criticise? You are a friend not my mother or my priest. You don't have carte blanche to say what you like. You never did! Do me a favour, Becky, keep your opinions to yourself and have a little respect for me and a man you clearly never knew.'

'Whoah! The worm has turned!'

'No,' snarled Sophie, 'the furry bunny has stopped being cute!'

'Okay, I'm sorry!' Becky put up her hand. 'It's true nobody does know what goes on between people. Sometimes they don't know themselves.' She got up from the sofa. 'I'll leave you to it. After the display earlier, your adoring public, I feel the need to offer myself up for a bit of the same.'

Sophie offered no comment.

Becky bent to kiss her. 'I didn't mean to hurt you.' She opened the door. 'Clearly I was mistaken. It wasn't one-way traffic at all, you loved him, which when you think about it, him being gone, and you alone, is an awful pity.'

~

Sophie stood in the wings peering through a notch-hole. She is dressed for the *Irma la Duce* number in a black velvet Teddy, a gold lame cutaway coat, killer heels, mesh tights, top hat and cane – the combined weight of the costume heavier than anything Abe put together, even so Sophie feels stripped naked, Becky's words – accusations, if that's what they were – ripped the skin from her hide.

She did try with Clyde! No one could have tried harder. Now he's on some covert operation murdering the innocent.

'I thought I was innocent,' whispered Sophie. 'I thought I did my best to make him happy. But if what she says is true then I gave him nothing.'

The orchestra is playing the opening chords of *Lili Marlene* the number chosen to introduce *Irma*. The houselights are down and with a single spot highlighting a lamp-post Sophie feels she's stepped back in time and almost expects to see Marlene Dietrich by the console sharing a cigarette with her dresser.

At the Waldorf Marlene talked of love and loss, that losing the one special person is like dying, you can't expect to recover.

Applause breaks out. A spotlight bathes the top of the stairs.

Sophie strolled into the light. Doffing the top hat she bowed low. In that moment, a furry bunny caught in the glare, she knew with absolute surety that whatever the outcome – one lover suspected of rising from the grave and another thought to be going to his death – she would never recover.

Chapter Thirty-Two
Kaleidoscope

'Hail Mary full of Grace the Lord is with Thee, blessed art thou among woman and blessed the fruit of thy womb, Jesus.'

The stick moved back and forth with the swaying of the ocean. Hilliard moved with it, an echo of his last words hanging in the air. Impaled on the stick – oversize flying boots twinkling with sea-shells dredged from the ocean floor – his flying days are over as is his need of a bottle and a Mighty Hand to tip it.

Back and forth the boots gain ballast. A drunk yet a brilliant flyer, Patrick Hilliard floated that metal bird down through the sky on nothing but bated breath. Thirty yards and they would've made it. Then a Puffin bounced against the cockpit window. Pat bounced with it. Now the plane is beached on a reef waiting like Clyde for the turning of the tide.

Grizz Hamilton said out of the frying pan and into to the fire, from the sky and into the Pacific Ocean closer to the mark. With nothing to do but die Clyde reflects on the week, starting with beating his wife and ending with empty fuel tanks and quadriplegia.

Drifting in and out of consciousness he has no idea how long they've been down. That it is daylight is all he knows, his watch, like his spinal column, beyond repair. The dial shows 0500. They left Udorn around 0300, Pat warbling 'Sheep shall safely graze' while Clyde slept it off among machine parts.

Clyde turned his head. His back is broken but his sense of smell intact. Flies are all over Hilliard but so far only the stench of desperation pollutes the air.

The window by his head is cracked. Sea water laps against the glass. 'Come on window,' he whispers, 'do an old sea-dog a favour. A chink is all I need, water to pour in, and I'm gone.

Fear and claustrophobia grabbed him. Gagging, he fought to keep nausea at bay. It's not good to vomit and the lungs fill with hydrochloric acid, though a paralysed man in a wrecked plane caring about the way he dies is a joke.

He once read an article on paralysis waiting on a sperm count in a London clinic. At the time the information, like his junk, was of little value. The consultant had frowned. 'A little on the light side I'm afraid, Commander.' Then he'd smiled; 'Sex with a caring woman twice a day before meals is my prescription, a sensible medicine offering pleasure if not absolute hope.'

Clyde got a caring woman but no hope. A child with Sophie would've been the best. He gave his spunk plenty chances. Adoption was mentioned but neither keen. With Clyde's death she'll be free to breed with the Ice Man. Not that that will happen. There'll be no reconciliation. Hooyah, it's a matter of honour. In saving Jake Frost's life Clyde sealed his mouth forever.

Strange how things work out, stranger still is the growing indifference. Clyde should rejoice at the SEAL's moral dilemma but has no feeling on the matter. A short time ago he couldn't think of the guy without wanting to crack his skull. Now, with his own spine cracked, he could care less what happens.

'Small mercies, huh?'

The Air Base has gotten a stiff neck since he was last there. Papa Joe didn't appreciate his humour. All he did was get up on the dais behind that girl and give a quick body search. How was he to know he'd busted in on a wedding. So, instead of trying another bar they went to hear a choir singing.

'Jar-heads and choirs?' he muttered. 'Times have changed, little seagull.'

A seagull pecks at the window, a razor sharp beak clearing algae.

A pretty creature with white fluttering wings, it reminds him of Sophie. She's appearing in LA but if folks are looking to see the darling of the Lido they're in for a shock. It's Sophie Hunter, prima ballerina, as she always wanted to be.

Clyde was at the Opera House at the Gala debut. Slick in white tie and tails he sat among pearls and furs. She danced *The Swan* from Saint Saens *Carnival of the Animals*. That performance sealed his fate. A sure-fire virgin, at first it was her pants he wanted into, but then, a spotlight illuminating her face, it was her soul he desired.

She is fabulous as Mamselle Perfidia. Not every dancer makes a great stripper. Any broad can shimmy down a flight of stairs wearing nothing but a grin, she can squirm round a pole, hang her ass out to dry, but unless she has that inner fire a man yawns and hangs a notice on his knob: 'Do not disturb.'

When Sophie dances he prefers to be up back with the lighting guys. Distance adds to a sense of mystery, you and her and no one else. It's you she sees and you she wants to touch. When she leans into the spotlight it's on your shoulder she rests her head. Yours are the lips she yearns to kiss. She has it all but unaware of her power gives it to you for free, the only man in the world.

It's starting to stink inside the plane. Clyde has a particularly sensitive olfactory system. He can spot a man at five hundred paces. It's what alerted him to the VC kid in the armoured car, fear and the need to make good coming through the planes and gunfire like a hand tapping his shoulder.

Water seeping through cracks is filling the belly of the plane, at every shift a tide of scummy water washing his body. The sun is high in the sky yet it feels dark. Maybe he ought to be feeling regret for the many men and women he has killed but the paralysis holding his body in check opened a door in his head, and like the gull, he hovers above, viewing all from a distance.

A thought nags his mind, something he forgot to do back in Virginia. It can't be the making of a Will, that's done, that old woman, Culpepper, insisting.

'Get your affairs in order, Commander, settle your debts.'

Settle his debts? Hah! There's not enough gold in Fort Knox to settle the tab he's racked up on earth. The loft in New York he left to Bryony, any money to Jamie and personal bits to Grizz Hamilton. Chrysalis he bequeathed to Sophie.

The past in the shape of betrayed husbands caught up with him. The Remote Viewing program didn't help. The Company saw it more of a joke than a serious endeavour – the KGB and the Stasi are doing it why not us! Clyde saw it as a way of keeping tabs on Sophie.

Overcome with bitter regret he cursed himself. Crazy! What is he doing lying here like garbage crapped up on the tide? A couple of days ago he was in Colorado unearthing a grave. He should've stayed put and let the gardener shovel shit over him. It would have saved time and energy.

~

They say hearing is the last of the senses to go. Clyde's sight is failing but he can hear plenty. The sounds of the sea are open to him. Parrot fish sculpt the coral, eels slide through dead men's bones. On the shore a turtle with boat-paddle claws gouges a nest in the sand for her eggs. The air hangs hot. The plane drags on the reef. Hilliard's boots tread the sea-bed.

Clyde needs a lock-keeper to open the canals in his heart or he'll explode.

Thank God for the window! Shadow and light play on cracked glass. Clouds drift across the sky, unidentifiable objects flash and flicker, the view changes.

Back home little Jamie has a kaleidoscope. Shake the tube and bits of plastic form a pattern. This window is Clyde's kaleidoscope – the Mill in Fredericksburg is God's. Seasons come and go, sails on the tower turn, coloured pieces inside change, another season, the sails turn again forming another pattern yet always with the same coloured plastic.

'Hey birdie! Welcome back! I wondered where you'd got to.'

The gull is here again. Bright eye staring, it pecks algae on the glass and then swoops away. Clyde likes birds. If he had his time over he'd swap the sea and the Navy for the air, infinitely preferable to his present waterlogged situation.

The plane shifted. Water swirled and rolled down his body.

Is this it, he thought, heart hammering? Am I about to die?

The plane settled, water rolling back leaving cigarette ends on his chest and a Playboy centrefold, Miss July's tits thrust under his nose, and headlines from the Washington Tribune telling how *Mount Etna Erupts*.

Clyde couldn't live on a mountain. Nature red in tooth and claw is not for him. He prefers the city. He never felt comfortable in Fredericksburg yet when he hit the fuselage and was knocked unconscious he thought he was back there.

When the fuel gauges showed empty Hilliard didn't panic. It's probable he knew they had no hope and like the captain of the Titanic meant to go down with the ship. The gulls hit the window. The rest was darkness.

That's when Clyde found he was outside the Mill.

Talk about a dump! He didn't recognise it. Sails on the tower were broken. There was a hole in the roof and tattered blinds at the windows, dirty green blinds behind which scores of empty eyes stared out.

Yard overrun with weeds and trees hung with moss, everything was dead or dying. He might have been back in Colorado in the cemetery among toppling monuments, only the gardener and his rotgut whisky was missing.

In the dream the door opened and Sophie's step-father, the drunk that haunts the turret room, barred the way. What a mess! None of the snazzy WW2 pilot, he wore a stained shirt and stank of sweat. Worms had been at his face, one of his ears was ripped off and a crater where his left eye used to be.

'What the hell happened to you?' Clyde seemed to think he said.

'The war happened,' was the reply.

'I need to get in.'

'Why do you?'

'I belong here.'

'Then give me the password.'

'Password? What password?'

'*The* password, the passport, you might say, the only way in.'

'I didn't know there was one.'

'Well there is. How else do guys like you and me get into heaven?'

'I don't have a password.'

'Then go your ways, Commander St John Forrester. This billet is taken.'

That's all Clyde remembers, one minute he's taking to a ghost, the next he's pretty much a ghost regaining consciousness in the wrecked plane.

Jeez! He shudders. If that's heaven he'll risk the other place.

Bobby Rourke flew with the RAF during WW2 and died in peacetime trying to avoid a dog. Not so long ago Clyde thought fit to mock him – would he go that way, crash and burn while trying not to kill a pet of hers. Now the words come back to bite him.

In all his wildest imaginings Clyde never saw this one coming, a shot from a sniper or a dark alley, sure, but never bathed to death in a piddling azure wash, better if water was to pour through the window sucking him under fifty fathoms below to be eaten by whales.

Once off the California coast a Blue Whale passed right underneath Chrysalis. The surge carried the boat for miles. It makes you wonder. Is God as man must seem to mouse a monstrous cloud or is He like Michelangelo's God leaning out of the clouds? If there's a choice Clyde is holding out for the good shepherd that little bat-winged soprano sang about, the guy who told a dying thief, 'this day you'll be with me in Paradise.'

Clyde is suffering. The Devil and his pitchfork couldn't be worse. There's a hole in his heart where hope used to bide and it is sucking everything good from life. It would help if, like Hilliard, he had faith in God, and real faith at that, not the mumbling of weddings and funerals – the faith that allows a man like Pat to look to the skies and know his Redeemer Lives.

But he can't be like Pat. After the things he's seen and done it's not possible to believe in anything. The hellfire and damnation Jehovah taught at Sunday school, the one that brings down plagues, he recognises that god. But his folks didn't go to church enough for that to bend his brain.

Grizz once asked what happened that he worked wet-slab CIA. Clyde had no answer. It's not that he was a product of a broken home, more that he was born broken. Sophie doesn't go to church though she must be a believer because she says grace before meals. Having gone without food during the war she said her mother insisted upon it. The first time she said it he laughed. They'd had sex earlier, her on her knees and his cock ramming into her.

'If you're asking forgiveness leave me out of it,' he said. 'I like me as I am, down and dirty.' He asked why she didn't go to church. 'Uncle Gabriel says God is everywhere,' she said. Then she glanced up. 'Even in the bedroom.'

Gabriel Templar is thought to be a brilliant sculptor. There's a piece of his in the Mill yard, an eagle carved from a single piece of wood that if you didn't know was wood you'd think a real bird hovered.

Sculptor, Knight of the Realm, convicted killer, the guy eats, drinks, and shits like any other, yet when you look in his eyes you see beyond human flesh.

Before Clyde left on this junket Templar sent a message via Sophie. 'Tell Clyde if he should need me I'm bound to be close by.'

The tide's turning. The plane won't hold out much longer. If ever an angel was needed it's now. Doesn't matter if he's only part angel, a percentage will do.

'Okay Gabriel Templar.' Clyde closed his eyes. 'You said you'd be here if I needed you. I do need you. You have the name of an angel. Live up to it!'

Chapter Thirty-Three

The Issue

'So what now?'

Sebastian turned. 'Sorry?'

'I was wondering what's on your mind.'

'Nothing much. I've got the washed out feeling I get after a mission. You know the "what was that all about and who gives a shit anyway,'' feeling.

'Yeah, I know that one.' Jake turned away from the Mess window. The view is as it should be. Gaze too long at acres of sea and sky you get a glimpse of how little you are. 1400 hours the Team heads Stateside. Once on American soil he's turning the mission off in his head. Success or failure, they did what was asked. One image will remain, Clyde Forrester slamming him to the ground.

Why do it? The VC had Jake in his sights. A twitch of the finger and it's done. Knee-jerk reaction is the only conclusion. Newton's Law of Physics states with every action there is reaction. How about this for a reaction, in saving his life Forrester killed any hope of Sophie. There can be no disclosures now, nothing of the marriage to Meg Lyle and Forrester's part in it. The Dirty Deal never happened. Puff gone, dead as the kid in the armoured car.

Jake is desperate for Seb's opinion on the issue but won't ask. If Seb brings up the subject then we'll talk. Three hours they sat in a bar last night nursing a beer. The beer got drunk but the issue remains unchallenged.

The fact is Jake can't tell anyone of the threats to Sophie's life, especially not Sophie. You don't spit on the man that saved your life no matter how low the man or how much you want to rip him and his reputation to shreds. You don't do it, at least a SEAL doesn't. 'It crosses a line.'

Seb yawned. 'What d'you say?'

Jake shook his head. 'Nothing worth saying again.'

Three hours in the same bar. There were reasons to stay, juke box jumping, plenty beer and plenty girls. It's been a while since either tasted what was on offer yet it was only beer they drank. Why is that? The place was packed with men seeking woman. Seb is as much in need as any. But his silence tells all and the answer to that question is in Virginia in an old Mill.

Seb sits in the Mess hall alongside but the way he leans away you'd think them strangers. Seb's feeling for Sophie is known. He said it, 'a close family friend.' Who better than a close friend to offer comfort when things go wrong.

This morning Seb was on the phone to his brother. The Farrell boys are close, what one knows the other knows. Something was said, lawyer to brother that gave Seb hope. Jake heard it in his voice: '*That right? Culpepper said that?*'

Whatever was said stayed with Seb. Now there's distance between them. He has hopes of Sophie and good man that he is he knows there's nothing he can say, no opinion to offer, without perjuring himself, so he says nothing.

Maybe if they hadn't run into Forrester last night he'd feel less constrained.

Monsoon threatening, it was a heavy evening, two seconds and your vest stuck to your back. They were out walking by the harbour trying to get a breath of air. Forrester was with a pilot attached to the base, a reported drunk, yet compared to Forrester staggering about Hilliard was stone cold sober.

It was Seb who saw them, every muscle stiffening.

'Okay,' says Jake. 'Just ignore him.'

Forrester didn't want to be ignored. 'Well, howdy-doody!' he'd grinned. 'If it ain't the Lone Ranger and his Yes-Boss sidekick!'

'Fucker,' says Seb.

'Forget it.'

There was no forgetting anything, Forrester walked alongside.

'I'm glad we bumped into one another,' he says. 'Me and Pat leave first light tomorrow taking the long route back via Okinawa and a little Geisha sight-seeing. I realise that once again this screws with your arrangements regarding Noah and his Ark but that's life, full of disappointments.'

Jake and Seb tried putting distance between them and trouble but trouble was what Forrester wanted. He pushed between them. 'In view of the change of plans I need a message going home to the little woman saying I'm alive and well and can't wait to see her? Maybe you could take it, Boss?'

No reaction, he tried for Sebastian. 'What about you, Pin-up-boy? You willing to oblige a comrade-in-arms? It's not like you're a stranger. Where she is concerned you're a regular little pigeon carrier.'

It was too much for Seb. 'What is your problem?'

Forrester smiled. 'I don't have a problem. I saw you guys and thought how dejected you both looked. It made me think of Robert Browning's poem *Home Thoughts from Abroad.* 'You know the one, Mister Farrell? '*Oh to be in England now that April's there.*' My wife loves that poem. She says it reminds her of Suffolk and cherry trees. Stuff like that gets to you. Browning and Christina Rossetti, old-fashioned poets, they knew how to stir the heart.'

Slick as a snake he switched to Jake. 'Do you like poetry, Boss-Man? See yourself as a scribe jotting down the odd ode? No? I guess you're more like me – careful about setting things down on paper. It's risky laying it out there, apt to fall into the wrong hands and get tossed on the fire.'

Granma's poem found and destroyed? Jake had wanted to stomp that smile into the dust but was stopped by the pain in Forrester's eyes.

'Why d'you do this?' he'd asked puzzled. 'What do you gain from it?'

'Light entertainment is how I try to see everything,' Forrester replied, his voice as empty as the words. 'One should never take life seriously. A short life and a merry one has always been my philosophy.'

'And how is that philosophy working out for you?'

Forrester shrugged. 'It's had its moments.'

A cab arrived and the pilot dragged him away. 'Sayonara, Ghost Man,' was his last word. 'I should say to the winner the spoils but looking at you and your buddy I don't see either of you winners.'

The Mayday message came while Jake was out running and though garbled was recognised as Pilot Officer Pat Hilliard. A seaplane was lined up to go.

Jake raced along to his CO. 'I need to be on that plane!'

'Why do you?'

'He was a member of the Team.'

The CO consulted a memo. 'I got him here as extra man. Central Intelligence it says, Commander Clyde St John Forrester.'

'That's him.'

'What's he to you?'

'He saved my life.'

'Ah, well then you have cause, I suppose. Aren't you due to shuttle out? You and your men back to Fort Eglin and if I'm not mistaken a week's pass?'

'Yes sir.'

'Then why bother with this. Okay, one must play by the rules but you've done your bit. There are plenty others able to search him out.'

'I know, sir, but he was a part of the Team.'

The CO smiled. 'You're a SEAL, aren't you?'

'Yes, sir! Hooyah, sir!'

'Never leave a man behind.'

'No, sir, never.'

'Not even a CIA spook with a bad smell attached to his name?'

'No sir.'

'Then I guess you'd better go.'

~

'Take a hit?'

'Thanks.' Jake took a swallow and passed the bottle back. Two hours he's been glued to his seat, a binoculars for eyes tracking mile-upon-mile of ocean.

Rarely does a mission go to plan, a SEAL hits the ground running and that's how he stays. What follows battle is not his concern. He takes what he must from the experience, accepts the positive, learns from the negative, and forgets the situations he cannot change, a compromise necessary to sanity.

This thing with Forrester is driving him nuts. They must find the guy because until they do the mission will remain unresolved. For God knows how long one thought has plagued him: 'I should've shot him.' It's what Sam Jentzen said. It's what Seb didn't need to say. Ethan Winter the Third made an error of judgement – he listened when he should have blown Forrester away.

Jake Frost would not have made that mistake. The older, wiser, man, the one who met death up close and personal, would've recognised the San Diego airfield and film script for what it was – stage props. He would've known Forrester for the actor who plays out his life in foot high letters. He wouldn't have parlayed with such a guy, wouldn't have doubted his own honesty wondering if he did steal another man's love. The first threat to Sophie – the first cynical test – he'd have pulled the pistol and shot Forrester dead. Then stood over him and shot him again for the fucking waste of a bullet.

During the mission, on the chopper in awaiting insertion, he had a pistol under his hand, thumb and forefinger loosening the safety catch, once drawn the gun would've fired and not a man aboard the Helo, Forrester included, supposed it any other way.

Later on the Laos Border, darkness and mangrove swamps, there were a million-and-one opportunities to kill and none to tell the hand that pulled the trigger or the knife that slit the throat. Jake's commitment was to the Team and the Mission and under orders made no such move. Forrester had no such loyalty and as many opportunities yet chose to save a life sooner than end it.

In '63 an Angel saved Jake's life. Now Jakes owes his life to the devil who stole Sophie thus he loses her again! It's crazy. What is he supposed to feel?

According to Forrester he never meant to save anyone's life. A mental aberration he called it; given another chance he'd fill him full of holes.

No one can follow that twisting and turning blue-print of a life. That a man can enjoy breaking the heart of those he loves while crippling his own makes no sense to Jake. Yet the devil must be found, dead or alive, it hardly matters, he is the last animal for the Ark and Jake owes him.

Closing his eyes, Jake sent out a prayer to the Dream Weaver – help me find this guy because until I do I won't be able to live.

Chapter Thirty-Four
A Cygnet

Granma Ellen and Aunt Sarah are arguing about Uncle Maurice and the party he's planning for his wife and their new baby. Granma says a baby at his age is nothing to shout about; he's too long in the tooth to be pushing buggies.

Aunt Sarah shuddered. 'Good luck to him! Measles, mumps, and formula bottles! I wouldn't go through that again if you paid me.'

Sophie wishes they'd all clear off! Twenty minutes before the second half of the show, the interval almost over, she needs a moment alone. This magpie gathering in the dressing room, Becky and Sue, her mother, drinking wine, Aunt Sarah at the mirror freshening her make-up, and Granma a Queen Bee buzzing about the flowers, demonstrates the family's opinion of Mamselle Perfidia.

That she wears a tutu and her hair bound in swansdown adds dignity to tonight's show but beyond that the fans queuing at the door with their teddy-bears is another example of a bizarre way of life. As for Ethan Winter and Clyde, they're another entry in a catalogue of errors and to be glossed over.

Daniel Culpepper rang yesterday to know if he might proceed with the divorce. Sophie told him to wait but for what she doesn't know.

If only Mom were here, she'd know what to do. As though catching the thought Gran nodded. 'If your mother could see you now she'd be so proud.'

'You think so?'

'I do and yet you're giving it up. It is a tough profession. Have you thought what you might do?'

'I haven't decided,' said Sophie.

'You could always go into the theatre.' Gran watched Becky down another glass of wine. 'Not as magical as the ballet or as prestigious but…!'

'But hard on the knees,' said Becky, 'the grovelling one has to do.'

There developed a debate – the theatre versus the ballet – until Sophie wanted to scream. There was a knock on the door. Karen Walker poked her head round. 'There's a right kerfuffle going on out here.'

Heads turn. 'Kerfuffle?'

'Gatecrashers, people saying they are in the wrong seats.' Karen shrugged. 'I thought I'd better tell you. You don't want to lose yours.'

On a scent of sparkling wine and *Je Reviens* the room is emptied.

'Gatecrashers?' Sophie enquired.

'I thought you could use some space.'

'You're a pal!'

'Well, they do seem inclined to take liberties.'

'Just a little.'

'Talkin' of pals,' said Karen, 'some good fairy decided me and Joe didn't need a bloody great mortgage hangin' over our heads. He or she waved a wand and hey presto the house in Hammersmith is paid for.'

'You don't say!'

'I do say, or rather the bank manager. He rang as we were leaving. 'Have a good trip, Mrs Walker.' I thought he was talkin' to someone else!'

'Seems you've had a bit of luck.'

'More a flippin' miracle!'

They smiled at one another in the mirror, a gorgeous English rose and a wounded swan. Sophie was tempted to share thoughts on Ethan but was afraid to speak in case of imagining things.

'Yes?' said Karen, ever in head. 'Was there something?'

'Not really.'

'Are you nervous?'

'A bit.'

'You'll be fabulous.'

'Getting through to other end without making a fool of myself will do. It's a long while since I danced this.'

'Yes but you do know it.'

'I've practised it enough and it was my debut piece at Covent Garden.'

'Now it's your finale.' Karen leaned on the door jamb. 'Seein' you like this, ballet frock and all, I realise the other stuff, the Lido and the fans was wrong. I didn't get it at the time, thought you were bein' a snobby bitch. I get it now.'

'Forget it. It's water under the bridge.'

'Sure but things between us might have been a lot easier if I hadn't been so far up my own bum. Same with Clyde! I leant on his bad side refusing to see his good. Right well, I'm off before someone does pinch my seat. I wanted you to know how grateful me and Joe are.'

'For what?'

'You know very well. Anyway go get 'em, Tiger! Show those folks what they've been missin'. And if they don't get it, show the bloke you loved! Tell him all the things you never got to say when he was alive. Let him be your swan song,'

~

Alone at last, Sophie read through the programme. The publicity people have her dancing the wrong piece. '*One night only at Caesars Palace a chance to meet and greet Mamselle Perfidia's exquisite alter-ego, the ballerina, Miss Sophie Hunter, of Covent Garden, London, England, as she performs the dance of the Sugar Plum Fairy from Tchaikovsky's Nutcracker Suite.*'
'So what?' Miss Kelly said earlier. 'Who cares what you dance? One look and the audience won't give a damn.'

'Alter-ego,' it says on the poster. Sophie is Mamselle Perfidia's alter-ego, a flesh and blood woman is perceived as a fictitious character, a shady gal who likes to prowl about in her knickers. If it wasn't so sad it would be funny.

Suddenly she is afraid and wishes Gran and the chatter back again. She stares into the mirror. A painted doll stares back against a backdrop of telegrams and flowers, the razzmatazz of fame.

Becky says she's done with men. You can't hold onto love or fame, they are flashes of lightning that leave you temporarily blind.

Where fame is concerned Sophie has few illusions. Love is the mystery. Mom and Dad, the Eyrie, Suffolk and Uncle Charles, were rocks on which she built a life. John Beaufort rattled that stronghold. Ethan Winter was the brightest flash of lightning. After his marriage and hitherto unchallenged death she was unable to see her way. One person took her hand, Clyde. His grip was painfully tight. She spent most of the time struggling to be free. Now that she is free her hand is cold.

'Miss Sophie?' There was a tap on the door. 'Do you need anything?'

'No thank you.'

The dresser left. Sophie had hoped it was a posy of white lilac. It seems whoever thought to send them has given up. What pity! Ridiculous to feel disappointed! It's flowers and doesn't mean anything other than good luck.

Everyone has a lucky mascot, a thing that helps them climb the mountain. Karen has a brass curtain ring she got when needing to pawn her wedding ring. She wears it, she says, to remind her of her roots. Becky has a plastic barrette her father left her. Sophie's usual mascot is a gold bangle engraved, '*to my little princess from Daddy Bobby*.' It's been worn so often the engraving is all but polished away. Tonight she wears another bracelet.

A coral bracelet was Clyde's last gift. She was fastening it about her wrist when the Remote Viewing Gate swung open and she saw Clyde.

'Oh!'

He was standing behind her. She could see him in the mirror

She stared. 'Wh...what?' she stuttered.

He was speaking but she couldn't hear what he was saying.

'What!' she said it again.

He was gone!

Sick and afraid, she snatched up the phone wanting Sam Jentzen's number. She stood swivelling the bracelet. There was no hidden message on this. This is made of coral, chipped from the sea bed it's too fragile to be engraved.

The General's service clicked in. 'I'm sorry to disturb you, General, but I am concerned about Clyde. Perhaps you'd let me know how he is.'

Heart crashing, Sophie stared at the door. There'll be another knock soon, the runner giving last call, and she will be expected to go out there and dance but how can she feeling like this? They parted so badly that last day. I love you, was the last thing he said before knocking her down.

People shouldn't part in anger, not when love has been exchanged. She never told Clyde she loved him. Nor did she tell him she is pregnant. She suspected as much that day but needed to be sure. He always said the chances of him becoming a father were rare, one in a million doctors said.

So much for professional diagnosis! If they wanted a truer picture they could've asked Clyde's former concubine, Emilia, she always knew everything ahead of time.

It's noisy out in the club. People come to Caesars Palace to have fun. No thoughts of a CIA assassin, no care for a murderer alone in the darkness.

Sophie slid down on her knees. 'I care,' she whispered. 'Lord, please help him. It doesn't matter who he is or what he's done he doesn't deserve to be alone. No one deserves that.'

It's true she doesn't feel for Clyde what she felt for Ethan. She'll never feel that again. Yet as Sue Ryland said you can love in a hundred ways. And you can regret not telling of that love. Sophie's belly is flat as a board, not a hint of a bump, yet she knows she is carrying a boy, a grey eyed son – Emilia said so.

There was a knock on the door. 'Last call, Miss Sophie!'

'Thank you. I am ready.'

At the mirror she undid the tight chignon letting her hair fall about her shoulders. Settling the swansdown cap again on her head she teased the pure white feathers over her brow. Eyes glowing like sapphires, she applied more mascara and more shadow and then slicking her lips a richer red.

'I'll do what Karen said but not for one man. I'll dance for Clyde and for John, and Sebastian and Ethan, and Tim and Josh, my brothers, and Uncle Charles, Gabriel and my dad – I'll dance for them all. I'll tell the world of my precious son so that wherever he is Clyde will hear. My swan song shall be his.'

Becky's scarlet shawl lay across the chaise. Gathering it up, blood red silk rippling against white, she flung it about her shoulders. Then she walked out into the light.

Chapter Thirty-Five
None Left Behind

Knock, knock, who's there? Apparently no one!
Shouting at God didn't work. The plane maintains a
precarious perch on the reef. Last minute distress calls
aimed at heaven and earth from this sinner are clearly
regarded as bad manners and as such to be ignored.

Clyde feels as though he's dissolving, everything rubbed
away by Jamie's magic eraser. Though there's no witness
he tries to make a brave end of it and makes jokes with a
seagull. And who cares what God thinks? In the end there
was only one opinion that mattered and she, bless her
pretty feet, is twinkling away on a stage oblivious of her
husband's introduction to Hell.

The sun has set and stars are out in their million.
Through the window they seem close together but they're
not, they're millions of light years apart.

It must be lonely being a star. Clyde wonders if Sophie
will be lonely when he's gone. She has friends, the English
stripper, and Sue Ryland and daughter Becky, who Clyde
had a thing with one night last September, curiosity on
Becky's part and idleness on his. A beauty like Sophie
won't be lonely for long. One thing for sure it won't be

her former passion that takes up the challenge – three in a bed, and one of them dead, makes for light sleeping.

Listen to those goddamn flies. Clyde hates flies. Afraid they'll lay eggs in his eyes he fights sleep. It's why he allows only the briefest glances through the window, the rest of the time his eyes are tightly shut.

It feels like he's been here forever. Where are the rescue teams? They should have been here by now. Hilliard's pain is over. Why is he left hanging about? If it's punishment for being a CIA Tidy Man he'd like to point out to whoever arranges these things he wasn't fulfilling a private urge, he killed in defence of his country: '*My country tis of thee sweet land of liberty....*'

Life as Tidy Man isn't easy, a lonely job with a quick exit at every corner you have to stay focused on the endgame, can't assume anything. Folks are always assuming. They see the outside and think they know. Take poor old Pat pickled in brine. Few people know why he drinks yet everyone offers an opinion. Once in a bar in Hawaii some kid gave him a bad time. The kid went to the head Clyde followed shoving his pretty face down the pan. 'Time you grew up, asshole, and learned you don't know a guy until you walk in his shoes.'

But where are the rescue teams! A Mayday would've been picked up. He was on the blower shouting co-ordinates until he was hoarse! A thought came to him that when the team does arrive five-will-get-you-ten the Ghost Man is aboard. Hooyah, sir! Never leave a man behind! It's a SEAL absolute. It's only a matter of time and he'll be free. They'll air-lift Pat first, he will insist on that. Then it's Clyde and back to the States and to a lifetime of pity.

'Oh Jeez!'

The reality hit him. Why the fuck didn't he die like Pat? He hit the fuselage with one mighty whack.

News of this will be filtering through the wires. He'll get back and she'll be waiting on the tarmac, her beautiful face a sculpture in ice. She does that when she is scared, freezes, her body twanging like a guitar string. It's like she's trying to assimilate the fear, force it through her system so she can move forward. From what he's heard her mother was like that and her pa.

Clyde will see it first-hand. Whatever went down before, jealousy, flying fists, it's forgotten. Caring for her crippled husband will be priority. From now on along with mutts from the Centre she'll shovel his shit. A ground floor room in the Mill will be his world, TV on and curtains drawn back so he can watch the seasons pass; temperature controlled, cool in summer and warm in winter, soft blankets to pad his shrivelled limbs, every care will be taken. There'll be nurses and dietary specialists, State-of-the-art spinal-injury bed and all mod cons. He'll want for nothing and be able to do nothing. Goodbye to ice-cold Budweiser and filet mignon, his food will be mashed by his wife's own fair hand. Come rain and weather, stoic British bulldog stock, she'll grin and bear it.

He made a promise not to hurt anyone or anything of hers, now she will promise not to hurt him, so help her God.

Goodbye hot young flesh. Goodbye Perfidia and Face-of-the-Month in *Time* Magazine. Hello Nunnery and a savage hair-shirt. To love, honour, and obey will be her reason for living. When she does need a break there'll be a motherly type taking her place, maybe Sexy Sue from next door sublimating a need for Templar by helping out a wounded vet. Who knows, Sue may offer the occasional hand-job, one crippled soul doing favour to another.

Year after year this *ménage a deux* will totter on until one day he and Sophie take up residence with the other ghosts in the turret room.

'No!' Horror filled his soul. 'Not that, Lord! Anything but that!'

~

Appalled by the possibility he must have passed out. When he came to the gull was pecking at the window again. It kept at it until head under its wing, and blood on its beak, it slept. Clyde has no idea why it stays. Most creatures give him a wide berth. He's tried taking in strays. They cower away like he's gonna beat them. Emilia, the tart with a heart, says it's because he's blood on his hands. Bullshit! He's never taken a stick to an animal, human animals, sure, those that threaten national security, but nothing that flies, honks, or crawls.

A teenager, his thirteenth birthday, he learned a lesson. Pa used to lay traps in the cellar. That night Clyde was down secretly smacking the pony and sipping JD. Whack! A trap sprung on a mouse.

He sat with it cradled it in his hands. The mouse died. Clyde cried over the squished body and as he did a mist rose up. Tiny ears, head and paws, another mouse, silver and shining, rose up into the air a tiny spirit going home.

That mouse went to heaven. When he dies he'll go to hell.

Military heroes get a fancy funeral, escort duty, quartered flags and limousines in motorcade. Though still attached to the navy he'll be lucky if he gets a Go-Kart. As for mourners who is there to mourn? Bryony will attend, Joanie and a couple of golf widows shedding visible tears. There'll be Grizz and his cute wife Beverley, and Sophie accompanied by Daniel Culpepper, and Emilia Sabri looking raunchy in widow's weeds.

Until now he thought he knew why he brought Emilia to Virginia. Now he's not sure. It surely wasn't sex. Sex is Emilia's stock in trade. Obstinate, and totally without scruple, she's more trouble than any two-minute fuck is worth.

Lying here he recognises another self in her. On the skids before they were born they were drawn together, plus she's easy as opposed to hard work. No need to worry about her feelings, passage to the USA, a pat on the head and booty in her purse, she'll come to heel.

No amount of booty buys Sophie. Fear for Ethan Winter and the Viscount kept her on a leash, yet her soul was never at risk. Eternally secure behind a Crystal Mountain her inner being has doors to which – as a drunken custodian of the Mill was eager to point out – Clyde has neither password nor key.

~

It seems the mind expands when in prison. Searching for a way out you hear and see things that aren't necessarily real.

Halfway in the body and halfway out, all and everything is in constant change. Clyde thinks of Sophie in Las Vegas and there she is pirouetting beneath sparkling chandeliers, patrons watching with sorrowful eyes, and the plaintive notes of the Saint Saens harmonising with the wash of surf on sand.

Does she know he's here alone and dying? Probably she does and is here in the darkness with him rather than the Ls Vegas Strip – prescient like her father, she knew things she shouldn't. Clyde would catch her oft times gazing at him with pity in her eyes. Maybe when she dies she'll come rescue him from hell, do a dance for the Devil. Five minutes of those feather fans trailing across his wicked ass and the Satan will be tossing Clyde out to keep Perfidia in.

The scent of roses fills the plane. Parisian cologne, light and sweet, Gabriel Templar had that about him. 'Tell Clyde if he needs me I'm bound to be close.' That was the message passed on. Bound? What does that mean? Does it mean hogtied and screaming, or leaping like a hare, or merely obliged to help.

Words! People do it all the time. 'We must meet. Let's lunch.' It doesn't mean a thing.

The gull is gone, stretched and flew away. Clyde watched it rise higher until it was a speck of nothing against the moon. Sadness overwhelmed him.

'Please don't go, little seagull,' he whispered. 'You're the only friend I have.'

Time passed, he slept and dreamt he was that gull flying in a clear blue sky, currents tugging back and forth, air pulling and pushing – what a feeling!

And what a range of vision! The bird can see everything, the whole of the blue planet and yet appears to be focussing on one patch of blue and on one man, Gabriel Templar.

In that bird's eye view he knew why the guy wasn't here to help. He lies unconscious on a mountainside. Clyde could see him crumpled in the snow and knew what had happened, a path gave way, and Templar fell.

He seemed to know and understand all of this as he knew and felt the pain of Templar's shattered leg. What's more he is aware that a rescue party is close by, can see them and hear them and feel their anxiety.

The gull hovered over the scene, Clyde hovered with it. The Golden Man they call Templar. There's nothing golden about him now. An empty shell, purple lips and face white as the snow in which he lies, he is alive but only just.

Clyde wanted to wake him. Sophie loves the guy. Alone and a widow she'll need help. He tried to shout, to tell him to wake up, that it's his leg that's broken not his back. But he couldn't shout – birds don't shout.

The rescue party was above, slipping and sliding, pebbles and broken branches showering down. Frozen ropes – unwieldy snakes – slide down the rock-face. The climbers discussed tactics, anxious voices rising above the rest.

Joshua, Templar's son, is there, and the other kid, Timothy. They were both there along with Beaufort risking life and limb.

Gabriel Templar is loved by many. When he dies there'll be banner headlines, 'famous sculptor killed in climb.' No child to love, no one will miss Clyde, maybe not even Sophie. Would you grieve for the man who stole your happiness and tied you to a promise you couldn't keep?

'Holy God!' Rage at the waste of a life, the loss of love, and the things he could've done but didn't, burst out of his soul. A bird, a man, a dream, whatever, swooped down and punched Templar on the jaw.

'Get up, dummy, and enjoy your life! You don't know how lucky you are!'

No fist connected. Nothing happened, only a single white feather spun slowly down through the air to land on Templar's cheek.

Templar opened his eyes. Those eyes filled Clyde's head until he's thinking like Templar and feeling like Templar, listening in on dreams and memories.

Dust under his boots, he's climbing a staircase. It's that other place, the Eyrie, the black and white Tudor house companion to the Mill.

The stairs he climbs are not the Eyrie of the '70s, the house of blue wisteria, Sophie's childhood home. This is a ruin of years gone by, the treads fallen through and the banister warped.

Gabriel's heart is pounding. His long hair is streaming with water, one thought on his mind as he runs, '*will she be there?*'

Up the stairs he goes to his secret place. Every inch of this room is known. Boy and man, Gabriel's been here many times before. The door handle is smooth to the touch of one hand, his hand.

Clyde is particular about his nails. He keeps them clean and polished. The hand that grasps the door-handle is worn, the fingernails cracked and broken.

The door opens. She, the woman he adores, is by the window. She turns and smiles. Slender arms reach out to hold him, warm lips caress him.

Poof! The house, the room, the woman, is gone.

Again Gabriel is climbing stairs. Time has moved on. It's the same staircase now polished and renewed as is the house. His heart pounds as before but not from running. Today he arrived in a limousine. He wears a Savile Row suit and Hermes tie. His hair is short and barbered. He smells of roses and money. His nails are manicured but his hands still the hands of a sculptor.

He taps on the door. 'Come in,' says a voice. The door opens. The attic is a painted blue and gold nursery. She stands by the window a baby in her arms. 'Come see your boy.' She passes the child into Gabriel's arms.

Passion, adoration, all rush upward but nothing is said.

Clyde is looking at Templar's past and along with those callused hands turns the pages of a brilliant scrapbook. With that knowledge memories cease. There is sudden darkness and a cable-car toppling down a ravine.

Templar's voice whispers in his ear. 'You said it yourself, Clyde, until you walk in another man's shoes you can't know his life.'

Poof! Clyde is alone in the wrecked plane. He is scared and cold but it's no use calling out for help. It's not coming. He's tried praying but flies drown out the words. Desperate, he tries again. 'I know I'm not much of a person but if there is a God out there will someone please tell Him I need help.'

It seemed to him then he was again inside the Eyrie but not walking in Templar's shoes, he was following those belonging to Sophie's mother.

Adelia Hunter stood outside the attic. He could see her; light from a lamp she carried illuminating her face. Photographs never do her justice. Like her daughter she was beautiful, as blonde as Sophie is dark and green-eyed where Sophie has blue.

She is gazing through the open door. Clyde kept his distance. He didn't want her to see him. Alive or dead she wouldn't approve of him. No mother wants a bully and a cheat for son-in-law.

For a time he bumbled in the shadows wondering why she was there. Drawn to that room he moved closer. A smell touched his nostrils, milk, baby powder and freshly laundered diapers; it was such a clean smell he hung back.

Wallowing in stinking sea water for hours, Hilliard's blood washing over him, you don't take that into a nursery.

Inside the room a woman hummed a lullaby. A cradle swung back and forth. Adelia Hunter sighed and Clyde felt that sigh as his own. She was thinking of her daughter, remembering her as a baby, the warmth of her body as she lay on her breast, tiny hand a delicate starfish.

Such sadness and yet, all while, a powerful sense of joy.

That feeling touched Clyde like no other, as did the smell of baby, new born and precious. He crept closer until he was seeing what this woman saw and knowing what she knew. A figure sat in a low chair with a baby on her knee.

The need to see and understand why the attic was so compelling his heart ached. 'Why can't I see inside? Am I blind now as well as crippled?'

With that, light flooded the room. He saw and knew what his mortal eyes didn't think to see – Sophie singing a lullaby and Sophie holding a baby.

Pain smashed into him. He staggered, tried to turn and run but his feet were lead. Forced to stand and watch, the grinding ache to his heart went on and on; questions, who, when, and what, until he thought he would die.

A hand slipped into his. Calm and steady, the hand held him still.

'Look,' she said softly. 'Look with your heart.'

Sophie held a baby, a boy of maybe four or five months old, a sturdy little thing bouncing on her knee, his chubby fists pushing against her breast.

'Whose baby is this?'

The thought whispered through the perfumed air. The baby turned and looked at Clyde. Grey eyes heavy with black lashes stared, dark brows and a single curl in a black thatch of hair quirked in question mark as though challenging daddy to know his own son.

'My God!'

Those eyes! Clyde knew them. He saw them every morning in the mirror when he shaved, same with the hair and shape of the face.

'Sophie was pregnant when I left.'

This can't be right! He didn't believe it, *couldn't* believe it! He shoots blanks! This is God taking vengeance, a cruel joke played on a dying man.

'Don't do this to me, God,' he begged. 'Please don't show me things that can't be true. You'll break my heart.'

As though sharing his pain the baby whimpered, his little hands waving.

'Oh look at him!' Clyde bit back his tears. 'Look at his hands and his fingers. He is beautiful. And he's m…mine! My son! My boy!'

'His name is Noah,' whispered Adelia Hunter, 'you know, like the story, the animals coming in two-by-two, all saved. None left behind.'

None left behind? All saved? What did it mean? He wished he could make sense of it but couldn't think. 'It's the flies buzzing. I can't get beyond it.'

'Is it flies making that sound or is it time to let go?'

It seemed to Clyde then he was two people, this man of light and air learning of his son, and a pile of rags lying in the plane.

'It's not flies buzzing, is it?'

'No. It's friends come to take you home.'

It was the buzzing of rotors. That was the sound he'd been hearing all along. It was a chopper, a Huey! The rescuers are here.

Panic rushed at him. He didn't want to be rescued. What for? He could never have a life with his boy. Never play soft ball together or catch a hoop. He'd always be 'Poor old Pa,' a crippled man tying his son and his wife to a cross they ought not to carry.

The Ice Man will be on that Helo. First man down it will be his arms that lift this broken body and his hands that support Clyde's useless head.

None left behind, it's the SEAL promise.

Weary, Clyde let go. 'I tried the Mill but Bobby said I couldn't get into heaven without a password. I have to say that Mill is not my idea of heaven.'

'What is your idea of heaven?'

'This! My boy! Keeping him safe! Watching over him and loving him as you watch and love.'

'Then this, where the heart loves, is the heaven you will find.'

'Truly?'

'Truly. And don't worry about Bobby. He's not really there. '

'He said I needed a password to get in. If you knew it would you tell it to me?'

'If I knew it I would but I don't.'

'How will I get in then?'

'It will come to you when you need it.'

'So it's too late for the chopper? They can't come and get me?'

'It was always too late.' She pressed his hand. 'No need to be afraid. You can leave this place. It did all you wanted it to do. The slate is wiped clean.'

Steam hissed. The plane tilted sharply. There was a violent shaking. Water sluiced one way and then turning sluiced back.

Clyde was alone again, memories of his little son wrapped tight about his heart. It's okay. If it has to be this way he wouldn't want his boy seeing it.

The slate's wiped clean, she said. Lord what a feeling! No more staring eyes to reproach him. No more questions to answer and none to ask.

The sun is splitting the horizon. Grief is like that sunlight. Sharp and white it cuts his heart into a million pieces. Emptied of all and everything he lay with his eyes closed, no coward but preferring not to see what's coming.

'Oh,' he thought. 'I forgot to send white lilac. I send a posy every show. She doesn't know it's me. Now she never will.'

The helicopter came out of the sun – rotors beating it hung over the wrecked plane like an eagle hangs over its prey.

Another bird sought the plane, a sea-gull, a small bird with a big heart.

Wings thrumming, it hovered poised and purposeful. Fulfilling a promise to love, honour, and obey, it has been waiting for this moment.

Below, the blue planet glows like a star-studded jewel, a miraculous creation, oceans and continents, a divine jigsaw puzzle. The bird sees only one target, one broken plane on a reef and one broken heart.

Once, twice she beat her wings and then spreading her wings flew down straight as an arrow speeding toward the cracked window.

Clyde heard it coming. He opened his eyes. Love was flying to meet him.

Boom! The bird hit the window. Glass exploded.

Water gushed into the wreck carrying the gull with it.

Broken wings outstretched it sank down on to his chest.

He knew the password. It was obvious. What else would it be?

Folding his arms about the dying bird he whispered her name.

'Sophie.'

Drawn into the tidal undertow the plane lifted off the reef and floated out into the ocean. Slowly and smoothly the wreck turned turtle and sank, nothing left on the surface but a handful of feathers.

Chapter Thirty-Six
Clear as Day

'Please, Madam Sophie. I sit at back. No make fuss. I behave.'

Sophie took a black moiré dress from the closet. Knee length sheath, fitted jacket with velvet collar, black silk hat and veil, simple yet chic, Clyde liked this. He said it reminded him of his Aunt Cristobel, a blonde with Marilyn Monroe giggle responsible for his first ever hands-free hard-on.

'Madame, you hear what I say? I sit at back. I just watch and weep.'

Red eyes and blotchy skin, Emilia looks as if she's done her share of weeping.

'Not at the back, Emilia. Sit up front with the rest of the family. You're practically one of us.'

That set Emilia off again. Sophie led her out onto the landing. 'Go have a cup of tea and then take a look in his study where I've set a few of his things out, cufflinks and such. There might be something you'd like as a keepsake.'

Emilia stepped back in horror. 'No keepsake, Madam! Mister Clyde not gone from me. He in my heart. I see him clear as day.'

'Me too, Emilia,' she muttered. 'Gone but far from forgotten.'

For the last eleven days Emilia has flitted between titles, Mamselle Sophie when she forgets Clyde is dead and Madam when she remembers. No point asking her to drop either. As usual all requests fall on deaf ears.

'You dead married lady now so you Madam.'

Dead married lady? Sophie stared into the mirror, a pallid individual stared back – rat's tails for hair and panda rings for eyes. Yes that is about right.

It's been a terrible time, Uncle Gabriel falling down a mountain in Nepal, a broken leg and severe concussion, the getting of him and the boys home to various points of the compass and the telephone calls to England, to Julia in Oxford and to Lady Beaufort in Suffolk – who also had a fall, broke a hip and is now in a nursing home – and the retrieval of poor Clyde's body caught up in a horrid jumble.

So much to do and unwilling to burden Sue Ryland, who had problems of her own, an ex turning up at the house, Sophie moved back into the Mill. General Jentzen brought news of the plane crash to Vegas. The funeral is at St Judes. Where else would it be? Bobby Rourke's funeral, Sophie's wedding, and Clyde brought to rest, the church on the hill is familiar with Hunter family tragedy.

Another church in Colorado has known Hunter tears Sophie doubts she will make that particular pilgrimage again, Clyde had such feelings about Ethan Winter, surely to go now would feel like betrayal.

The phone has been busy, messages of condolence, the most moving from Clyde's step-daughter, Bryony, who wanted to come to the funeral with her boy, Jamie, who loved Granpappy. Many of the callers were strangers, men with whom Clyde had served. Yesterday men from the Navy called with forms to sign, and other than an official message of condolence, brief to the point of indifference, that's all the Defence Department had to say.

General Jentzen accompanied her to the airfield to collect Clyde. A dreadful day filled with unspoken questions it rained heavily, the wind turning umbrellas inside out. Frankly, she'd have done better without Sam Jentzen for company. He never cared for Clyde and beyond remarking of the weather he contributed nothing to the journey only sat whistling through his teeth the expression on his face, she felt, one of grim satisfaction.

The funeral arrangements were hit-and-miss no one seeming to know who was doing what. Aunt Sarah thought the Navy arranged such things. 'He was a sailor, wasn't he, though other than the Americas Cup and that boat of his, did anyone ever see him set foot on a boat?'

The men in heavy overcoats waiting at the airfield didn't appear to represent any branch of the military. They certainly didn't behave as servicemen. They lacked propriety, another day and another body; the casket taken from the plane and dumped on a metal gurney. Then shoulders bunched against the rain, wheels on the gurney wobbling, they raced to the funeral car.

Sophie watched all with growing resentment. How different a homecoming compared to that of Alexander Hunter. Dad was a General and deserved civility, nonetheless, Commander Clyde St John Forrester served his country for more than two decades and was worthy of equal respect.

Where before there had been a dull ache in her heart not easily recognised as grief, at the airfield there was anger and sense of affront. Why here in the back of beyond and why men in black loafers and no flag draped coffin? Anyone would think they were ashamed of Clyde!

To make it worse the skies opened and the leader of the pack seeking shelter under an awning. Nobody seemed to care that the casket was out in the open raindrops bouncing off the metal. As for the General he consulted his diary, while, goddamn it, still whistling between his teeth. The only person to show respect was a lone Navy officer standing to attention by the plane.

A radio was playing, the song echoing about the airfield, 'Spirit in the Sky', the lyrics so wrong and yet so right Sophie hadn't known whether to scream or join in. Then the driver of the funeral car lit a cigarette.

'I say you!' She saw it out the corner of her eyes, the glow reflected in her dark glasses, and marched forward. 'Put that cigarette out!'

The cigarette ground under his heel she turned on the director. 'I don't know who you are, or who employed you, but you're done here. Take your men and go. Your services are no longer required.'

He protested, or tried to. 'But ma'am, I assure you…!'

'Don't you ma'am me! I am Mrs Clyde Forrester and I could care less about your assurances. Do nothing more with my husband's body. Leave the casket on the gurney. I'll have it dealt with more respectfully by another firm.'

General Jentzen gaping, she pushed through to the terminal building. 'A phone if you please.' A phone and chair appeared. Kicking the chair aside she called Frank Bates. 'Oh hello Frank. Sorry to disturb you. I'm phoning from the Arlington airstrip. I need your help.' A few words and he was on his way, the situation restored to more capable hands.

Fighting anger and nausea, not sure whether she'd wanted to pee or be sick, she'd then asked for the casket to be moved out of the rain. 'Don't worry, ma'am,' someone said. 'It's being attended to.' Trembling, she looked through the window to see the gurney guided into a hangar and the unknown Navy Officer draping his mackinaw over the casket as a mark of respect.

Terrible anger replaced by terrible grief, she wanted to thank the stranger but couldn't walk a step. All she could do was lift her hand, and he, God bless him, bowed in response his startling white hair glittering in the sun.

The General was desperate to speak. 'Sophie, there's somethin' you oughta know. Some weeks ago I told you I needed to talk about Clyde and that it was in your best interest to listen.' A clerk offered Sophie a glass of water, the General still talking. 'I guess, I should've told you earlier seeing as it's as much about the Navy guy over there as it is about your husband.'

When Sophie asked for a cab Sam Jentzen almost exploded. 'Will you please listen to what I have to say? It's something you must hear!'

Seeming to know what he had to say would bring her world further to its knees she denied him. 'Don't say any more I beg you.'

'But I need to tell you, honey! It's buggin' my mind.'

'Then I'm sorry for you as well as for me.' She'd reached up to kiss him. 'You are a good man and I'd hate anything of mine to distress you. But on my honour I do not want to hear. It's as you said, Dear Sam. It's too late.'

~

The General is here now in the church. Poor old man looks quite worn out. There was a time when he might have been a relative, Aunt Sarah for a time involved with his youngest son. But that was then and the younger son too young and Aunt Sarah too sensible and who having made the cut found the same glamour in another pilot but with added years and income.

The weather has taken a turn for the worse, not so much raining as sleet, everyone bundled up. Churches are always cold, St Judes no exception. Sophie wishes now she'd worn a heavier coat. The family are all here minus Granma Ellen and Uncle Gabriel, Granma not too well and Uncle Gabriel unable to fly. Such a darling always thinking of others, he called this morning.

'How you doin', honey?'

'Never mind me! How are you?'

'Mendin' now but not fast enough to be with you.'

'That's alright. I know you're with me in your heart.'

'Always, Sophie, always.'

At that her feelings ran away with her. 'Oh Uncle Gabriel, I feel so bad! I don't think I treated him right.'

He clicked his tongue, a thing he did when annoyed. 'I don't aim to speak ill of the dead but bein' dead don't make a man invisible. His faults remain as do his favours. Keep the balance, don't lean on one while forgettin' the other.'

'But did I let him down, Gabriel?'

'Lord, you remind me of your ma. It could be her in that pew, black hat and wispy veil hiding' her bruises, worryin' about a guy who didn't know when he was lookin' at pure gold. Bobby Rourke's gone, Sophie, dead and buried years ago. You don't need his ghost hangin' over your life any more than you need create a new. Do you understand me?'

'Yes.'

'Your mom couldn't fix it. Neither can you. Let go the past and the men. It's time to look to the life growin' in your belly. That train we used to talk about has left the station. Love will be offered again'. Choose wisely. As for Clyde you treated him as you treat us all with lovin' kindness. It's not your fault if he couldn't handle his own darkness.'

'Is he in darkness now?'

'No, honey, he's not. He's where we all long to be, in the Light.'

~

Sighing, Sophie, gazed round the church. Ten minutes she's been sitting in the pew. Ten minutes, that's all, and yet it feels like ten hours. But for the family the church is empty, poor Clyde, a loner in life and lonely in death.

The cortege is on the steps, the bearers sorting themselves out. Tim and Josh will be the cause of delay. Having elected to be among the bearers there'll be some rearranging. She was so terribly moved when they said they wanted to be bearers. Joshua insisted. 'We are kin. We should do it.'

'Joshua, that is so kind.'

'Not kind, Sophie! A few days ago I came close to losing another father. I've a lot to be grateful for. Bearing a brother to his rest is the least I can do.'

Dear Tim nodded, so quiet and within, he and Joshua so changed she can't think of them as boys as she can no longer think of herself as a girl.

The flowers are lovely. Two large urns filled with yellow roses either side the bier Sophie did them early this morning, the exquisite hot-house blooms brought in from 'Forget-Me-Not' in Richmond.

Roses were Daddy Bobby's thing, especially red roses. 'Better red-red than dead-dead,' he would say. He came last night to make a last visit while Sophie was following a family tradition of hanging a lamp on the veranda.

Mom used to do this. A nightly ritual along with checking the doors and putting the cat out, so to speak, it became such a habit if Mom was busy you'd see Dad setting light to the wick, a golden glow cherishing his face.

Bobby stood by the water-butt. So long since the last visitation Sophie was startled. Handsome in uniform, it was the same Bobby yet thin and insubstantial. 'Yeah, it is me,' he said. 'Bad penny turned up one last time.'

'You okay, Bobby?

'I'm chipper as ever. How about you?'

'Well, you know.'

'I do know. I can't say I'm sorry for your loss. Let's just say I'm sorry you're unhappy. Anyway, I came to say cheerio. I'm movin' on.'

Sophie didn't like to ask where since in her heart she didn't really believe he was here. It was her imagination just as the RV Gate and the Otter and so much more were always imagination.

He smiled. 'Is that what you think, imagination?' Then a hand across his brow and scarf tossed about his neck, he quoted Shakespeare, ''*There are more things in heaven and earth, Horatio, than are dreamt of in your philosophy*!'''

'I'm sure you're right.'

'I am right and as time goes on you'll realise how right. Okay then, I got people to see and places to go. Two bits of wisdom to pass onto my Princess, keep runnin' and keep the lamp burning. It will help keep bogies away.'

With the feeling of a kiss on her cheek and a squawk from a rubber duck he was gone. That night she cried herself to sleep – another chapter of life closed.

The same might be said of Sebastian Farrell. He came by Wednesday. She was parking the Corvette at the time reversing into the garage and making a hash of it, whacking the fender against Clyde's Buick for a second time when a voice said, 'you'd do better if you swung out wider.'

'And you'd do better not telling a woman how to park.'

'Yes ma'am! Thank you, ma'am!' he said, palms uppermost as though pacifying a wild beast. 'Just offering an opinion.'

They took tea in the cottage sitting-room.

'I came to offer my condolences.'

'Thank you.'

'I never got to know Commander.'

'He didn't have a great many friends.'

'We served in different branches of the military.'

'Indeed.'

There was long silence, Sebastian seeming to search for words. Then the Gate tried to open. Tired of resisting she didn't try shutting it out. It juddered once, twice, and then closed – it was Sebastian's hand that kept it closed.

Sophie knew it and had looked at him in a questioning manner.

'We can't like everyone, Sophie, and they can't like us,' he said. 'One thing I can say, the Commander was a brave man. He recently saved the life of a friend of mine. It was under what you might call exceptional circumstances.'

'Clyde had exceptional qualities.'

'I wish I could say more but it's not my story to tell.' Again Sophie was aware of suppressed information. She felt it with the General and the funeral team at the airfield. They knew things she did not.

He didn't stay. Sophie was glad when he left. She liked him more than she could say but tied as he was to memories of Ethan Winter she was never sure if the attraction was real or a need to transfer one love to another.

Sebastian made his feelings clear. 'If you should need me, if you're in trouble, or need a friend to talk to I am here.'

She gave him her hand. 'Goodbye, Sebastian, and thank you.'

He'd paused on the steps adjusting his cap. 'Just one thing, that box my brother sent, the gift from the old lady? Did you ever get to open it?'

There it was again, hidden knowledge and the Gate a magical doorway into Never-Never Land. This time it was Sophie that closed it. 'I might have but then again perhaps not. Like Pandora's Box some things are best left unopened.'

~

'I am the Living God, the resurrection and the life, whoever believes in, even though he dies, he shall live.'

The cortege entered the church, the padre leading the way and the bearers following. Clyde's friend, Grizz Hamilton, is up front with a Navy man, Josh and Tim support the centre, John Beaufort and another Navy officer to the rear.

John may well be another good thing to leave the circle of her life. He arrived yesterday at the airfield out of the blue – how he knew she was marooned out there down to Aunt Sarah's constant quest for a foothold in ancient Suffolk.

Lord John de Beaufort knew how to make an entrance, British Blue-blood guns blazing, pennant flying and coat of arms emblazoned on the doors, a Rolls Royce Phantom swung through the gates. The car cruised to a halt. Out jumped George Allen, a wizened monkey in grey suit and chauffeur's cap. Savile Row suit, cashmere overcoat, and dark glasses, plus that indefinable touch of breeding, John then unwound his long length.

Having popped a vast umbrella George scuttled forward.

John didn't seem to care about the rain. 'How are you, Sophie?'

'I'm alright. It's this.' She'd gestured. 'It's all a bit of a mess.'

'So it would seem.' He took her arm. 'You should wait in the car.'

'But what about Clyde!'

'I can't think he'd want you out here in the rain.'

'It does seem rather silly.'

Good manners, commonsense, and centuries of being used to people doing as a Beaufort bid, he had the situation snagged and tagged in less than five minutes. Soon the Rolls is bowling back down the highway, Frank and the casket following close behind. It was then John took off his dark glasses.

'Oh my word!' Sophie had winced. 'Is this what happened on the mountain?'

Eyes disappearing into puffy flesh, his smile was rueful. 'It happened as I was climbin' back up. I managed to hook Gabriel to a line but then had to climb back up, and as you see not as agile as I thought.'

'Are you in pain?'

'A couple of ribs, Gothic eyes, and badly dented ego, apart from that I'm fine.'

'I'm glad you're here.'

'I couldn't have stayed away.'

Conversation was difficult. So much had passed between them there was little either could say without treading old ground. John wore the same silence as Joshua and Tim, a cloak of reserve that covered him so completely she might have sat with a stranger. When the car pulled up at the funeral parlour he asked if he might be a bearer. 'Obviously you've the Commander's friends to consider but I was wonderin' if…'

'I'd like that,' said Sophie.

'It's a bit of a cheek, I know, but I'd feel so much better if I could.'

'I understand.' She did understand. He was suffering the same sense of responsibility that comes with the death of people like Clyde. 'And John?'

'Yes?'

'You are a friend.'

He'd paused, handsome face so very still. The old John Beaufort, the Hon John of boots and spurs and TV smile, would have a quirky quip guaranteed to throw a girl off course. This man bowed. 'I am glad to be so.'

~

It was a brief service, no eulogies, no one saying what a good man he was and how he'd be missed. Sophie asked for a choir but that was more for her than Clyde. She couldn't bear the idea of anyone going to God unnoticed. The choice of music was simple, a soprano singing an aria from Handel's Messiah. There is a promise in 'I Know My Redeemer Liveth' from which even an unbeliever like Clyde St John Forrester might take comfort.

Clyde once said he preferred cremation. 'Don't put me in no mouldy soil. Burn, baby, burn! But it's your choice, Sophie. It will always be as you wish.'

As she wished? Life with Clyde was one compromise after another. Now she's alone and pregnant with his baby – is that as she wished?

She will love this baby even though he causes her to throw up in the morning and last thing at night. Clyde is happy about the baby. He told her so.

It happened the night she moved back to the Mill. She couldn't sleep, the same broken sentence going round in her head. '…regret to inform you… regret to inform you…'

Just before dawn she slept and dreamed she was in the Eyrie, in the nursery, the same blue teddy-bear motifs dancing about the walls but not the same baby in the cradle. Mum was there, Sophie couldn't see her but could hear her and smell her perfume. 'His name is Noah,' she was saying. 'You know, like the story, animals coming in two-by-two, all saved, none left behind.'

Then she heard Clyde, his voice choked with love. 'Look at his eyes! Yeah, that's my boy, handsome as all get out.' Then for a second, no more than that, she felt Clyde's kiss on her lips, heard him whisper. 'Thank you, Sophie.'

Now not only does she know she's carrying a boy she knows his name. It's a good name as is the idea of giving life to one whose destiny is to save animals.

Mom would like that, and Dad, who, God bless him, never seems to show in dreams and yet is always here, blue eyes gazing back from a mirror.

Noah's life and happiness is paramount. She will do what's best for him as Mother did what was best for her. In 1946 Adelia Challoner left England and all she knew for the sake of her daughter. Might it not be better for Noah if

Sophie was to reverse the process leaving the New World for the Old?

'It's about signs!' Aunt Sarah stayed over last night. 'You mustn't rush into anything, dear,' she said. 'Just take your time and look out for signs.'

Weary, Sophie had yawned. 'What do you mean by signs?'

'What I say!' Sarah was brushing Sophie's hair, the brush emphasising every word. 'Things that come to you, you know, suggestions from above.'

'You mean suggestions from God?'

'I was thinking more your Guardian Angel. You must keep your eyes open, look for the signs, and when they come grab 'em and don't let go.'

'You mean a Phantom Rolls Royce with plush interior kind of sign?'

'Exactly!' Aunt Sarah didn't bother to blush. 'There is such thing as a second chance, you silly stubborn girl. Your mom and dad had one such lucky chance and never looked back. Who knows a Phantom Rolls might be yours.'

'And how do you think Clyde might feel about that?'

'Are you kidding? He'd love it!'

'He would not! He couldn't bear the aristocracy. Another life, he'd be the guy that chopped off King Charles' head, the original Roundhead. That I should inhabit that kind of world he wouldn't have a minute's rest.'

'Rubbish! He might have thought that before but not now.'

'What do you mean not now?' Sophie had pushed the brush aside. 'Have you been talking, telling people things they don't need to know?'

At that Sarah did blush. 'I might have mentioned you were pregnant to the odd person.'

'How odd?' Sophie's blood had run cold. 'John Beaufort odd?'

'Possibly! I can't recall exactly who I told. Not that it matters. Sooner or later everyone will know.'

Lord! At that moment, Aunt or not, Sophie could have gladly strangled the woman. 'That means he knew when he came to the airport.'

'Again, possibly! But if I did tell him, and if that is why he came to rescue you, then doesn't that tell you something?'

'Yes! That my one-and-only Aunt is an interfering busy-body who can't be trusted to let me run my own life?'

Sarah didn't turn a hair. 'I'd add an i in that if were you – make *run* into ruin, because that's pretty much what you've done so far with your life.'

'You know nothing of my life. Like all the rest you look from the outside in.'

'Yes and see a goddamn mess you're making of it! Sure I've looked as your grandmother has looked and sweated and worried! And we weren't the only ones doing the worrying. Your mom and dad were right there with us!'

'Well they, and you, don't need to worry anymore. The cause of the mess, if it was a mess, is dead and lying in the chapel. We lay him to rest tomorrow. From then on any mess that's made will be down to me.'

'Yes and your boy suffering because of it! It's not about you now, Sophie, anymore that it is about your mother coming to Virginia. She left her home to make her child safe. You have to do the same. This place!' Sarah waved her hand. 'Stay here and it won't be you paying the cost, it'll be your boy and therefore Clyde. If you ever loved that man now's the time to show it.

~

'I know that my Redeemer Liveth and that He shall stand at the latter day upon the earth, and though worms destroy this body yet in my flesh shall I see God.' The soprano is singing, purple velvet drapes closing the casket from sight. Sophie struggled to rise and the prayer book slipped from her hand.

John Beaufort caught it, an echo in her ear, Dear Uncle Charles and a cricket catch, 'Howzat sir!' Aware of his hand under her elbow, the way he'd stood at another funeral, she stared at the altar. Somewhere in the world a man lives who she once thought dead; swans they were and as swans partnered for life. She used to dream of searching and finding him and loving him again, but that was yesterday's dream. 'I was a girl when I dreamt that. Now I am a mother.'

A sign, she thought, I need one sign that says, go that way, Sophie.

Closing her eyes, she prayed. Not to God! No! This was too mortal a prayer and therefore not worthy of His ears, she prayed to Clyde.

'Send me a sign. Doesn't have to be earth shattering, no thunderclap or a lightning bolt. Just something human that says 'go that way Sophie.''

She waited. There was nothing. Not a murmur, just the soprano reaching for a high C and not quite making it. It was John Beaufort's hand that guided her out of the pew. There were her brothers, sunbeams slanting through the window making a helmet of Joshua's hair. The Navy officer at the airport had hair like that. There was something about him, something heartbreakingly wonderful.

A tear slid trickled down her cheek. 'Goodbye love,' she whispered. 'So sorry we didn't make it.' Behind her a woman burst into tears. She probably thinks I'm talking of Clyde, thought Sophie, then who shall say I am not.

They walked out of the church into bright sunshine. The rain had stopped and the air smelt sweet, like white lilac. I will go to Colorado, thought Sophie. I can at least do that. The lilac will have sprouted. I'd like to see that.

Earlier this week when choosing the wreath she did think white lilac might be the thing but then chose forget-me-nots, a blue velvet rug to cover the casket.

Tired, head aching, she would've preferred to go home but they'd a small reception in town. 'Are you coming with us, John, for a cup of tea and a bun?'

'Perhaps for a moment, yes.'

'I guess you have to get back, things to do at the Abbey.'

'There are always things to do at the Abbey. Proppin' somethin' up, pullin' somethin' down, it's part and parcel of the job.'

'You love the Abbey.'

'Yes, for my sins. It is my home. I wouldn't want to live anywhere else. So may I drop you in town?'

'Thank you.'

They walked to the car, George already waiting.

'I see you kept George.'

'Of course. He and Betty are necessary to my life. They know more about the Abbey than anyone. We'll get old together. I couldn't possibly part with either.'

Sophie nodded. 'I know what you mean. Such things are precious. You can't ever let them, no matter how ruinous.'

'Indeed.' There was a moment then, a brimming over in John's eyes, when he might have said more, but today is not the day. 'After you, Sophie.'

John helped her into the car. A thought passed through his head, a memory of something said and believed above all else; 'My word as an Englishman. My house is your house. My life, is your life.'

George leaned in with a rug laying it across Sophie's knees. 'It's a bit nippy today,' he said. 'Don't want you catchin' cold.'

Sophie smiled. 'Thank you, George.'

Face crinkling he smiled back, a singular sign shining down from heaven through a million wrinkles. 'Thank you, my Lady.'

Chapter Thirty-Seven
Appointment

He saw her again today. Last time it was in Greeley, Colorado, the old cemetery. This morning it was the Guggenheim.

Jake was there picking up a leaflet for his daughter, an exhibition on Cubism next week. Indigo's into Dali, Braque, and Deschamps and if not that then a dozen other oddballs, in particular the tree-frog.

'Did you know, Daddy, the tree frog was on earth before dinosaurs?' He didn't know any more than he knew a frog could see in all directions and that its tongue is attached to the front. Indy is a wealth of such information. Jake quite likes frogs but is less happy with Cubism. He prefers stuff he recognises as human, Monet and Renoir, real people with real faces and not 3-D chequer boards and a woman with a beak for a head.

He called in the Museum after dropping Indy home. They'd been on the lake fishing, his weekend to have her, Carey, her mother, attending a lecture at the Shriner's hospital on the reconstruction of cleft palate.

Dr Carey Jane Roberts is a brilliant doctor. Indigo is not yet twelve so he mustn't count his chick til fully hatched yet so far, thank God, a brilliant mind and red hair is all

Carey has passed on. For sure Indy doesn't need the other stuff, the quivering nerves and self-repression.

Seven years ago Cary left him for another man. Jake was relieved. No more hysterics over ill-judged comments. No more hurt silences or explanations as to why he did this, or said that, and 'would he have said that to the other woman who ruined his chances of ever having a normal relationship!'

He did nothing to prevent Carey leaving, though to be fair she wasn't alone in causing the twanging nerve that was their marriage. He was at fault, him and his everlasting passion for the woman he saw this morning.

She was signing autographs at the Guggenheim. Why she wears dark glasses is a mystery. Five ten of female elegance and extreme beauty, six foot plus when wearing heels, high cheekbones and sexy full-lipped mouth, who wouldn't turn and look? Then there's the hair, don't forget the hair! Piled on top of her head, or drawn back from her face, it's a trade mark, the one seen in the glossies advertising the perfume that carries her name, Lady Perfidia.

This morning she was waiting for someone. Twice she was offered a seat, first the doorman, his jowls quivering, and then by a quartet of Guggenheim heavies hustling through to bend the knee.

A gaggle of kids stood bottom of the elevator, balloons in their hands and Moms in fur jackets they were having a day out. The doors swing open and coat tails flying, in she strides. A ripple passes through the group. One mom whispers to another. There's a brief huddle, a decision made and a little girl shoved forward. A teddy-bear held up as visiting card the kiddie tip-toes forward. She smiles, child and bear receiving a kiss. They gather round laughing and exchanging pleasantries. That's how easy it is to meet and greet Sophie de Beaufort, wife of Lord John Beaufort of the Abbey, Suffolk, England.

How he felt about seeing her again can't be put it into words, Renoir or even Braque could say it better. First there's her beauty, a creamy wash settling over the soul and then before becoming the familiar blue of regret the cream deepens to golden yellow acknowledging the kindness she shows, her smile caressing their faces, her lips curving in that look, 'Oh, so there you are!'

She wore that same delight in her eyes when they met in Paris. Seeing her this morning ripped him apart, yet in time that smile, and Indigo, his darling daughter, will help him mend.

In Paris he was Lieutenant Ethan Winter the Third, Navy SEAL and all-round good guy. These days he's Commander Jackson L Frost, Special Attaché to SECDEF, Washington DC, divorced these three years, now single and meaning to stay so. Difficult to tell how he arrived at this point other than to say he was led, a Wurlitzer ride beginning after the Search and Rescue mission in North Vietnam. A four-star military hand gave him a push. In a series of moves he was promoted Commander then bumped out of active service into the Pentagon and from there to an office in the White House, an apartment on Capitol Hill, a cabin by the Lakes, and a padlock on his heart.

Carey happened the spring of '73, a business lunch, medics looking for government support in the manufacture

of high quality prosthesis. Jake was there as guest of Sam
Jentzen. Carey Jane Roberts MD was on his right. A
vivacious redhead, sparkling green eyes and a seductive
smile, Jake was not above being seduced especially as it was
the day Sophie got married.

Several bottles of wine, eye contact plus an enthusiastic
fuck in the hotel laundry room and like Barkis he was
willing. Sometime between Indigo's second birthday and a
permanent post with White House Staff he lost the will.

If he could've loved Carey it would've been the day she
gave him Indigo. Such a gift is worthy of any man's love and
he did try. God damn it, he wanted to love her! It would
have made life so much easier.

Carey wanted more. She wanted to exorcise the dead.

'How come you're such a mystery?' she would say.

'What's mysterious about me?'

'Everything! No previous wife seeking alimony, no kids
to drag through high-school, no police record, not even a
DUI or parking fine, you're a modern miracle,
Commander, and frankly too good to be true.'

'What can I tell you, what you see is what you get.'

'Yeah that's right! Tell me about the girl.'

'What girl?'

'The girl you love.'

'There is no girl.'

'Of course there's a girl. I see her in your eyes and hear
her in your voice. And don't tell me I'm crazy. She was
here before me and still is.'

'Don't start with this again, Carey. It doesn't help.'

'Doesn't help? How can you talk of not helping when every second of every day you're chasing away from me and this marriage!'

'I'm not chasing anywhere. I'm here aren't I? I'm not out cruising bars!'

'It might be better if you were. You don't care about me or this marriage. All you do is mine treasures from the past. She must really have been something that woman. Either she broke your heart or you broke hers.'

'Nobody broke anybody's heart.'

'Then what is it? Tell me about her, tell me what happened and then I might at least understand.'

He couldn't tell her. He couldn't tell anyone. There are no words. They dried up when Ethan Winter ceased to be.

So what d'you know, Sophie married John Beaufort. Man, did that one knock him out of the park! Without knowing the details he always figured he was yesterday's man. Goes to show how little we know of people and feelings.

It was the sculptor, Sophie's Uncle, the one he thinks of as the Dream Weaver, who told of the marriage.

April '73 Jake made the cut to Commander and was planning to take the boat out on the Lake when he saw Templar walking toward him.

What a shock! You dream of something. Then one day you look up and the dream is walking toward you.

The dog saw him first and tail wagging raced away. The guy was leaning on a stick, a problem with his leg, a fall on a mountain about the time Forrester died. Jake remembers reading about it. Apparently it was Beaufort who saved him, climbed down a ravine and hauled him out.

Jake tried fetching the dog away, it fawning over the guy's feet as if meeting an old friend. 'Sorry about that,' said Jake. 'He's a good dog but a little crazy.'

Templar had nodded. 'You saved him and he's grateful.'

Jake did save the dog, he and Pick Madsen fetched it back from Laos. They went specially to get him. Crazy bastards! They could've been killed never mind given time in Leavenworth. Henry's gone now yet he had nine good years with Jake. How Templar knew they saved him is another thing.

'Jackson L Frost?'

'Gabriel Templar.' The hand was out, no hesitation, expecting Jake to know who he was and what. Jake touched that hand and did know. Whatever he'd dreamt, whatever fancy in his head, this was a man, flesh and blood.

Templar spoke, Jake hearing the same voice that once quoted the bible, saying how vengeance belonged to the Lord. Jake has excellent memory retention. You can't have a poor memory and sit behind the Secretary of Defence with a wire in your ear hour-after-hour translating one language for another. You have to be able to reach into nothing and pull out precise verbs, nouns and inflections. Jake knows what the Dream Weaver said there by the water's edge, reflections coming and going, but can only remember part.

'I came tell you Sophie's gettin' wed next Saturday. I'm givin' her away.'

'Can I ask who you're giving her to?'

'John Beaufort.'

'John Beaufort?'

'They're gettin' wed in the Abbey. The Suffolk Abbey not Westminster. I thought you ought to know. No one else could have told you, surely not Sophie, you bein' what you are.'

'And what am I?'

'I'd say somethin' of a miracle.'

That was the gist of the conversation, a brief dialogue is how Jake's brain recalls the encounter yet his soul remembers so much more, and sometimes when waking in the morning, when he's caught between worlds, he gets the whole package, Templar's drawling voice offering comfort to his heart.

'To understand the daughter you have to understand the mother. One and the same those gals, suckers for the weak and needy! Dogs and cats, houses, trees and land, they see somethin' sickly and can't help tryin' to make it better. A man or woman comes with blistered hands, they take those hands and bless them. Don't matter that the blisters burn! They hold on until the hand lets go of them. Same with a heart! It may be black and filled with tar. They just keep pumpin' light into darkness. They don't know any different! If you see that, Jake Frost, then you'll know no matter how short the time or how bumpy the ride, you were blessed to share the light, because once lit it never goes out.'

Sucker for the weak and needy? At the time Jake thought he meant Beaufort, a decade on he sees that isn't so. Knowing what he does for the World Health Organisation and wildlife you couldn't think him needy. The guy is a real dynamo. Bit between his teeth, he's at one with the tigers he fights for, up to his neck in political deep water pissing off people and governments.

His face used to be on billboards advertising razor blades. Now you're likely to see him on News night getting up front and personal with heavyweight lawyers disputing oil spillage and fishing rights. A group of men and women marching down a road protesting anti-vivisection and Acid Rain, he's prowling the front row, a modern gladiator, eyes flashing and fist clenched: '*Ave Imperator, morituri te salutant.*'

He's here now in Washington attending a convention banning the import of Ivory, and according to White House Press being a right, royal, pain in the ass.

That'll be why Sophie is here supporting her husband.

The tabloids love stories of blue blood, the scandalous the better. They dig up any old dirt. These days the Beaufort name is relatively free from scandal. When first married you couldn't open a paper without Mamselle Perfidia's electric eyes giving you a jolt. They named a perfume after her, a percentage of the profits going to her Animal Centre. News now is scarce. If there is anything in the society columns she's likely scissors in her hand cutting a ribbon or a spade planting a tree. Occasionally there's a shot of her climbing out a cab or newsreel of her nipping past cameramen in that Mini Cooper she drives.

Beaufort inherited the family aristocratic good looks. Leather jacket, denims or white tie and tails he turns heads. In the rare shots of him and Sophie together you get a glimpse of what Templar meant by 'shining a light'.

Christmas and Thanksgiving all in one is the expression on his face when looking at his wife. Thankful is how Jake would describe the look, maybe in the same way the stray, Henry, was thankful of a second chance.

~

If there was any hope of getting back with Sophie it died with Forrester. Looking back Jake knows why he pressed to be part of the rescue team. At the time he believed it was SEAL honour, none left behind. It was that, it was also the hope that in saving the man he, life-for-life, repaid the debt.

Four hours after the radio Mayday message the wreck was sited. Difficulty landing a plane they had switched to a Huey. The wreck shone silver in the sunlight. Rescue imminent, he along with the others watched horrified as a great well of water bubbled up dragging the wreck off the reef.

'No, no, no!' he heard himself mutter as the plane was sucked into a whirlpool. Evac of bodies proved it was always too late. Forrester was killed in the crash. Post-mortem confirmed he'd been dead some time his neck broken.

If there's one memory he'd sooner lose it is of that guy suspended in space. Jake acted as diver. The first glimpse through the window was of a body floating in green water. He might've been looking through a porthole in time at a marble effigy in a medieval church – a knight slain in battle, helm laid aside and long hair floating like weeds, a dog at his feet and shield on his breast.

'What the fuck is that?'

Jake recalls the shocked gasp as the body was hauled aboard the SDV. No dog at Forrester's feet but a seagull clasped in his arms. Locked tight to his chest it took a while to free it. The pilot of the Huey wouldn't touch it. 'Leave it,' he'd said crossing himself. 'Let some other guy chance his luck.'

That image, and the look of Forrester's face, quietude rarely seen in life, sent Jake back to Laos dog-hunting. It was the badge of honour jibe Forrester made in North Vietnam. Jake had to bring something back alive if only a mutt.

There was a time when Seb Farrell had hope of Sophie. Jake doesn't know if that hope was ever given voice. Seb is in civvies now practising law alongside his brother. Married with kids and living the American Dream in Connecticut and seemingly happy he has little time for old comrades. When their paths do cross at SEAL reunions neither mentions Sophie. It is as if she never existed, time past and the woman a mirage too distant to grasp.

That was no mirage this morning in the Guggenheim any more than Easter Sunday in the cemetery in Greeley.

Carey claims she married a mirage. When she left in she took Indy with her. When Jake said he wanted Indy to stay Carey laughed. 'Are you insane?'

'Must I be insane to want my daughter with me?'

'Yes. if you think it would work.'

'I know it would be difficult but with a little forethought and organisation.'

'Forethought and organisation? Is that how you do it?'

'You know what I mean.'

'I do know what you mean but do you? Let's give it a run through and call it Monday, first day of the week. With appropriate forethought and organisation you wake Indigo at 7. You wash, dress, and feed her, and since it's share-day, and you the communal chauffeur, you collect the Hanley kids and the Johnsons and drive them to school. At 3-30 on the dot, parking an issue at her school, you collect her and share kids and drop them home. And then… and then…!'

On and on it went, her voice a dentist's drill, how difficult it is raising a child on one's own, how much it takes out of life and the professional sacrifice, on and on and all discussions and debate coming down to one thing, how like her ex-husband he was, the selfish sonofabitch. 'George was the same, couldn't keep it in his pants, always sneaking around with some whore.'

'I'm not George,' Jake would say.

'You're worse! At least George was screwing flesh and blood. Not jerking-off to a dream.'

Carey is a good mother. The political scene being what it is – a new Russian premier and President Reagan's advisors taking advantage of *Glasnost* – Jake can't be far from a phone. When it does ring, day or night, he has to respond. It might be the White House, or the Pentagon, or Airforce One and a flight half-way round the world. It's no life for a kiddie.

Indy was in no doubt. 'It's okay, Daddy, I'll come see you. We'll take Henry and go fishing. You don't need to worry about me or Mummy. We have everything under control.'

Indigo had everything under control. It was her pa that was floundering. All these years on and he's still floundering. Since the divorce he's been on dates. He's seeing someone now, a White House librarian, pretty and clever and not too pressing, you never know it might end happily ever after.

Indigo and the cabin on the lake is his salvation. Time out and you'll find him on the water fishing and feeding the swans. Trumpeters, they come in off Pagosa Springs, the same pair nesting these three years. He has another sideline where twice a year he spends time in Greeley at the old cemetery.

It was there in December '78 he saw Sophie.

He made the trip to Colorado to lay a wreath for Granma. Sentiment took him on to the old cemetery where EW3 is supposedly buried. When he got there he found the gardener struggling with broken gravestones, the same guy that years ago gave Sophie directions to Blue Farm.

The cemetery was a mess, kids gotten in and creating damage. A lot of work for one man Jake rolled his sleeves to help. A couple of hours later he was about to leave when the gardener said. 'I'd bide awhile if I were you. Maybe take a rest here by the Morton family tomb.'

Jake had smiled. 'Will the Morton family mind?'

The gardener shrugged. 'Andrew Morton's been gone these hundred years, knocked down by a fire truck out walkin' his dog. A hundred years of dust and cobwebs is too late to mind about anythin'. Hush up, Mister, she's a-comin'.'

She was indeed a-coming, Sophie in a dark anorak walking through the graves a bunch of roses in her arms.

Seeing her there gave Jake such a pain he thought he was having a heart attack and head down crouched behind the stone.

'Nervous kind a guy ain't you,' the gardener offered a flask. 'Take a swaller of this and steady your nerves.'

Jake took more than a swallow. Rotgut whisky, it burned his throat.

'She comes every year 'bout this time,' the gardener continued. 'Christmas and Easter never misses. She brings flowers to a grave, not that there's much of a grave. It ain't like this vault crammed to the gills with caskets. There's only the one occupant and him under consideration.'

Jake's ears had burned. 'What do you mean under consideration?'

'The usual stuff, who is it down there and why?'

Hope rearing up in his head Jake got to his feet. 'Did she, that lady over there, ask such questions?'

'Why would she do that?' the gardener replied. 'She's comes a long way to leave them flowers, all the way from London, England. I know 'cos she told me. Seems to me anyone makin' that kinda journey knows who's lyin' in a grave.'

Jake wasn't able to answer. Head spinning, he'd knelt here, crazy thoughts running through his mind – mad ideas like dashing out and saying, 'don't look down there, beloved! I'm here! Come with me and we'll start over!'

Thoughts built up until he was in danger of being seen.

'Hold on there, Mister!' The gardener had touched his arm. 'Don't be doin' anythin' hasty. Dead is dead and should stay dead.'

Jake had stared.

'You stare but think about it. A grave wrongly marked can cause all manner of heartache. Say there's been a mistake and the person you love ain't buried under the sod. In fact, he ain't dead at all. He's alive and waitin' for the day when he can rise up like a livin' nightmare.'

'Why would it be a nightmare?'

'It couldn't be anything else. Like I said, think about it.'

Jake did think. He thought about the mess that was his marriage, the silent partner ever sharing the bed, and the hurt inflicted on people like Carey.

'I suppose it would be one hell of a jolt. It's been years. She's got a family, a husband and kids. The truth coming to light now wouldn't help anyone.'

'No help at all. People get hurt. They try rebuildin' a life. It takes time but if they're strong they manage. They even begin to be happy. Then one day bam! A skeleton chooses to pop out the cupboard and it's all wrong again.'

'So why does she come here if she's happy?'

'For the same reason all folks visit a grave, to remember the dear departed and honour the time spent together.'

'Is that why she comes?'

'I don't know!' The gardener turned away. 'I'm a gardener. I know nothin' about anybody. I'm just sayin' if there was a mistake then a man with a heart and a conscience wouldn't try correctin' it. He'd do the right thing, the only thing. He'd let sleepin' dogs lie.'

'You think a dog lies under that soil?' Jake had said bitterly.

'From what I hear tell he was a hero. A SEAL, she says, one of them Navy lads with green faces. You heard of them boys?'

'I've heard of them.'

Sophie left soon after, a chauffeur waiting by the car to drive her away. The gardener was gone, lumbered off to trouble some other sinner's soul. Jake vowed never to go again but couldn't stay away not with the hope of seeing Sophie. As it turned out other than last Easter he missed her every time.

He won't go again. Skulking about a bunch of tombs feels all wrong. There was a moment at the airfield the day Forrester's body was brought home when it could have gone another way. Good manners prevented it then. Necessity determines it now.

Okay, so he will go back to the cemetery. Last time he went a passer-by said they don't have a gardener. Apparently, there never was a gardener, or the old boy that was there had disappeared and the place falling into greater decay.

Jake doesn't mind giving the odd weekend. He could rent a room at the farm now that's been sold. Who knows, he may become another old guy propping up tombs and giving advice to fools. As for Sophie she doesn't need to bring flowers to that grave. It isn't a grave any more it's an oasis. A tree rises from the earth, six-foot or more of pure white blossom blooms through a desert of stones as a flag of peace.

~

It's 2145 hours. The moon is rising. Jake shoves his feet into running shoes. Twice round the Lake tonight and no stopping. It's the right distance. If he runs hard it will get him to the point where blood is pounding in his veins and his head is light, ideal conditions on an evening like this.

It's drizzling rain. That's okay. It keeps him cool. Stripped down to sweats he stretches his muscles easing the iron out. A bottle of water in his hand and a towel about his neck he starts out, clockwise as ever.

Sanguine, he accepts that whatever he saw today it changes nothing. He's made no new decisions about his life. Other than to keep going there's nothing to decide. It's as Granma says, 'it ain't over 'til it's over.'

The moon is a spotlight over the Lake, the pair of breeding swans like Tall Ships gliding through reeds. He loves swans, they mean so much. He still has the photograph, the little kid in ballet skirt. It is worn now, the little girl's face changed, yet it's still his baby cygnet. He looks at it and wonders if in time little Maisie Beaufort will follow in mammy's footsteps to point a dainty toe.

It was for her children she waited in the Guggenheim, some kind of celebration afoot, more guys in suits shaking her hand. It was then the doors buzzed open and the family arrived, a whole parcel of them, smiling and hugging and kissing. First there's Milord bending to kiss his wife, toddler Maisie caught up in her daddy's loving arms. One-by-one the rest approached. Two strapping guys closed in, her brothers Jake seems to think, one guy razor sharp in Army greens the younger, the artist and writer, Joshua Hunter, a blond Apollo in jeans and linen jacket, his face seen on book covers and magazines.

There were others, relatives, kissing cousins, the actress Rebecca Stone, wife of Sol Stone, the theatrical impresario, and a British couple, talking and laughing, their strident cockney accents raising smiles.

A photographer tried herding them together but someone was missing. The doors swung open; hands in his pockets and smiling the cause of the delay, and the darling of the media, Noah St John Beaufort ambled in.

Sophie's smile was dazzling. No question she loved her daughter yet this boy with smouldering eyes and coal black hair had her heart in the palm of his hand. No real hurry, he'd strolled forward to suffer a kiss from Mom and a high-five from Pa. Centre of the group, everyone shuffling to accommodate him, he grinned. 'Okay guys,' he'd drawled. 'Let's rock and roll.'

In that moment, cameras flashing and John Beaufort ruffling the boy's hair, Jake knew why she chose the man. It was for this, her son, the future Lord of the Abbey, and for his blood father – a wound healed forever.

One guest late arriving missed the photo session. Gabriel Templar arrived through a side door. In his 60s, yet still tall and straight, he cut an elegant if lonely figure. Sophie was first to greet him. They hugged, his hair whitened straw against her glossy locks. Then she was swept away through the Gallery and lost to sight.

Hampered by a limp, Templar was slow to follow and was walking through the archway when he paused, hand raised as if signalling doubt. A thought had flashed through Jake's head: 'Hello there Commander. Good to see you. Is there somethin' you wanna say?'

Lord, how Jake wrestled with the need to speak, to say something even if it was only thank you. The moment passed and with it the need to say anything.

~

Jake was working up a real sweat. This nightly routine is a must. It doesn't matter where he is or with whom, he needs to get out and run.

It used to drive Carey crazy. 'What do you mean going out? It's snowing! You'll freeze to death.' Three times last winter he was stuck indoors. Eleven inches of snow in a day, not even a snow-plough could get out.

Indigo's been out with him and understands why he loves it. 'It blows through your head, doesn't it, Daddy, and makes everything clean.'

It doesn't make everything clean for Jake but it helps. He loves Indigo and is grateful to her mother. Carey deserved better and does seem happier with her new guy able to talk to Jake these days rather than yell – she even offered to make the scar in his eyebrow disappear.

The scar is a reminder of another time and another man. He doesn't want it to disappear. Same with the gold ring bought for five hundred dollars. Indy has it in her trinket box, a gift from the Great Granma she never got to meet. Again, but for indecision things might be different. He might have another daughter now with blue eyes and raven hair instead of green eyes and freckles. That's okay. Indigo will do fine, thank you, Lord. He wouldn't swap.

Most nights Jake runs alone with only his shadow and swans chanting on the Lake for company. Bang, bang, feet beat out a rhythm, a Jodie cadence in his head, Navy stuff, slightly blue round the edges but it keeps him going.

Months go by, years, he runs alone, and then one night when he's feeling really lucky, or conversely really lonely, someone will run alongside.

Tonight he is awake to every sound, the splash of an otter seeking a late supper in the reeds and the beat of wings as a swan lifts into the sky.

Shadows lengthen and stars fill the heavens. Jake remembers Versailles and the Hall of Mirrors, their brave young faces replicated in glass – how they wondered at the future, the gift they'd been given and the price to be paid.

'I shouldn't be doing this,' he said.

'No nor me,' she replied.

He was thinking of Seb at the time. 'There are others to consider.'

'Yes others,' she'd said, stealing her hand away his doubts becoming hers.

'I told myself I wouldn't.'

'Did you?' Cold and suddenly small her hand is creeping back into his.

'Yes,' he'd nodded, 'because of the others.'

'But you couldn't help yourself… could you?'

'No.'

Jake doesn't know if Sophie suspects he's alive but thinks in her heart she knows. Maybe it's as the gardener said, she comes to the grave to honour the memory of the love they shared. Jake doesn't know if she ever knew he loved her, yet thinks that in her heart she knows and chooses, as the old man said, to leave that particular dog to rest in peace. One thing is sure there's a place in time and space where everything is known, no secrets, only the truth. It's in that place they meet, and in that place they continue to love.

Tonight that place is here by the Lake.

'Hush!'

Someone is coming! There it is! The echo of another footfall!

A perfume drifts through the night, Lilac, clean and sadly somewhat bitter.

'I'm here!'

Ponytail flying she slips in beside him, long legs reaching out, her stride matching his. Heart thrashing, he smiles. She smiles.

They don't speak. They don't need to. It's been said a million times before. It will be said a million times again.

'I love you.'

'Remember me.'

Fragile

Blossoms

By

Dodie Hamilton

(extract)

Prologue
Kill or Cure

A dainty little china cup was the first to go – a pretty thing, so fragile and fine one could see candle light shining through.

She ran to the shed and finding the biggest, heaviest hammer, went back to the cottage. A sun-beaten arm across the door, he tried barring the way.

'What are you going to do?'

Scornful, she ducked under his arm. 'I'm going to rid myself of a problem. I've borne the damned things long enough.' She set the cup on the table and swung the hammer. Always a good shot – Daddy used to say she could've played Hurling for Ireland – the cup exploded, sending costly porcelain flying.

Next to go was a triple cake-stand, a delicious thing, rose-sprigged with gilt edging. Plate, hammer, and table, she weighed up distance.

'Oh don't, madam!' the maid wailed. 'You surely can't mean to do that!'

'I surely can, and will, so, if you don't want to watch I suggest you leave!'

The maid ran weeping, her apron over her head.

One blow and the cake-stand disintegrated, gold metal pegs used to support the plates lethal bullets flying every which way.

Eyes as green as the seas he travels, he leant against the door-jamb, so handsome and so perfidious. 'You should cover your eyes. What you're doing is dangerous as well as foolish.'

'And you shouldn't be here!' she said. 'The cottage may be on yours, yet I am in possession therefore you trespass.'

'It's not my cottage.'

'Whose is it then?'

'Yours! I willed it to you this morning.'

'Why would you do that?'

He shrugged. 'I am a sailor, madam, my life in the hands of a ship's crew and Lord God Almighty – I thought to make your life more secure.'

'Am I supposed to thank you?'

Again he shrugged. 'It wasn't done with gratitude in mind.'

'Good because I'm not grateful. I don't want the cottage and I don't want you. You are here at your own invitation. Please leave! In staying you take advantage of your position.'

'And what is my position?'

'Where I am concerned it is nothing and nowhere.'

It's warm and the evening sultry. What they need is a storm to clear the air. She is aware of another watcher, a girl, a would-be woman who brought the village screaming to this door, and now unable to do worse peers through a spy-glass. I'll give them a storm, she thought. I mean mercy's sake, why waste time taking items down one-by-one when every shelf on the dresser is full.

Lace tearing, she pushed back the sleeves of her gown. 'If as you say this is dangerous you'd better stand back. I wouldn't want to hurt you.'

'Wouldn't want to hurt me?' He laughed. 'You hurt me every second of every minute of the day. You stab me through the heart and then you stab me again. Go ahead! Do your damndest! Kill the Meissen as you are killing me.'

She gazed at him. Unshaven and great coat travel-stained, he looked weary. Back from the farthest reaches of the earth, ship duly docked in Southampton, it's likely he's travelled all day, the horses sweating out in the yard.

'You called here first?' she said. 'You didn't climb the Rise?'

'I always call here first, don't you know,' he said his mouth tight. 'It's the rules of the game – the beloved first and the family second. I thought you knew that. Indeed, I thought it was what you wanted.'

It was too much. That bitter tone and seeing of himself the injured party was the last straw. How dared he blame her for this? How dared he!

Screaming, she ran at the dresser, the hammer a lot heavier than thought, she mistimed the shot, catching the middle shelf. It leapt up in the air, tipped and struck the top shelf, which began to slide – plates falling and smashing on the stone floor like a deck of brilliantly painted playing cards.

Weeping at such destruction, she struck again and again, until there was nothing but razor sharp porcelain, and the knowledge that, even as she struck, the shards would pierce her heart throughout this lifetime and the next.

Printed in Poland
by Amazon Fulfillment
Poland Sp. z o.o., Wrocław

62076575R00324